BITE THE HAND

Alix comes to Gridley Nelson as a neighbor more than a policeman—their children are friends. She is being blackmailed over an indiscretion that occurred early in her marriage. Captain Nelson is in charge of Homicide so he shuttles her problem over to a colleague, who quickly determines that it is her husband Richard who is doing the blackmailing. This doesn't jibe with Nelson's take on the husband, but the evidence does point to him. Then Richard is struck by a taxi in a hit-and-run accident. That's when Nelson meets Lilith, Alix's friend, who comes to her rescue when Richard is whisked off to the hospital. However, Nelson suspects that this hit-and-run was planned, and that the real victim here might not be Alix... but Richard himself.

DEATH OF THE PARTY

It's a snowy night, and while walking the streets after a terrific argument with his girlfriend, Matt is knocked down by a car. The driver insists on taking him with her. She drops him off at a doctor's office where there is a party going on. Avoiding the merriment, Matt finds himself in a back room where there is a body laid out. But this body did not die of natural causes. There is a scalpel plunged into his chest. And when Matt tries to alert the partygoers, they accuse *him* of being the murderer! After all, they were all friends of the deceased. What motive could they have? To the cops it looks open and shut. Only Gridley Nelson doubts Matt's guilt. But who could have killed the late, lamented partygoer—and why?

RUTH FENISONG BIBLIOGRAPHY (1904-1978)

Gridley Nelson Mysteries:
Murder Needs a Name (1942; UK edition, 1950)
Murder Needs a Face (1942)
The Butler Died in Brooklyn (1943; UK edition, 1946)
Murder Runs a Fever (1943)
Grim Rehearsal (1950; UK edition, 1951)
Dead Yesterday (1951)
Deadlock (1952)
The Wench Is Dead (1953)
Miscast for Murder (1954; reprinted in PB, 1956, as *Too Lovely to Live*)
Bite the Hand (1956; UK edition, 1958, as *The Blackmailer*)
Death of the Party (1958)
But Not Forgotten (1960; UK edition, 1960, as *Sinister Assignment*)
Dead Weight (1962; UK edition, 1964)

Unrelated Mysteries:
Jenny Kissed Me (1944; reprinted in PB as *Death is a Lovely Lady*, 1944)
The Lost Caesar (1945; reprinted in PB, 1950, and UK edition, 1946, both as *Death is a Gold Coin*)
Desperate Cure (1946)
Snare for Sinners (1949; UK edition, 1951)
Ill Wind (1950; UK edition, 1952)
Boy Wanted (1953; juvenile)
Widows' Plight (1955; UK edition, 1957, as *Widows Blackmail*)
The Schemers (1957; UK edition, 1958, as *The Case of the Gloating Landlord*)
Villainous Company (1967; UK edition, 1968)
The Drop of a Hat (1970; UK edition, 1971)

Plays
The Boiled Eggs: A Federal Theatre Project Play for Young People (1937)
Katcha and the Devil (1938)
The Speckled Band
The Mighty Mikko
A Valiant Little Tailor
The Totem
Babar the Elephant
The Children of Salem

BITE THE HAND
DEATH OF THE PARTY
RUTH FENISONG

Introduction by
Curtis Evans

Stark House Press • Eureka California

BITE THE HAND / DEATH OF THE PARTY

Published by Stark House Press
1315 H Street
Eureka, CA 95501, USA
griffinskye3@sbcglobal.net
www.starkhousepress.com

BITE THE HAND
Originally published by Doubleday & Company, Inc., Garden City, and copyright © 1956 by Ruth Fenisong. Copyright © renewed January 5, 1984.

DEATH OF THE PARTY
Originally published by Doubleday and Company, Inc., Garden City, and copyright © 1958 by Ruth Fenisong. Reprinted in paperback by Zenith Books, New York, 1959. Copyright © renewed January 6, 1986.

Reprinted by permission of the agent on behalf of the heirs of Ruth Fenisong. All rights reserved under International and Pan-American Copyright Conventions.

"Ruth Fenisong" copyright © 2019 & 2024 by Curtis Evans.

ISBN: 979-8-88601-103-6

Book design by Mark Shepard, shepgraphics.com
Cover art by Shootelkora
Proofreading by Bill Kelly

PUBLISHER'S NOTE:
This is a work of fiction. Names, characters, places and incidents are either the products of the author's imagination or used fictionally, and any resemblance to actual persons, living or dead, events or locales, is entirely coincidental.
Without limiting the rights under copyright reserved above, no part of this publication may be reproduced, stored, or introduced into a retrieval system or transmitted in any form or by any means (electronic, mechanical, photocopying, recording or otherwise) without the prior written permission of both the copyright owner and the above publisher of the book.

First Stark House Press Edition: October 2024

7

Introduction:
Ruth Fenisong
by Curtis Evans

13

Bite the Hand
by Ruth Fenisong

161

Death of the Party
by Ruth Fenisong

Ruth Fenisong
By Curtis Evans

Ruth Fenisong, a popular and prolific twentieth-century American mystery novelist hailed in her day as a "virtually faultless pro" by Anthony Boucher, dean of American crime fiction critics, published twenty of her twenty-two crime novels in the very heart of the mid-century, during the two decades falling between 1942 and 1962, beginning with *Murder Needs a Name* and ending with *Dead Weight*. Only a poignant children's story, *Boy Wanted* (1964), and a couple of additional crime novels, *Villainous Company* (1967) and *The Drop of a Hat* (1970), appeared from the author's hand in her later years; and, even before Ruth's death in 1978, her name had almost fully faded from the mystery field, with all of her books having gone out of print. Yet in her heyday as a crime writer, from the early Forties to the early Sixties, Ruth Fenisong was a component part of that remarkable corps of women mystery authors who flourished in America, right alongside the more attention-grabbing hard-boiled boys, during World War Two and the early years of the Cold War.

Over these creatively fertile years Ruth Fenisong published non-series mystery novels as well as her Gridley Nelson detective series, the latter detailing the murder cases of an empathetic, prematurely white-haired and Princeton-educated New York City police investigator, Sergeant (later Lieutenant and Captain) Gridley "Grid" Nelson. During the course of the thirteen novel series, Nelson acquires an indomitable housekeeper and cook named Sammy (a black woman who is closely involved in his earliest cases), a lovely wife named Kyrie (first encountered in the fourth novel in the series, *Murder Runs a Fever*) and a lively son named Junie (Sammy's nickname for the boy, derived from Junior); yet as Nelson rises up life's ladder of success he never loses his intelligent sympathy for the unfortunate individuals thrown willy-nilly into the monstrous maelstrom of murder. Although Ruth Fenisong somewhat romanticizes Grid Nelson, who as one of fortune's favorites is even blessed with an independent income in the fashion of the charming aristocratic gentleman sleuths associated with the British Crime Queens Dorothy L. Sayers (Lord Peter Wimsey), Margery Allingham (Albert Campion) and Ngaio Marsh (Roderick Alleyn, himself a cop too, however improbably), the world which Nelson inhabits nevertheless is a grittier one than that of Wimsey and his gang, more akin to that which one finds in the American mid-century police procedurals of Ed McBain and Hillary Waugh. Fans of American police procedurals and British manners mysteries alike should find much to their taste in Ruth Fenisong's appealing crime fiction.

Ruth Fenisong was born on April 29, 1904 in New York City, under the name Ruth *Feinsong*. Although the author's deliberate transposition, later in life, of two letters in her surname obscured the telltale traces of her actual ethnic identity, Ruth in fact was one of two children of immigrant Jews: Maurice Feinsong, a tailor and clothes designer originally from Russian Poland, and his wife Janie (or Jennie), who had been born in Whitechapel, London to Simon Bobbe, a cloth cap maker, and his wife Martha, both of whom came originally from the Netherlands. (Janie would have been nineteen at the time of the Jack the Ripper murders that terrorized the East End of London.) As a child Janie had attended a charity school housed in a great three-story Jacobean Revival structure, the Jews' Hospital and Orphan Asylum (later the Norwood Home for Jewish Children), indicating that her parents were possessed of no great means. In New York in the 1890s Janie joined her elder brothers Samuel, a tailor, and Louis, an advertising manager for the department store Koch & Co. and wed Maurice Feinsong, a successful clothing shop owner, in 1895.

Ruth's sole sibling, her elder sister Martha, married Edmund Theise, a movie theater projectionist, and with him had one son. Ruth herself never wed, although for some four decades she resided in Greenwich Village with her life partner, native Irish schoolteacher Kathleen Gallagher (1901-1980), the daughter of a lace importer. In the first years of their relationship, Ruth and Kay, as Kathleen was known, lodged with Phil Berry (aka Sverre Filberg), a prominent popular women's magazine illustrator originally from Norway, and his wife, Evelyn, but from the 1940s onward they resided at an apartment in a five-story, turn-of-the-century row house at 227 Sullivan Street. "I have many fond memories of my Aunt Ruth and her dear friend 'Aunt Kay'," recalled a great-niece of Ruth's (although unfortunately she to date has never related any of these memories to me).

How Ruth supported herself in her twenties is unclear. Throughout the 1930s she traveled in Europe, to England (1930), France (1932) and Italy (1937), on the latter trip in company with Kay Gallagher. This suggests she enjoyed either her own independent means or the indulgent support of her father Maurice, or "Pop" as she called him. (Her mother had passed away in 1928.) After the Second World War, Ruth and Kay resumed traveling, though to Bermuda and the Bahamas rather than the war-ravaged nations of Europe. By this time Ruth was enjoying a steady income from the sales of her popular crime novels, many of which were published not only in hardcover but in paperback. Before she began writing crime fiction in the Forties, however, Ruth in the Thirties found herself, as the Depression tightened its dreary grip in the United States, rewardingly (if not necessarily remuneratively) employed with the Federal Theater Project (FTP).

Launched under the Works Progress Administration in 1935, the FTP at its peak provided creative work to over 13,000 jobless actors, artists, writers, directors and stage workers. Despite the success it enjoyed with the public, the FTP was terminated in 1939 after the organization came under blistering attack from the House Un-American Activities Committee (HUAC), an investigative arm of the United States House of Representatives that was tasked with rooting out political "subversion" in the United States. (In practice this came to mean anything, in the eyes of the reactionary gentlemen who led this committee, deemed critical of capitalism and sympathetic to racial integration.) As far as I know, Ruth Fenisong was never singled out for attack by notorious red-baiting HUAC committee chairman Martin Dies, as was future one-shot mystery writer Irving Mendell (who hid under a playful anagrammatic pen name, "Amen Dell"), then head of the FTP's "Living Newspaper" (an innovative theatrical form designed to present factual information on current events to a popular audience). However, during the few short years that she worked with the FTP, Ruth did much interesting work, and her political perspective in that work, when it is discernible, is discernably Left.

As one of the more than three hundred and fifty people in the FTP who worked with marionettes, Ruth wrote and staged Puppet Theater in collaboration with such notable artists as the great Puppeteer Remo Bufano, Director of the FTP's marionette projects. Ruth's marionette plays included *Katcha and the Devil*, *The Mighty Mikko* and *A Valiant Little Tailor*, all adaptations of European folk tales (the last of which her father should have particularly enjoyed); *The Totem*, concocted from Iroquois tribal legend; *Babar the Elephant*, based on the beloved (and then contemporary) children's books by French writer Jean de Brunhoff; and classic English tales by literary giants Charles Dickens (*Oliver Twist*) and Arthur Conan Doyle ("The Speckled Band"), the latter of which of course is one of Sherlock Holmes' most famous and thrilling adventures. More provocative to the likes of Martin Dies, no doubt, were the allegorical *The Children of Salem*, about two children who nearly provoke the killing of a purported witch (the play was billed as "a strong indictment of superstition"), and *The Boiled Eggs*, in which a ruthlessly scheming restaurant owner ("Landlord") and his equally atrocious Wife, attempting to fleece a simple Farmer of $2000 for a meal of a dozen boiled (and very rotten) eggs, have the tables deftly turned on them by a wily Lawyer and a goodhearted Waiter. By the end of the play, the waiter has joined a union and is picketing the Landlord's restaurant, which in a burst of poetic justice is destroyed when the remaining rotten eggs explode. Evident throughout these works is Ruth Fenisong's ardent sympathy for the different and the downtrodden.

With the demise of the FTP in 1939, Ruth, now thirty-five years old, launched out on a second career, one suggested by her composition of the puppet play *The Speckled Band*: writing mystery fiction. In 1942, she published two Gridley Nelson detective novels, *Murder Needs a Name* (dedicated to "Pop") and *Murder Needs a Face*, the latter of which makes estimable use of her background in Puppet Theater. Two more Gridley Nelson novels, the cleverly titled *The Butler Died in Brooklyn* and *Murder Runs a Fever*, appeared the next year, followed by the non-series *Jenny Kissed Me* (1944), *The Lost Caesar* (1945), *Desperate Cure* (1946), *Snare for Sinners* (1949) and *Ill Wind* (1950), rounding off a prolific and highly praised decade for the author. 1950 also marked the welcome return, after a seven years absence, of Gridley Nelson, in the novel *Grim Rehearsal*, which also made excellent use of the author's theatrical background. Eight more Gridley Nelson mysteries followed over the next dozen years, which would prove the perceptive policeman's busiest period: *Dead Yesterday* (1951), *Deadlock* (1952), The *Wench Is Dead* (1953), *Miscast for Murder* (1954), *Bite the Hand* (1956), *Death of the Party* (1958), *But Not Forgotten* (1960) and *Dead Weight* (1962). Interspersed among these winning works was a fetching pair of non-series crime novels, *Widows' Plight* (1955) and *The Schemers* (1957).

In addition to clever mystery plots, Ruth Fenisong's impressive crime corpus offers readers sensitively rendered portraits of people from a variety of social and ethnic/racial backgrounds—or, as an admiring Anthony Boucher in his 1952 review of *Deadlock*, the seventh Gridley Nelson mystery, memorably put it, "beautifully realized [characters], on every level of Manhattan from café glitter to basement sordidness."

Dead Weight, the final Gridley Nelson novel, takes readers back to a milieu which has more in common with the murderous comedies of manners of the British Crime Queens, though there is seriousness at its heart. The last pages, which take place in the Nelsons' cozy living room as Grid and Kyrie discuss the recent case, have the feeling of a coda, as indeed they were, *Dead Weight* turning out to have been Grid's last recorded case. "Capt. Gridley Nelson is as quietly perceptive a detective as ever," noted Anthony Boucher in his review of the final Nelson novel, neatly bookending his 1943 observation, in his review of *Murder Runs a Fever*, that then Sgt. Gridley Nelson was "one of this department's favorite gentlemen coppers."

Over his twenty-year recorded career Grid Nelson remained one of the most likeable and appealing of fictional American detectives, a testament to the admirable creative vision of his idealistic and kindhearted creator. "Will you please stop trying to remake the world?" a lovingly exasperated Kyrie asks Grid, in the novel's closing lines. "Sometimes you seem to have a sneaking idea that you can change it singlehanded." There doubtlessly was a limit to what Grid Nelson—or Ruth Fenisong for that matter—could accomplish in society singlehanded, but in their mysteries, at any rate, Grid and Ruth made pieces of it better for a time, giving Ruth's readers a reassuring feeling that there could yet be some measure of justice meted in an unjust world, to both the guilty and the innocent.

—August 2019/May 2024

....

Curtis Evans received a PhD in American history in 1998. He is the author of *Masters of the "Humdrum" Mystery: Cecil John Charles Street, Freeman Wills Crofts, Alfred Walter Stewart and British Detective Fiction, 1920-1961* (2012), *Clues and Corpses: The Detective Fiction and Mystery Criticism of Todd Downing* (2013), *The Spectrum of English Murder: The Detective Fiction of Henry Lancelot Aubrey-Fletcher and G. D. H. and Margaret Cole* (2015) and editor of the Edgar nominated *Murder in the Closet: Essays on Queer Clues in Crime Fiction Before Stonewall* (2017). He writes about vintage crime fiction at his blog The Passing Tramp and at Crimereads.

BITE THE HAND

RUTH FENISONG

Chapter One

Gridley Nelson looked at the woman and listened to her with something more than professional interest. Her face and voice, the beauty of her quiet hands canceled out his dingy little office. He might have been sitting in a theater enjoying a play performed to enchanting music. He had only one fault to find. The lyrics were commonplace.

He said, "Lieutenant Danzig is the man for you to see. It so happens that he's been given temporary space here because of a fire at his own headquarters. He's on this floor. Go through the squad room and turn left." He had a mental glimpse of the men in the squad room as she walked among them, their eyes traveling the exciting course from ankles to soft red hair, or vice versa, their mouths incipient whistles.

It took her a while to accept dismissal. She sat on in the hard straight chair as though it had been especially designed for conformation with her graceful body. "Your wife seemed to think—"

He thought of Kyrie's almost embarrassing confidence in his ability to put everything to rights. He thought that her confidence stretched even further. Few wives would willingly have subjected their husbands to the shortest of contacts with Mrs. Richard Hildebrand. He smiled and said, "For once my wife was wrong. My work is confined to Homicide."

"Blackmail might lead to homicide," she said.

"When it does the blackmailer is usually the victim. Extortion might—but in your case it isn't extortion." He looked at the reports that covered his desk. He tried to look as though he were itching to tackle them.

"I'm a bit confused about the difference between blackmail and extortion."

"Extortion threatens bodily harm. The letters you received threaten only to reveal an incident you prefer to keep to yourself."

"Only?" she said. Her beautiful face clouded. She managed to look as though he had failed her. He thought that she managed it skillfully, considering that her recitative had contained no particular emotion. She might at least have had the decency, he thought, to color it with a little shame or regret.

"It's simply," she said, "that I want to spare my husband the unpleasantness of hearing such things about me from such a source."

"I understood you to say you have no idea of the source."

"I—I haven't."

"You've come this far, Mrs. Hildebrand. You might as well go the whole hog."

"No—I just meant that blackmailers in general must be a pretty contemptible lot."

"There's generally a way to disarm them."

"You advise me to confide in my husband?"

"I'm not in a position to give you advice. That was a suggestion. You're the only one who can evaluate its worth. I don't know your husband."

"My husband is as nearly a saint as a man can get to be. He wouldn't break up our marriage because I'd been guilty of an indiscretion. But—but I can see no point in telling him something that's over and done with—something that would hurt him unnecessarily. He's been troubled enough lately—he—" She let it stand.

Nelson said he saw, and had a troublesome desire really to see. He told himself that it was none of his affair. Nothing, he thought, would break up any marriage of hers unless she herself wielded the hammer. Any man, saint or sinner, would do his all to keep the hammer from falling.

"No," she said, "I don't want to tell him. If it comes to that I'd rather obey the instructions in the last letter. And yet—I've always been sure that people who allowed themselves to be blackmailed were fools." She read agreement on Nelson's face. "That's why I made myself come here. I've heard that as far as possible the police keep matters of this nature quiet—and if that's true it wouldn't be good sense for me to attempt to cope alone. It seldom stops at the first demand—does it?"

"You were wise to come," Nelson said, "but not to me." He drew one of the telephones on his desk toward him and asked to speak to Lieutenant Danzig. It was a defensive action. While he engaged in the brief exchange with Danzig he was wishing that Mrs. Hildebrand did not provide such gainful employment for at least three of the known five senses, and he was trying not to imagine what it would be like to touch and taste. Not since Kyrie's advent had he been prey to what he now categorized disgustedly as either adolescent or goatish responses to other women. He had looked, of course, and taken pleasure in looking, but without marked stirring of the blood. He was very much surprised at himself.

She arose as he replaced the receiver. "I'm sorry I wasted your time." Her voice had stiffened to a formal mold.

"It's the other way around." He got to his long legs. "On second thought I'd better take you to Lieutenant Danzig. Our corridors are devious unless you're familiar with them."

The reaction of the men in the squad room was not quite as expected. An unnatural hush had descended before the opposite door was reached, and Nelson could detect no mouth shaped for a whistle. So are great moments received, he thought, only half amused.

He left her with Lieutenant Danzig, not waiting to observe what her effect might be upon that tough old bachelor.

Back in his own office, he could not immediately concentrate upon the laden desk. First he had to open the window to permit the faint but heady scent of perfumed flesh to escape. That left two of his senses still engaged by her. His eyes retained her image, his ears her voice. Implicit in that voice was the vibrato of a fine instrument, yet she had played it carelessly, using none of the stops to draw sympathetic response to her predicament.

"It happened soon after I married," she said with a peculiar air of detachment. "My husband was called away suddenly." Here she had paused and looked at Nelson. Apparently she mistook some involuntary shift in his chair for impatience. After that there were no more pauses. "We've enough money to take the mechanics of housekeeping off my shoulders. To occupy myself I started to attend some classes at an art school. I met a young man there. He came from a small town and had no friends in New York. He seemed lonely and I suppose I felt sorry for him. It was no more than that. I asked him to the house to have a drink. He wasn't particularly attractive. He was just there. To avoid meeting him again I never went back to the school—and even now I am unable to explain to my own satisfaction why I went to bed with him."

Up to that point Nelson had believed that, like most of the people who found their way to his office, she wanted to offer information pertinent to a current case. His habitual tact deserted him. He said bluntly, "Why do you tell me this?" and experienced a curious sense of betrayal, not because she was keeping him from his work but because the facade she presented should have housed a treasure-trove of rare secrets rather than the shoddy lapse she had produced for his inspection.

She had raised an exquisite eyebrow. "As background for the

letters—naturally." She took them from her bag and placed them before him.

There were three in number. They were printed in purple crayon on the reverse sides of the second-class mail that chokes any mailbox any day of the week. The first was a free soap coupon, the second an announcement of a new beauty salon, and the third an invitation to sample the food at a midtown restaurant. In each instance the crayoned text was predominantly Anglo-Saxon. The one bearing the most recent date concluded with "Pay—or else," and stated where and how the sum of two thousand dollars was to be delivered.

"That business in the record shop has an amateurish ring," Nelson said.

She seemed startled. "Has it—why?"

"A professional would have weighed every contingency— including the one that you might go to the police. He'd have given himself more protection."

"Oh."

A number of obvious questions had risen to Nelson's lips: the name of the young art student—if she remembered it—the names of the servants in her house when she had "entertained" him, the names of those of her immediate circle who needed money or who needed to express hatred for her. But he repressed the questions. Lieutenant Danzig would obtain the necessary information. He had made certain that she arrived at the lieutenant's office because occasionally people on similar errands changed their minds midway and did decide to cope alone.

That should have ended it so far as he was concerned. And did—and does, he told himself firmly. Thereupon he devoted his full attention to the reports on the ninth murder to come to his desk that week. It had been an uncommonly slow week.

No personal preoccupations, however strong, could survive the pressures of even a routine day at Homicide. Presently his phones began to ring and his office became the scene of many entrances and exits. By evening he had buried Mrs. Hildebrand beneath the exigencies of his job.

It was Kyrie who resurrected her that evening. They had finished dinner and were in the living room. Junie, their small son, was upstairs, asleep. Sammy, a combination of cook, housekeeper, nurse, friend, and adviser, whose accomplishments put modern inventions to shame, had gone to the movies.

Kyrie said, "Would you like to see my new spring coat?"

"Spring?"

"Why do you sound as though I'd bitten you? It is spring. Haven't you noticed?"

"Well—yes—in a way."

She gave him a quick glance. "Did you have a rough day?"

"No—where's that coat?"

"Upstairs. I'll get it."

"Don't move. I'll see it later." He came and sat beside her on the sofa. "It couldn't make you look any better than you look now."

"I do like a well-turned compliment." She rested her ash-blond head against his shoulder.

"Spring," he said, as though he had found a satisfactory solution to a puzzle.

Kyrie drew away from him. "Delayed reaction or something?"

"Or something." He felt at peace there in the warmly colored room, and Kyrie its warmest note. "Obviously Junie's in tune with the season," he said. "Who's his new crush—the one he kept hurling into the conversation. I was sure that any minute I'd be asked for my blessing."

"Don't worry. Nora's half past six and looks it—at least fourteen months older than he is."

Nelson laughed. "He might be developing into a gerontophile."

"Your Princeton vocabulary would floor me if I couldn't piece the word together from freshman Greek."

"Does this ancient crone live in the neighborhood?"

"Across the street and six doors down—and she goes to Junie's school. Oh—that reminds me. Her mother was going to visit you."

"Her mother—?"

"Mrs. Hildebrand. Did she?"

"Yes." He lit a cigarette. Kyrie took it from him, ruffled his prematurely white hair, and said, "Mind your manners." He lit another cigarette, staring at her.

"Grid—you're gawking as though you don't know me. Is it because I snatched your cigarette?"

"You can snatch anything I've got," he said.

"Then why gawk?"

"Every so often a check is necessary to see if your eyes are really violet."

"And you're the man who didn't smell spring in the air." She kissed him lightly, but quite strongly enough to reduce Mrs. Hildebrand to the status of a fleeting aberration.

He found that he could say with healthy annoyance, "You should have known better than to send that woman to me."

"I didn't send her. I told her blackmail wasn't your pigeon —but apparently she had heard Junie brag that his father was the boss of the whole police force—and in the minds of most people the departments are lumped together anyway. So she was sure you could advise her."

"I advised her to see Lieutenant Danzig. The desk sergeant could have done as much."

"I'm sorry. Was she a nuisance?"

"Yes," he said, "or, to put it more gallantly—a distraction."

Kyrie's voice was thoughtful. "If I weren't the overconfident type I'd examine that statement minutely."

He curved an arm around her slim pliant waist. "Examine it for what?"

"Never mind—just don't bother to put things so gallantly. Did she manage to say her piece before you got rid of her?"

He nodded. Then he said, "Surely she didn't run through it for you. You can't know her that well."

"I met her only yesterday. I'd have mentioned it last night, but you came home late and it slipped my mind. Nora performed the introductions. We were near the house, so I asked her in. I almost asked that man in too. I thought he was with her, but I took a second look and decided he couldn't be—a flash type—waiting for someone— I guess. Well, Nora went upstairs to watch television with Junie— and Alix—that's what Nora calls her—let down her hair. Beautiful hair—isn't it?"

"For people who like redheads."

"Do you? No—don't answer. Anyway, I was as surprised as you seem to be. She looks so reserved. But of course when I realized that she knew about you it didn't seem so strange."

"It does to me. If she thought it necessary to explain why she wanted to see me she could just have told you she was being blackmailed. What was your reaction to the tale of the art-student lover?"

"The art student—? But she *did* just tell me about the blackmail. Oh, Grid—your face! Honestly—I wasn't trying to pump you."

"I know. Well, I suppose it's better for me to be a complete cad than for you to burst with curiosity." He told her the rest of it.

She made no comment. She said, "You don't have to swear me to secrecy. Even if I were the gossipy type I wouldn't consider it worth circulating."

"Has she lived in the neighborhood long?"

"Quite a while, I imagine."

"Funny—I don't remember seeing her around."

"You *would* remember—wouldn't you?"

He said virtuously, "Of course. I have a trained eye."

"And a glib tongue. Well, she might never have crossed our paths if Nora hadn't come home. Children and dogs are almost the only way people get to know their neighbors in a city. A week or two before we moved here Nora was sent on a visit to her grandmother. Junie spotted her the day she returned and fell hard."

"Is she a pleasant child?"

"She's a love—all big gray eyes and beautiful manners." Kyrie added, "She takes after her father."

"You've met him too?"

"No. I'm quoting Mrs. Baldwin, who lives next door to them. It isn't exactly hearsay. I saw for myself that she doesn't take after her mother."

"Nora's a love," Nelson said. "Nora doesn't take after her mother. Conclusion—Nora's mother is not a love."

"That isn't what I meant. I was speaking of physical resemblance." Kyrie shrugged her pretty shoulders. "No I wasn't —not entirely."

"There's my fine honest girl."

"There's your fine honest cat. Maybe her being so wonderful-looking has something to do with it. You know—the stock feminine reaction you read about. Did you like her, Grid?"

"I had the stock masculine reaction you read about," Nelson said.

"I wish I didn't believe you."

"It's more important that you believe I have reactions that aren't in stock—and that I reserve them for a special customer." He got up. "Don't I hear the doorbell?"

"Oh dear—just when you were getting interesting. I guess it's the Blakes. Adele called and said that they might drop in."

In the weeks that followed, business picked up at Homicide, and Nelson spent few evenings at home. On one of those evenings he met and made friends with Nora Hildebrand, who had stayed to have supper with Junie. Nora, a charming pigtailed child, insisted upon addressing him as Mr. Grid-dely because that was what Sammy called him. Later Nora's father came for her. Nelson liked him and the little girl so well that he made a mental note to ask Lieutenant Danzig how the blackmail case was progressing. What he learned from Danzig shocked him. It was the first of a series of shocks.

Chapter Two

He dropped in on Danzig during lunch time. The massive-shouldered lieutenant was having coffee and sandwiches in his temporary office. He gestured at Nelson with a powerful arm. "If it isn't the brand-new captain hisself. Be my guest. You won't be depriving me. This bread is pure cardboard."

Nelson straddled a chair. "I'm on a cardboard-free diet. I stopped in to ask about the client I brought you—Mrs. Hildebrand."

"That case is closed." The gloom on Danzig's seasoned face might have been due to the mouthful he swallowed. "As of ten days ago."

"Quick work. Congratulations."

"Nothing to it—at least from our point of view. From where the lady sits it's another story. She got a hell of a scare." He gulped pale coffee. "Maybe she had it coming—but she couldn't have been more than a kid when she slipped. If I'd've been her husband I wouldn't've left her alone in the first place—and in the second place I wouldn't blame her—"

"You're an old bachelor," Nelson said, "which disqualifies your opinions on that subject." He was glad that Richard Hildebrand would not be given the option to blame or not to blame. In the act of rising he said, "Who was the foul fiend?"

"Sit down—I haven't told you the half of it—not by a damned sight. Truth is I'm not at all comfortable about the lady."

"Your discomfort is probably shared by every man she meets."

"Sure—glands will be glands." He looked pleased. It was like seeing an impregnable fort look pleased. "Jokes aside—once a screwball's unwound, there's no telling who'll be hit."

"You said the case was closed."

"Did I say I had the blackmailer under lock and key?"

"Haven't you?"

"She wouldn't prefer charges. She wouldn't even let me tax him with it."

"The art student?"

"No—the husband."

Nelson said incredulously, "You've lost me."

"Give me a chance and I'll find you. The husband wrote those letters. How about that for a lousy way of getting even?"

Nelson wished he had stayed lost. He said, "You're certain?"

"Here's how certain. For a starter we got his thumbs off the letters."

"Mine too—no doubt," Nelson said.

Danzig grinned. "Not a whorl or a loop. You couldn't have been as rattled as you thought. Only two sets—his and hers. We checked his with the prints on his desk. She'd tipped us when he'd be out—not that she suspected him—but so he wouldn't wonder why we were there. We didn't suspect him either. We were just doing a thorough job. The main purpose of the call was to talk to the servants. But they were clean."

"And on the strength of the prints Mr. Hildebrand wasn't?"

"I follow you. The ads could have come into the house and been handled by him. I'd buy that except for the rest of it. We found a purple crayon in his desk. It was sitting on top of a stack of ads he'd salted away for future use."

"You're describing a fool."

"I'll go you one better—a crazy fool. Most blackmailers are foxy. This one didn't even bother to brush up on his work."

"There's something wrong somewhere. I've met Hildebrand. He's sane and quite intelligent."

Danzig scratched his head. "Far be it from me to question your judgment. It's the evidence talking."

"What about the evidence that all this happened more than six years ago—presumably before she presented him with a child? Why should he drag it out now?"

"Search me. Maybe he just got wind of it—or maybe it's been gnawing at his mind. Anyway—it was five years ago. Seeing you're pitching for him, how come you're not more in his confidence? The little girl's none of her doing—his by a former marriage." He stared at Nelson's face, at the hand that rose to tug at the oddly vital white hair. "Hold it—I thought of that too. The kid's about six or seven—but nowadays they come precocious—"

"I'm not thinking of it," Nelson said, and purged it from his mind. It was difficult to swallow Hildebrand as a blackmailer. It was impossible to associate either the content or intent of the letters with that nice sensitive child.

"Also—the angle of her hating her stepmother is out. I make it they get along real good. I had other ideas when I found the crayon matched a set the kid had in her room—but that was before I heard she was visiting her grandma in California at the time the first letter arrived—and you saw for yourself all three were delivered by hand. They weren't postmarked, so it stands to reason Hildebrand shoved them into his own mailbox. I'm telling you he's a real dog—using his daughter's playtoys for his dirty work."

"I suppose you were too satisfied to dig up the art student?"

"You sure are a die-hard. I not only dug him up—I spoke to him."

"I'm surprised she remembered his name."

Danzig frowned. "What gives? You got a down on the lady—or a notion Homicide's the only squad knows its stuff? The art student's name is Myles—Leon Myles. Not being one to sneeze at a likely candidate, I located him before I did anything else. All I had to do was look in the telephone book. It's the same fellow, so don't climb on your horse again. He's got a store on Washington Heights where he does picture framing—with a side line of greeting cards and stationery. I hiked myself up there and rigged a tale to explain being nosy. He made no bones about admitting he'd attended the Fiftieth Street Academy at the time in question. In fact, he was tickled to reminisce about his bohemian days. If he's a man with a chip I'll drum myself out of the force."

"Did he reminisce about Mrs. Hildebrand?"

"Nope. So help me, I had to jog him with a description of her before he clicked."

Nelson, who was becoming sick of the whole business, picked up interest. He said, "She told me he was a small-town boy—alone—without friends in the city. Didn't it occur to you that in similar circumstances even a kind invitation to a drink would stand out in anyone's memory?"

"Why don't you quit and open up a law office? He wasn't putting on an act. I can spot an actor in a thick fog." He thought for a moment. "Or if he was it had nothing to do with the case. He'd introduced me to his wife—a nice hefty piece of goods who was lending a hand in the store. And with her around he might have thought it smart to soft-pedal a caper like that. He's a respectable married man and he likes the status quo fine—a going business—an A-1 credit rating—and fat twins sitting out front in a baby carriage." Danzig offered the twins triumphantly, as though they were conclusive proof of the ex-art student's probity.

"What of Hildebrand's credit rating? Does he need money?"

Danzig dusted crumbs from his desk and threw the remains of his lunch into the wastebasket. "I'm glad you asked that question. If Dun and Bradstreet haven't flipped, he needs money like I need you to heckle me. He's the president and biggest stockholder of one of the top real estate outfits in the country."

"A very crazy fool."

Exasperation seamed Danzig's face. "Didn't they teach you about the human brain in college? When it gets fouled up its right cells don't know what its left cells are doing. Take you, for instance. Nothing personal—but it's been no secret you're well-heeled—not since that dough you inherited was made public by the commissioner when some crank wanted to start an investigation to prove your scale of living spelled graft—"

Nelson stirred restively.

"Okay—don't take off. It's no crime to be rich—not yet." He was enjoying himself. "And I'm not pasting the screwball label on you for working at a job like yours when it's not a matter of bread and butter—like you was a priest with a calling. What I'm getting at— suppose your wife came to you empty-handed—and every cent she used was out of your pocket? Being in your right mind, can you imagine yourself putting the bite on her for your own dough?"

"Didn't Mrs. Hildebrand bring anything to her marriage?"

"Nothing but herself." He added truculently, "And isn't that plenty?"

Nelson had no answer. He did have another question. Danzig anticipated it.

"So's you won't go away dissatisfied," Danzig said, "here's the clincher. You know Agnes Beal?"

"Yes." Agnes Beal was a young policewoman, personable, and for the most part equal to the roles that were thrust upon her.

"Well—to drive in that last nail, I assigned Beal to follow through on the pay-off. The Music Mart on Fourteenth Street is a kind of self-service joint—a barn for size—stacked with old records, sheet music, and songbooks, plus all the latest stuff. There are booths in the back to try out records, and the place is usually full of hipsters buying or browsing. Mrs. H. was to enter carrying the money boxed and wrapped like it was something she'd bought on the way. She was to choose a bunch of records, hand them to the clerk, and ask him to bundle her package in with them. Then—"

"I read the instructions. She was to plead further shopping and leave the package there with her name on it to be picked up later."

"That's right. Which we had Mrs. Hildebrand do on the given day— and which she only consented to do to prove us wrong. Beal staked out where she could cover the entrance. She was about ready to call quits when he showed."

"Hildebrand?" Nelson was unable to accept it.

"In person. Talk about your screwballs! He could have sent a messenger—or at least he could have staked out himself to make sure his wife didn't cross him. But no—he walked right into it—and Beal watches him make a bold-as-brass exit with the whole kit and caboodle." Danzig's grunt was pure frustration. "If the lady didn't have such a forgiving nature we could have nabbed him good. Care to make another speech on how sane and intelligent he is?"

Nelson did not. He said lamely, "I guess there haven't been any more letters. Whatever you substituted for money would tell him the game was up—if it was a game."

"Yeah—if it was a game. That's what's eating me. Once they start cracking they generally break. He might try something more dangerous than a purple crayon on his next go-round—and what can I do about it? My hands are tied."

"But if he's as mad as you seem to believe there must have been signs for his wife to notice."

"There were. She told me he hadn't been his sunny self for a spell—but she's too loyal to connect it up—"

"Did she go into detail?"

"Not after I added all the twos and twos. Before that she'd said she didn't want him to know about the blackmail because he'd been moody and jumpy lately. I could see she was holding back a lot and I didn't press her—that end of it not being my department. Still—I'd sure hate to see her come to grief. What about you dropping him a hint he should get himself psyched?"

"He'd have to recognize the need—for it to do any good. Besides, I don't know him well enough to drop that kind of hint."

"I'll be damned. I thought you were his lodge brother at the very least."

"Your tone when you mention Mrs. Hildebrand is misleading too," Nelson said.

He carried a small formless weight of depression from Danzig's office. He was far less concerned with the threat that hung over Mrs. Hildebrand than with what might be in store for young Nora. In the little he had seen of her there was no indication that she came from a disturbed household. At first he had thought her somewhat grave for her years, but that effect had been dispelled when he caught in transit a pixyish smile sent Junie's way. Moreover, her relationship with her father seemed normal and unstrained. She had greeted him affectionately and at once launched a chronicle of her activities. Hildebrand, on his part, had been an indulgent listener and, after granting her an extension of her visit so that she could assist Julie in rounding up scattered toys, had helped her into her coat and hat with practiced skill.

The extension had stretched to nearly an hour, in which Hildebrand accepted a drink and offered pleasant lucid conversation in return. His words and manner during that period were the sole basis of Nelson's assessment. But summing up people was his job, and a large percentage of his success depended upon quick and fairly accurate estimates of those with whom he dealt.

It was true that he had not been deliberately seeking defects in the character of a chance guest. But neither had he been seeking the qualities of balance and integrity, which prior to Danzig's report he would have sworn were there.

That night before they went to bed he told Kyrie of Danzig's findings. She too found them hard to accept.

"I watched him with Nora," she said. "I remember thinking what a pleasant man he was—and hoping we'd see more of him."

Both of them were silent for a few minutes, like people standing before a picture in a gallery. The picture showed a stocky dark-haired man of average height, not handsome, but with fine gray eyes and a firm generous mouth. It was a good-natured face—a good face....

Nelson said, "Has Nora been here recently?"

"More than you have. Tonight's dinner was the third in a row you've missed." It was a comment rather than a reproach. "But I haven't seen either of her parents. A maid calls for her when she stays to eat with Junie. Oh, Grid—I hope Nora isn't in for a bad time. Is there anything you can do—?"

"If there is it eludes me. I can't very well walk up to a man I hardly know and beg him to consult a psychiatrist. It wouldn't exactly come under the heading of small talk."

"Suppose I invite them to dinner? It would give you a chance to—"

He vetoed it. "No, Kyrie. Say that a second look altered my opinion—what else would it achieve? I still couldn't give the man unsolicited advice. Let's continue to invite people here for purely social reasons."

"But that poor baby. I wonder if her own mother is alive or if she—" Kyrie looked at him. She said nothing for a while. Then she suggested that they go to bed for purely social reasons.

His opportunity for a second look at his neighbor came without being contrived. He was leaving headquarters one evening when he saw Hildebrand making for the exit. Not stopping to weigh the pros and cons, Nelson called his name.

Hildebrand turned. It took a moment for his eyes to clear. In that moment Nelson noted that he seemed to have aged since their first encounter.

"Good to see you again." He was making an obvious effort. "I promised myself that pleasure but I didn't think it would be here."

"Can I be of any help—or is your mission accomplished?"

"No—yes—I—if what I've heard about you is correct it wasn't anything in your line."

"That's good. Homicides are a glut on the market these days. My car's outside and I'm homeward-bound. Like a lift?"

Hildebrand looked as though he needed a lift. "Thanks—perhaps I could buy you a drink on the way."

Nelson said, "Good idea," and asked him to wait a minute. He phoned Kyrie, who expected him, and said that he would be a bit delayed. A short while later he steered Hildebrand to a table in a quiet hotel bar. Conversation en route had been heavy going. Scotch did not further it. Nelson offered Hildebrand a cigarette and watched it burn unsmoked as the man fumbled for something to say.

"I don't believe I thanked you and your wife sufficiently for being so charming to my daughter. Her talk is full of Junie and Mrs. Nelson and someone called Sammy who appears to do nothing but feed her. I hope she isn't making a nuisance of herself."

"If she is we'll have to put up with it," Nelson said, "or disinherit Junie. I'm quite sure his intentions are serious."

Hildebrand laughed. Nelson, who had judged him to be in the early forties, lopped off a few years and had to replace them as soon as the laugh died. He thought that he had never seen more distress or defeat on anyone's face. The compulsion to alleviate it was too strong to resist. He said abruptly, "What's wrong?"

"I—I beg your pardon."

"You went to headquarters—and it's plain you got no answer to whatever took you there. I don't say I can give you an answer either, but I'll be glad to take a stab at it."

"You're right I got no answer. I went to the precinct first and was sent down to see a certain lieutenant. He was—rude would be putting it mildly—so would contemptuous. He hardly listened. He treated me like a criminal—a particularly vicious criminal of the type he hated most."

"Was it—do you know his name?"

"Danzig. Never mind—I don't intend to make trouble for him."

Nelson thought Danzig would appreciate that.

"Maybe he believed it was a matter for a private detective,"

Hildebrand went on, "and that I was taking up his time unnecessarily when I could afford—"

"Police officers don't think that way," Nelson said.

Hildebrand was wrapped in his own thoughts. "As a matter of fact, I was considering a private detective. There's one named Lindstrom who rents office space in one of my firm's buildings on Seventeenth Street—the one where I have my offices." He shrugged. "But—"

"Too close to home?" Nelson said.

"Not only that. I happened to see a man coming out of his office—someone I'd encountered on the street one day talking to—to a friend of my wife's." He seemed to have difficulty with the word "friend."

"Perhaps you could recommend another—"

"I'm recommending myself."

Hildebrand stared at him, really met his eyes for the first time since he had come to take his daughter home. Then he said, "It's my wife—I don't think you've met her—" Nelson made no disclaimer. Psychotic or not, it was unlikely that Hildebrand could know that his wife had come to Homicide with her complaint. And if he did know that she had gone anywhere, and yet insisted upon pretending otherwise, Nelson still wanted to hear him out.

"Quite accidentally," Hildebrand said, "I discovered that she was being blackmailed."

Nelson had difficulty with his facial muscles.

"She has no idea that I'm aware of it—or that I know the precise nature of the hold the blackmailer has upon her." He had been fingering his glass. He drew his hand away and clenched it to a fist. "I'm not a violent man, Captain, but ever since morning when I realized what was going on I've been afraid of myself. I have a terrible feeling that if I find the one who's subjecting Alix to this—this indignity—I'll kill him." He added softly, "Or her."

"You suspect a woman?"

"It's not that cut-and-dried. It's simply that I can't think of anyone else to suspect." He misread Nelson's wooden expression. He shook his head. "It won't work, Captain."

Now it comes, Nelson thought. He knows I know. "What won't work?" he said.

"Dumping this in your lap."

Nelson wondered fleetingly if they had switched roles, if his own sanity hung in the balance. He said, "I'm asking for it."

"Yes—I know—but I shouldn't take advantage." He was striving to make his voice light. "I'm a hardheaded businessman, Captain, but even the most realistic of us get fanciful ideas. We meet someone and—well—right from the start he seems to have all the earmarks of an old friend. It isn't just your asking for it—it's—never mind—" He pushed his chair back. "We'd better be getting along. I've kept you from your dinner—"

"Sit down," Nelson said.

Chapter Three

Hildebrand sat down again. He looked away from Nelson. A waiter interpreted the turn of his head as a signal and brought replacements. Hildebrand said abruptly, "I can't help believing that Lilith is at the bottom of it." He seized upon and gulped his second drink as though the words had burned his throat.

For Nelson the name he had spoken immediately conjured up demons and strange medieval rites. He fought his own sudden thirst. He saw Hildebrand set down his empty glass and stare at it in astonishment. He could not help thinking what Danzig thought, but he censored it from his voice. "Ready for another?"

"No, thanks. If that doesn't generate enough steam to get me started, nothing will."

"Lilith seems a better than average start." Nelson leaned back in his chair with the air of a man relaxing.

Hildebrand said, "She probably has no more right to call herself Lilith than she has to any of her little affectations. For all I know, Greenway's a phony too."

"Is Greenway her husband?"

"No—sorry—storytelling's not one of my talents. I've never even been able to tell a joke without putting the point first. Greenway's her last name—Lilith Greenway. She's not married. At least there's no husband in the picture. She's the woman I referred to—the one who might be blackmailing Alix. Don't ask me why I'm accusing her—except that when trouble brews she's the type you automatically look to as the cause. Alix knew her long before she knew me. They went to the same neighborhood school as children and grew up together. That doesn't seem a sufficient basis for friendship since they have nothing else in common—but Alix is extremely loyal. She says that Lilith has had a hard time and that it would be cruel to drop her."

"A hard time money-wise?"

Hildebrand shrugged. "I didn't encourage Alix to give me the details. I only know that the moment she turned up in New York she started to haunt my house."

"She lives with you?"

"No—thank God. She lives with her brother—uptown. Before that she lived on the Coast—and before that in Shenanga, Pennsylvania, where she and Alix were born." He lit a cigarette, drew on it, and said, "She might as well live with us. She's there all the time. You'd think she'd have the grace to leave when I come home—not because I don't make every effort to hide my distaste for her—but because she can't hide hers for me. She goes out of her way to make me uncomfortable."

Persecution mania, Nelson thought. And then he thought angrily, To hell with labels. To hell with being influenced by Danzig.

"I don't take rabid dislikes to people often," Hildebrand said. He held his cigarette before him and stared at its glowing end as though he were trying to quell an evil eye. "There's her brother too. He makes my skin crawl—but not for the same reason. It's the way he looks at Alix—yet I'm sorry for him—poor devil. I think he's mentally out of whack. He manages to hold a job though—which Lilith obviously doesn't. I've often wondered as to the source of her income. Still—whether I'm right or wrong about the blackmailing, there's Nora. She shouldn't be subjected to either of them, and I wish Alix would realize it without my having to point it out. It makes me sick—"

He was sick all right. Sweat had broken out on his forehead. His generously formed lips were ridged in white. Nelson waited, wanting him to continue at his own gait, trying not to let the word "obsessional" gain a foothold in his mind. But when the pause gaped dangerously he had to fill it. "I wouldn't worry about Nora. She seems so entirely claimed by her own little world that I doubt if the fine shadings of adult behavior affect her."

"Fine shadings," Hildebrand muttered.

"Not to you, perhaps. But whatever's going on can't possibly be obvious to her, because I've seldom seen a child who shows more evidence of well-being."

Hildebrand's mouth was less taut. "I've tried to make her feel secure. So has Alix." Speaking normally, he recalled and confirmed Nelson's first impression of him. "Alix loves her as much as I do. That's why it's so difficult for me to lay down the law—or even hint that her friends aren't good enough for my daughter." Again the darkness descended. He made a painful effort to dispel it. "I don't believe I told you that Alix is Nora's stepmother."

"No—you didn't tell me."

"Well—my first wife died when Nora was an infant." The words carried the gentled sadness of an old grief.

Nelson wondered among other things how soon after the first wife's death he had remarried. He received a vivid image of a baby crying upstairs in a house visited by an art student. Because almost any question would have revealed foreknowledge, he said noncommittally, "If Mrs. Hildebrand has had Nora since infancy she's probably forgotten that she isn't her own child."

Hildebrand looked pleased. "She really has—although Nora was nearly three when I brought her home. She lived with my parents for a while after I remarried. They wanted her and it seemed a sensible arrangement. It was hardly fair to saddle Alix with a ready-made family at the outset—although she's since told me that I cheated her out of Nora's first years."

Nelson hit upon a question he thought was safe; one that would lead back to the reason for his presence in this bar while Sammy's excellent food waited. "Did you know of the blackmail the night you called for Nora at my house?"

Hildebrand said, "No. I learned about it this morning." He took out his wallet and extracted a crumpled sheet of paper that had been smoothed and folded. "It's a circular from a dry-cleaning company. Don't bother about that part of it. Turn it over."

Nelson saw what he expected to see and tried to look as though it were spot news. The purple legend lacked the obscenities of the preceding messages, but it was in the same vein.

"Surprise—Surprise! I know all about your games, Sweetheart. How crazy can you get! Scream to the police again and take the consequences. I can be plenty artistic when it comes to dealing with your kind. But I've got a big heart. I'll give you one more chance. Instructions coming up in my next."

Nelson lifted his eyes to Hildebrand's watching face.

Hildebrand waited for comment, received none, and said, "I suppose it needs a preface before it can make sense to you." He went through the motions of drinking from his empty glass, swallowed dryly, and set the glass down. "Right after Alix and I were married I had to make a trip to California. It was urgent—my father was critically ill there. Alix decided she'd only be in the way, so she didn't accompany me. We both thought the separation would be no more than a few weeks—but as it turned out I was gone for two months. As soon as I got back one of the maids came to me with a tale. Most likely she believed she'd be rewarded for keeping tabs on my interests. I dismissed her." He took a match folder from the table and tore out the matches one by one. He laid them on top of each other in a neat structure, razed it, and went through the process again. The second time he let the structure remain. "Alix was—is—a great deal younger than I." He spurred himself to go on, grimacing as though the spurs hurt. "Nothing had changed about her that I could see. We've all—at some time in our lives—performed unpredictable acts that are foreign to our usual behavior."

Nelson thought unhappily of the use Danzig would have made of that statement. He said, "Didn't you have to give a reason for dismissing the maid?"

"I told Alix the truth, hoping she would deny it. She did. She explained that she'd been attending some art classes during my absence and that she'd invited one of the students in for a drink. I believed—" He corrected himself without appearing to notice that he had done so. "I chose to believe her—and we went on as before. She was and is the best of wives. She has never—I was never given cause to remember that there had been the slightest rift between us until"—he looked with loathing at the circular—"until I discovered this."

"How did you discover it?"

"I happened to be at home this morning when the mail arrived. I went to the box and found it in with the rest."

"No envelope?"

"No—so of course the postman hadn't brought it. Someone must have stuck it in earlier." Hildebrand was busily striking matches on the denuded folder and pinching them out. "It's decent of you to be interested enough to ask questions. The officer I spoke to wasn't. All he wanted was to get rid of me."

"It isn't usual for you to be at home when the mail is delivered?"

"No—it isn't. There's no law that says I have to be at the office at a given time—but I'm an early riser and since my work is sedentary about the only exercise I get is a long walk or a ride in the park before I settle down for the day. But last night I took Alix out to celebrate her birthday. It was pretty late when we got home. We so rarely visit night clubs that I hated to spoil her pleasure by suggesting I'd had enough. As a result I overslept—"

Nelson said, "What I'm getting at is that the letter must have been written by someone who is familiar with your habits." He did not say, You—for instance. He saw that Hildebrand was arranging the burnt-out matches into a careful design, and had to remind himself that the act would have seemed ordinary in one whose sanity was not impugned.

Hildebrand addressed the matches. "Nobody outside of the household knows my habits better than Lilith Greenway." He punched the table with his fist and the design was no more. "There's irony for you. Lilith is the trusted confidante—not me." He jerked his head at the circular. "There must have been more of these. That's obvious. Yet—shouldn't my attitude toward the maid have given Alix faith enough to realize that she could tell me anything?" His voice had swelled, and suddenly he became conscious of it. With a look of distaste he muttered, "Sorry—I didn't intend to broadcast. You can see—can't you—why it's impossible for me to bring the matter up when Alix is trying to keep it secret—thinking God knows what effect it will have on me?"

And judging by the look of you, she's right, Nelson thought. He said, "What I can't see is why you're so certain your wife's friend is the blackmailer. Ruling out your personal feelings about her, aren't there more logical suspects? Disgruntled servants have been known to strike back. The maid might be in need of cash—or she may have repeated the story to someone who saw a way of capitalizing on it."

"At this late date?" Hildebrand shook his head. "She's a Swiss girl—of German parentage. When I fired her she informed me that she'd had enough of this country and would return to Switzerland as soon as she could. As a matter of fact, I arranged passage for her instead of paying the usual notice."

"She must have been a high-priced maid."

Hildebrand said sheepishly, "At the time it seemed worth the extra money to avoid any chance of running into her again. I hated the sight of her—but after I'd simmered down I realized that she was only acting according to her lights—doing what she called her duty. I don't think she was dishonest—just smug and self-righteous."

"Do you remember her name?"

"Knobler—Gertrude Knobler—and I'll save you the trouble of bringing up the next logical suspect. Naturally it occurred to me that the art student could have authored this—" He gestured at the note on the table, quoted the purple scrawl. "'Plenty artistic' certainly calls attention to him—yet it might be exactly what Lilith's type of mentality would look upon as a really subtle touch to put Alix off the track—so—"

Nelson finished it for him. "So your money's still on Lilith." He was thinking that his delayed dinner had served no good purpose. Danzig had looked up the art student, and he himself would check to see if a Swiss girl named Gertrude Knobler had re-entered the country. He would also check on Lilith Greenway or anything in her past that might support Hildebrand's suspicion. But he had no optimism in regard to what these checks might unearth. As Danzig put it, the clincher seemed to be Hildebrand's visit to the Music Mart.

Hildebrand said, "Yes—my money's still on Lilith. Don't ask me to explain why. How can I list intangibles? Anyway—where am I going to dig up the art student? I didn't ask Alix for his name. I wanted to keep him as anonymous as possible." He produced a bleak smile. "Isn't there a gag about a policeman moving a corpse to another street because he couldn't spell the one where the accident had taken place? I suppose you'd have some justification for putting me in the same category—thinking I'm fastening on Lilith for the convenience of it—" He foundered on. "Well, whichever way you look at it, Frank isn't much to go on—"

"Frank?"

"The maid had heard Alix call him Frank."

"You're sure?"

Hildebrand was startled by the sharpness of the query. "She pronounced it 'Fronck'—but I put that down to her accent. I can still hear her growling it out. Now that the whole thing's revived, all the gruesome details have come back to me. I thought I'd succeeded in forgetting them, but it seems I couldn't—"

Not according to Danzig you couldn't, Nelson thought, not more than a man with a festering sore. He puzzled over the fact that Frank or Fronck was a far cry from the Leo Myles of Danzig's report.

"Of course it might have been his last name," Hildebrand said, "except that—" He bit his lip. The words he could not bring himself to say were plainer than speech. A woman does not call her lover—even of brief standing—by his last name.

Nelson wished he could give the reassurance demanded by the unhappy eyes. He said, "I can't make any promises, of course, but at least you've got it off your chest—and if you can get it off your mind until I've had a chance to mull it over I'll try to come up with something."

Hildebrand's formal expression of thanks carried no hope. He closed it with, "I've been a rotten host. Another drink? Well—" He summoned the waiter and paid the check.

The business traffic had been replaced by theatergoers. Nelson, a practiced hand at outmaneuvering other vehicles, drove by reflex, his thoughts fixed upon someone called Frank or Fronck, who might or might not be a product of Hildebrand's imagination. He felt uncommonly low in spirit. His ambivalence in regard to Hildebrand had taxed him more than a full day's work. It was as though the repeated exercise of drawing toward and retreating from the man had been a physical rather than mental or emotional process. At their first encounter there had been no ambivalence. He had merely made natural response to a likable human being, and he wondered now how he would have reacted to Hildebrand's story on that evening. He was unable to arrive at any conclusion except that the issue seemed clouded enough without the introduction of "Frank." There was, for example, that business of the Music Mart.

He said, "I had quite a discussion with Nora about music."

Hildebrand, shrouded in his thoughts, answered, "Yes—she loves music. She has her own record player and we're always adding to her collection." Then he said, "I'm beginning to wish I hadn't run into you tonight."

"Why?"

"It's hard for me to say."

Nelson waited, glanced at him, and said with considered lightness, "Isn't it too early to decide I've been a washout?"

"I didn't mean that. I meant I'd have preferred to keep our relationship on a purely social plane. I was looking forward to having you and your wife meet Alix. You'd have liked her—"

Nelson's collar clutched his neck. It took will power not to loosen it.

Hildebrand said haltingly, "But after what I've told you—knowing what you know—it wouldn't be fair to Alix. It's not much of an excuse—but if I hadn't been bowled over by that police officer's attitude I'd never—"

Nelson stopped him. "Can you be under the delusion that you've behaved like what our British cousins refer to as a 'bounder'?"

"It's not a delusion."

Nelson cursed himself for his inadvertent use of the word. He cursed Danzig because of the significance it assumed on Hildebrand's lips.

"Besides," Hildebrand went on bitterly, "now that I've presented a neighbor with the intelligence that I'm what all our cousins refer to as a 'cuckold,' further association with him will be awkward—to say the least—"

"Look here—you didn't consult me out of bounderism or anything else you want to call it. You talked to me because you have a problem that's too big for you to handle alone. You weren't gossiping about your wife—or about yourself. You were trying to protect your marriage—so—" The ambivalence took hold again. Or were you? he thought. What was your real motive? For all I know, the blackmail might have been motivated by obsessional hatred for Lilith. You might—in your sickness—think it enormously clever to write the letters—fix the guilt on her—and so remove her from your wife's orbit. "I'm a policeman," he said, and self-anger tinged his voice. "I take such matters as you've confided to me in stride."

"I'd have talked to you no matter what your profession happened to be," Hildebrand said doggedly.

"All right." Nelson made deliberate burlesque of it. "We won't speak as we pass by."

"You make me sound like a blushing schoolgirl—but this is something I *can't* take in stride."

"What you sound like is a man under a strain. I'd get a good night's rest if I were you—even if it's necessary to use a barbiturate. Sleep will help you more than anything you can possibly do for the time being." He listened to the insipid words without pride. He thought disgustedly that with his training and experience he should be able to deal out something more potent than the stock advice so cheaply vended by every amateur do-gooder who walked the earth. But he could find nothing to add to it, and if it reached Hildebrand at all it received the silent treatment it deserved.

Halted by a traffic light, Nelson examined an impulse to tell Hildebrand that he had met Alix, and give a full account of the meeting. He rejected it because he suspected that it was based chiefly upon his dislike of playing false to Hildebrand's instinctive trust in him and would accomplish nothing but his own peace of mind. As shock treatment it might produce interesting results, but if Hildebrand were in no condition to receive shock treatment it could bring on a crisis best postponed until further exploration had been made.

When they were a few blocks from home Hildebrand asked to be let out. He said he had an errand to do and would prefer to walk the remaining distance. Before Nelson drove on he saw him turn at a florist shop. For no explainable reason this caused his spirits to drop another notch.

He braked savagely in front of his lighted house. Kyrie answered the door before he had time to produce a key.

"I was watching from the window," she said. "I sent Sammy out for a walk."

"Is she annoyed with me?" he said, and meant, Are you?

Kyrie kissed him. "We thought when they promoted you from lieutenant to captain that we'd see more of you—on the theory that the bigger the shot the less he works—I guess. But both of us learned the futility of being annoyed with you years ago. Anyway, dinner was nothing that had to be served on the dot. Sammy knows better than to cook souffle-type dishes until you're safe on the premises."

He tried to meet her cheerfulness. "What are we having?"

"Ragout—it improves with reheating. I thought it would improve with company too—so I waited."

"I've got a wife as is a wife. I'll be down in a minute." He ran up the stairs.

She called after him, "Look in on Junie. He's been put to bed twice. Maybe you can make it stick."

Nelson took a quick wash and went to his son's room. Junie breathed regularly, half on, half off the bed. Nelson removed from the blanket a wad of modeling clay, a bent screw driver, one boxing glove, and a drunken-looking hand puppet, straightened the little boy out, and tucked him in.

"All quiet," he said as he reached the foot of the stairs.

"Well—it was a good fight while it lasted. He seemed determined to stay awake until you came."

He told her about Hildebrand as they ate. He seldom talked shop at table, but Hildebrand was not exactly shop. For once Sammy's skillful cooking was wasted. He and Kyrie swallowed large helpings of the ragout, but neither of them tasted it.

They carried the coffee service to the living room. Kyrie was filling the cups when Sammy returned. Sammy stood tall in the archway, distress printed on her handsome apricot face. Nelson knew at once that something very serious had happened.

Her deep rich voice confirmed it. "I glad you here, Mr. Griddely. You better go right outside. That poor child's daddy, he look to be in bad trouble."

Chapter Four

About halfway up the street two policemen were engaged in diverting traffic and pushing back a small crowd. Nelson worked his way to the cleared area. He cut short the protests of both policemen by identifying himself. He was thankful that Kyrie had not insisted upon rushing out with him.

Part of the contents of a squashed cardboard box was strewn freakishly over the inert figure on the asphalt. Someone in the crowd said, "Nothing like supplying your own flowers," and someone else tittered nervously. Another voice demanded to know why the handsome white-haired boy was being given special treatment, and another asserted confidently that he was either a relative or a politician. Still another complained about ambulances always taking forever and added with unctuous pessimism that it was probably too late for an ambulance anyway. There was a surge forward as Nelson dropped to his heels. He saw what was to be seen by the street lights, scanned the surrounding asphalt, and arose nursing the hope that it was not too late.

"Think there's a chance, Captain?" one of the policemen said.

"He's breathing. How long ago did it happen?"

"Ten-twelve minutes. I rang Bellevue soon as I could whistle up a stand-by. I didn't want to risk anyone trying to move him. Name's Hildebrand. Lives on this street. A woman recognized him and hot-footed it off to give his family the bad news. Funny the wife or someone else from his house hasn't come out. Just as well though. Being loaded, they might balk at Bellevue. People get an idea it's strictly for bums. But any hospital nearer mightn't act quick enough to—"

"Has he been conscious at all?"

"He opened his eyes and closed them again like the pain hit him where he lived. If it's a faint I figure he's more comfortable that way."

"Where's the car?"

"Gone, Captain. A hit-and-run."

"Any witnesses?"

"Two. One was a little old lady—a cleaning woman in an office building on Madison. The other was a middle-aged gent dressed like he still thought he was going to college. I took their names and addresses and let them run along."

"Did they get the license number?"

"They couldn't even come near it between them. They couldn't even agree on the color of the taxicab. One said orange—the other said red." He scowled to show what he thought of witnesses in general. "The middle-aged college gent was one of them nuts—cultists, I think you call them. He swore he saw two heads at the wheel and that one of them was Death. So how could you expect him to bother about a little thing like getting the license numbers?" He added glumly, "There was a third—a colored lady—but she got lost before I could nab her."

Nelson cheered up a little. He had not waited to question Sammy, but if she were the lost witness everyone but the hit-and-run driver would be a gainer.

"Both witnesses swear the man was jay-walking. They thought maybe the hackie couldn't help coming at him." The policeman scratched his nose. "But if they're right, why did he take off?"

"They're sure it *was* a taxi?"

"So they say—only what with all those two-tone cars around, they could've missed up on that too. They make it a red and white or an orange and white—" He broke off to discipline an aggressive member of the crowd. "Hey—get back till I build you a grandstand."

A flashbulb exploded and Nelson turned, recognizing and addressing the news photographer who had used it. "If I'm in that, Biff, you can cut me out. Did you come by flying saucer?"

"Nope—by grapevine, Captain." He pointed to his companion. "Mortie and I happened to be attending a shindig on Park."

The policeman elbowed him. "Don't bother the captain now."

"Who's bothering him? Say, Captain, he must be more important than I thought if they called you out."

"They didn't call me. I live on this street."

"That's right—so you do. For a minute there you had me wondering what Homicide would be doing at a vulgar street accident—top Homicide at that. You're sure there isn't more to this?"

Nelson said, "A serious murderer doesn't ordinarily depend on a car for a weapon. The results are too uncertain."

"Check. Not on a city street, anyway—and not with anything less than a truck—though it's been known to happen on a country road where more than one try at the bull's-eye doesn't pull an audience. Too bad. I was starting to dream I had a beat. I guess I hoisted a few too many—or else I was influenced by some whack in the crowd who said he saw Death in the front seat. We sure meet some interesting—"

The ambulance came screaming down the street and the crowd scuttled out of its path. It was waved to a stop, and two interns descended. Wasting no words, they went about the business of transferring the unconscious figure to a stretcher. When the doors had closed upon Hildebrand, Nelson conferred briefly with the intern in charge. Then he stood watching as the ambulance streaked off, carrying in addition to the patient the policeman who had put in the call.

He himself felt rather like a deserter, thinking that should Hildebrand recover consciousness he might benefit by the sight of a friendly face. But then, it was unlikely that he would recover consciousness en route. The interns had not attempted to determine the extent of his injuries, nor had they commented upon the stains where his head had struck the asphalt. It might be no more than a slight— Well, no profit in sending the mind on that sort of tour.

For the second time Nelson inspected the asphalt, seeking traces of shattered glass or any trace to lead to a vanished taxi. Absently he picked up a bedraggled spray of white lilac. Come to think of it, why had there been no trace of the friendly face Hildebrand would most need? Where was the beautiful Alix—or had the neighbor changed her mind about being the bearer of ill tidings? He straightened up, did a little jig step to flex his long legs, and pivoted toward Hildebrand's house. Six doors down and across the street, Kyrie had said. The lights were on, but that did not necessarily mean that the mistress was at home. Nelson stared morosely at the white lilac and cast it from him. He shook his head to clear it of extrinsic matter. Hildebrand had mentioned an errand, not errands. He had insisted that he wanted to walk home. But after he left the florist's he had perhaps decided that a longer walk was indicated before he could return to the bosom of his family. Nothing strange about that. People often used exercise as a palliative for inner turmoil. If I had waited for him, Nelson thought. Dropped him at his own door…? He shook his head again. How often in the course of his work had he tried to relieve some suffering soul bowed under a burden of guilt because of an innocent omission? And here he was, shouldering a similar burden, who should and did know that the consequences of such an omission were impossible to foresee.

The west-bound traffic was on the move again, by-passing him with oaths or curiosity, according to the humor of its drivers. The crowd had dispersed as quickly as it had gathered, the newspapermen along with it. He went to join the remaining policeman on the sidewalk.

He saw the small white figure flying toward him and thought sympathetically for a moment of the witness who had seen death in the taxi. He thought that his own imagination was tricking him.

The child was bareheaded and barefooted, and her nightgown billowed out behind her like the gauzy drapery of a Christmas angel. Only it was nobody's Christmas.

Intent upon her mission, she would have flown past him, but he shrugged out of his coat, stooped, caught her, and wrapped her in it, and lifted her in his arms. She struggled, twisting and kicking, butting her head against his chest.

"It's all right, Nora." He held her close, making soothing sounds.

"Let me go," she sobbed. "A car hurt my daddy—Josephine said he was in the middle of the street. I have to find him—"

"Stop crying and listen to me. They're taking good care of your daddy. They've put him to bed and I wouldn't be surprised if he weren't sound asleep by this time." He thought that over grimly.

She quieted in his arms. He tilted her face back and mopped it. Her long dark lashes were like beaded curtains over the salt-washed gray eyes.

She stared at him. After a moment she said apologetically, "At first I didn't recognize you, Mr. Grid-dely. Have they put my daddy to bed in your house?"

"No—in a great big hospital." He made it sound like a palace.

"Will you take me there?"

"Not tonight. You're not dressed for visiting."

"I know. I was in bed—but something woke me up and I went to the stairs. I thought it was Lil talking in her loud voice, but it was Josephine telephoning in the hall to Dr. Falvey about what happened to Daddy and how he must come because Alix had fainted when the lady from next door told her. Josephine doesn't like the telephone, so she always yells at it. Then she saw me and hung up and took me back to my room. She said everybody was having their night off except her and she had her hands full enough without me being naughty and I was to go back to sleep like a good girl. But I didn't want to be a good girl if my daddy was hurt—and I couldn't sleep—and after Josephine went away I got up again and tiptoed to Alix's door. Her light was off and I couldn't hear her breathing—and she couldn't hear me when I said 'Alix' twice—so I was frightened and I ran downstairs and out the door and—"

The tears were not all shed. He saw more coming and forestalled them. He said quickly, "And you flew straight to me like a smart little pigeon."

She smiled heartbreakingly. "I didn't really fly to you on purpose—I wasn't really trying to find *you*—"

"That makes you all the smarter. You found me without trying."

She was not to be diverted for long. "If my daddy's in bed in a hospital he'll be wearing pajamas—so I don't think he'll mind if I have my nightgown on—"

The policeman coughed to attract Nelson's attention. "It's nearly time for me to report back to my precinct, Captain. Would you want me to take the little girl home first?"

"No, thanks—I'll attend to it. Good night."

"Good night, sir."

As the policeman walked off, Nelson saw that a strolling elderly couple had halted in their tracks. He heard the woman say, "I don't know what explanation he gave that policeman, but it doesn't satisfy me. What's he doing with that barefoot child?"

Nora whispered in his ear, "I guess they think it's funny for you to be carrying such a big girl." Then she said, "Don't attend to it."

"To what?"

"To taking me home. If Alix is still fainting and Josephine is still cross, I won't like it there—especially without my daddy."

Undecided, he glanced toward the Hildebrand house. Two more people had halted to stare. It looked as though they might form the nucleus of another crowd. He muttered, "We'll talk this over in private," and struck out for the opposite side of the street.

Nora, when she realized where they were heading, said reproachfully, "You told me I wasn't dressed for visiting."

"I meant not in a strange place. It's different in my house where you're well known."

Sammy opened the door. Nora deserted him to plaster herself against the compassionate breast. "Sammy—my daddy's hurt—you'll take me to him—"

"Your feets dirty," Sammy said calmly. "Cold too." She nested them in one of her long-fingered hands. "We got to attend to that before we study about anything else."

They walked into the living room where Kyrie waited. Kyrie's eyes asked questions and lip-read Nelson's mute answers. The voice she used for the child was one of pleased acceptance. "Hello, Nora. Have you come to spend the night with us?"

Nora shook her head vehemently and followed it by a gallant effort to remember her manners. "No, thank you—but I'd be glad to some other time. Mr. Grid-dely brought me here to talk in private because everybody on the street kept looking and looking and we didn't like it—" The tears began to flow again. She struck at them with little fists. "S-so if you'd please lend me some visiting clothes I c-could—" The hiccup took her by surprise. She looked shocked and managed to gasp, "Excuse me," before the next spasm shook her. Then sobs and hiccups mingled to inhibit further speech. Frustrated, she turned her face to Sammy's shoulder.

Sammy patted the small heaving back. She said, "My friend and me need a drink of something," and carried her from the room.

Kyrie said as soon as they were alone, "Sammy didn't dream it was anyone we knew until she heard some woman tell the policeman his name. She wasn't here the night he called. How serious is it?"

"I don't know." Briefly he told her what he did know. She said somberly, "This isn't his lucky year—is it?"

"No. I'd better call his house before they think they've lost Nora too."

The maid who yelled at telephones answered the call. She was a poor listener. Before he had time to make the situation clear she asserted that Nora was safe in bed and rushed off to confirm the assertion. He hung on patiently. He heard the distant shriek and was struck by the irrelevant thought that if this did not bring Alix Hildebrand out of her swoon nothing would. Then the word "kidnaper" rushed through the open line to explode against his ear.

"Be quiet," he said, "I'm not a kidnaper.... No—I'm not asking for a ransom.... Will you listen? ... I'm Junie Nelson's father—Junie—the little boy Nora plays with. Nora was on the street—I saw her and brought her here—"

He was no longer speaking to the maid. The receiver had been taken from her. A clear cool voice said, "I'm sorry—there's been so much confusion tonight—"

"Mrs. Hildebrand?" He knew it was not.

"No—a friend of hers—Lilith Greenway. Do I understand that Nora's with you? If you give me your address I'll come for her."

Chapter Five

He hung up, stared at the telephone, and then called Bellevue. By a series of steps he reached the doctor in Emergency who had ministered to Hildebrand.

The doctor knew him and supplied what information was available. Hildebrand had recovered consciousness while he was being examined. His mind seemed clear but his pulse and general manner indicated abnormal excitement. This, of course, the doctor said, was not uncommon in accident cases. Now he slept, assisted by morphine. He had been in considerable pain but was less concerned with his injuries than with the worry he had caused his wife and daughter. He had begged that his wife be permitted to visit him no matter how late she came. He wanted to assure her that he was safe to prevent her from spending a sleepless tormented night. He looked to be such a decent type that the doctor had humored him by promising to give his wife more than the "patient is resting nicely" routine. He had even left these instructions at the desk. So far he had not been informed that anyone was trying to storm the iron gates.

Aside from the head injury, Hildebrand had two broken ribs, assorted contusions on limbs and body, and a torn ligament in his shoulder. The head injury appeared to be superficial, but the doctor admitted that the examination had been superficial too. It would be completed in the morning. Until then he preferred to withhold his opinion. The cab had apparently struck Hildebrand with such force that it rolled him over. It did not look as though he had been run over. After the impact the driver must have been able to skirt him. When pressed, the doctor said that he did not think Hildebrand's condition was critical.

Nelson considered calling headquarters but decided against it. He interfered as little as possible in matters outside his own sphere, and the first policeman would have set in motion a routine search for an orange and white or red and white taxi which showed signs of uncommon wear and tear. He would call later if Sammy had anything to add to the sparse record. He went in search of her and met Kyrie near the stairs.

"Sammy's got things well in hand," she said. "The hiccups have stopped and Nora's being fed hot milk. I don't think she'll keep her eyes open long enough to finish it."

"That's good. Did Sammy actually witness the accident?"

"Only the tail end—literally. The tail end of an orange and white taxi speeding from the scene. She got part of the license. I jotted it down. Here—on the hall table. Does it help?"

"It might. Anything else?"

"She got an impression that the lamp thing on top was unusually large with a funny shape. Pyramidal—from the way she described it to me."

"I'll pass it on to headquarters. Be back in a moment."

When he rejoined Kyrie she said, "Did you call the Hildebrand house?"

He nodded. "Bellevue too." He gave her the doctor's report.

"Do you know him, Grid. Is he good?"

"Yes on both counts. And from where he practices he gets about as much experience in a week as most doctors get in a lifetime."

"That makes it sound pretty hopeful, doesn't it? Maybe they *will* let Nora see him tomorrow."

"Maybe."

"Did Mrs. Hildebrand come to the phone when you called—or is she at Bellevue clamoring for the right to nurse her husband?"

"Do I smell the scent of irony?"

"You do if your nose is working properly."

"She fainted when she heard the news. Her doctor has probably given her a sedative."

"I wouldn't allow myself to faint or be stuffed with sedatives if you'd been rushed to the hospital."

He believed her. He found it unnecessary to comment.

"Who did answer then—the maid? I hope you managed to reassure her. If she's the one who comes to take Nora home, she's kind—but a bit slow. She must have been absolutely frantic when she discovered—"

"She got frantic. Up to the time I called, Nora hadn't been missed."

"For heaven's sake—what kind of a household—? Doesn't anyone ever look in to see if the child's covered or—"

"What happened tonight would put any household at sixes and sevens."

"All right—I'm unjust—and the worst of it is I know what motivates it. I can't even plead the fine virtuous excuse of being narrow-minded enough to scorn Mrs. H. for her self-confessed sin—because nothing short of meanness and cruelty has ever shocked me. I'm just plain jealous and you might as well know it."

"You've seen beautiful women before."

"Yes—but I always imagined you hadn't—not really seen them, I mean."

He touched her warm smooth cheek. "It would be dull being married to a saint. Besides, most saints die young. I can't tell you how relieved I am when you produce a few human failings. That should cut both ways."

"Sophistry—pure cold sophistry. It doesn't comfort me a bit."

"Then be comforted with this. You imagined wrong. I really do see beautiful women. I always have and I always will—because how else could I have judgment enough to award you the golden apple?"

They drew apart as Sammy came down the stairs. Sammy smiled benignly.

"How's Nora?" Nelson said.

"That poor baby sleeping—and I hope she dream good. I put her down in the little room next to mine. Junie sleeping like a soldier too. He going to be mighty happy when he find her here. How about I make you that coffee you missed at dinner?"

Nelson glanced at his watch. "Swell—add another cup, Sammy."

"We expecting company? It going on for eleven."

Kyrie looked at him. "You didn't mention it, Grid. Someone to do with work?"

He did not know how to answer. He did not know whether anything more than simply curiosity had prevented him from staving off Lilith Greenway. Certainly he had no intention of permitting her to disturb the sleeping child. He said, "When I phoned to say Nora was here a friend of Mrs. Hildebrand's offered to come and get her."

Kyrie was the first to launch her protest. "Grid, why didn't you tell her we'd keep Nora for the night? It doesn't make sense to wake her—"

Sammy said, "'Scuse me, Miss Kyrie, but nobody's waking nobody. She going to stay right where she is till daylight come."

Under their accusing glances he felt like a mustachioed villain. "Foiled," he said. "Spare me and I promise not to send the chee-ild out into the night."

Kyrie's eyes were puzzled. "Shouldn't you phone again so that whoever it is won't have to come on a fool's errand? Oh—!"

The doorbell rang. Unhurriedly Sammy went to answer it. Nelson walked with Kyrie to the living room. Kyrie said quickly, "She's the Lilith woman Mr. Hildebrand told you about."

"Yes—this seemed like a good opportunity to meet her."

"Would you like me to disappear?"

"No—I'd very much like you to stay. Two opinions are better than—"

"Shhh." Kyrie sat down, a golden note on the coral cloth of the sofa.

Sammy ushered the visitor into the room and said with dignity, "I explain to the lady how it bad to fuss that child now and make her remember all over again. I going to serve coffee directly unless the lady fancy a highball."

Lilith Greenway said, "No, thank you," either to the coffee or the highball or both. Her voice was as clear and sexless as a choirboy's. The rest of her was not.

She was a small woman, scaled to size, her figure roundly emphasized even beneath a severely tailored suit. Emphatic, too, were the features of her pale triangular face eaved by a thick glossy fringe of black hair. Her eyes were narrow ellipses, so dark that pupil seemed to merge with iris, her nose sharp-cut and straight, her mouth made interesting by the sensual fullness of lower lip above a short firm chin. She wore no make-up. The fringe was her sole departure from severity. In her stark presentation of herself it was as though she stated, I am Lilith Greenway, and quite good enough as is for you and you.

She said as Sammy left the room, "I didn't know servants like that existed any more," and managed to convey a lifetime of coping with hired help. Then she smiled at Nelson without parting her pink lips, and he found himself speculating about the hidden teeth and hurriedly disavowing the obvious symbolism.

"Please don't stand," she said. "I mean to make this as short as possible. You've had your share of intrusion tonight. It was very wicked of Nora, but at least she had the sense to place herself in good hands."

"I'm Kyrie Nelson," Kyrie said firmly, because the dark eyes had not once strayed from Nelson's face to accord her any status at all. "I do wish you'd sit down. Otherwise my husband won't."

Lilith turned toward her. She was undoubtedly a quick study. Nelson could almost hear the click of her brain as it photographed Kyrie, couch, and room, in sharp detail. "How rude of me, Mrs. Nelson. But I'm sure you'll make allowances. First Richard—then Nora. We were beside ourselves." She did sit down, plopping soft as a cat on the cushioned chair. "I never want to go through that again." Her hands, with their short unpainted nails, lay lax upon the chair arms. A lamp beside her cast light unreflected by her eyes.

Nelson sat down too, and arose immediately to help Sammy. with the tray. When he had taken it from her, Sammy announced that if

Mr. Grid-dely promised to attend to the locking of doors and windows she would retire. Assured of his promise, she commanded that cups and plates be left for her to clear away in the morning and said, "Good night." Nelson, observing her straight-backed departure, suspected that she had it in mind to guard the upper regions against invasion should the visitor decide to complete her mission.

He took soundings. "I've been strongly criticized for causing you inconvenience, but Nora was so upset that I didn't realize Sammy would succeed in getting her to sleep before you arrived. I hope Mrs. Hildebrand won't mind her spending the night here."

"I'm sure she'll be grateful," Lilith Greenway said. She accepted a cup of coffee from Kyrie, devoured one of Sammy's inviting sandwiches, and reached for another with the dedicated greed of a child. Between mouthfuls she made cool explanation. "I hadn't realized I was hungry until that tray appeared. It made me remember I'd skipped dinner."

"Were you with Mrs. Hildebrand when she learned of the accident?" Kyrie asked.

She raised her cup and drank. "This is delicious coffee. Yes—we'd delayed dinner, thinking that Richard would turn up any minute. He has a habit of phoning even if he's to be only a little late. They're a very devoted couple—Alix was beginning to get uneasy long before we knew there was anything wrong. After we heard, of course, there was no thought of eating."

"It must have been a terrific blow," Kyrie said. "Nora told my husband that Mrs. Hildebrand fainted."

"You can't keep a thing from a child, can you?" Lilith paused to consume the last bite of her second sandwich. "I suppose that idiot maid wove it into a bedtime story for her—complete with harrowing details."

Nelson said, "Not exactly. She overheard the maid telephoning. After she'd been tucked in again she crept to Mrs. Hildebrand's room and called her name—and got frightened because there was no response."

"Oh—I see. If no one's going to eat the last sandwich, I will. I'm not superstitious." She helped herself. "That must have been while I was downstairs with Alix—trying to get her to take some brandy and wishing the doctor would come so that I could rush outside to Richard." She shrugged. "But that Cassandra from next door had said there was quite a crowd and probably I couldn't have broken through it anyway." Her pink lips smiled again without parting. She looked like a toy in the lap of the large chair. "I'm not built for tackling crowds. They frighten me."

Does anything? Nelson wondered.

She said, "It's just as well I couldn't force the brandy on Alix. It might have interfered with the sedative the doctor gave her."

"In a way," Kyrie said, "it was a blessing she fainted. At least she was spared the shock of discovering Nora's absence."

"That's true. She does take the responsibility of Nora very seriously." She surveyed her empty plate with an air of regret. Or perhaps the regret was for what she felt compelled to say next. She ignored a cigarette box extended by Kyrie and took a flat gold case from her pocket. She inclined toward the match that Nelson held and nodded perfunctorily. "I'm fond of Nora, myself, but just between us she's quite a handful. I suppose a certain amount of imagination is natural in a child of that age—one hesitates to call it lying, but—" Her straight black eyebrows rose almost to the edge of the fringe.

Nelson saw Kyrie's lovely mouth go mutinous. He forestalled a spoken comment. "Our son comes up with some fantastic yarns on occasion too. Psychologists agree that it's the nature of the beast."

Kyrie's eyes called him Judas. He went on quickly, "Did you manage to worm any information out of Bellevue?"

Lilith said, "Why on earth did they have to take him to—?" She did not finish it. She said, "No—we couldn't find out anything more than that bit about the patient resting comfortably. If Alix is well enough she'll go there first thing in the morning. If not, I'll go alone. It might be best at that. Alix is terribly sensitive to surroundings. It would spare her a great deal if Richard could be moved to a decent hospital before she visits him."

Kyrie said sweetly, "You're exactly the kind of friend I'd expect Mrs. Hildebrand to have."

Lilith looked at her and murmured a controlled "Thank you."

Nelson, who had learned to control himself without revealing any of the signs, said, "Bellevue may not be a show place, but that's because its funds are spent on equipment rather than frills. You may assure Mrs. Hildebrand that her husband is receiving excellent care."

"You speak as though you have firsthand knowl—?" Lilith made an abrupt spring to the chair's edge. "Of course—I know who you are now. You're Alix's handsome captain. She's told me about you. Your name sounded familiar, but I didn't put two and two together until this moment. Oh, please, since you have authority, won't you call

Bellevue and get some definite information for me? I'd appreciate it so much—and Alix will be in your debt forever."

"I have called—"

"And yet you allowed me to sit here making idle conversation to distract myself from the most awful fears for Richard—and all the while you could have eased my mind. Please—?"

On the whole, he did not agree that the conversation had been idle. He said, "I'm afraid I took it for granted that you'd been told I was a police officer."

"Then you must have taken it for granted that I was terribly callous not to bombard you with questions." Her mouth drooped to the classic lines of tragedy. Her dark eyes tried to convey reproach. They conveyed nothing that warmed the air around her.

"My cook witnessed the accident," Nelson said, "and routed me out to offer my services. That's how I happened to be on scene when Nora appeared." He summarized what had taken place and what the doctor at Bellevue had said.

She came in on cue with "Thank heaven he's not on the critical list." But again the warmth was noticeably absent. "Did he say anything that would explain how the accident had come about?"

"No—but as soon as he recovered consciousness he asked for his wife—so if it's at all possible for her to see him in the morning, I recommend it."

"I'll tell her—and I'm sure if it's at all possible she'll be there." She flicked something off her blouse. "You say your cook was a witness? The woman who opened the door to me?"

Kyrie said, "Yes—Sammy. She's our entire staff—except for a cleaning woman."

Lilith took another lightening invoice that covered Kyrie's clothes, accessories, and the room's furniture and fixtures. It was as though the fact of only one servant was forcing her to revise her original estimate. Apparently the revision was automatic and did not employ her full mind. "Mrs. Baldwin—the neighbor who came galloping with the news—told us that Richard had been struck by a hit-and-run taxi. Is that true?"

"Sammy confirms it," Nelson said.

"I hope she had something to add—something more definite."

"Not a great deal."

"No? Well—I'm not surprised. It's been my experience that even the best of them are apt to lose what wits they have in an emergency." The quotation marks that set off "them" were clearly indicated.

Both Kyrie and Nelson stiffened. On Kyrie the process showed. She said distinctly, "Sammy observed more than the other two witnesses. At least she got several figures of the license number."

"Oh? Well—I suppose that's something—provided she didn't invent it to give herself importance."

"She *is* important," Kyrie said, "vastly."

Lilith stretched and yawned. The glimpsed teeth were small and slightly irregular. "Sorry—I seem to be making myself completely at home—and I know you're both wishing I *were* at home—but I'm so bone-tired I hate to stir. Tonight's events took more out of me than I realized."

Kyrie said politely, "Would you like a drink?"

"You're too kind. In the mood I'm in one drink would be enough to make me break down and tell you my life's history."

Nelson doubted it. Kyrie said, "I'm sure it would be very interesting," and said it too sincerely.

"I really will go," Lilith said, rising. "You've put up with me above and beyond the call of duty. Thanks—and thanks for keeping Nora."

"We love having her." Kyrie put no emphasis upon "her," but for Nelson, receptive to every inflection of her husky voice, it was heavily underscored.

Lilith said, "Obviously the little imp must have a full set of company manners. I'll send Josephine for her in the morning. I'm spending the night at the Hildebrands' in case I'm needed. I really shouldn't have left Alix alone for this long, but you were so easy to talk to." She confined the compliment to Nelson.

"I'll walk you over," he said, and turned to Kyrie. "Would you like some fresh air?"

"No, thanks," Kyrie said. She added softly, "I'll just open all the windows."

Out on the street he observed that Lilith had an incongruously long stride for a small woman. He forced her to slow down by substituting a leisurely amble for his habitual gait.

"I should have protested this added strain on your good manners," she said, "but the truth is I'm glad of your company for even a little while longer. I don't look forward to being alone with my thoughts."

"Your thoughts shouldn't trouble you too much," Nelson said. "The doctor's report was fairly optimistic."

"It isn't that—it's—" She broke it off. "We're walking in the wrong direction."

"Just as far as the corner. I can't risk crossing in the middle of the street with you after what happened tonight."

"Oh. I wouldn't have given it a thought. But then I'm not accident-prone. I'll bet you aren't either."

"Do you think Richard Hildebrand is?"

"That's just it. He doesn't appear to be the type—but—" She blurted it out with an impulsiveness that did not match her air of cool containment. "Was it an accident? Was it really?"

He could not see her face when he looked down. All he could see was the top of her head. "What else could it have been? I can't remember a case where a taxi driver deliberately used his cab as a lethal weapon—not even when he'd been undertipped."

She seemed startled. "Of course not." She repeated it. "Of course not." She was quiet for a few steps. Then she said, "Some weird notions have crossed my mind since Mrs. Baldwin spoke her piece. I know Alix has more or less confided in you, so I won't be telling tales out of school if I say that Richard hasn't been himself lately. Naturally I didn't want to mention it in front of your wife—"

Nelson said dryly, "Alix has more or less confided in my wife too."

"Which just shows how upset she's been—and with reason. It makes me wonder—"

Between the intermittent sounds of the quieting street he heard her quick-drawn breath. She was like, or she wanted to seem like, a novice on the edge of a diving board.

He said, "It makes you wonder what?"

"If Richard—" She dived. "If he wasn't trying to commit suicide."

"That *is* a weird notion."

"Maybe—yet there have been things—his depression—bursts of temper—you don't know him well, do you?"

Nelson said, "I haven't met him more than twice."

She nodded. "So you haven't any means of comparing the way he was and the way he is."

"No—I'll have to take your word for it." He crossed his fingers. "Has his business suffered by the change you speak of? I understand that the firm he heads is one of the largest in the country."

She raised her head. Now he could see her pale triangular face, but he could not read it. She seemed to be trying to read his, with as little success, he trusted. She said, "It wouldn't necessarily affect his business. Am I boring you?"

He could assure her honestly that she was not.

"Oh, I admit," she said, "that because Alix is such a dear close friend I might be exaggerating—it might seem worse to me than it is. In fact, I've been frightened enough to bone up on it." She waited for his question.

He asked it. "Bone up on what?"

"I hate to name it—yet I'm afraid it isn't as farfetched as—well—as I could wish." She was on the diving board again. Again she plunged. "Do you know anything about schizophrenia?"

"Nobody does." He knew as much as a layman could, and more than some professionals.

"I suppose that's true—yet for what it's worth, it's generally granted that the symptoms are far less recognizable than in other forms of mental illness—which means that it's often impossible to tell schizophrenes from normal men."

"Until they go over the edge," Nelson said.

"Exactly—only—well—aren't those letters a sign that Richard has gone over the edge?"

"There's no real proof that he wrote those letters," Nelson said.

"I thought—at least Alix told me the police officer you sent her to was convinced of it."

Nelson did not want to go into that. He said, "One of my good friends is a psychiatrist at Bellevue. I might ask him to have a talk with Mr. Hildebrand." He was speaking more to see what her reaction would be than out of conviction that any psychiatrist living would base an opinion on a single interview.

Her hand was on his arm. She removed it suddenly. They had reached the Hildebrand house. Light from the vestibule outlined the large man on the top step. He stood a little away from the door, unbraced by it, yet curiously rigid. Lilith said, "Damn!" and Nelson thought it was the most uncalculated utterance he had yet heard her make. The man, as he swiveled toward her, was like someone emerging from a trance. His mouth, which had hung slack and stupid, closed. He descended the steps in slow motion, and when he reached the sidewalk the alcoholic smell of his sweat tinctured the air around him.

"Lil," he said, peering at her, "you been to a beauty parlor or something? I was waiting inside but—"

Her voice rang loud and clear. "This is Captain Nelson, Herbert. The captain is on the police force but he happens to be one of Alix's neighbors. This is my brother, Captain Nelson. Herbert Greenway—"

She went on talking while Nelson shook and dropped without regret the large flaccid hand of her brother. "Sorry, Herbert. I should have phoned to let you know I wouldn't be home tonight." And to

Nelson, "You'd never think he was my junior, would you? He acts more like a father—stews if I'm two minutes late. Well—good night, Captain. I don't want your wife to start stewing too. Families are the bitter end, aren't they? Thanks again."

Continuing her monologue, she hooked arms with her brother and, like a pygmy leading an elephant, steered him up the steps. "Herbert—worried or not, you might have stopped to change your clothes. They may be all right for that constant tinkering you do, but—"

The vestibule door closed upon the "but." Nelson carried it home with him.

Chapter Six

Kyrie had gone upstairs. Before he joined her Nelson toured the lower floor, switching off lights and checking upon windows accessible to the street.

On the second floor, Sammy, who kept no regular hours, had as usual left her door ajar to extracurricular demands. But Junie and the small guest in the house were sleeping soundly.

Kyrie was reading in bed. She lowered her book as he entered the room they shared. "I didn't expect you for hours," she said.

"Lilith wasn't that fascinating."

"I know it. This time I'm not jealous."

"What are you this time?"

"Prejudiced. First—I like Mr. Hildebrand and he doesn't like her. Second—I don't like his wife and Lilith does. Third—how dare she say such things about Nora? Fourth—I have no use for women who have no use for women—and if Alix is Lilith's exception to the rule, that makes it worse—"

"You've certainly been giving it thought."

"I'm not finished. Fifth and last, I wouldn't like her anyway—and stop grinning. You wouldn't either. You just don't have my gift for putting it into words."

"I think I'll take a shower."

"There—that proves it—that's exactly the way I felt. I put out clean pajamas in your dressing room."

When he came back Kyrie said, "Those silly bangs."

His hand rose absently to his wide brow.

"Not yours—you're always beautifully brushed after a shower—

hers. She sheds too."

"What?"

"Well, she does. There were tail ends of hair on her suit."

Nelson said, "She'd stopped in at a beauty parlor—maybe to settle her nerves—the way some women buy hats."

"Grid, you're tired. There aren't any beauty parlors open at this hour." Kyrie watched him fish in the pocket of his robe. "If I were a decent wife I'd tell you you'd smoked enough for tonight." She added with mock resignation, "But if you must—there are cigarettes right beside you—or if you'd like another brand for a change she left hers downstairs. Monogrammed. The case—I mean."

He took a cigarette. He lit it and sat down in a chair near the bed.

"Not her monogram either," Kyrie said. "Alix's. Shall I give it to the maid when she calls for Nora or would you like to return it in person?"

He closed his eyes.

She said softly, "To be answered at your earliest convenience."

"Huh?"

"Oh—I thought you were asleep. I was thinking of taking one of those quick muscle-building courses so that I could hoist you into bed."

He opened his deep-set eyes. They were clear as he looked at her. "Stay as sweet and feminine as you are. I'm not a bit sleepy."

She wriggled. Determinedly she returned to the subject. "I wish I could keep Nora here until Mr. Hildebrand's well enough to come home. Without him I can't help feeling it's not a very sympathetic atmosphere for a child."

"Feeling," he said. "That's what it boils down to—nothing concrete at all."

"Did she say anything on the way home?"

"She expressed a fear that Hildebrand was schizophrenic."

Kyrie said hotly, "I won't believe it. If I'd believed it before she said it I'd change my mind on general principles. It's on a par with calling Nora a liar—and if you want my opinion, about that, she did it because she's afraid Nora will drop a few truths and she thinks it wise to prepare the ground for skepticism. What else did she say?"

"She said 'Damn.'"

"Really? I had an impression that she was much too controlled to swear. Somehow it isn't consistent with whatever role she thinks she's mastered."

"I guess the control slipped for a moment. Her brother was waiting for her on the Hildebrand steps and she didn't seem pleased to see him—or perhaps to have me see him."

"What's he like?"

"Large—extremely well built—dressed in work clothes—active work, I gathered—less intelligent than she—and that might be understatement."

"What else did you gather?"

"Practically nothing. She broke out in a rash of small talk and brushed me off and whisked him indoors too fast."

"Maybe having a brother in work clothes doesn't suit her look. Maybe she's just a plain snob."

"Maybe." He put the cigarette out. He took off his robe and came over to her.

"That's better," Kyrie said. "I was beginning to think I'd broken out in some kind of rash too." She disengaged an arm to deal with pillows and bed lamp.

Morning began with Junie clamoring like an alarm clock and Sammy padding into his room to turn him off. Nelson awoke to these sounds, hushed Kyrie's half-waking murmur, and slid out of bed.

Junie came to his dressing-room door while he was knotting his tie. Junie had violet eyes and tow hair. Otherwise he was a miniature version of his broad-shouldered, narrow-hipped father. He stood quietly on the threshold and when Nelson greeted him he said, "Shhhh," very sternly.

"What for shhh?" Nelson asked.

"Sammy says we mustn't wake Nora because she's company."

"If Nora slept through that racket you made a while ago, the danger's past."

"I didn't know she was here then. Nobody told me. Did you know?"

"Yes, I knew."

"Will she stay for always?"

Nelson said, "It would be nice if she could, but she'd be missed—just the way we'd miss you if you went to stay at her house." Junie's rebellious expression told him that it would be politic to change the subject. He hoisted the little boy to his shoulder. "Who's going to help me eat breakfast?"

"Me." He had buckled a holster belt around his robe and thrust his pajama legs into cowboy boots. He dug the boots into Nelson's ribs and gave a war whoop.

"Who let that maverick in?" Nelson said. "I thought we had to protect the little lady's rest."

Junie stepped out of character. "Nora's not a lady—she's a girl. We're staying home from school today because she's tired."

"You never told me she went to Mrs. Merriam's too."

"Everybody knows that. How long will she sleep?"

"As long as she wants to."

"I think she'd like to eat with us. I think she's hungry."

"Let's not tell her. Let's keep it a secret." He carried his rider out of the danger zone.

They breakfasted in the kitchen, Sammy catering to their wants.

Junie looked at her angelically and reached for his fourth muffin. "I think I'll have breakfast with my dad every day."

"Watch you don't trip over them eyelashes," Sammy said, "and leave that muffin be. You stuffed. You going to get up as early as your daddy you got to study about dressing yourself better. You don't catch him wearing no crazy boots with his night clothes. He a big important man."

"Why did he let Nora's daddy get run over?"

"'Cause he can't be every place at once."

In the spirit of quitting while he was ahead, Nelson chose that moment to depart. He intended to get the latest report on Hildebrand and on the errant taxi, but he walked into what he called a bargain-basement day at Homicide West, and had no time for anything beyond the immediate demands of his job. It was well that the morning fare provided by Sammy went a long way. He did not take a lunch break until after two, and then he could face neither the telephones nor the coffee and sandwiches that staled upon his desk. He decided to drive to Bellevue and pick up his information at first hand. He could eat en route. He was about to exit from the building when the desk sergeant shouted to him.

"Telephone, Captain. I wouldn't have stopped you except it's the missus."

Kyrie seldom called him at headquarters. He talked himself out of a slight case of apprehension before he picked up the receiver. "Kyrie?"

Her warm pleasant voice was apologetic. "Are you busy?"

"Not now. Make it as long as you like."

"It's Nora. No one's come for her. She's been as good as gold, but she has such an orphaned air that I can't bear it. I phoned the house, but the maid who answered told me it was Josephine's day off and nothing had been said about arrangements for Nora. She offered to take her off my hands if I was busy, but of course that isn't the point. Here at least she has us. Alix and the girlfriend are both out. They left the house early this morning."

"They're probably at the hospital."

"What hospital? Have you called Bellevue?"

"No—I'm on the way there now."

"Then it's as well I caught you. I called to find out how Mr. Hildebrand was and after a few stops and goes I was told he'd been moved. They couldn't or wouldn't tell where."

Nelson said slowly, "Well—that's reassuring. It means he hasn't taken a turn for the worse. And our guest last night hinted that Alix wouldn't be able to stick the thought of his being at Bellevue."

"Yes—but what about Nora? She's going to take a turn for the worse unless she visits him soon. I've never seen such a worried child. She's scarcely touched a bit of food although Sammy's done her wonderful best to tempt her. Junie's been divine too—gone through his whole bag of tricks—but even he's beginning to act downed—like a jilted swain. She won't go further than the backyard for fear of missing news—"

"All right. I'll see what I can uncover."

Kyrie sounded relieved. "That's what I hope you'd do. When I find out where he is I can take Nora there myself. I'm sure he needs her as much as she needs him. Sammy's just gone across to pick up some clothes for her to wear. I've dressed her in Junie's, but the shoes are too big and the pants a spot too tight in the seat. Somehow they emphasize that orphaned look. Will you call me back?"

Nelson said he would. He returned to the telephones in his office, rang Bellevue, and was told that the patient had been signed out at ten-thirty. He himself had wanted to leave and there was no reason to detain him, not with the bed shortage at an all-time high. No—there was nothing at hand to show where he had been taken. If the captain would hang up, inquiries could be made and the results sent on to him. Nelson hung up. He did not wait for the results to be sent. Nora had overheard the maid talking to a Dr. Falvey. He consulted the telephone directory and discovered a Dr. Enoch Falvey on Park Avenue in the Sixties. He dialed the number and a crisp female voice responded.

"Dr. Falvey's office. Good afternoon."

"Is the doctor in?"

"No—his office hours are from three-thirty to six on weekdays. Would you like to make an appointment?"

"Is he the Dr. Falvey who attends Mrs. Richard Hildebrand?"

"Yes—did Mrs. Hildebrand recommend you? May I have your—?"

"Is he connected with any hospital?" Nelson sounded like a cautious shopper.

"Dr. Falvey is connected with Garde Medical." Her tone rebuked him for unpardonable ignorance.

"Thank you very much," Nelson said, and did not wait for her to reopen the conversation.

Three minutes later he was in possession of the fact that Mr. Richard Hildebrand was "resting comfortably" at Garde Medical. He turned down the offer to connect him with Mr. Hildebrand's room and thought as he replaced the receiver that the sensitive Alix had wasted no time in wresting her mate from Bellevue's clutches. On the surface this evidenced a praiseworthy concern for his comfort, since the luxury of Garde Medical was comparable to that of a class-A hotel. Not for the first time Nelson asked himself if there was any real need to look below the surface.

Kyrie, when he had relayed the information, said, "Well—that's a step up the social ladder—in fact, it's a whole flight of steps. I'm not knocking Bellevue, but I'm glad Nora will see him in prettier surroundings." She hesitated. "Perhaps I should call before I trot her there. I don't want them to think I'm being officious."

"Good idea." He too hesitated. "Or this might be better. Their visiting hours aren't rigid. If a definite promise will hold Nora I'll try to get home early and act as her escort. It will save you the trouble."

Kyrie was not fooled but she was tactful. "At least it will save me the trouble of convincing Junie that there's a good reason for leaving him behind. Do you want me to call Garde Medical anyway?"

"Yes. He might even be well enough to speak to Nora. Hearing his voice should help."

"Suppose Alix or Lilith answer? I don't want to tell either of them that I employed a detective to track him down."

"Aside from the responsibility of Nora, inquiring about him at Bellevue was a neighborly gesture that shouldn't warrant any explanation. Let it be assumed that's how you discovered his whereabouts."

Kyrie said, "I haven't had so much fun since I worked for the FBI." He could almost see her nose wrinkling with distaste. "Don't take it to heart," he said.

And that advice goes for you too, he told himself. But he could not follow it.

He ate a worse-for-wear sandwich and washed it down with cold over-sweet coffee. That took no more than five minutes, during which he remembered his promise to Hildebrand. Since he had forgone a legitimate lunch hour he felt that he would not be wasting the department's time if he submitted the name Greenway, Lilith and Herbert, to Records. The check was negative, yet inconclusive if Hildebrand had been right in thinking the name a false one. While he was at it he called Immigration for information on Gertrude Knobler, Swiss maid. He was assured that the data would be sent to him as soon as possible.

Still unsatisfied, trying to seize upon some other means of keeping faith with Hildebrand, he reviewed the scene in the hotel bar, recalling as nearly as he could Hildebrand's words and how he had looked when he uttered them. He had started with Danzig. Danzig, he said, had made him regret not consulting a private detective. He had mentioned one named Lindstrom in his building on Seventeenth Street. He had not gone to him because he had seen someone entering or leaving his office—someone associated with a friend of his wife. He had said "friend" as though he were saying "enemy." Could he have meant Lilith? Had he seen Lilith in company with some doubtful character and decided that if he was a sample of Lindstrom's clientele Lindstrom was not for him? No stone unturned, Nelson thought, sneering at himself. But he reached for the telephone directory and called Lindstrom, John, in the building on Seventeenth Street.

Lindstrom sounded wary. "What can I do for you, Captain?"

"What sort of cases do you handle?"

"Nothing illegal—divorce evidence when I'm hard up—finding missing persons who've skipped for one reason or another when their wives or husbands or whatever don't want to lodge a complaint against them. The depression's set in though. I haven't had but one new customer in the past ten days. If it keeps on that way I'll retire to a chicken farm."

"Who was the new customer?"

"Uh-uh—something tells me I'm about to lose him too. Well—that's the way it goes. Matter of fact, I've been wrestling with my conscience. Maybe if the police hadn't called me I'd have called them. I wanted to be sure first—is all. It's a story I better tell in person."

"All right. Can you stop in to see me at Homicide West—at about five-thirty?"

"I'll be there. Business isn't likely to interfere."

"Did he have a woman with him—a small dark—?"

"No—he was alone."

Nelson hung up, thinking that for his pains he had accomplished no more than inadvertently uncovering something with which he had neither personal nor official concern.

Until three-thirty the Hildebrands and their associates walked in and out of his mind. Nothing sufficiently engrossing occurred to keep them long at bay. Nelson tried to shift the blame for his preoccupation to Danzig. Danzig had been too ready to lay the blackmail letters at Hildebrand's door. He should have carried the investigation further before he wrote "closed." Then I could have written it too, Nelson thought.

He knew that he was being unfair. Hildebrand, not Danzig, was responsible for this busman's holiday. Considering the shortness of their acquaintance, his sympathies had made a record leap toward the man. Danzig had taken all the steps that were indicated at the time. He had performed his full if unimaginative duty, and that being so, he had undoubtedly construed Hildebrand's appearance in his office as an outstanding example of bravado. Nor was he likely to be influenced by later events. What right-thinking member of the police department would connect a hit-and-run taxi driver with blackmail?

Which puts me in my place, Nelson thought. Not that I really do believe there is a connection. And in the next breath he went on to wonder if the quick removal from Bellevue had by any chance been instigated by Lilith as a result of his random offer to send a psychiatrist to Hildebrand's bedside. Everything pointed to the fact that Nora was no more than an excuse for Lilith's visit last night. That she was up to something he had no doubt, whether or not that something involved the services of a private detective. And even ruling out that it was something criminal, it boded no good for Hildebrand. Her every mention of Hildebrand's wife had expressed a strong sense of possession. What little he, Nelson, had seen of her was enough to convince him that she would make the rules for any game she played. Should she seek to discredit Hildebrand, say because he stood between her and the object of her possessiveness, there would be no holds barred. She had wanted the question of Hildebrand's sanity to be well established. Was it farfetched to assume that she could not permit him to remain in a hospital where psychiatrists might have free access to him and form opinions contrary to her interests? Quite probably she shared the common view that madness and Bellevue were synonymous and that psychiatrists lurked behind every door of that institution, waiting to pounce upon unsuspecting patients.

At that point his mind mounted a favorite hobbyhorse and galloped away from Lilith down more familiar lanes. The general public did not trouble to instruct itself upon the true state of affairs. It did not realize that Bellevue had to stand in line with government hospitals throughout the land for an inadequate share of the some five thousand psychiatrists turned out per annum. Far from waiting to pounce, these men had all they could do to cleanse the surface of an ever-spreading fester. Seven or eight million dollars a year was set aside for research upon the care of the emotionally ill. And this money, spent to oil the laboring brain, was less than the sum allotted to the search for a satisfactory lubricant for machines. And it was less than the sum spent for state highways, and less than— The hobbyhorse threw him, but at least it had outdistanced thoughts of Lilith.

At three-thirty he drove to the Police Academy to deliver a scheduled talk before an assembly of rookies. He avoided such assignments as much as possible, but this one had been commanded by the new commissioner. His subject was the use and misuse of guns. He made it brief and pointed and, returning to a desk cluttered with files and memoranda, he envied all the stalwarts who had been forced to drink at his "font of wisdom" and looked back with yearning to his own start on the force, when action rather than briefing others for action had been the order of the day.

He sorted the immediate from the less immediate, distributed assignments, spoke to some people who had been waiting to see him, and tried to find the right words for a woman whose husband had been arrested on suspicion of murder. When he had ushered her out, a clerk appeared with yet another piece of paper to deposit on his nearly cleared desk.

"This was phoned in a half hour ago, Captain. They buzzed you but your lines were busy."

"Thanks." He glanced at the paper, and the Hildebrands were with him again.

The message informed him that an orange and white taxi had spent the night in a used-car lot on Amsterdam Avenue near 100th Street. He spent the next twenty minutes on the telephone asking for details.

The cab, he was told, had a large pyramidal-shaped lamp. It also had a cracked windshield and several suspicious dents. Someone had tried and failed to remove the license plate. It hung by one hook. Its first three figures and the one after the dash corresponded to those supplied by Sammy. The glass over the driver's identification card had been smashed, the card removed. The cab was an independent. The Motor Vehicle Bureau had come up with the name of the licensee. He had been found and questioned. His insistence that he had not been driving the cab at the time of the accident was substantiated. In more or less his own words his statement was relayed to Nelson.

He lived at an address in the West Nineties. At six-thirty last night he had left the hack in front of his apartment house and gone upstairs to have supper. As a rule this meal was consumed inside of thirty minutes, but last night a quarrel with his wife had prolonged it. It was about eight when he reached the street again, and the hack was gone. At first he thought that someone was playing a trick on him. He had canvassed a group of teen-agers with whom he was on friendly terms, but they professed innocence and even helped him to scout the neighborhood. No one seemed to have witnessed the theft, or if they had they must have assumed that the man behind the wheel had every right to be there. The driver had not immediately reported his loss. He had meant to do so. To avoid facing his still angry wife he had stopped in a bar to use the telephone, but some tomato had taken a long lease on it. He felt low, what with the quarrel and missing the theater trade and who knew what more, because if the hack was gone for keeps the insurance company would be in no sweat to make good. So he had ordered a drink while he waited. Then he had ordered another and another. He seldom got the chance to tie one on. Driving from morning to night was a sober job. It was a quarter after ten before he connected with the local precinct. That was on record. But his alibi for the time of the hit-and-run was unbreakable. Sure he had locked the ignition. The high iron fence around the used-car lot had been locked too. Locks were a belly laugh to the crooked so-and-sos that ran loose these days.

No one at the used-car lot had been able to account for the presence of the orange and white taxicab. It had been parked behind two sizable jobs, a station wagon and a pick-up truck. It had come to light three hours ago when a customer moved the station wagon. Yes, there had been a night watchman on the premises. He would be given his walking papers. He had slept it off once too often. Nelson's obliging informant, whom he thanked, asked respectfully if there was anything else the captain wanted to know.

Nelson said, "Not at the moment."

"Well—no doubt we've got the hack that did the trick. Now all we have to do is get the man. I want to thank you for your co-operation. There's a memo here says you phoned in the description last night and were to be kept posted. I would have called you earlier but—"

"I'm sure you had more important things to do."

"Well—" He seemed disposed to continue the conversation. "About you being interested, Captain. This wouldn't tie in with something Homicide's working on—?"

"No—the victim just happens to be a neighbor of mine."

"Oh. We'll keep after it. He shouldn't have crossed in the middle of the street, but he shouldn't have been left for dead either. Can't afford to take hit-and-runs lightly."

Nelson could not top that. He said good-by and sat pouring over a file that had been brought to him, until he became aware that the air in the office had been used by too many people. As he got up to raise the window the door was once again pushed inward.

A short wiry man with a simian collection of features stood on the threshold. "Captain Nelson? My name is John Lindstrom."

"Oh yes." The clock on the dun-colored wall said exactly five-thirty. "You're on the dot. Come in and sit down."

"I really was figuring on coming to you—even without the call. I'm kind of glad you didn't give me any choice. Maybe I got mixed up on whether or not it would be ethical to split to the authorities—but I'm not a priest or a lawyer. If I get a client who stinks, I don't want any part of him."

By way of encouragement Nelson offered him a cigarette. He hung it on his lower lip and told his tale. A "Fred Hicks," he said, had engaged him to trace a missing "pal." The description of the "pal" tallied more or less with a mugshot circulated by the police of a wanted criminal. The name of the "pal" rang a bell too. It sounded like one of the aliases under the mugshot. Furthermore, from a couple of slips the client had made, Lindstrom suspected that he was implicated in the same job and that his "pal" had vanished with the loot.

"What was the job?" Nelson said.

"The Fromm Drug Company robbery—the deal where a night watchman was clobbered."

Nelson leaned across the desk. He muttered, "Tease a cat and be clawed by a lion."

"What's that?"

"Old Chinese proverb." His department along with every other department had worked vainly to solve the Fromm robbery. A man had been murdered and two hundred and fifty thousand dollars' worth of drugs had disappeared into thin air. He drew a pad toward him. "Have you worked on it—found any trace of the pal?"

"I worked on it—but how would I get anywhere alone if the whole police force came a cropper?"

"What name did he call the pal?"

"Melvin Johnson."

"I see what you mean. The initials are the same as those of our chief suspect."

Lindstrom looked uncomfortable. "It could still be coincidence. That's why I didn't—"

"You should have—but never mind. You're here now. Give me a description of Fred Hicks."

"Dark brown hair—what I saw of it—he didn't take off his hat—blue eyes—average height—compact built—sharp dresser—camel's-hair coat—English shoes. No scars—nothing special—just an all-around sharpie."

"I suppose it's too much to expect that he left his address with you."

"He was dumb for a big-time operator—if he is one—but not that dumb. He's to contact me Sunday—day after tomorrow—at my office at five o'clock to ask for a progress report. You could have one of your men standing by to trace the call."

"I'll have the building covered as well. You might be able to tempt him with a hint that you've got something too precious to trust to the wires."

"I'll go along with that. Just give me notice of your arrangements. I guess he's not so dumb at that. You'll have to go some to hide your plants in an empty office building."

"Don't worry about that."

Lindstrom arose. He made a monkey face. "Do I take it my nose is clean?"

Nelson nodded. He rather liked the little man. "You were late with a lot."

"Could be. So long. Meeting you wasn't as bad as I expected."

"Wait a minute."

"Anything you say."

"How would you like to take me on as a client? At your regular rates, of course."

"Are you kidding—with the facilities you command?"

"This isn't a departmental matter. The people I'm interested in aren't on record with us." He wrote three names on a sheet of paper. "As far as I know they had their beginnings in Shenanga, Pennsylvania. What I want are salient points that might have but probably didn't occur in their history to date."

"I get you—salient dirty work." Lindstrom looked at him curiously. "I still don't see why—?"

"Call it an after-hours round of cops and robbers that doesn't justify wasting Homicide's time or resources."

"They in New York now?"

"Yes." He gave Alix Hildebrand's address and reached for the telephone directory. "The other two are brother and sister. They live at—" The listing was in Herbert Greenway's name. Nelson repeated slowly the number on West Ninety-first Street.

Chapter Seven

He called Kyrie to say that he was leaving. It was good to get out into the cool evening. He would have liked to take a long leg-stretching walk, but Kyrie had told him that Nora was ready and waiting and that her anxiety was at high-water mark. He got into his car.

Nora had not been granted the reassurance of her father's voice. When Kyrie called the hospital she had spoken to Alix. Alix had set the seal of approval upon the proposed visit, apologized for the advantage taken of the Nelsons, attributed it to a mix-up in arrangements, thanked Kyrie profusely, and asked to talk to Nora. Judging by Nora's responses, Alix had done her best to be comforting, but after the conversation Nora had continued much as before, wrapped in a kind of shattering silence.

At the sound of Nelson's key in the lock Junie came to the door. "They're in my study," he said aloofly, and led the way.

His study was a small library designed for Nelson. He had preempted a corner of it as an auxiliary playroom. Prominent among the toys favored at the moment were a small easel and a finger-paint set.

As soon as Nelson appeared, Sammy started to button Nora into her coat. Kyrie, who had been writing a letter at the desk, looked up and murmured, "I thought you'd never make it."

Nelson said loudly, "Is there a young lady here who wants an escort?"

Nora wriggled away from Sammy. Her eyes were too big and too bright. "Are you ready to go, Mr. Grid-dely—or does Sammy have to give you your supper first? She gave me mine—"

"Least I tried to," Sammy said. "Hold still for your hat. Mr. Griddely ready soon as you are. He going to eat in peace when he come back."

Junie had detached himself from the proceedings. He was back at his finger-painting. Nelson glanced down at the easel and shuddered. "Isn't that a lot of red, old man?"

Junie ignored the criticism. He said in an injured voice, "Why didn't *you* get taken to the hospital so that I could come and see you?"

Nelson took a deep breath. "Wouldn't you rather go to the zoo—maybe Sunday morning?"

"When is Sunday morning?"

"Soon." He knew that according to Junie's calendar the day after tomorrow was light-years away.

"Are there animals in the hospital?"

"None to speak of."

Thoughtfully Junie rooted among his paints. "I *might* rather go to the zoo," he announced. He added a gob of yellow to the angry canvas.

Nora tugged at Nelson's sleeve. Kyrie said to him, "Dinner will keep. Take your time—but don't try to make time. She's only beautiful."

He was grinning at the caution as he helped Nora to the front seat of the car. "All set?"

"Oh yes."

During the drive she did not stir an inch to the right or the left, but he sensed the tight springs within her set to go off at the instant of reaching goal.

He tried to ease her tension. "It isn't very far. We'll be there almost as soon as you see the river. In fact, I wouldn't be surprised if you could see the river from your daddy's room."

"I think I'll be too busy," Nora said. Merely by way of indulging him she twisted her rigid little body toward the window.

Garde Medical was a group of freshly sanded modern buildings on East End Avenue. Nora's thumb was poised on the door's release button before he had braked in the curved drive of the main entrance.

"Hold it," he said. "A lady's escort must help her out."

She sat still until he had walked around and assisted her to the paving stones. He said, "Have you ever been to a hospital?"

"Alix says I was born in one but I don't remember."

She had grown wings. Only his hand held her to the ground. He maneuvered her through a revolving door into a softly carpeted lobby. "We'll have to stop at the desk first and get a pass," he said.

She whispered, "They won't not let us—will they?" and reassured herself. "They've got to because you're a policeman—but you'd better say so. I wouldn't have known it myself if Junie hadn't told me. Frank knows too. I heard Alix tell him."

He kept his voice even. "Who's Frank?"

"That funny man. I'm glad Miss Kyrie didn't ask him in. Hurry—ask—"

"Does Frank come to see Alix?"

"I guess so." There was no more to be had from her. She kept a tight grip on his hand and did not loosen it until the visitor's slip had been surrendered.

"It's on the third floor," he said, "Room 301."

Her lips formed the number repeatedly as they ascended. He did not try to restrain her when she darted out of the elevator. He merely indicated a corridor and followed slowly in her flying steps.

As he reached 301 a nurse's aide was wheeling out two supper trays, each still bearing a quantity of food. He stepped aside to give her clearance, surveying the scene from the open doorway. The room was spacious, well furnished, and generously windowed. Except for the hospital bed and table, it had no clinical notes. Richard Hildebrand lay partly on his side, an arm encircling Nora. Nelson heard him say, "I'd hug you with both arms, but one of them's silly enough to hurt."

A tall nurse beamed down at the tableau. She said, "We couldn't have found a better cure for the hurts, could we?" And a musical voice said from a large armchair, "Are you sure she isn't tiring you, Richard? Come over here and sit with me, baby."

Gently Nora disengaged herself and stood up. She looked satisfied, yet somewhat doubtful, as one who reaches home after a long hard journey to find a few minor changes. "What hurts besides your head and your arm, Daddy?"

"Don't let the bandage on my head bother you. It looks more important than it is."

"It looks very important. Have you any others?"

"I've got some stickum stuff on my ribs. That's why I can't move as much as I want to. But I'll be as good as new soon."

"I tried to find you last night but—"

"Is Mrs. Nelson waiting downstairs for you, baby," Alix said, "or did she send the maid?"

"Mr. Grid-dely brought me he— Oh—there he is." She ran to the door. "Did you get lost, Mr. Grid-dely?" She tugged him into the room. "Here's my daddy—he's glad I came—so is the nurse—her name's Miss Leeds—"

"I'm here too, baby," Alix said.

Nora said without enthusiasm, "This is Alix, Mr. Grid-dely."

Silently Nelson thanked the child for the introduction. It gave Hildebrand no way of knowing that this was not a first meeting. Nor could it be guessed from his wife's manner.

She looked slightly haggard. There were faint circles beneath her eyes. But it would have needed a major plague to impair her beauty. Quickly he released the hand she extended.

She said, "We'll never be able to thank you for your kindness to Nora."

Hildebrand, watching from his pillow, seemed to have discarded the scruples he had expressed prior to the accident. He said serenely, "Any time you're short of sitters, Captain Nelson, send Junie to us. He's our nephew from here on out."

Alix said, "I didn't realize you'd met the captain."

"I called at his house for Nora one night. You were at that literary club dinner."

"Oh—I see. Darling—I'm afraid you've had enough excitement for one day."

"I'm fine—I'm enjoying my visitors—but I'm afraid you need a change of scene." He smiled at Nelson. "She's been stuck here with me since morning. I can't get her to leave even for meals—and I must say she's done less than justice to the fare here."

"She can leave now that I'm with you," Nora said. "I'll stay, Daddy."

The nurse saw fit to take a hand. "Nobody can stay very much longer. It's a rule."

Nora said, "Alix stayed long, Miss Leeds."

Alix was tactful. "Only because it's a strange place for your daddy and I had to help him get used to it—you know—the way I stayed with you on your first day at nursery school."

Nora looked stormy. "But I didn't want you to—and my daddy wants me."

"That's unkind, baby."

There was a diversion. Framed by the doorway, the small form of Lilith Greenway cast a shadow that reached as far as Hildebrand's face. She said, "I've been eavesdropping and I think Richard is right, Alix." She came in and sat on the arm of Alix's chair. "You do need a change of scene—and he needs a little peace and quiet."

The tired lines that appeared around Hildebrand's mouth bore out the last half of the statement. He moistened his lips. The attentive Miss Leeds said, "There's orange juice in the thermos jug. Would you like—"

Nora was there before her. She had to stand on tiptoe to reach the jug on the night table. She poured the liquid as carefully as though it were a priceless cure-all and held the glass to his lips. "See, Daddy, I can take care of you."

"I'll tell you what, Nora," Lilith said. "We three girls will have dinner in a nice restaurant, and after that—"

Nora set the empty glass back on the table and stared at her coldly. "I've had my dinner."

"Ice cream too?"

"Mr. Grid-dely's house is full of ice cream."

Lilith cast her black eyes upward. "How can I buck such competition? I hope you're not being spoiled."

Nora ignored that. She said, "You look funny with bangs." She resumed her protective stance at the bedside, engaging her father in whispered conversation. Alix made soft-voiced apology to Nelson. "There's no mistaking the fact that Lilith and I are in her doghouse, is there? Lilith by association—I suppose. She's usually such a reasonable child and I can't really blame her for being stubborn now. She's too young to realize that I didn't mean to neglect her. I only hope no lasting damage has been done. I'd hate to lose her affection—"

"You're just too angelic," Lilith said. "A few wallops in the right place would be my prescription."

Nelson answered Alix. "I wouldn't worry about Nora—she's merely asserting what she believes to be her rights—but I haven't that excuse. I read somewhere that five minutes was the decent limit for a hospital visit, and I'm afraid I've gone beyond it."

Alix had turned her head away. All he could see was the incredibly pure profile capped by the blazing hair. She said, "Well—if you must go—"

Hildebrand stopped whispering to Nora. He said, "Must you?" and there was more than formal protest in his voice.

"I'll drop in again."

"We think it's wonderful that you dropped in at all," Alix said, "We realize from what Nora's told us that you're an exceedingly busy man. Say good night, Nora."

Nora looked lost, as though an ally was deserting. "Are you going because I whispered, Mr. Grid-dely? It wasn't rude—like secrets—it was just—just that my daddy and I hadn't seen each other in a long time."

Hildebrand smiled. His eyes suggested that he was fighting sleep. "Everyone will understand that we needed a bit of privacy. But we've exchanged all our news now—and tomorrow's another day. So after Miss Leeds takes you to have a look at some very new babies on the fifth floor you can come back and give me a good-night kiss. All right?"

She nodded. "Will you wait for me, Mr. Grid-dely?"

He promised. When she had left the room with the nurse Lilith said, "There'll be fireworks when we try to pry her loose from you. She seems to thinks she's moved into your house for the duration."

"She could," Nelson said. "It would make it simpler for Mrs. Hildebrand, since she'll probably spend most of her time here." He thought that Hildebrand looked relieved. He also thought that Lilith's glossy finish had been subject to wear and tear since last night.

Alix said. "But we couldn't possibly let you—"

"It needn't be settled this minute. If you do plan to leave soon I'll drive you home—and then you can decide."

Hildebrand's eyelids were drooping. He forced them apart. "I guess you're wondering how you happened to let yourself in for all this?"

"No—I'm wondering how my household will get along without Nora once you're on your feet."

"You're very good." His voice thickened a little. "If we had relatives in New York who could take over I wouldn't consider—"

"Richard," Alix said anxiously, "Dr. Falvey's orders are that you're not to bother about anything but getting well." She moved to a straight chair near the bed. The hand on the white coverlet turned up to enclose hers. "You feel chilly," she said, "shall I shut the windows?"

"No—sit still. Captain—about that taxi—" he winced. "Entirely my fault—I was so wrapped up in my—"

Alix stroked his hand. "You mustn't think about it. Captain Nelson hasn't come here to talk shop. Besides, minor traffic accidents aren't his province—and thank heaven it was minor."

Nelson said easily, "But it took place so close to home that I can't help being interested. Did you notice the driver at all?"

"No—" Hildebrand swallowed dryly. "I only saw—I—"

"Are you thirsty, Richard? More orange juice?"

"Yes, please."

She poured some and he sipped it. He mumbled, "No more—been

standing too long."

"I'll get some fresh—"

"Don't bother."

Lilith touched Nelson's arm. "Do you have a cigarette?" As he bent to light it she said, "Has the cab been found—or don't you know?"

"I've been making a few inquiries. Yes—it's been found."

She drew hard on the cigarette. Smoke drifted toward the bed. "Well?"

"But the driver hasn't been found," he said.

She flicked ashes to the floor. "Do you mean to say—?"

Alix said in a muted voice, "Lil, if you have to smoke in here use an ash tray."

"Do forgive me. I'm not hospital-broken." She turned back to Nelson. "When Alix starts to pick on me it's a sure sign that her nerves are frayed—and I don't wonder. It's high time I got her out of here. Richard won't miss her—he's gone bye-byes. Where were we? Oh yes—that cab. By the way, did I leave my case at your house last night?"

"Yes—sorry I didn't think to bring it."

"That's all right. I'm relieved. I thought I'd lost it and Alix might have been annoyed. She gave it to me." She flicked ashes again, caught herself at it, and said, "Let's take a turn in the corridor until Nora comes back. It will save me another bawling out." She got up off the arm of the chair. "We'll meet you outside, Alix."

"Shhh—"

Hildebrand opened his eyes. "They tell me the driver ran away."

"We'll find him," Nelson said.

Lilith killed her cigarette in a tray on the bureau. "What's stopping you? If you have the cab and you have his license number and his picture, what more do you want? How easy does it have to be for the police?"

"Unfortunately neither the license nor the picture means anything. The man who was driving had stolen the cab."

The words did not reach Hildebrand, who mumbled in a sleep-clogged voice, "Don't blame him—jay-walking—maybe trying to make a train for—passenger—"

"Passenger?" As Nelson watched, the heavy eyelids fell.

"Richard—does that light bother you? Shall I—?" Alix used her handkerchief to dry his moist forehead. She smoothed the coverlet, straightened gracefully, and came over to Nelson. "He's had several shots to relieve pain. I guess they've caught up with him. Perhaps it will disturb him if we stay here and talk. Let's wait in the corridor for Nora so that she doesn't burst in."

Outside the half-open door they waited quietly until Lilith said, "That child must be memorizing the pedigrees of every infant in the nursery. Why don't we see what's—?" Alix shook her head. "You may if you like. I don't want to go too far until the nurse gets back."

"All right, I'll go— Oh—at last!"

Nora and the nurse approached, stepping sedately to the rhythm of their surroundings. Nora seemed to have thrust off her resentment toward Alix. "We saw them through a big window," she said, "little tiny ones. They look like this." She illustrated by measuring the air and screwing up her face. "We couldn't go behind the window to touch them because we're full of germs, but as soon as my daddy's well I'll ask him if he can't get one for me."

Lilith snorted, "Do that."

"Baby," Alix said, "can you—"

"You wouldn't call me baby if you saw them—they—"

"All right, dear, but do you think a big girl could kiss Daddy without waking him? He's gone fast asleep—and he needs a lot of sleep if we're to have him home soon."

Nora seemed to be searching the words for flaws. Apparently they passed inspection because she laid a finger to her lips and tiptoed into the room.

Alix said to the nurse, "Do you think he'll sleep through the night, Miss Leeds?"

"He'll be aroused for medication and for the usual routine—but there's no point in waiting, Mrs. Hildebrand. Your presence might only stop him from dropping off as quickly as he might if you weren't here. Come as early as you like in the morning."

"Well—"

"If you want me to I'll give you a ring later—just to report that all's well." The nurse looked at the beautiful troubled face and smiled. "It's bound to be, you know." She seemed a kind, competent woman, Nelson thought. Possibly the best woman on scene.

Alix said, "Are you going to remain on night duty, Miss Leeds?"

"I think so—unless other arrangements have been made. It was pretty late when I came on."

"I know. I'm sorry the other day nurse got sick, but I can't help being glad someone like you took her place."

"Thank you, Mrs. Hildebrand." She said a general good night and went into the room. A moment later Nora tiptoed out.

Nora said, "I didn't wake him. I only put a little kiss on his cheek and whispered in his ear that I'd come back tomorrow."

"That's a good girl," Alix said. The music of her voice was sorrowful.

Nora said slowly, "If you're lonesome, Alix, I won't go to Mr. Griddely's."

Lilith snorted again. "Little Miss Importance. Isn't a kid's ego something?"

Nelson thought her ego was something, but kept the observation to himself.

They walked toward the elevators, Nelson absorbing by habit the smells and sights and sounds along the way. A loudspeaker gave tongue, paging monotonously a Dr. Rasselman. Two interns, dignified by dangling stethoscopes, chatted before the wide doors of an operating room. An old man halted at a closed door and peered up worriedly to read its number. A student nurse whose face was as starched as her uniform filled vases at a water tap. And as they passed the floor's reception desk a woman whose cap and manner proclaimed authority cited the law to one of her underlings.

In front of the elevators they became part of a larger waiting group. Lilith said loudly that the service was certainly not in keeping with the fees charged and expressed her displeasure by pressing her finger to the bell. To disassociate himself Nelson gave her the back of his head. He faced the desk, hearing behind him Nora's total recall of the tiny tiny babies. He thought absently that uniforms were great equalizers and that even at a short distance it was hard to tell nurses apart. For example, the one turning out of the corridor as though she were being chased looked exactly like Miss— He craned his neck.

Behind him the doors of the elevator opened to take the waiting load. As he stepped forward he thought he heard Nora call his name, but he did not look back. The elevator descended without him.

Before his stride brought him to the desk the head nurse had arisen. "Three-o-one?" she said. "I'll take a look." She struck out briskly, with Miss Leeds pacing her.

To Nelson who had followed, the cheerful room was exactly as it had been a short while ago. Hildebrand lay in quiet sleep. Too quiet?

Nelson lingered just inside the door, nerves stretched, eyes strained, trying to assure himself that he actually saw what might be merely imagined, or at best barely perceptible, the slight irregular rise and fall of the covers. Both women had made straight for the bedside. The head nurse held Hildebrand's wrist

With her eyes still on her watch she said, "Nurse—tell Dr. Courtland or Dr. Benjamin to come at once—whoever's nearest. Then call his own physician."

Miss Leeds nodded and whipped past Nelson, giving no indication that she saw him. He spoke to the head nurse. "What is it?"

"I don't—" She had started to reply automatically. She collected herself. "I didn't see you come in." Her voice was polite but dismissive. "I'm sorry, but the patient won't be permitted any more visitors tonight."

Outside, the voice of the loudspeaker made a throttled sound, cleared, and went into a repeated demand for Drs. Courtland and Benjamin.

Nelson went to the bed. He stooped over to raise one of the bluish eyelids.

The nurse said uncertainly, "Are you a doctor?"

"I'm a police officer. Do miscalculations in the administering of drugs happen often at Garde Medical?"

She drew herself up. "I've been here fourteen years. Such an error has never occurred."

"Then I think this is a case for the police." He said it with a kind of comfortless vindication. He felt rather like a hypochondriac whose fears have been confirmed at last by the visitation of a real ailment.

Chapter Eight

The summons of the loud-speaker was answered within five minutes. It seemed much longer to Nelson. Waiting, he tried to recall what he had learned about opium derivatives during his apprenticeship in the laboratory of a criminologist. Mentally he applied every known treatment, going through all the remembered steps, issuing commands to a conjured horde of assistants.

Potassium permanganate to neutralize the dose, he told this unseen band. Even given hypodermically, morphine enters the stomach. Add dilute ascetic acid to the antidote to change the drug to soluble salt. Remove by pump or emetic—zinc sulphate or mustard will do, a tablespoonful in a cup of water—repeat if necessary—follow by more water to encourage results. Inwardly he cursed the bound ribs—the injuries that would add to the awful pain of the process. Ice to the nape of his neck, alternate with hot compresses. Dash cold water to face and chest—careful, too much will bring collapse. Dry him—get him on his feet—walk him—give him strong coffee—pinch him—slap him—keep him awake—KEEP HIM AWAKE—

Frustration brought sweat to his forehead. He cursed again because here in this place he wore no vestments of responsibility. He was a layman. His diagnosis was not to be trusted. If he were wrong, if he attempted to arouse Hildebrand by so much as lifting him to sitting posture, it would kill or cure. But if a doctor did not come soon—?

He pushed past the silent nurse. He sprinted to the door. He sprinted smack into a thin bushy-haired man who was dogged by Miss Leeds.

"Dr. Courtland—" the head nurse said. But the doctor had no time for her. Neither did he take time to question Nelson's presence, according him no more than one alert glance. "Nurse here told me what she could," he said, bobbing his head at Miss Leeds. From then on he concentrated upon the work at hand, issuing real orders with real authority, commanding real assistants who did what he bade them do. He wanted more space, and the patient was rushed to the operating room on the floor. Nelson went too in the superfluous role of observer.

Later he left the room of his own volition, and for reasons that were shameful from a policeman's viewpoint. The truth was that he had found it uncommonly hard to witness the indignities inflicted upon Hildebrand. These would have been an ordeal without the damage previously wrought by the taxi. As it was, Hildebrand's valiant efforts to co-operate as soon as he opened his guileless eyes had even pierced the professional detachment of Dr. Courtland.

Empathic to a high degree, Nelson was always moved by the suffering of others, but repeated experience had provided him with an outward seeming of immunity. He could not account for the fact that Hildebrand had somehow managed to strip him of this protection. It must, he thought, be something to do with the ambiance of the man, a composite of simplicity, integrity, and extreme vulnerability.

Outside, he justified his retreat by a return to business. This took him back to Room 301, which showed signs of a hurried exodus. The pillow of the unmade bed lay upon the rug. The visitors' chairs had been pushed aside to give the stretcher clearance. One of the bearers had knocked over a vase of flowers. In passing, Nelson picked up the pillow and righted the vase. In passing he remembered that flowers had also been on scene at the first "accident" and wondered grimly who was responsible for this lot.

He picked up the thermos jug neatly stamped with the room number. He lifted its cover. The level of orange juice was low. He sniffed it and the glass beside it. He went to the bureau and looked at its spread of toilet articles and at the contents of the drawers. Whoever had packed a bag for Hildebrand had brought everything necessary for his comfort, he thought. And there was a possibility that something which did not fit into the category of comfort had been brought as well.

He looked into the clothes closet. The emptied bag was on a shelf. He inspected it and replaced it. Hangers bore a stained topcoat, a torn wrinkled suit of clothes, a pressed suit, and a heavy silk robe. He went through the pockets of each garment. In the jacket of the pressed suit he found a medicine bottle containing a residue of white powder. The bottle was unlabeled. There were raised figures on the glass bottom, but they were probably the code numbers of the manufacturer. Last he investigated the adjoining bathroom. He found nothing of interest there.

He weighed the advantages of the police laboratory with the facilities at hand. He voted in favor of the facilities at hand since there was scant hope that the objects in question were marked by significant fingerprints. He had seen Nora and Alix handle both glass and jug. Unquestionably Miss Leeds had handled them too, all of which added up to one amorphous smear.

He pressed the buzzer attached to Hildebrand's bed. Too soon to be an answer to the summons, a nurse entered the room. She was a fresh-faced young girl with large blue eyes that grew larger as they went from Nelson to the unoccupied bed.

Nelson smiled at her. "Did you happen to be passing as the light flashed on?"

"No—I'm a private nurse. I was notified this afternoon to come on at seven-thirty for night duty. I told Dr. Falvey's secretary I'd have to be a little late because it was short notice—and she said that was all right. This is Mr. Richard Hildebrand's room?"

Nelson nodded. "He'll be back after his treatment."

"The thing is," she said, "there's been some sort of mix-up and I don't know whether I'm to stay or not. You see—originally Miss Leeds was supposed to be on night duty, but she came on at three because the day nurse took sick—at least that's what they told me downstairs."

Nelson said, "Why not talk it over with Miss Leeds when she comes back? Meanwhile there's something you can do." He had wrapped glass and thermos jug in a towel. He held the bundle out to her. "Careful—keep it upright. Dr. Courtland, wants the liquid analyzed. Do you know where to take it?"

"Oh yes." She added with pride, "Mr. Hildebrand will be my fifth case at Garde Medical." Then she said doubtfully, "Shouldn't I put the room to rights first?" Her eyes did not know what to make of its general air of disorder.

"You'll have time to attend to it before the patient gets back, Miss—?"

"Watkins—Jean Watkins." She stared up at him, frankly puzzled. "I thought Mr. Hildebrand was Dr. Falvey's patient."

"He is. Dr. Courtland is the house physician."

"I know that but—" She blurted it out. "Who are you?"

"Mr. Hildebrand called in a specialist." He said it forbiddingly. He fixed his expressive face to discourage further questions.

"Oh—I see—well—excuse me—I'll take this down at once, Doctor."

When she had gone he allowed his facial muscles to relax. If Hildebrand's condition was the result of a hospital error, he supposed that everyone connected with Garde Medical would learn of it, either directly or by grapevine. If it was not a hospital error, everyone who read the newspapers would learn of it. Meanwhile a premature broadcast was to be avoided even at the cost of rebuffing the pardonably curious Miss Watkins. It should be left to the doctors to give her what information was necessary.

The telephone had been plugged into an outlet near the bureau. He unwound its long cord and gave the operator his own number. Kyrie answered and he said he was sorry that he could not be home for dinner. She said that since it was after eight she had figured that out for herself. She sounded much farther away than the short distance between Garde Medical and home. She inquired about Hildebrand. He hesitated because the privacy of the line was moot, and said, "As well as can be expected." She asked stiffly if Nora was with him. He said no, and intimated that he would elaborate when he got home. She told him that by that time she would probably be asleep. He asked if he had been paged by headquarters. She said, "No." He asked if everything was all right. She said, "If you mean here, yes." Then she wished him good night and hung up.

His mind had moved so far from her real or pretended jealousy of Alix that he could not understand what had bitten her. She was accustomed to his irregular working hours, which often necessitated a change of plan without notice, so it could not be that. He completely forgot that she did not realize he was working.

He left 301 and walked along the corridor that was beginning to seem all too familiar. He came to the beneficent torture chamber but did not enter. He paced back and forth between its wide doors and the elevators. After a while the girl who had replaced the head nurse at the desk did not look up when he passed.

The hospital began to quiet down for the night. Visitors straggled toward the elevators. Nelson envied them. At intervals he halted to deposit half-smoked cigarettes in a convenient sandbox. He felt queasy and the cigarettes did not help, but he continued to light them. He thought that it had been a lean day, foodwise. He thought of his offer to drive Alix and Lilith and Nora home and wondered what they, and particularly Nora, had made of his defection. He hoped that the child was faring well and regretted that he had not asked Kyrie to make certain of this. He thought of Kyrie. He wondered if while he was engaged in 301 Dr. Falvey had come. He thought it quite likely that Dr. Falvey had communicated with Alix and hoped that Nora had not repeated her eavesdropping act. He wondered if the news had caused Alix to swoon again or if, in line with her exemplary behavior of the day, she would come back to the hospital. He thought of Hildebrand. He thought of Lilith and of the man she had introduced as her brother. He closed his eyes and tried to visualize 301 as it had been at his initial entrance, his object being to recall if the arrangement of chairs had suggested other visitors before his arrival. He opened his eyes in time to avoid collision with the reception desk. The nurse was watching him with alarm. He made a right about-face, and if she spoke to him he did not hear.

Time passed. He outlined tomorrow's schedule, contingent upon the night's developments. His thoughts retraced their torturous course to Alix, to Nora, to Lilith, to her brother, to Hildebrand. Always they returned to Hildebrand and to the battle that waged behind the wide closed doors.

The exodus began at half-past ten. The first to emerge was an orderly carrying a tray of covered white utensils. Nelson challenged him in a crisp professional voice. "Is this for the lab?"

The orderly conferred a medical degree upon him. "Yes, Doctor—stomach contents and etcetera." He went his way.

A few minutes later Dr. Courtland came out. He wore a clean white coat and had evidently just scrubbed. The smell of disinfectant rose from his strong bony hands. He looked tired but not grim. He seemed charged with nervous energy.

Nelson intercepted his dash toward a closed stairway. "Dr. Courtland —"

"Yes?" He came to a reluctant stop. "Oh—so you're still here. Well—the worst is over. After he's been walked another mile or so he'll be allowed to rest. His own physician is with him." He was trying to be courteous. He was also trying to be bluff and hearty in the manner of doctors everywhere who had to deal with the friends and relatives of patients. "I don't mind telling you luck was with us. If his legs and feet had been injured it could be a different story." He waited for Nelson to step aside, visibly containing a will to bolt. "You can go home now with your mind at ease."

"I'd like a talk with you, Doctor. I'm—"

"Sorry—but there's nothing else I can tell you. Different people react differently to certain drugs." He tapped his foot impatiently. "Or possibly there are other factors involved. After the accident he was taken to Bellevue. The treatment he received there might have conflicted with ours."

"Wasn't Bellevue asked for an account of what had been done?"

Dr. Courtland chose to disregard the question. He said, "I assure you that, whatever the cause, all precautions will be taken to eliminate it. Naturally I understand your concern, but I've had an exceedingly heavy day. Good night—"

Nelson said, "I'm not accusing Garde Medical of carelessness, Doctor. Neither am I an overanxious relative of the patient. I'm a police officer, and up to a certain point my interests run parallel to yours. I have no desire to give a good hospital a bad name."

The doctor's pores seemed to open to absorb the information. In the act of reappraising Nelson he said, "Did you just happen to be in the building or did someone send for you?"

"It's a mixture. Could we continue this in private?"

"Come along."

Nelson followed him up a flight of stairs and was led to the sitting room of a small apartment. His host pushed aside a screen that hid kitchen facilities, measured coffee precisely, lit one of the stove's burners, and set the percolator upon it, muttering that anyone would think he had seen enough of the brew in the past few hours to turn him against it. Then he sank into a leather chair, removed his shoes, sighed, and said, "All right. I'm listening." He motioned Nelson to a companion chair.

Nelson explained as much as he thought was necessary. He started with the blackmail letters but did not cite the nature of the blackmailer's hold. Nor did he mention Alix's friends. He sketched in his ideas about the hit-and-run and concluded with an observation that tonight's episode could be a sequel to the first attempt upon Hildebrand's life.

"But surely none of this is more than suspicion," the doctor said.

Nelson got up to take the bubbling percolator from the stove. The doctor demanded cream, sugar, cheese, and crackers, as though he were demanding instruments. He caught himself at it and apologized. "Sorry—being an unchallenged power in a large establishment does odd things to a man." He had a thin sharp face. His smile improved it. "Get another cup and join me."

Nelson was glad to join him. Coffee and cheese and crackers had never been more inviting. His queasiness left him after the first few mouthfuls. He said as though there had been no interruption, "I expect you'd rather have my suspicions justified than yours."

The doctor's "What's that?" was defensive.

"As head physician of the staff here you wouldn't like it much if there'd been a nearly fatal error. I gather that's the conclusion you jumped to—and of course it may be the correct one."

"Just a minute! It doesn't have to be either foul play or error. The man could be allergic to even a small quantity of morphine."

Nelson shook his head. "I think that's ruled out. When it was given hypodermically at Bellevue he had no unusual reaction. By the way—I took the liberty of sending a donation to the lab in your name." He told him about the thermos jug. "How long will it take them to analyze that and the contents of the tray you sent?" He had pocketed the bottle found in Hildebrand's jacket. "The reports should put both of us on a more solid basis."

Dr. Courtland said dryly, "You haven't wasted much time, have you? Hand me that house phone on the desk behind you. The cord will reach. Thanks."

Nelson heard him speak briefly. Then he gave a series of pointed orders. He hung up and said, "They'll start on it at once. It shouldn't be a long procedure. That fool orderly didn't make it urgent enough."

Nelson replaced the instrument on the desk. "I don't suppose you get many emergencies," he said idly.

"No. Few of our patients put off attending to themselves until the last minute. They can afford to anticipate their ills."

Nelson said, "Was it you or an assistant who examined Hildebrand after he was admitted?"

"I didn't set eyes on him until tonight. Judging by the fight he put up, I'd say he was a man of considerable character."

"Is he really out of the woods?"

The doctor's shrug was not callous. "I think so. If he survives the next twelve hours I'll know. After what you've told me I won't feel out of the woods myself until he's been discharged from Garde Medical. What happens to him here—murder by an outsider included—will be a black mark against us, whichever way you look at it."

"If you're thinking of the publicity angle, we'll do our best to—"

The doctor made angry interruption. "I served throughout the war. When it was over I felt entitled to sink into a comparatively easy berth—but it hasn't made me as cynical as you might suppose. I'll let the Board of Trustees worry about unfavorable publicity." He talked down Nelson's polite disclaimer of intended slight. "Perhaps the war gave me a murder phobia. But prior to it and since, I've seen death come by many different routes—and sometimes I was even able to stop the train." He glared. "You may not believe it, but I still like to try—and tonight's effort had better not be wasted."

Nelson said, "Amen," and thought that the doctor improved upon acquaintance.

The doctor measured him, his glare fading. "As good a way to end a sermon as any. Ascribe it to guilt. Every so often I ask myself what I'm doing in this plushy place."

"There's no valid reason why minority groups like the rich shouldn't be entitled to good medical attention," Nelson said.

They both smiled. Nelson returned to the subject. "About how long does it take for the symptoms of morphine poisoning to appear?"

"They can become manifest from a quarter of an hour to an hour," the doctor said. He elaborated upon the answer, but Nelson paid only minimal attention. Lilith did not go near the thermos jug while I was in the room, he thought. Still—she could have been in and out all day. She could have been there a few minutes before I came, for all I know. So could her brother. Alix—?

The doctor was saying, "... fatal results have been known to occur in three quarters of an hour—but as a rule not until eight to twelve hours have passed. Mind you—I'm not worried so much on that score. I doubt if there's a vestige of the stuff left in him, but—"

Hildebrand seemed quite calm, Nelson thought. No undue mental excitement—no noticeable contraction of the pupils—but of course I wasn't alert for symptoms. I chalked the flush that came later to Lilith and his dislike of her. Was he drowsy before or after he drank the orange juice? Nora gave it to him the first time—then Alix—

"... a wonderful machine, the human body," the doctor was saying. "Too bad it's governed by that mess of imponderables we call the human mind. As soon as he's capable of sustained thought he'll want to know the whys and wherefores, and I haven't enough of his history to guess how he'll thrive on the answer—especially if it turns out to be your answer. I can't guess how I myself would react under the same set of circumstances. The injuries he had to begin with wouldn't make for a rosy outlook in any man—and being dragged from his bed for a gratuitous workout as though he'd fallen into a nest of sadists—well—" He grimaced. He moved his hands along his rib cage as though he were testing it for soundness. "Add physical pain to the mental torture of being told that a vicious faceless enemy will keep trying—and you don't get a reassuring total."

"It won't come as a complete shock to him," Nelson said. "The fact of blackmail made him realize he has an enemy."

Dr. Courtland said resentfully, "It didn't do him much good to notify the police about it, though."

Nelson took remarks like that in stride. "The pace of life is usually slower than the pace of television or theater," he said. And he thought, Life isn't as well written as a prepared script either. Too full of coincidences and of characters that dime novelists would scorn to use—and of static intervals in which even the leading players lost interest.

The doctor looked at him and said pacifically, "I should know better. I've received the same kind of heckling—but there's something about that man. Befuddled as he was, he projected decency. I've been meaning to ask you about his family. The nurse kept droning stuff about a wife and daughter into his ear to make him take notice. What are they like?"

"Very devoted." Nelson thought that no amount of preparation would help Hildebrand if the wife he loved proved treacherous.

"That should rule out suicide—unless the blackmail was enough to discourage him. Of course he could have troubles we don't want—"

"I don't think it was suicide."

"Neither do I. His will to live seemed too strong. I was merely—" He jumped up and reached around Nelson for the ringing telephone. He grunted and listened. Nelson left his chair to prowl the room. The doctor's end of the conversation consisted of grunts and gaps until he said, "Who's there with you? ... All right. I needn't advise you not to dine out on this.... Yes, he is. No thanks to your findings.... Yes—they'll want that."

He replaced the receiver. He turned and said, "A copy of the report will be typed for you."

"Thanks."

"Meanwhile I can see that it isn't necessary to spell it out. I almost wish it could be laid to our door." He added grimly, "If so, I can tell you the chance of a repeat performance wouldn't exist."

"Orange juice?"

The doctor nodded. "An indicative residue in both glass and jug—and over two grains in the stomach contents. One sixth to one half grain subcutaneously have produced fatal results." He sat down to put on his shoes. "I'll have another look at him. What do you intend to do?"

"First of all I'll station a guard outside his room—plainclothes—"

"Station an army in battle dress if it will do the trick. This phone has no outside line, but there's one in my bedroom."

He stood by while the call was made to headquarters. Then Nelson accompanied him to the door of Hildebrand's room. He was not asked to enter and he did not solicit an invitation. He waited outside.

The doctor rejoined him in a few minutes. "He's dropped into a normal sleep. Dr. Falvey is with him and will stay for a while longer. He informs me that he has the case well in hand." The words were said without expression, but they pulled the long lips to one side.

"Was Dr. Falvey present during the workout?"

"For the best part of it. He did some expert supervising. Dr. Falvey's patients swear by him. He has the kind of bedside manner that's almost vanished from the profession."

Nelson said, "Thank you for the coffee," because there was nothing else to say. He was trying to make up his mind as to whether or not he should wait for Dr. Falvey, who was on his list of people to see. He decided that it might be more rewarding to beard that particular lion in his habitat.

"Good night, Dr. Courtland."

"I suppose you'll be around."

"I suppose so. Sorry."

He was given another glimpse of the attractive smile. "I've had to take worse. I'll walk you as far as the elevators."

He had to take worse before they reached the elevators. The girl at the floor desk stopped them.

"Dr. Courtland—the lab has been ringing you— Oh—here's—"

A white-coated technician came abreast of the two men and drew the doctor out of earshot. Nelson saw the intent poise of the bushy head as the man talked, saw his lips move at intervals, but could not hear the syllables he uttered. Yet even from where he stood they sounded explosive. Then he saw the doctor look his way and beckon. He hurried over.

The doctor was breathing fire. "The lab's had a busy night," he said. "They've just finished an analysis of vomited matter. Dr. Ballard here thought the results might interest me. I'm afraid it will interest you."

Nelson's brow shirred.

"Morphine," the doctor said. "The patient is no longer with us—"

Nelson said stupidly, "Hildebrand? But you—"

"No—not Hildebrand. Not a patient either, come to think of it—a nurse—age twenty-nine—a private—not attached to the hospital. But a friend of hers lives in the nurses' home in the next building, so she went there to lie down. Nobody thought anything about it except that she'd been out last night and was succumbing to a hangover. An hour ago her friend's roommate came in and discovered her—dead. She'd been vomiting. The doctor who was called too late didn't like what he saw and had the wits to verify his suspicions." He pointed a finger at Nelson. "Would you call that a coincidence?" Nelson did not answer. Scenes flashed across his mind. Alix Hildebrand telling Miss Leeds that she preferred her to the nurse who had been replaced; the night nurse entering 301 and explaining that there had been some confusion in the schedule. The doctor was staring at him as though he were a jinx. He said in a repressed voice, "I don't know what's going on here. I only know nothing like it ever happened until you appeared. Well—say something. It's either murder or a suicide—which makes it your specialty, not mine. I give it to you."

Nelson thought drearily, You're too late. It was given to me earlier—twice—and the second time might have been soon enough to save the girl. I knew about the orange juice then—I— The back of his neck felt tense. He raised a hand to rub it. But I'm not a soothsayer—I do the best I can. He said quietly, "I'm pretty sure it was Hildebrand's nurse."

It was the doctor's turn to look stupid. "How the hell can you know?"

"Never mind." He was a homicide officer on the job again. "I'll have to go over there."

"There's a bridge on the seventh floor that connects the buildings." Nelson nodded abruptly and walked away.

"Wait—I'm going too." The doctor caught up with him. "Isn't there a chance she got the poison somewhere else?"

"I'll make inquiries." He was pressing the elevator bell as impatiently as Lilith had pressed it.

"An autopsy will supply more answers than you're likely to get by asking."

"An autopsy will be performed—by us. I'll have the body removed to the morgue."

The doctor groaned. "That means we'll be overrun by your men—reporters—God knows who else."

"Everything will be done before daylight."

"Well—that's something. If I were in a thankful mood I'd give thanks for the hour."

The hour, as an operator slid back the doors of the only elevator in use, was midnight.

Chapter Nine

By the time Nelson had recrossed the seventh-floor bridge and descended to the lobby of Garde Medical, his mind was like a house rudely used by too many visitors. Deliberately he shut the door upon it, postponing the labor of putting it to rights until he was rested. Now he was too tired to give himself to anything but the anticipation of a hot bath, a drink, a light meal although he was not hungry, and perhaps a bit of reading before he tried to sleep.

The lobby was not quite deserted. A cluster of nurses near the desk talked softly and sent occasional glances at a woman who occupied one of the upholstered chairs. Her mouth was scarlet in a mat-white face. Her hair shone brighter than the few subdued lamps that had been left burning.

He sent a glance of longing toward the exit, sighed, and crossed the invisible circle of loneliness in which she sat. "Mrs. Hildebrand."

She seemed to take his presence for granted, showing no surprise, wasting no words on a greeting. "You knew something was wrong before we left. That's why you didn't come with us. How is he now? Why did you let me leave when—?"

He said, "It's all right—he's sleeping. May I drive you home? This time I'll make the offer good." He did not feel gentle toward her and yet his voice was gentle. You could pay tribute to a work of art without liking it, he thought defensively.

She looked up at him, and he was suddenly impelled to touch his chin to learn just how badly he needed a shave. She said, like a child complaining of grave injustice, "They won't let me see him."

"How long have you been sitting here?"

"I don't know. Dr. Falvey had left word with his secretary to notify me—but Lilith took the call and said nothing because she didn't think I could stand any more bad news after last night. Later my maid happened to ask if the call from Dr. Falvey meant that Richard was worse. Then Lilith had to tell me and I dressed again and came here." He had to bend over her to catch and separate the notes in the low swift flow of her voice. "Someone had given orders that nobody—not even me—could go up—and while I argued about it visiting hours were over for all the patients and only the staff elevator was running. So I found the stairs and walked to the third floor—but Dr. Falvey came out of Richard's room and told me it would be better not to disturb him and told me to go home. Dr. Falvey hadn't meant for me to come at all. He just wanted me to be ready—in case—in case—" She swallowed. "Well—he said the crisis had passed and I was not to worry—but how can I help it?"

Nelson did not have time to speculate upon what else Dr. Falvey had told her. She said, "It never occurred to me that Richard could have a relapse. According to Dr. Falvey, it often happens after an accident—something to do with delayed shock. Still—I can't help thinking I'm responsible—letting him see everyone—tiring him—"

Her perfume was insidious. Nelson sat down, almost as though a lower altitude might raise his boiling point. I must be more tired than I realize, he thought hazily.

He said, "You trust your doctor, don't you?"

"Yes—yes—I do, but—"

"Then obey his orders and go home."

"I can't—I tried to get a room here, but there isn't one free—"

"That should settle it—or do you intend to sit in the lobby for the rest of the night?" Purposefully he arose.

"I'll—anyway, I'll wait until Dr. Falvey comes down."

He was reluctant to touch her, but he did. Her hands felt boneless in his and fleshed with silk. He said, "Besides—there's Nora," and pulled her to her feet. His own ears caught a confusion of meaning behind the words. Besides—there's Nora. Besides—there's a helpless husband who has been fighting for his life. Besides—there's Kyrie—

She took only the literal meaning. "Nora's safe in bed."

"She was safe in bed last night—which didn't prevent her from setting forth on her little excursion. If she should get it into her head to try it again it might not end so well."

"Lilith promised to keep an eye—" Unexpectedly she capitulated. "Very well. If I can't be with Richard I guess it doesn't matter whether I'm here or home. Tell me the truth. You're sure—?"

"I'm sure." He made a mental reservation. As sure as a policeman standing guard can make me.

She laid a hand upon his arm. Guiding her to the exit, he told himself that he should have quit while he was ahead, that it would be better to question her when rest and daylight had restored his wits.

Winter had made a return engagement. The rush of cold river air cleansed him of the hospital smells, and of the smell of the poisoned body in the nurses' building, and of the nervous exudations of those among her white-clad sisters who had not managed to take her death in professional stride. And anticlimactically it rid him of Alix Hildebrand's scent, so that in the covering dark he grinned crookedly at the fool who was Grid Nelson, and pushed him aside to make way for the Homicide captain.

He did not start the car at once. Something was happening in the driveway of the next building. Shadowy forms strained under a shadowy burden. His mind's eye saw what the night obscured, men bearing a wicker basket, property of the morgue. The wind muted such sounds as attended their grim activity. It was like watching a drama in dumb show as with skilled, rehearsed movements they lifted the basket to the waiting vehicle.

He looked sidelong at Alix Hildebrand. She had not stirred since entering the car, except to make a tighter sheath of her coat when he lowered the window. Her eyes were closed. She might have been asleep. Everything about her was still, the scarlet mouth, the hands in her lap, everything but the glistening wet that crawled from beneath her eyelids.

He tried to attribute the tears to self-pity or to a bid for attention. He remembered her air of detachment the day she had come to his office and how she had impressed him as a woman of little feeling. He clung to his role as officer of the law.

The morgue vehicle went by, turning west at the corner. He set his car in motion. Driving along the river, he framed and discarded questions, seeking the one most likely to provide the opening he needed. The next time he glanced at Alix Hildebrand her face was drowned. Yet no sound came from her.

The quietest bid for attention on record, he thought. His compassionate "Here—don't—" was involuntary. It startled him, and it startled her. She turned toward him blindly, and blindly threw herself against him.

He almost lost control of the wheel. He was unaware of sending a message to his feet and hands. They seemed to take independent action, pulling the car to the curb, braking it to a dead stop.

Gaining control of himself was harder. It was he who needed a brake. His heart raced. He was shouting, You might have killed us both—and the people behind and ahead—what kind of mad trick—!

But the shouting was inward. Aloud he made soothing mutter to lull her racking sobs. The private citizen of the sensitive nose was in again, breathing her, holding her close, suffering sweet agony in all his nerve centers.

Cars detoured around them, the lights picking them out and casting them back into the darkness. He did not hear or see. He did not know how many moments passed, and would have disbelieved the few it had taken to cancel reason.

A driver slowed and yelled, "Are you in trouble, Jack?"

That reached him. That was like a whip laid across his back. "Yes—no—"

"Say no more. You picked a fine place. My advice is don't wait for a cop to come along."

"All right," he said, "all right. Thanks." His arms slackened and emptied. She went away to huddle in her corner. Her back was toward him, curved ungracefully to the posture of an old woman.

He gripped the wheel. The anonymous driver's cop was there inside him as he joined the moving traffic. The cop engaged in fleeting and none too pleasant speculation. One day, he thought, she'll pour out a dispassionate tale of how she nearly seduced another poor slob flung by circumstance within her orbit. He wasn't even particularly attractive, she'll say. He was just there.

He knew he was being unfair. True, he was just there, but not as a male to be ensnared. Probably not as a human being. A tree, a pillar, the nearest symbol of support to lean against in her extremity. She had not tried to be provocative. Tears like that were not summoned at will. Nor was she trying to be provocative now. The average woman would be at her purse, madly eager for the restoratives of powder puff, lipstick, and comb. But although she no longer huddled and had gone so far as to blow her nose, she had not even dried her face, and the wind blowing in would chap her delicate skin

He said, "Put the window up on your side."

She obeyed. She produced a tremolo. "I'm sorry."

"No damage done." Surely tears and the handkerchief were responsible for her smeared lips. Everything that had happened, he told himself firmly, had happened within him. She could have no inkling of the havoc wrought.

"No damage done?" She repeated it on a keening note, much too intense to be a by-product of the recent storm. "I wish I were dead. The river was there all the time I sat waiting. I should have—" She stopped. She said again, "I'm sorry."

"I don't know of any reason for you to entertain thoughts like that," he said.

"No—how would you?"

"Would you like to tell me?"

"Tell you?" He realized from the sound of her voice that she had herself in hand now. "You know more than I do. You were upstairs—they allowed you to stay."

He saw that if he was to gain any ground at all it would have to be by inches. He said, "Who else visited your husband besides Miss Greenway?"

"Herb—" She tripped over it, changed it. "Her brother—only for a few minutes. He left a little while before you came—and Richard's secretary, Miss Garvey, and two of the men in his firm—Ken McClean and Charlie Phillips. They just dropped in to pay their respects. None of them stayed long, except Lilith—she was in and out all day—but I suppose even that was too tiring."

"Did the doctor or the nurse complain?"

"No—"

"Then there's no sense in reproaching yourself."

"But there is," she said. "Why do you pretend there isn't? You can't have forgotten what I told you the day I came to your office."

Again he thought that she might be on the verge of some revelation, but dared not rush her. "I haven't forgotten," he said. He was marking time, and wishing that there was more time to mark.

They had left the river and soon they would be at her door. To give her leeway he managed by a series of nice calculations to hit every stop light. He knew from experience that the combined spur of moment and mood was unlikely to operate twice in the same case. He said, "When you gave me your confidence that day it was because you misunderstood my position—so I thought it only decent not to remind you of it." Between lights he let the speedometer drop. She did not notice the fact that they were crawling, and the few cars that shared the avenue did not call it to her attention.

"You may stop being a gentleman," she said. "Don't you see—I want to talk about it. I've got to. That officer you took me to—did he tell you the outcome?"

"He told me of the circumstantial evidence that pointed to your husband and that you had urged him to let the matter drop—which means, of course, that you accepted your husband's guilt."

Her denial was fierce. "No—no—that's not true."

"It was the impression you gave him."

"I had to get rid of him somehow. He meant well—but what good was he to me? He made it plain that he was satisfied—that he had no intention of looking further."

"He's a man who takes his job seriously," Nelson said. "His record shows that."

"And Richard's record? From what you've seen of him, can you possibly think he'd send blackmail letters to anyone—let alone me?"

"Not unless he's—"

"There's no unless. If you're against him too I won't go on with this. You've been prejudiced by that lieutenant—so has Lilith—but there's an excuse for her—she's—oh, I don't know."

"She's what?"

"Nothing—she's my friend. She—she wouldn't want anything to happen to me. What's the use—you wouldn't understand. Richard's the sanest human being I've ever met. I thought you were sane too. I thought—I thought I could talk to you, but I can't—I can't."

He had seen and heard much, but he had never seen the tables so completely turned or been robbed so completely of his own side of an argument. She was Hildebrand's wife. She had every right to take up the cudgels for him. He only wished that the cudgels did not have such a rubbery look. He said, "Didn't you admit to the lieutenant that your husband had changed—was moody—given to irrational bursts of temper?"

"I told you I wanted to be rid of him. I don't remember what I said but I'm sure I didn't use the word 'irrational.' He probably used it himself and I agreed—just to get him out of the house. My biggest mistake was in expecting help from the police. I'd never have done it except that—well—your wife and son are so—so—" She could find no descriptive words for Kyrie and Junie. "Seeing them made me think you'd be more than run-of-the-mill. I thought you'd be interested and not shunt me off on—"

"I'm interested now."

"For the wrong reasons."

He wondered guiltily what she meant.

"Richard didn't have a relapse. You wouldn't have hung back when we left—or stayed all that time—if it was anything like that. I'm not a fool—"

He agreed. He thought that she might even be too clever for her own good.

"I have a right to know," she said. "You have no right to keep me from knowing—not you or Dr. Falvey or anyone else. Doesn't it occur to you how cruel it is to let me imagine all sorts of—?" Imagination seemed to take over, closing the door on speech.

"What have you been imagining?" Nelson said.

"Things—crazy things—that Richard took some drug in an attempt to commit suicide. That's considered a crime, isn't it? It would account for your being there—only it can't be true. He wouldn't—not Richard. No matter how I'd failed him he wouldn't leave Nora to carry that weight for the rest of her life. And anyway—we—it was all right between us."

"I thought you told me he wasn't aware—to use your word—that you'd 'failed' him."

"He wasn't—not when I spoke to you—but since then he found one of the blackmail letters. He wasn't going to tell me. He was waiting for me to tell him." She sat immobile, a work of art defaced by the elements of her own nature, cheeks salt-encrusted, mouth smeared, hair tossed. She was like a stage-set ravaged by storm machinery which, bogus or not, lent drama and pathos to what had been static perfection. As he eyed her obliquely Nelson's heart leaped forward. His mind shied.

"If I had told him before," she said, "there would have been no accident. He wouldn't have been so worried that he didn't know what he was doing or where he was going. He wouldn't have crossed in the middle of the street—"

Nelson tested her preoccupation by driving past the street on which they lived. No protest came. She went on talking. "But he scolded me for saying that. He said that in a way the accident had been a good thing—it had cleared his head—given him back his perspective. He said that it was easier to bear broken ribs than wounded pride—and that nothing had ailed him before the accident but wounded pride because I hadn't turned to him when the letters started coming. So the first moment we had alone today he brought the whole business out into the open—and we discussed it—and he felt better." She halted. She nodded her head. "He *did* feel better. That's why I —"

She leaned toward Nelson. For a moment he thought there might be a repetition of the storm scene. But she only said prayerfully, "Could it really have been a relapse?"

"I'm not a doctor." He was glad that he no longer had to pose as one. "Did you discuss the possible identity of the blackmailer with him?"

"No."

"Did either of you mention Frank?"

"Fr—" She started to repeat the name. She shook her head.

"Did he visit the hospital today?"

She took her time. "No—my husband doesn't know anybody called Frank. Why should you think—?"

"Do you?"

"W-what's his other name?"

"I'd like you to tell me."

"I—I really can't."

He recognized the answer as equivocal but he saw no future in sparring with her. "Have you thought of any explanation for the purple crayon or the circulars in your husband's desk?"

"Just—just that somebody must have put them there."

"Who, aside from the servants, had the opportunity?"

She appeared to misunderstand. "The servants were questioned. They didn't do it."

"That isn't what I asked. I excepted the servants. Lilith Greenway—"

"Lilith wouldn't!"

"I'm not accusing her. I'm merely pointing out that she and her brother and probably other of your visitors have the run of the house—and that among them there may be someone who wishes you or your husband ill. I've mentioned the Greenways specifically because they're the only close friends of yours I've heard about. Who else?"

"I don't know what to say. We haven't really close friends in New York. We're friendly with neighbors and business acquaintances but—"

"Which leads us right back to your husband." He made it as brutal as he could. "Even if we concede that the purple crayon and the circulars with his fingerprints on them were planted, we're confronted by the more damning evidence of the payoff. Your husband was seen going into a record shop and coming out with the records." He was trying to construct a trap that would either choke from her that something which he sensed she was suppressing or end her pretense, if it was a pretense, of defending Richard Hildebrand.

She cried out, "Why have you suddenly turned inquisitor? You said that blackmail wasn't your department."

"And it was you who pointed out that blackmail could lead to my department."

"But I tell you he didn't—I don't care if a hundred people saw him coming out of the record shop—"

"Have either of you patronized that shop before?"

"Yes—often. Nora has a subscription to a children's magazine that's always recommending records, and she picks out the ones she'd like to have and we buy them for her there because they have a full stock. The letter had instructed me to buy ten—so automatically I picked the ones I knew she wanted." She stopped. She said in ringing triumph, "It was nothing but coincidence that made Richard go there that day. He just remembered Nora's latest list and thought he'd do something about it—and I suppose the clerk recognized him and told him I'd been there first—and handed him the package. That must have been the way it was."

"Mrs. Hildebrand, did he bring the records home?"

"Why shouldn't he?"

"Did you see them?"

"They're kept in Nora's playroom. She has so many. I didn't think to look."

"But if they were unwrapped in your house and your husband is as innocent as you profess to believe, wouldn't he or Nora have asked you about the extra packet that the police told you to enclose?"

"Not necessarily. He might have thought the packet had something to do with the records—booklets, perhaps—and when he saw it contained blank paper he'd think it had been put there by mistake and he'd discard it."

Nelson did not comment. He said, "We can check to see if the records have been added to Nora's collection."

"And if they are, do you think it will prove to me that Richard had any part in it? Don't you understand? The blackmail has stopped being important now that he knows of it. He says that if the letters keep coming we'll just ignore them until he—until whoever it is gets tired." A moment later she gasped, "Oh no—it's impossible."

"What is?"

"I was—it just struck me that maybe—somehow—another letter arrived at the hospital and was brought to him while we waited for the elevator—and it—it was worse than the others and made Richard sick all over again in spite of his—" She seemed to be pleading for Nelson's denial.

He would not give it. He thought, I can be as equivocal as the next, and said, "It's not impossible."

He tried to see her face, but she had turned away. She was peering out of the window. She said shakily, "Aren't we almost home? What street is this? Stop—you've driven past the—!" Her voice accused him. "I might have missed a call from Dr. Falvey."

"I doubt if the situation has changed any."

She moaned, "If I only knew what the situation is."

He wanted to say that she could read all about in in the papers. Not because he trusted her but because he would not be there to observe her when she did read all about it, he said, "You were at the hospital when the first day nurse felt sick and went off duty?"

"Yes." She seemed to search for the question's relevance. "Why?"

"She's dead."

"De—? Oh no! The poor girl. What was?"

"Poison."

There was poison in his delivery of the word. Her lips moved against each other as though they tasted it. "Liquor?" she said. "Bad liquor?"

"What makes you think that?"

"I—I don't know. I don't mean to be unkind. Lilith—Lilith thought there was nothing wrong with her except a hangover."

"It was drink all right," Nelson said, "but a soft drink. A drug intended for someone else had been added to it." He waited fruitlessly for her to ask what he was sure she must ask, the name of the intended victim. He said, "So you see—you were quite right in thinking I had a professional reason for remaining at the hospital."

She said wonderingly, "And it never occurred to me that you weren't detained because of Richard. All my thoughts were centered on him. I guess even now I'm too full of my own troubles to take it in. It just seems strange that a nurse would make a mistake like that—wouldn't notice—"

He bore down hard on the gas pedal.

"You'll think I'm shameless," she said, "but I don't care. It's a terrible thing, of course, but I can't help being relieved that—well—it explains the relapse, doesn't it?"

His "Yes, it does," was flat.

She reproached him gently. "Couldn't you have told me sooner instead of keeping it to yourself? Do you know—if you hadn't been so good to Nora I'd begin to think you were unfriendly to us. How

Richard came to hear of it, I can't imagine. Surely they don't go out of their way in hospitals to give the patients distressing news. Naturally he'd be affected—to have her right there in the room with him, alive and cheerful at first, and then to learn she'd died. He's so kind—so sympathetic—he was the first to realize even through his own pain that she felt miserable. Tell me—is that why you—rather than Mrs. Nelson or your maid—brought Nora to the hospital? Had you been sent for?" She reined herself in. "Well—that doesn't matter now." When she started again it was along the road he had mapped for her. "Did you say the drug had been intended for someone else?"

"That's right."

"Prescribed for someone by a doctor, you mean?"

"It wasn't a doctor's prescription."

"A drug put into a soft drink and left around for anybody to take? I guess I must be too muddled at this point to grasp what I'm sure you're explaining quite clearly. It—it sounds weird to me."

"Insane would be more apt."

"If you'd rather not discuss it I won't press you. I know your work is confidential."

"Ask anything you like." And I'll answer, he thought. But until I'm satisfied as to exactly where you stand, what I won't do is give you gratuitous information.

"Not a prescription," she said. She might have been playing Twenty Questions. "Oh—I really am muddled."

"You must be—knowing my job is murder, and yet not making the obvious connection."

Her hand went to her brow to rub at an incipient crease. It was the first fidgety gesture he had seen her make. "Of course. I don't know why it is that I should keep remembering it one minute and forgetting it the next. But then—it isn't easy to think of murder in connection with you *or* with Garde Medical." She treated him to another of her consistently unexpected reactions. "Garde Medical seems so safe—so insulated. I do hope it won't get any publicity. That would be unfortunate, wouldn't it? Not only for the hospital but for the patients. Sick people are apt to magnify everything—"

"Murder is one of the things that can't be magnified or reduced." He used the flat voice that had marked his responses for the past few minutes.

"I didn't mean—I've told you I can't take it in. Tomorrow, perhaps, it will register and I'll be able to feel sorry for the nurse and wonder if she was alone in the world or if she left a family to grieve for her—

things that Richard would have thought of instantly. He—" She sighed. "You must be sick of listening to me go on about Richard—especially with all you have on your mind." He heard the faint susurrus of her clothing as she moved on the car seat. She said, "What was it? Some sort of feud between staff members?" And now she was a woman desperately airing her social graces to draw out a boring guest.

Nelson said, "No—it had nothing to do with the staff."

Her "Oh" was detached and meaningless. It issued no invitation for him to elaborate.

He ached from head to foot with paying out rope that never touched bottom. He ached with shame, too, not because he had been unfaithful to Kyrie for a little moment, but because the object of his desire seemed cast of such hollow stuff. Even her love for her husband, the one apparently genuine emotion that rattled about in her beautiful head, cried out for appraisal. Yet, pending appraisal, how could he say bluntly, Someone wants to kill your Richard. He himself, or you, or Lilith, or Lilith's brother, or a man named Frank, or, for all I know, his secretary or assistant, poisoned his orange juice. And the nurse drank some and died. And he drank some and lived. And what have you to say to that? If it were not news to her he would be tipping his hand prematurely, and if it were news it would serve no purpose but to keep her from needed sleep.

He took her home. He saw her safely into the darkened house, bade her "Good night," and wished he could make it "Good-by."

Chapter Ten

Nelson opened the bedroom door. The lamp that burned all night on the second-floor landing presented Kyrie's slim body rough-sketched by a closely gathered blanket. Not only was she asleep but she had moved her pillow to the center of the bed. Thoughtfully he retreated.

He carried out his program of bathing and of going down to the kitchen to forage. Sammy's plenty stocked the refrigerator, but the small effort required to assemble a meal was too great. He drank a glass of milk, went upstairs again, and entered the room he used out of consideration for Kyrie, and in spite of her protests, on nights when work detained him beyond a reasonable hour.

The room was pleasant, and Sammy always had the bed made up

with fresh linen. So there was no cause for him to feel disgruntled as he plucked a book from the shelves, adjusted pillows and coverings, and tried to unwind. No cause except that heretofore he had been exiled by choice, and in this instance he had been given no choice.

Kyrie was a quiet sleeper. Once settled for the night, she stayed put. Which meant that if she was in the middle of the bed she had started out in the middle of the bed.

He chewed on this new problem. It assumed sufficient importance to take precedence over the book he held. A hell of a detective you are, he told himself. Eight years of marriage and you can't even solve your wife. After a while he closed the book, tossed his extra pillows on the floor, and put out the light. He stretched to full hard length between the sheets.

The room began to crowd. He wished that all those people would take their faces from behind his eyelids. Hildebrand—Lilith—nurses—*the* nurse—Dr. Courtland—Alix. He said to Kyrie, Who needs her? She's only skin-beautiful. You're Kyrie. I hoped you'd wait up for me. I didn't get a chance to give you the latest developments. I couldn't even tell you I was working—but you must have guessed. What else did you think I was doing? It's not like you to—

Kyrie remained a tragic ash-blond statue until sleep came and carried him off. Sleep was a fast train. It bounded over the rails, passed his usual station, and deposited him in the middle of morning.

So rarely had he failed to awaken on schedule that he could not believe the hands of the bedside clock or the corroboration of his watch.

No one interrupted him as he shaved and dressed. Before he descended the stairs he stuck his head into the rooms of Kyrie and Junie. Both were deserted.

Sammy was in the kitchen. That much was usual about the cloudy Saturday. She wished him a good morning and said that it was fixing to rain. She did not sound very outgoing. He put it down to the weather and watched her as she busied herself at the stove.

"Where's my family?"

"Miss Kyrie taken Junie to his appointment at the dentist."

"Funny I didn't hear Junie—"

"Ain't funny. It mean you bone-tired not to hear that little boy—especially when he acting up."

"Acting up? Because of the dentist?"

"Dentist don't fret him. That dentist smart—he got a moving-picture screen front of the chair—but Junie, he plain mad 'cause you didn't bring Nora back yesterday."

"She chose to go home."

Sammy said tepidly, "Well—I expect that where she belong."

He frowned at the kitchen clock. "Somebody should have awakened me."

"What for?"

"Because I picked the wrong day to oversleep."

Sammy looked at him and shook her head. "You call that oversleep, Mr. Grid-dely? Seem to me like I only just hear you come home. Now you sit down and eat yourself a big breakfast. We going to keep you alive someway."

Grapefruit, grilled chicken livers, and hot rolls improved his morale. He took a final swig of coffee, finished his cigarette, and arose. "That was wonderful, Sammy. Please tell Miss Kyrie I'll call her first chance I get."

"In your shoes I'd make a quick chance," Sammy said.

He smiled, wondering if Kyrie had been acting up too. Her performance would be far more subtle than Junie's, yet not too subtle for the discerning Sammy. Not, he thought, that there was anything subtle about that bed routine. At the kitchen door he turned. "Has Miss Kyrie seen the morning papers?"

"No—they inside. You want me to fetch them?"

"Don't bother. I'll pick them up at headquarters." If there was an item concerning Garde Medical he wanted Kyrie to read it.

Sammy kept him a few minutes longer. "They find that taxicab yet?"

"They did—and thanks to your memory of the license number, there's no doubt it's the right one."

If she was pleased she did not show it. "Well—that part of it settled anyhow. When you phone Miss Kyrie last night you still at the hospital?"

"Yes."

"Nora's daddy—he coming along good?"

"Yes—he's coming along."

"I glad to hear it. But if he doing good why his wife have to hang around him so late? Miss Kyrie call her last night to see could we spare her some by keeping Nora here. Only she ain't home. Her lady friend say she back at that hospital."

"It's a long story, Sammy. I'll tell you about it later."

"You tell Miss Kyrie come dinner," Sammy said firmly. Then she came to the point. "Miss Kyrie, she feel more like she do this morning than she did last night." While he was sorting that out she said, "Just before she taken Junie to the dentist I in your dressing room gathering the clothes you shuck off for the wash. And she come in to talk and she happen to catch me holding your shirt. She don't say nothing, but it appear to me like she studying how that red paint get smeared on its front."

He said, "I'd better do some studying myself," and made a hurried exit.

He drove through a fine drizzle to headquarters. As soon as he was within sight of working territory his mind obliged him by sloughing off personal matters. He glanced at the old brick Records building across the street from Homicide. Yesterday, at his request, a superficial search had been made to see if the indices contained any reference to the Greenways or to Alix Hildebrand, whose maiden name, Voelker, they had got by way of the marriage license bureau. Unless John Lindstrom came up with something in short order a more thorough exploration would have to be made. Row upon row of files weighted every floor of Records, and each file contained prints, mugshots, descriptions, and the modus operandi of prisoners, released prisoners, wanted criminals, parolees, degenerates, et cetera. In short, of every shady character who had ever reached the blotter and of many who had managed to avoid it by a hairbreadth. No one in the department envied the keepers of Records' unsavory preserves. Nelson decided not to add to their labors until he had produced fingerprints and photographs. These would simplify matters should Greenway prove to be a brand-new alias.

On his way to his office he surrendered to a messenger Lilith's forgotten cigarette case and the small bottle he had found in Hildebrand's jacket. He asked that the bottle be subjected to laboratory examination and that the case be returned to him as soon as it had been tested for prints. He doubted that it still retained what he wanted, especially if Kyrie had picked it up to look at it. But if the off-chance materialized, he would be saved the nuisance of seeking Lilith's prints elsewhere.

His office had never seemed less inviting. He was glad that most of his work that day would be accomplished out of it, but after his first automatic glimpse, the dirty window, dreary walls, and scuffed linoleum faded from his consciousness.

He had been handed several yellow memoranda as he passed the switchboard. There was an answer from the Immigration Bureau to his query concerning Gertrude Knobler, former lady's maid in the

Hildebrand household. She had not re-entered the country. There was a routine "check-in" from the detective covering Hildebrand's room at the hospital. Nothing significant had occurred during the hours of his watch. Dr. Enoch Falvey had left at one thirty-seven, pronouncing the patient out of danger. The detective's relief had come on at 9 A.M.

The remaining yellow sheets did not relate to the poisonings at Garde Medical. Nelson dealt with them rapidly. He also dealt with his own note to arrange a stake-out at John Lindstrom's office against an appearance by one "Fred Hicks." He submitted "Fred Hicks" along with Lindstrom's description of him to B.C.I., explaining the suspected tie-in with Mike Jarmon, wanted criminal, alias Mort Jasper, alias Melvin Johnson, alias legion. He suggested that in Jarmon's file there might be information supplied by stool pigeons to indicate Hicks as an accomplice in other crimes. For the stake-out he was forced to choose men who had made other plans for Sunday. They were not pleased, but the prospect of a long-sought break in a celebrated case of homicide and grand larceny reduced their grumbling to a minimum.

That much accomplished, Nelson officially assigned himself and other members of his staff to the Hildebrand affair. As a first move he sent Clevis, a detective he held in high esteem, to see what he could discover at first hand of the occupation and habits of Lilith's brother, Herbert Greenway.

Next he called the City Mortuary and received from an assistant pathologist a preliminary report on the deceased Edris Hogan, R.N., age twenty-nine. Only wordage distinguished the initial findings from those of the Garde Medical technicians. As he hung up, Lilith's cigarette case bearing Alix Hildebrand's monogram was placed upon his desk. No note accompanied it.

He called the laboratory. "Did you bring out anything worth preserving?"

"Can't say. Photography will send you some eight-by-tens as soon as they're developed. We're not through with the bottle yet, but we thought you wanted the case back right away."

"I did. Thanks." Half amused, half concerned by the possibility that if Kyrie had fingered the cigarette case her prints might find their way to B.C.I., he asked to be connected with the Photographic Department. He was assured that both negatives and pictures would be sent directly to his office.

Before he dropped the gold oblong into his pocket he scrutinized it for telltale traces of gray powder. He wanted to take no chances with the owner, who might have reasons for being more than average observant. But someone in the laboratory had evidently been so impressed by the case's value as to buff it to a high glow. Even the tiny hinges shone. He thought that if the polish aroused comment he could attribute it to Sammy's housewifely zeal.

He succeeded in quitting the building without interception. Except for the times when it was advisable to call attention to his presence, he did not travel in a department car. The missions that engaged him now indicated his own Buick. He drove it uptown and found parking space near Ninety-first Street and Central Park West.

He went on foot toward Amsterdam Avenue, passingly oddly assorted line-ups of modern apartment houses, remodeled tenements, small and mostly seedy shops, and decaying structures of the type instantly brought to mind by the mention of slum clearance. The faces of the adults and children he encountered on the streets were predominantly Puerto Rican, but on the whole it was a mixed local boasting representatives of almost every nationality in the cosmopolis. The newer buildings, instead of elevating the neighborhood, emphasized its shabbier aspects.

Albert Ross, owner and operator of the stolen cab, lived in one of the in-between houses, but its freshly decorated halls boxed the smells of a former era. Nelson, permitted to enter by a buzzer that released the vestibule door, looked doubtfully at the proportions of a miniature self-service elevator, inserted his wide-shouldered frame, and arose to the third floor, his object being to determine whether anything other than coincidence accounted for the proximity of Albert Ross to the Greenways.

Albert Ross answered the bell in person, summed up Nelson, and said with bitter disgust, "You ain't from the police."

Nelson was surprised. "As a matter of fact, I am. I didn't know you were expecting me." He produced his badge of office.

Ross did not give it a glance. Eagerness replaced disgust on his long thin face. "Okay—okay. Did you bring the cab back? Is it downstairs?"

"No—"

"What's the big idea? How long—?"

"May I come in?"

"Why? I got a clean bill of health. What are you trying to do—strangle me with that lousy red tape?"

"I'd like to ask you a few questions."

"I'm sick of answering questions." He wore baggy slacks and a singlet. Nelson could see the tightening cords of his lean bare throat. He was obviously a nervous man, either by nature or by strain of coping with New York's traffic. "Let me tell you, things are tough enough the way they are—laying around here counting the money I'm losing."

Not to bribe but to soothe, Nelson said, "I'll do what I can to get the cab back to you today."

"You got influence—or just oil?" He looked Nelson over again, plainly evaluating the value of the promise. Then he shrugged and stepped aside. "All I can say is you're lucky my wife went out. She'd give you some real loud views on why there ain't enough cops where they ought to be to see innocent taxpayers don't get the bread taken out of their mouths because some joker decides to treat himself and his girl to a joyride. And what's worse, they go to work and tie up the cab, which if it's ever returned will need dough and work to get it back in shape. Sure—step right in—sit down—put your feet up. Why not? You won't find another guy living with more time to waste than me."

There was no hall. The door opened directly onto a small living room. Nelson sat down in an overstuffed chair. His host took to the couch, putting his feet up on its Kelly-green upholstery with such an air of defiance that Nelson was willing to bet he would have made less free if his reputedly vocal wife were present. But she undoubtedly had her points. The apartment was spotless and, except for an empty cigarette pack and a filled ash tray on an end table, in stiff order. From his chair he could see by only slightly shifting his position both the gleam of the kitchenette and a smooth area of bedspread in the second room.

Ross picked up the empty cigarette package, crushed it in his fist, and threw it back onto the end table. He accepted a cigarette from Nelson with the grudging nod of a man who cannot afford to be choosy. Nelson said, "It shouldn't be a major repair job to hammer out a few dents."

"Are you trying to be funny? What about the windshield—what about my back seat?"

"What about it?"

"Polka dots—that's what. Red polka dots. Listen—if you're interested enough to push in here you should've been interested enough to take a gander at the cab. The seats ain't plastic—see? So the stains won't come out. Also, there's one on the floor—and what about the glass on my identification card?" He puffed violently on the cigarette.

The report on the stolen cab had mentioned nothing about bloodstains. Either the cab had not been given a thorough going over at the time or no significance had been attached to the rear seat.

Nelson said, "You're certain the stains weren't there before the cab was stolen?"

Ross looked furious. "Certain? It's an old hack but I nurse it like it was my mother. There ain't a night I don't give it the works inside and out. Why? Because where will I scrape together the down payment on a new one?—and even with spit and polish mine ain't got the trade-in value of a go-cart. So help me, I wouldn't be this burned if them stains were at least big enough to show she was hurt real good. That would learn her. Or do you think maybe she's anemic?" He paid tribute to the intended witticism with a yellow grin.

"She?"

"Sure 'she.' Unless the punk's a pansy who else would he be taking for a joyride?"

"That's an interesting theory—except that partners to a joyride usually sit side by side."

"Sue me. Breaking that glass and stealing the ident card was a dame's work. Dame's always have to overdo it. You'd think she'd've let that go and spent more time trying to remove the license plate—not that the description alone wouldn't tag it if it was parked anywhere in the vicinity."

"Was there any blood on the front seat?"

"Naa—why would there be? The windshield ain't broken—just good and cracked. I tell you, she got cut from flying chips when she smashed the glass and stole the card—or he did if you have to argue. Who cares?"

Nelson cared. He was beginning to evolve his own interesting theory. "Is there a glass partition between the front and back?"

"There was once, but I took it out to make it more like the jobs they're building now." His voice yearned for one of the new jobs. "Maybe my wife's got something. She says it should be a lesson to me to take her advice and hack for one of the big fleets. But I been my own boss so long I can't see it—even if working for myself is full of drawbacks. This has been a hell of a winter." He stubbed his remaining inch of cigarette and took another from the proffered package. He seemed to have forgotten that Nelson had any status besides that of a sympathetic ear. "The way it's shaped up, I would've been ahead if I'd listened to Doc and stayed in bed a couple of weeks longer. But you know how it is."

Nelson went the long way around to find out how it was. "Were you in the hospital?"

"Not me. Not while I've got a say-so. But it sure looked like I was headed for one." He went on with the mixture of pride and complaint that people use in citing their ills. "I got an ulcer. Doc said if I kept to a diet and rested they wouldn't have to operate. Course I did myself no favor by drinking that night. You wouldn't believe what's going on inside me this minute—"

"And the cab was inactive while you rested?"

Ross shook his head. "I paid a guy to drive it. There wasn't no fortune left over after he got his forty-two and a half per cent of the take—but it was better than a hit on the head."

"It couldn't have been easy to find someone you trusted."

"For once I struck it lucky. Bert happened to be out of work."

Nelson controlled his breathing. "A friend of yours?"

"Kind of—but not so friendly he did it for less than scale. He lives around here. We got pally in the stationery store on account of the fellow who owns it calls us both Bert. Everybody else calls me Al—"

"Is his name Albert too?"

"No—Herbert. Herbert Greenway."

"What does he do for a living when he isn't working for you?"

"He's a hackie—or anyway an ex-hackie. His license was in order is all I know. I didn't ask no questions why he's out of work. I ain't nosy." The antagonism returned. Ross sat up. "You ain't asking no questions either—none that will get us places."

Nelson disagreed. He said, "He was probably disappointed that you were able to take over again as soon as you did."

Ross showed extreme boredom. "Could be." Footsteps went past the door and continued on up the stairs. "Say—my wife's liable to be home right away and, the chip she's carrying, you'll give yourself a present by disappearing. It wouldn't bother me none to see you get your ears pinned back with her song and dance about where's the cab—except I'm sick of hearing it myself."

"You'll get the cab back," Nelson said. He thought that Ross had earned it.

"Today?"

"Yes—today."

Ross did not go so far as to look pleased. He merely looked less cynical. "You got another cigarette to spare?"

Nelson glanced at the stuffed ash tray. "It won't help your ulcer. Here—you might as well keep the pack."

"Thanks." It was economical, but it stretched to acknowledge the promised return of his livelihood. With another look at the door he got up, carried the ash tray to the kitchenette, and brought it back empty. "Honest—I'm not trying to brush you off but—"

"I'll leave in a few minutes. Did this man you employed give any evidence of ill will because the job ended sooner than expected?"

"Why should he? I didn't give him no guarantee—" Understanding broke out on his long face. It left a scowl. "Nix—forget it. Bert ain't the type to hold a grudge—and I ain't the type to frame a pal. I might have known there was a catch to you being so ready to oblige—"

"There's no catch. A criminal act has been performed. You're not a stupid man. You know that one of the ways to fix guilt is to eliminate the innocent. If Greenway is innocent he won't be persecuted."

"If he's innocent? It's not like he's a spic or something—he speaks English even better than I do. I tell you he's okay."

It was said with conviction. Nelson dug to see if the conviction had a reasonably sturdy foundation. "What makes you so sure? He worked for you. He lives in the neighborhood. He's aware of your habit of leaving the cab downstairs while you eat dinner."

"Yeah—putting it that way, it sounds cut and dried all right. But just the same Bert wouldn't do it. Working for me, I'd swear he didn't chisel so much as a loose nickel—and without me getting wise he could've snatched the pants off me. There are plenty of tricks to the trade, but he didn't use any of them. Why? Too dumb. Honest and dumb. That's Bert. He wouldn't know how to gyp a grape off a fruit wagon—let alone pull a trick like this."

"Whoever smashed the glass in your cab didn't strike you as being too intelligent."

Ross said stubbornly, "A dame—look for a punk and a dame and you're home."

"Can you suggest any particular punk?"

"Naah. The woods around here are full of them. But take it from me, Bert's out. It don't even need a man with my experience who's got a ringside seat on human nature to spot how Bert operates. The big dumb lug is like a window with no shade on it. A six-year-old could watch his wheels go round without even standing on tiptoe. Tell me something—will you? What's all the shooting about? So my hack was stolen. So it's important to me—but that don't make it no

Brinks robbery. I don't get it. Maybe I would if they sent a harness bull or one of them J.G.s to lean on me, being they had nothing else on their minds—but it don't take four eyes to see you're something else again—especially when you make me a promise I almost believe—and I ain't the easiest man to convince."

"Weren't you told that your cab had injured a pedestrian?"

"Sure—but hit-and-runs happen all the time—and they're caught or they ain't—and that's that." Then he said, "He died?"

"No." Nelson wanted to touch wood.

"Well—so who is he—the mayor or something? I didn't go out to buy a paper in case I missed—" As Nelson arose, he returned to his primary concern. "You on the level about putting me back in business?"

Nelson nodded.

"Prove it. The phone's in the bedroom and it's on the house. I'd feel better if I could hear you start things rolling."

Nelson obliged. He went into the neat bedroom and picked up the phone. His end of the conversation was not informative, but it reassured Ross, who hovered in the doorway. He hung up and gave Ross an address. "You're to call for it at four o'clock." He could have made it earlier, but he wanted to give himself time to inspect the cab first.

Ross, in a sudden blaze of good will, tried to reward him with a glass of beer. That was the moment that Mrs. Ross appeared. She looked small and wholesome and harmless, but Nelson did not put this observation to the test. He eased himself out of the apartment.

Chapter Eleven

The building in which the Greenways lived boasted a doorman, but its two elevators were operated by the tenants. As soon as Nelson entered the lobby the detective he had sent to hold the fort materialized. Clevis had bright button eyes in an otherwise undistinguished face. He looked deceptively small and nondescript, but the baggy clothes he affected concealed a full set of well-trained muscles. He carried a black bag.

"Where did you come from?" Nelson asked.

"The stairs." He jerked his thumb at a fire door. "I propped it slightly open so's I can see the elevators—indicator and all. The doorman thinks I'm here to fix the Greenway television set. He tells me the lady's out. But Greenway's in." He gave an accurate description of Greenway.

Nelson nodded. "That's your man."

"Yeah—I went upstairs with the paper boy and saw him take them in. He's not alone. I heard a man's voice talking to him."

"All right. I'll go up. When and if he's flushed out, you follow."

"Will do. It's fourth floor front—4-B."

Nelson took an elevator. He rang the bell of the Greenway apartment and, waiting for it to be answered, speculated as to how and where an unemployed taxi driver and his lady sister managed to scrape up a rent which even in this neighborhood would be sizable. The building was one of the newcomers to the street, splendid with glass and metal. Undoubtedly it featured all the latest electronic inventions designed to save time that would be squandered on pursuits far less important than household chores. But no money had been invested in soundproofing. He could hear footsteps approaching the door and words flung over a shoulder to a second occupant before a hoarse "Who's there?" reached his side of the barricade.

"I've something for Miss Greenway."

The coppery knob turned on the last syllable and Herbert Greenway crowded the frame of the door. He said, "Is it paid for?" Then he looked at Nelson's empty hands. "I don't see any package."

"I have it in my pocket—it's a cigarette case that Miss Greenway left at my house." Nelson opened his damp topcoat and made a pretense at searching his person.

"Oh—I thought you meant something from the stores. My sister's not home."

"The doorman told me she was."

Greenway said without animus, "He made a mistake. She's been stay— She's out. Listen—maybe you forgot to bring it." He had been holding the door open. He stepped back, prepared to shut Nelson out. "Don't bother—another time—"

"Do you mind if I come in? If I shed this coat perhaps I'll find—" He stepped into the apartment. He gave the door a hard backward shove so that the resulting click of the snap lock was clearly identifiable to whoever kept Herbert Greenway company.

A male voice called out, "What was it, Bert?"

"Nothing—nobody." And belatedly, "It's still raining."

To Nelson the weather announcement sounded like a prearranged signal. A quietness followed it. Greenway stood staring at him dully in the indirect light of the foyer. Quite evidently Greenway was not a master at dealing with unexpected situations even when he did not exude alcohol. Now he smelled soapy. The stubble of a recent crew cut was damp, and above his bathrobe rose the clean powerful neck of an athlete. His build and features were good, but a squat brow and a slackness of mouth invalidated the claim to masculine beauty.

Nelson said, "Your sister didn't mention that she had two brothers."

"Huh?" He swiveled his head toward the rear of the apartment. "You mean him? He's not a brother. He's a fellow from out of town who's parking here for a couple of days. He's not up yet—he's—he's on vacation." Then he said, "No use you waiting. Who knows when Lil will be home?" A puzzled frown indicated cerebral labor. "Haven't I seen you someplace before?"

"Yes. Miss Greenway introduced us when I walked her home the other night."

"The other— Huh?" There was more laboring behind his low brow. He panted with it. "Your name's—"

"Nelson. I'm a neighbor of the Hildebrands."

"You're—wait a minute—you're that police fellow!"

"If we talk here," Nelson said, "we'll disturb your guest from out of town." He started across the foyer to what was obviously the living room. He boned up on judo holds as he walked, expecting at any moment to be seized from behind by Greenway's large hands. But Greenway, although he dogged him closely, created no incident.

The living room, Nelson noted, was aggressively stark. No drapes or rugs relieved its modern furniture. An abstract portrait of Lilith, he thought, except for the untidy litter of newspapers, soiled cups, plates, and glasses that had probably gathered in her absence. He turned to face Greenway. "You have a nice place."

"Don't make yourself comfortable. I didn't invite you in." It was a weighty pronouncement with no intended humor. Greenway loomed over him, yet in spite of his bulk he did not look menacing. He looked as though he might burst into tears. "You can bet you wouldn't have got this far if I'd recognized you."

Nelson used a tone of polite interest. "Why not?"

"Why not?" He seemed floored by the simple query. "Because— because I'm busy. I've got stuff to do." He produced it triumphantly and appeared to be listening for commendation from an unseen mentor.

"Do you have to go to work?"

"Work?"

"You said you were busy. Are you employed?"

"I meant— No, I'm not employed. I'm taking a rest."

"Good. Then a talk won't interfere with anything important. Sit down."

"I will not—and you won't either."

"I don't understand," Nelson said. "I entertained your sister the other night. I'm sure that if she were here she'd be glad to return my hospitality."

"That was a dirty trick—saying you had something for—"

"If it will make you feel any better—I have." He took the cigarette case from his pocket. "Your sister left it at my house." Albert Ross was only half right, he thought. The man's more than average stupid.

Greenway had snatched the case from him. "That's Alix's—!" Then he grimaced, and his slack mouth performed a sucking operation as though it were trying to draw the words back. He peered at the case, fingered it, and set it down on a chair arm.

"I noticed the monogram too," Nelson said, "but I thought Mrs. Hildebrand might have given it to her. If it was only borrowed I might as well return it to the owner." He scooped it up and dropped it into his pocket.

"No you don't—give me—"

"Why should I ask you to assume responsibility for anything so valuable? It won't inconvenience me. The Hildebrands live on my street."

"I ought to slug you—"

"Sit down. You don't want violence in your house—especially with a guest present." He found himself pitying Greenway. This was the kind of hunting he hated. It was comparable to shooting a sleeping animal. Hildebrand had mentioned feeling sorry for Greenway too. Mentally out of whack, Hildebrand had said. Nelson stiffened. Was that it? Did that provide a better explanation for Hildebrand's quick removal from Bellevue than Lilith's tale that Alix could not bear to leave her husband in such surroundings? Had Lilith's brother been a patient there, and did she fear that either of them might be recognized by doctors or attendants? Farfetched? Well, so were the numerous guises of family pride. And the theory might also account for the tags of knowledge she had picked up concerning schizophrenia. It would be easy enough to verify—

All this went through his mind as Herbert Greenway dropped to a chair and sat gazing at the floor with the sullen defiance of a scolded child.

Nelson himself remained on his feet. Looking down at his prey, he could almost feel the air seeping out of his theory. Greenway, he thought without conscious levity, did not have enough of a brain to support one personality, let alone split two ways.

Greenway was squirming, shifting his eyes every way but up. He harked back to his main theme. "Why did you have to bust in here?"

"I was in the neighborhood. I made another call first—on a friend of yours."

"You don't fool me. I have no friends in the neighborhood."

"Albert Ross would be hurt by that statement."

This time nothing came of Greenway's attempt at a comeback. His eyes popped as he swallowed and tried again. "Albert Ross?"

"That's right. The man whose cab injured Hildebrand. He's a friend of yours—isn't he?"

"Hildebrand?"

"Both." It was beginning to sound like a vaudeville skit. "Or perhaps I should have said that Ross is an ex-employer. At any rate, he spoke of you in a friendly way."

After a pause Greenway said, "Why shouldn't he?"

"But you evidently don't reciprocate his friendship."

"Who says so?"

"Where were you employed before you worked for Ross?"

"None of your business."

"What source of income do you have now?"

"That's none of your business either."

Nelson moved a chair to a strategic position and sat down. "Take your time. I'll wait all day."

"No you won't—you'll get right out of here." His hands clenched. He got up swinging, but his robe was too tight across the shoulders. The rip of parting seams halted him. He bellowed, "Now see what you made me do!" Mislaying his original intention, he reached a hand behind him to investigate the damage.

Nelson, who had not stirred beyond the reflex of tensing his muscles, said, "Does Lilith work?"

"You leave her out of this."

"All right. Let's get back to you. Did Ross treat you badly?"

"Huh?" Craft lit a small spark in the dull eyes. "Do you think I'd have stood for it? He treated me the same as I treated him. I've got nothing against Ross."

Nelson honed his voice. "Then why did you steal his cab?"

"Why did I—?" Greenway sat down slowly. He repeated, "I've got nothing against Ross. What's he want to blame it on me for?"

"What have you got against Hildebrand?"

"Nothing—not a thing—"

"Why do you want to kill him?"

"Kill him—me? I swear—"

"If it was an accident why did you run?"

"I didn't—I—" His mouth closed. All his efforts were expended upon keeping it closed.

Nelson got up and turned toward the foyer. He called out, "You'll be able to hear better if you come in."

Herbert Greenway's guest emerged from hiding and stepped jauntily into the room. He was a man of medium stature, compactly made. His face started with a cleft chin and ended in a satanic widow's peak.

The sight of him seemed to revive his host. "He pushed in, Frank. Before I knew it he pushed in. He's a detective."

Frank dusted an imaginary speck from his sharply cut lapel. He said in a tone of exaggerated culture, "Do tell?"

Nelson said, "If you missed anything else while you were listening outside I'll be glad to bring you up to date."

His insolent blue eyes made a slow tour of Nelson. "All I missed was proof of the accusations you've been throwing around."

"I was hoping you could help to supply the proof. Witnesses state that Mr. Greenway had a passenger in the stolen cab on the night of the accident."

"What accident would that be?"

"You disappoint me. You seemed so well informed." Nelson glanced at the pile of newspapers.

"Those belong to Bert." Bert's guest took a pipe from his pocket and bit down on it with strong glistening teeth. The pipe was as empty as the gesture. "Bert's a great reader. I gave it up long ago. Even the comics scare me to death. So do you."

Greenway, at the mention of his name, came to attention like a trained dog. "Listen—what does he mean about witnesses?"

"Don't break your head. You're doing fine." He spoke around the pipe. A dangling cigarette would have looked more at home between his full bold lips. He said to Nelson, "Are we supposed to take your word for it that you're a detective?"

"No. We'll continue on a basis of mutual distrust." Nelson offered his badge and the wallet containing detailed credentials. They were subjected to studious inspection.

"Satisfied?" Nelson said.

"Satisfied?" He snickered. "Sure, Gridley, if you are. Your old lady must have hated you on sight to stick you with a handle like that."

"Did your old lady entitle you to a second name—or should I call you Frank?"

He jerked the pipe from his mouth. "I've seen comedians come and go." He kept his voice soft. "My name is Henry Francis Hacket. Don't bother to shake hands. Just count me out of whatever it is you're trying to pin on my friend. I wasn't here."

"When weren't you here?"

"Any time you want to mention in the last couple of months. I only hit town last night."

"Last night?"

"You heard me."

"The term is rather loose. Some people use it to mean early afternoon or late evening."

"I said last night and I meant last night."

"Can you prove it?" Nelson took a small notebook from his pocket. He wrote busily.

"Can you prove otherwise?"

"I'll work on it. Occupation?"

"Retired."

"Your last job must have been profitable." Nelson's face was as bland as he could make it. "Were you self-employed or a member of a gang?"

Successfully Hacket converted a snarl to an elaborate yawn. He said through the yawn, "Wrap it up—save it for the next sucker who tries to help a pal. I horned in because I don't like to see anybody being pushed around—and all of a sudden I'm it."

"Occupation?" Nelson said.

"Traveling salesman. Have you heard the one about—"

"What firm?"

"You won't find it listed in the New York book—um—Hickson's Novelties. It's in Keokuk."

"Keokuk, Iowa?"

"Is there another Keokuk?"

Greenway kept turning his head from one to the other like a man refereeing a ping-pong game. He looked as though he had lost track of the score.

Nelson said, "What's your home address?"

"Keokuk."

Nelson continued to play it straight. He was pleased to note that his activities with the notebook seemed to be taking toll of Hacket's nerves. "Did you come to New York by train?"

"A friend drove me—man by the name of Frammis—in the fish business." Hacket fought to regain his jauntiness. "He said something about going on to Canada—or maybe it was Alaska."

"I suppose you have a sample case of the novelties you sell?"

"No—this is a pleasure trip—or it was." One of his blunt manicured hands tugged at the knot of a hand-painted tie. "Anyway, you couldn't buy anything. I don't take retail customers."

Nelson said without altering pace or voice, "How long have you known the Hildebrands?"

Hacket put the pipe between his teeth again, took it out, stared at it, and said peevishly, "Hey—Bert—what the hell happened to my tobacco?"

"I don't know. Listen—"

"Skip it." He thrust the pipe into his pocket. "The Whodebrands? Never heard of them."

Nelson caught Bert Greenway with his mouth wide open. "How long have you known this man?"

Bert became a staunch champion. "I've known him for years—that's what. He comes from my hometown he—"

"Okay, Bert. You got it across."

"So you come from his hometown," Nelson said. "Then of course you know Alix Voelker."

It was Greenway who reacted to the name by screwing up his face. Hacket said, "Confidentially—no. Confidentially I don't come from Bert's hometown either. The part about him knowing me for years stands. But he's got me mixed up with some other fellow. Think back, Bert. Don't you remember—we met right here in New York—let's see—when was it? Nineteen-fifty—somewhere around there."

Obediently Bert presented the picture of a man thinking back. Hacket's voice dwindled to a murmur. "I wouldn't like to say he hasn't got all his buttons—but they're sewed on kind of loose."

Nelson said, "Have you any identification?"

"What do you want—a passport? I thought I was still in America."

"A driver's license—even an envelope addressed to Henry Francis Hacket will serve."

"Come back with a search warrant and you might find something like that in my luggage."

Nelson wrote, "Search Warrant" in large letters. Hacket seemed fascinated by the course of the pencil.

Nelson put the notebook away. "How long do you intend to stay in New York?"

"As long as I'm amused—which reminds me—" He looked at his wristwatch. "I've got a date. Any objection?"

"No. You're excused, Frank." He almost pronounced it 'Fronck.' Hacket, he thought, would have undeniable attraction for certain women. A certain woman? Could she have thought it less indelicate to admit to an affair with an art student rather than with this—?

Hacket looked astonished, then victorious. He turned and walked toward the foyer.

It was Greenway who voiced the objection. "Hey—wait— stick around, Frank. He—"

"Don't worry, Bert. He's strictly windville. Be seeing you."

Nelson said, "That's right, Bert. Don't worry. You've got a date too. Get dressed."

"Me?"

Hacket had stopped in his tracks. "What do you think you're pulling? What's the charge?"

"The charge for what?" Nelson said.

"Shove it. I don't have to be a lawyer to know you can't walk into a man's house and arrest him just like that. We don't buy it."

"You can always protest to the police department—provided it doesn't inconvenience you. Of course it might mean more time than you're prepared to spend—"

Bert Greenway made pitiful appeal. "Time? Listen —"

Hacket yelled, "Shut up."

"He means shut up and get your clothes on, Bert," Nelson said pleasantly. "Since you're both such strong upholders of the law, I'm not making an arrest. I'm merely taking you to headquarters for a quiet talk. There are too many interruptions here."

Hacket said, "And if he won't go?"

Greenway followed the leader. "Yeah—if I won't go?"

"You'll go. And when you get there I'm sure you'll be most co-operative."

Hacket looked hot, literally as well as in the slang sense of the word. "Sit tight, Bert. He can't make you budge without a warrant."

"Warrants seem to be an obsession with you, Mr. Hacket. Suppose I phone and have one brought here? Suspicion of theft will do for a starter. The more serious charges will come later. We may have to wait a little while, but that doesn't matter. There's such a lot to talk about."

Greenway said in a high voice, "Frank—you've got to get me out of this—Lil—"

"Take it easy. Go along with the gag—and, believe me, it is a gag. He knows you won't be inside ten minutes before I have you sprung. Here's what it amounts to—that two-bit hackie turns sour because someone relieves him of his broken-down heap and parlays the play into an accident. So the hackie wants company in his misery and sics the cops onto you—and right away, because you happen to live in the neighborhood and there's nobody else handy, you're the goat. That's all they've got on you and all they're going to get—and if they can make it stick I'll bake you a cake with a file in it."

Nelson said admiringly, "Why—Mr. Hacket! You knew about the cab and the accident all the time. In fact, I wouldn't be surprised if you were just as well informed about the Hildebrands."

"Be surprised. They're news to me."

"Alix Voelker too?"

Again it was only Greenway who reacted to her name. Nelson would have paid cheerfully to know what inspired that sick grimace.

Hacket said, "Why don't you give up? I told you I didn't hit town until last night. I haven't had time to make new acquaintances."

"Or renew old hometown ones?"

"Come again?"

Nelson considered the advisability of repeating the questions he had asked and of interpolating those he had withheld. But he thought that such a course would tip his hand and so defeat his purpose. He wanted to make Hacket uneasy. To panic him might prove disastrous. He said, "Very well, Mr. Hacket. Don't let me detain you any longer—unless you insist upon riding to headquarters with us to see that your friend gets fair play." He primed himself. If Hacket left he would take the elevator. There would be time to streak down the stairs and give Clevis the signal to tail him.

Hacket said, "I'll do better than ride with you. I'll go right out and find a lawyer. Don't worry about a thing, Bert." Jauntily he left the room, and almost at once the apartment door slammed.

Nelson did not think that the sprint down the stairs would be necessary. Hacket, he believed, was still with them. Deliberately he played the dumb cop. "Now that we're alone, do you want to reconsider and talk?"

The miserable hulk in the chair did not answer.

"All right. I'll give you ten minutes to dress."

Greenway lunged. The tackle found Nelson unprepared. He had forgotten that what was evident to him would not be evident to his slow-witted adversary. He crashed to the rugless floor. As he tried to rise, Greenway picked up a metal table lamp.

Nelson shouted, "Hold it!"

He did not know if Greenway heard or if he had listened to some inner warning. He saw him gaze stupidly at the weapon and slowly set it down. In that space of time he regained his feet and collected his muscles. He was ready if not eager, but Greenway, without so much as a glance at him, turned and lumbered from the room.

Chapter Twelve

Nelson selected a listening post to the right of the room's exit. From where he stood he was invisible to anyone passing through the foyer. He did not move except to massage absently the shoulder that had struck the floor. The sounds that reached him indicated a feverish haste on Greenway's part. Either he was not slow in all departments or he was receiving assistance. Perhaps Hacket, undoubtedly a man of parts, had offered himself as valet.

Hacket, for all his glibness, was not overburdened with brains either and, common to his type, he held in contempt the brains of society in general. His timing of the slammed door had borne that out, if for no stronger reason than that the day's drizzle had changed to hard rain heard plainly against the windowpanes. Nelson had reasoned that a self-advertised dandy in a hand-painted tie would have delayed for the few minutes required to protect his sleek hair with a hat, his sharp creases with a waterproof, and probably his polished shoes with rubbers. Nelson had seen none of these articles within reach in the foyer. But if his reasoning was faulty, and Hacket, under stress, had been willing to let the elements ruin his clothes, there was more substantial cause to believe that he was still among those present. He had made it clear that he rated Greenway's mentality lower than most. He had come out of hiding to support him, not, all things considered, as an act of altruism, but as insurance against some threat to his own safety. Would he then be willing to subject Greenway to a session with less forbearing inquisitors than the ineffectual specimen he had so cleverly outsmarted? He would not. He would lurk, as he was lurking. He would try to spirit

Greenway to a safer place until he could work out a plan or bring to fruition the plan that was afoot.

It was Nelson's intention to give him leeway. Greenway should have leeway too. He was glad to be spared the nuisance of taking either or both into custody on a charge that as yet lacked adhesiveness. So he waited and strained, and before the specified ten minutes had passed they had stolen away like the Arabs. The faint and final click of the door told him so.

He went to the window, raised it, and looked out and down. Presently they emerged. He discounted the chance that they would look back or up, since it would not occur to them that he had deliberately played into their hands. He was right. They looked straight ahead. Both of them wore raincoats, and the shorter of the two had further armed himself with an umbrella. He also carried a small suitcase.

They did not hail a cab. They started walking east at a fast clip. Nelson grinned when a third figure emerged to follow in their wake. Then his face sobered.

He had firm respect for the Fourth Amendment, but his conscience gave him little trouble as he engaged in a methodical search of the apartment, beginning in the living room and working back to the two bedrooms. He had not broken and entered the dwelling of a private citizen. He had been admitted, though grudgingly, and after a fashion entertained. Moreover, he had not asked to be left alone to divert himself as best he could. And if this search was the form of diversion he chose in his loneliness, who could blame him, considering that he had practically been invited to make free of the premises? The speciousness of his logic did not bother him. What rankled was that the search netted little. The suitcase carried by Hacket might have accounted for that.

It developed that Hacket had risked practically nothing by engineering the stealthy exit. His deserted effects bore no labels, and if he transacted any business, including blackmail, by way of the written word, there was no record of it in evidence. There was not so much as a bill or a postcard. Nelson explored the unmade bed to make sure, although by that time he was calling himself rude names for the wasted effort.

The room Hacket had used was Lilith's. Nelson doubted, for what it was worth, that it was the first time he had slept there. His clothes, hanging beside hers in the closet, looked too much at home to be transient. So did the shoes in the shared rack and the mingling of possessions in bureau and dresser drawers. It seemed almost impossible that he could have taken over as fully without being a permanent resident. But if "Frank" was Lilith's lover—?

It seemed that Lilith, too, was chary of committing herself to paper. She neither saved letters nor kept copies of those she might have sent, and if she owned address book, checkbook, or passbook, she carried these items with her. He did find a receipted rent bill and a bill from a department store, both too high for anyone in the middle-income bracket. He also came across a picture of Lilith, recent, to judge by her clothes. Her suit was the one she had worn on the night of her visit, but her hair was different, brushed straight back off her forehead. In his considered opinion it suited her better than the heavy fringe. Yesterday at the hospital she had worn a dress, which meant, since she was too small to borrow Alix's clothes, that she had come home to change. He went to the closet again. The suit of the snapshot was there. He brought it over to the window for scrutiny.

Her brother's room was a shambles, attesting to the haste with which he had made ready to depart. Its sole yield was a small flat key, interesting because it was fairly new and because it opened no lock in the apartment.

The bathroom, adjoining the master bedroom, and the kitchen were innocent of anything more revealing than milk and eggs and an uninspired stock of canned goods in the one and a slopped floor and dirty towels in the other. Nelson threw in his own towel.

He made certain that all was as before and left, well content to hear the spring lock snap behind him.

He sloshed through the rain to his car. He drove to the police garage that held the delinquent cab, only passing conscious of his wet clothes and of his aching shoulder.

Substantially the condition of the cab was as reported. The thief or thieves had been thorough in destroying clues that might give aid and comfort to the law. The steering wheel had been wiped clean to inhibit a test for latent prints. Even the ash trays were empty, so that if the theft involved a smoker, his favorite brand remained secret and, more important, the science of serology was robbed of a means to determine his special blend of saliva.

Assuming that Albert Ross's joyride theory held water, his "dame" ran counter to stereotype. She had shed no bobby pins, dropped no handkerchief, left no scent that could be separated from the prevailing musty odor. Blood had indeed been shed, but not generously. Nelson's last moments in the garage were devoted to studying the location of the stains. Then he signed a release, called Ross, and informed him that he need not wait until the promised hour to fetch his property.

It was nearing three o'clock. He drove back to headquarters and, without removing his wet coat, buzzed for a clerk. He told him to call Bellevue and ask if they had a record of a former patient named Herbert Greenway. He added, "Or Lilith Greenway," because it occurred to him that Lilith might possibly have got her smattering of information about schizophrenia at first hand. He instructed the clerk to stay with the call until it produced results.

He himself called the lab for a report on the bottle he had taken from Hildebrand's pocket. He was told that the residue contained morphine. That was not news. The fact that the code mark on the bottom of the bottle could be traced to a definite source was. He hung up, thinking that, after all, the Fromm drug robbery might not go down in the books as unsolved.

He went through the material that had accumulated on his desk. It consisted mainly of yellow slips bearing telephoned messages. There was one from the man on duty at Garde Medical.

Hildebrand had been awakened and given light nourishment. He was very weak, but according to the house physician and to his own doctor, who had called early, his condition was satisfactory. The "special nurse" replacing Miss Leeds said that he was depressed and uncommunicative. His wife had appeared in the morning, bringing the child with her. The nurse had allowed them only a brief visit and had not left the room while they were there. The child had taken well the explanation that her "daddy needed rest and sleep so that he could come home faster." The wife had seemed harassed. She had spoken little except to ask questions concerning his health. He had looked at her a lot and she had avoided his eyes.

Nelson put the message down, pondered about the part that was unstated, and reached for the next slip. It told of repeated calls from John Lindstrom. He picked up a telephone.

Lindstrom said, "Did you make the arrangements for Sunday?"

"Yes. Describe your man again—will you?"

Lindstrom obliged with height, weight, and coloring. "Okay?"

"As far as it goes—but it goes for a great many people."

"Well—let's see. One of those virile beards that leaves a blue shadow right after shaving. No scars on face that I could see, but there might have been one under his hat. He had it on—pulled down—and he didn't remove it. Nothing else I can think of—just a man of distinction along corner-cigar-store lines. Why? Do you think you've got him pegged?"

"I'll tell you later."

"Wait—don't hang up—what I really called you about was the job you gave me. I couldn't make a trip to Shenanga and get back in time for the Sunday party but I—"

"That's all right. Send me a bill for thinking about it. Something's come up that makes it official business now, so I'm putting it through the regular channels."

"You are?" Lindstrom sounded disappointed. "Okay—I'll send you a bill, but it will be for more than thinking. I've been warming up the Shenanga telephone wires."

"Oh? Then I might as well hear the results."

"Don't raise your hopes—and stop me if I bore you. The police had nothing. Neither did the town clerk—except confirmation that the subjects were born there. But it's one of those very small small towns—and the operator horns in and puts me onto a Mrs. Dixon who turns out to be aunt to Lilith and Herbert Greenway. It seems their mother died four years ago and their father a year later. Mrs. Dixon's a friendly soul—not the kind you have to be original with—so I gave her the chestnut about representing a law firm that wants to find Alix Voelker because they have beneficial tidings for her. The name 'Alix Voelker' doesn't hit the jackpot from your point of view, but it rings a bell and something comes out. I don't even have to reintroduce the Greenways—they being tied in with Mrs. Dixon's recollection of Alix. She 'ohs' and she 'ahs' and hopes the poor child will have good fortune at last. She says she was a foundling—taken from the town orphanage and adopted by the Voelkers, who didn't treat her right. They worked her hard, kept her out of school a lot, although she was a great one for reading and such, and were too stingy to pony up for medical treatment when she needed it. The neighbors saw what was going on but they couldn't take steps because the Voelkers were within their rights and stopped just short of out-and-out cruelty. Anyway, every chance the girl had she'd sneak away to the Greenway house, where they fed her and were nice to her. Compared to the pinchpenny Voelkers, the Greenways lived high. Too high, maybe—it was a good thing his wife had gone before him and his children had left Shenanga to strike out for themselves—quote—unquote." Lindstrom stopped to draw breath. "Say—do you really want this stuff?"

"Yes—I want it." He could hear the crackle of paper as Lindstrom went back to his notes.

"It's mostly quotes from here on. Bert—that's the Greenway boy—was always sweet on Alix Voelker—and no wonder. She was an intense little thing—bound to make something of herself—but a real beauty. The clothes she had to wear would have broken any child's heart, but she wore them like a princess. And Bert wore his heart on his sleeve—so for a while it looked as if she might marry into the family. Bert's mother wasn't too pleased. For one thing, they were both young—Alix couldn't have been more than sixteen when it began to seem serious—for another, coming right down to it, she didn't know what kind of folks Alix had come from—could have been riffraff just passing through the town. Not that Bert was such a much. Being his aunt, she shouldn't say it, but all the same he was backward in some ways. His sister Lil always had to do his homework for him—and a lot of other things, too, she wouldn't be surprised. Still—he was a good boy. He had a sweeter disposition than Lil. Lil could be pretty nasty when she wanted—but come down to Bert, you couldn't deny she was a real little mother. Well, anyway—Alix could have done worse. He had a good build—and he played a smart game of football in high school. But be that as it may, it never came to anything. The Voelkers picked up and left town, taking Alix with them. No—she couldn't say where they went and she hadn't heard hide nor hair of them since. She hadn't heard much from her niece and nephew either. Children grew away from you and there was nothing you could do about it—and Lil and Bert weren't much for writing."

Nelson said, "I know."

"How's that?"

"Go on."

"I've come to the end of it. I told you it wasn't worth—"

"At least it's unexpected. What's Mrs. Dixon's first name? I might want to get in touch with her."

"The operator called her Belle. Her husband's name didn't come up. But if you ask for the aunt of Lil and Herbert Greenway you won't have any trouble—not in such a chummy place."

"Thanks, Lindstrom."

He sat revising his conception of the way it had been between Alix Voelker and the Greenways. He had pictured Alix as a sheltered, well-nurtured child bestowing largess upon two kids from the wrong side of the tracks and later, for her pains, being cursed with a pair of incubi who intended to hang on until she was drained dry. Hildebrand had conveyed that impression in the hotel bar. *"Alix says Lilith has had a hard time and it would be cruel to drop her.*" But Alix should have said, "Lilith and her family were kind to me when I needed kindness. I'd be ungrateful to drop her."

He shook his head. Gratitude was a fine simple theme. Unfortunately, in this case it was swamped by an excess of strident variations. His imagination elaborated upon the phrases used by Mrs. Dixon. "A beauty—an intense little thing bound to make something of herself"—something more than a physically neglected drudge in hand-me-downs. The Greenways lived high. They would symbolize her earliest level of aspiration. She ran to them for solace—found warmth and comfort in their family circle—and food for her starving ego in that she became the object of the son's doglike devotion. But she was whisked away before—?

The clerk who had called Bellevue came into the office. He said there was no record that anyone named Greenway, Lilith or Herbert, had been committed as mental patients or entered as any other kind of patient. They had checked back five years and would check further. Nelson said it would not be necessary.

There were a number of questions he wanted to put to Mrs. Dixon. He wrote them down, called the ready room, and summoned a detective named Judd, who was experienced at the type of assignment he had in mind. Judd, freckled and forthright, looked as though he had never left the small town of his birth. He listened solemnly to the briefing and went off to make his arrangements for a trip to Shenanga.

Nelson arose to put his coat on and discovered with surprise that he was still wearing it. At once he became so acutely conscious of discomfort that he decided to go home and change his wet clothes before he did anything else. The next call was in his neighborhood, which meant that very little time would be lost. Besides, he owed it to Kyrie and Junie to keep free of colds. Not, he thought, that he was likely to give one to Kyrie if Sammy had correctly analyzed her mood.

He did not announce his arrival. He let himself into the house quietly and went upstairs without encountering anybody. His family, plus one, were in the living room. He had heard their voices as he passed, and glimpsed a warm glow from the fireplace. At any rate, he was no longer in Junie's doghouse because the third voice he had heard was Nora's. He wondered, as he put on dry socks and shoes, whether she had been fetched by Sammy or deposited by someone in her own household. He routed out a Burberry that Kyrie had presented to him a long time ago. It was as good as new because he rarely wore it, and as he took it from the closet he thought of the waterproofed Henry Francis Hacket and hoped that Clevis had managed to keep up with him and with his lumbering companion. He wished that he had assigned two men to the job, but of course at the time he had been unaware of Frank's proximity. He was cheered by the fact that Clevis was often as good and occasionally better than any two men on the squad.

As he walked toward the stairs a tantalizing odor rose from the lower regions. It smelled as though Sammy had just removed pastries from the oven. He hesitated on the landing. His late breakfast had made lunch at the usual hour unnecessary, and as the day progressed he had been too occupied to give a thought to food. Perhaps it would not be indulging himself to sit by his hearth for a little while and ask Sammy to bring him a sample of her baking along with a hot drink. He shook his head. It would be more than a little while. Junie and Nora would make irresistible demands upon him, and Kyrie would make no demands. And that would take even longer. He wanted to postpone a talk with Kyrie until he could devote his whole heart and mind to it. He had better leave as quietly as he had entered.

He was too late. Kyrie was coming up the stairs. She was taken aback to see him. Then she hurried to join him on the landing, but before she reached his side some of the lights in her face went out. He had a feeling that she had turned them off deliberately and that whatever had caused her to "act up" was no longer valid. He also had a feeling that she did not intend to let him down easily.

"I'm sorry," he said. "I didn't mean to startle you."

She said coolly, "It's just that I'm not used to a man in the house. Have you been here long?"

"No. I got a bit wet and stopped in to change."

"Did you change your shirt too?"

"It wasn't essential. I didn't meet any crying women today who mistook me for a blotter. You can be mulling that over until we meet again."

After a moment she said, "You're going out again?"

"I would have been gone—but I was trapped by that maddening smell coming up from the kitchen. I guess I'm hungry."

She declared a temporary truce. "Grid—didn't you have lunch?"

"Big breakfast."

"So Sammy told me—at half-past ten—nearly six hours ago."

"I'm pleased to know that even if you've renounced my bed you're still concerned with my board."

"I didn't renounce your bed," Kyrie said, "I hogged it."

"And you're glad—glad—glad!"

She set her wavering lips primly. "My emotions haven't crystallized yet. But no matter what happens, you're the father of my son and I have to protect his interests. Come downstairs. It won't take Sammy a minute to bring you tea and a sandwich."

He glanced at his watch. It was twenty minutes after four. If Dr. Enoch Falvey kept regular office hours on Saturday he should be at his Park Avenue address until six. "I'm a weakling," he said.

Kyrie muttered, "Poor man—you can't resist anyone at all." She left him at the living-room door and went to see about tea.

The children sat on the rug playing a game that involved a board and counters. They were evidently playing it by ear. Junie swept all of Nora's counters off the board and announced that he had won.

"No—I won because I'm out. You've got all yours left."

Junie looked exactly like a man on the verge of saying, "Isn't that just like a woman?" Then he saw his father and ran to him. "She's come to stay with us," he said, as though he had just discovered that it was a mixed blessing.

Nelson tousled his hair. "I can't think of a nicer surprise on a cold wet day."

Nora came over and held up her face for his kiss. "It surprised me too, Mr. Grid-dely. I was taking a nap because we got up very early this morning to see my daddy—and then I woke and heard Bert. And Alix came and packed my suitcase and brought me here. I asked her if I shouldn't say good-by to Bert, but she said he wasn't there and I must have been dreaming—"

Junie said loudly, "I was dreaming too. I dreamed it was Sunday and I was at the zoo."

Nora said, "I'm going to live with you, Mr. Grid-dely, until my daddy gets out of the hospital. Alix said so."

"That's fine."

"Yes—Sammy let me bake a cake all by myself almost—but Alix looked sorry. She hugged me to death."

Nelson said with no zest for pumping the child, "Did you dream you heard anyone besides Bert?"

She shook her head. "I don't think so." Then she said, "I didn't say good-by to Lilith either. Alix wouldn't let her go to the hospital with us this morning and she was cross—so maybe she went home."

Junie said, "I'm getting cross, Mr. Grid-dely. I want it to stop raining. If it rains on Sunday I'll—"

Kyrie came in with a tray. She said, "Sammy just took a little cake out of the oven. She wants to know if it belongs to anyone in here." The room was cleared of children before she had finished.

She sipped tea while Nelson ate and drank. He said the sandwich hit the spot. He praised the fresh strawberry tart. He lit a cigarette for her and for himself and said, "I suppose this is what's known as a pregnant silence."

"You're in a hurry—and one word will lead to another."

"Come off it, Kyrie." He told her what had occurred at Garde Medical, condensing the account but omitting nothing of importance. "That's why I couldn't call you sooner last night and why I couldn't say much when I did call. Haven't you seen anything about it in the newspaper?"

She nodded. "How is Mr. Hildebrand? Nora says she visited him this morning. That sounds hopeful."

"His physical state seems to be satisfactory. I won't know what his mental state is until I see him—which will probably make me late again tonight—so don't look for me at dinner-time."

"All right."

"Is it? I mean are you?"

"Quite. I wasn't last night, but I am now."

"You baffle me. I can understand you being miffed when you saw the lipstick on my shirt this morning—but why last night? Did you think Alix Hildebrand and I had set up a love nest at Garde Medical?"

"I don't know what I thought or why I thought it—or even if I did think it. It was more of a feeling than anything else."

"Do you still have it?"

"No—but I'm a bit shaken because—well—it can happen so easily—and to anyone—can't it?"

He said firmly, "Not to us."

She sighed. "The truth is I'm more annoyed with myself than I am with you. I always believed I was completely sophisticated. Have you seen her today—or spoken to her?"

"No, I haven't seen her—or called her—and she didn't call me—at least not while I was in my office—nor was there any message to say that she had—and no reason why she would—"

"Don't look so put upon. If it's any comfort to you, I didn't need your explanation. I'd stopped suffering before you came home. I just thought it would be fun to see *you* squirm for a change."

"Is it fun?"

"No. For one thing, you aren't squirming—and for another, I've lost the art or the zest I once had of making men jump through hoops. Besides—" She shrugged.

"We'll get back to your lost art when there's more time. What was the 'besides' leading up to?"

"Alix Hildebrand."

He groaned.

"I'm not being snide. She brought Nora here. She said you'd offered to take her yesterday, and I said I was glad to have her—and we talked—"

He raised an eyebrow. "What about?"

"Nothing really—not half as much as you've told me—and not much more than that vague little item in the newspaper. I said something about the nurse being poisoned, hoping she'd cast some light on it, but she didn't. She looked so haunted that I stopped being your little helper and changed the subject. Grid—I've never been more sorry for anyone in my whole life. Oh, I know it doesn't make sense, but I'm so ashamed of being catty about her. She's frantic with worry—an entirely different woman from the shallow beauty who stopped me on the street that day—eyes swollen as though she'd been weeping since birth—nose red—"

He stared at his wife suspiciously, but her violet eyes held real distress. And knowing her as well as it was ever given one human being to know another, he knew that she had no ulterior motive for the picture she was painting.

"I kept thinking—not that she'd brought Nora as an excuse to see you—but that she had something terribly urgent to tell you that she couldn't tell me—and that somehow she hoped you'd be here. That's why I asked if she'd called you."

"Another one of your feelings," he said. "She couldn't have expected to find a workingman at home in the middle of the afternoon. If she did have anything urgent to tell me I gave her all the opportunity in the world when I drove her home last night." He half expected that to draw sparks, but it did not.

"Maybe you're right—but it was the way she jumped when someone rang the bell—anxiously—and yet sort of hopefully—it even made me mention you although I hadn't intended to because I didn't want her to—well—"

"Blush or look coy?"

"Something like that," Kyrie admitted. "But you're evidently not as fascinating as I thought you were. Sammy came in while she was here and asked something about dinner and I segued into the matter of your crazy hours and said something to the effect that at least I could always reach you at headquarters when it was necessary. But she had no reaction at all. I don't even know if she heard me, and right after that she left."

"How long ago?"

"About half-past two."

He got up and went to an extension phone near the fireplace. He made two calls, put two questions, and waited until the answers came. He hung up and said, "She didn't call me and she isn't at the hospital. Did she say anything about going there?"

"No—she just kissed Nora as though she never expected to see her again and thanked me and went out into the rain."

"You're developing a nice talent for melodrama," Nelson said. He drew her to her feet. "I'm going out into the rain too. How about pretending you'll never see me again?"

Chapter Thirteen

He put on the Burberry and an equally unaccustomed hat. This was by way of concealing his white hair from anyone who might be inclined to regard it as a danger signal. He left his car where it was and walked down the street behind a couple of other pedestrians. A casual glance gave him the Hildebrand house on the opposite side. Its windows were closed, its blinds drawn. He continued on toward the corner. He passed a boarded-up brownstone and almost immediately had the sensation of being followed. When he was beyond window range of the Hildebrand house he turned on his heel.

Clevis quickened his pace and joined him. Clevis was crestfallen. "You knew I was tailing you?"

"Only because I knew where Bert had gone—and hoped to draw you out of cover. Where were you?"

"In the areaway of the brownstone. It's made to order. Its only drawback is no roof." He shivered. His baggy clothes were drenched.

"Everything else under control?" Nelson looked over his head at the Hildebrands' fronting pavement.

"Yep—they're both inside. Is the chum important?"

"I think so. Go back to my house. Use the kitchen extension and call headquarters for relief. Tilman will do if he's there. Then ask Sammy to give you some hot food, but don't be tempted to dawdle over it. I'm in a hurry."

Clevis was off before he had finished. He stood still for a moment, melted into a group, and when it came level with the boarded-up brownstone he dropped out of sight.

The areaway was a catchall for the rain. Nelson was grateful for the Burberry. He tried to think pleasant thoughts. The only thing he could think of was that he had forgotten to ask Kyrie for a description of the flashy character she had seen loitering near Mrs. Hildebrand. He had removed the hat and poured water from its brim for the third time when Clevis returned, legs first. The ladder he carried missed Nelson by inches.

"Disguise," he said, propping it against the wall. "I thought I'd be a workman for a change if anyone cared. You can charge the department for it. Did I miss anything?"

"No. Did you see my wife?"

"Not a soul. Sammy let me in. She's a pal. I'm a new man inside and out." He struck a match. "How do you like it?"

"The coat doesn't fit any worse than your own."

"Yeah—but you got awful big feet. She dug out shoes and rubbers too. But I didn't mean that. I meant this little home from home. Before I recognized your long pins I was thinking if I didn't starve to death I'd freeze to death—and the chance I'd get to a telephone to beg relief was nil. Also, I got nervous about who should I tail if they both came out and went in opposite directions on account of I had no instructions there'd be two of them."

"I didn't know it myself. Has anyone else come in or out?"

"Only a high-class female construction job with red hair and a kid—a half hour after I got here. She turned toward your end of the street. She was carrying a suitcase and I made her the lady of the house off on a trip. Nobody else came or went."

"You're sure?"

"Unless there's a back way—and if there is I'm risking pneumonia for nothing. The front door is above street level, isn't it? You can see for yourself I got a full view of it and the steps. Of course they could come up out of the basement, and if they crouched they'd be hidden by traffic—but why should they if they don't know I'm here?"

Nelson had looked at the houses on that side of the street when he was shopping for his own. There were doors leading to backyards which most of the tenants had tried to transform into gardens. The yards or gardens were walled in by high fences. Short of climbing them, to use a back door as an exit meant to end up at the left of the front entrance by way of the service alley. He said, "Do you think they spotted you?"

Clevis said indignantly, "They did not."

"Well then—your argument about the basement holds. The only other means they have of leaving is a climb behind the house with practically no toe holds. They wouldn't try it unless they suspected that they were being watched—but I'll arrange to have the area covered anyway. Could you see who let them in?"

"Looked like a maid. The door opened and closed too fast for me to be sure."

"Did you see anyone at the windows?"

"Someone closed them and pulled the shades right after I ducked in here—but whoever it was kept out of sight."

"Any detours before you arrived?"

"Nope—we came by subway—and so far this has been the first and last stopping place. From that angle it's not a bad assignment—anyway, not since you catered to my creature comforts."

"Good. Then hang on with the relief when he gets here. That point you raised about a departure in opposite directions is sound. I don't want to take any further risk of drawing attention to your 'home from home,' so I'll send reinforcements to a different stake-out. If your business hasn't taken you elsewhere by the time they come you'll receive a signal."

Both men had been watchful as they talked. No life was visible within the house across the street. No shadows fell upon the blinds, no curtains stirred. Nelson's rise to the pavement was protected by a collection of legs. The owners of the legs gave him no more than incurious glances. That was New York.

He regained the shelter of his car, tossed his hat on the rear seat, and stepped on the gas. He made one stop to telephone headquarters, and reached Dr. Falvey's address at a quarter to six. It was a large apartment house typical of the buildings along the avenue. Aside from the main entrance there were two outside doors bearing metal name plates. Dr. Falvey's door was on the latch. A bell tinkled as Nelson pushed it inward.

He found himself in an empty waiting room furnished with standard lamps, a couch, a number of upholstered chairs, and a scattering of small tables covered with magazines. Before the echo of the bell faded, a woman with blued hair came out of an adjoining office.

She said, "Good afternoon," and looked at him inquiringly.

"Good afternoon. I'd like to see Dr. Falvey."

"I'm sorry—the nurse should have locked the door when she left. His hours are from nine to one on Saturday." Her eyes protruded rather like the eyes of an insect and were a hard bright brown. They missed no detail of his appearance. She went on doubtfully. "Unless it's an urgent case—"

"I'm not a patient, but it is an urgent case. Are you Mrs. Falvey?"

"No—the doctor's been a widower for some time. I'm Miss St. Clair—his secretary."

He thought the statement sounded aggrieved. He gave his own name and occupation. "If he's in will you tell him that my visit concerns Richard Hildebrand? If he isn't in please give me his home address."

She seemed at a loss for a moment, made partial recovery, and said, "This is his home address—he has an apartment on the tenth floor—but I don't think— Would you mind waiting? I'll see—" She turned and walked through the adjoining office to the recesses beyond.

He picked up a copy of *Vogue* and noted with some astonishment that it was the latest issue. He flipped the pages, stared at a redheaded model, and put the magazine from him. Then he diverted himself by filling the room's upholstery with patients in various stages of real or imaginary ailments and gave the air conditioner an approving nod.

Miss St. Clair returned. She said, "The doctor's very tired. I hope you won't worry him or keep him too long. This way, please."

She led him to a walnut-paneled room containing shelves of fat important books and centered by a large modern desk. Dr. Falvey rose from behind the desk, offered his hand, barely made contact, and sat down again. His "Good day" sounded as meaningless as it was. His "Won't you be seated?" made the most of a bad bargain. He waited until Miss St. Clair had closed the door behind her, and said across the stretch of polished wood, "I'm afraid I can't cast any helpful light upon this matter. If I were asked to list the best hospitals in the country I should include Garde Medical without hesitation." His fine long fingers drummed on the desk. His face was like a room that had not been designed for hard living. The visiting disturbance sat ill at ease upon its clean-carved features. He said, "I simply don't understand how an accident like that could have occurred." Preoccupied as he was, habit worked upon him. While he talked he subjected the man in the patient's chair to professional scrutiny.

By way of diversionary tactics Nelson said, "What's the verdict, Doctor?"

"I beg your pardon?"

"You make me want to apologize for occupying this chair. I'm beginning to feel almost obscenely healthy." He was rewarded by a faint smile.

"I diagnose that your white hair is hereditary rather than the result of age or serious illness. You show no alarming symptoms, but of course my opinion can't be confirmed without examination—and even that doesn't always reveal the whole story."

"No. I expect a general practitioner is called upon to practice a certain amount of psychiatry—especially these days."

"That's true enough. The mounting tensions of the average existence—" His own tension returned. He smoothed his iron-gray hair. He played with a paper cutter. He said, "I was informed by Miss St. Clair that you wished to see me about Mr. Hildebrand. Please understand that a member of my profession is not free to discuss his patients. I can merely state that he is on the road to recovery."

Nelson said, "Edris Hogan, the nurse who attended him, won't recover."

"That's unfortunate. I'm deeply upset by it—but beyond the fact that I was responsible for recommending her, I fail to see—"

"I agree that you're not responsible. Her death was accidental. Poisoning Richard Hildebrand was not."

"I can't believe that anyone would deliberately—"

"Nevertheless, it's true. How long has he been a patient of yours?"

"For several years—three, I think."

"And Mrs. Hildebrand?"

He did not answer that so readily. He spun the paper cutter on its handle. He shifted the position of a framed photograph. His attention seemed riveted to these tasks. "For approximately the same time—perhaps a month or so earlier. Then I was called to treat Nora for German measles—and after that I became the family physician."

"When Mrs. Hildebrand came to you what was the nature of her illness?"

A flush crept along the doctor's cheeks. He seemed to be struggling with the ethics of the situation. He said, "I am extremely reluctant to bandy information concerning my patients. What bearing—?"

"I'm not here to gratify idle curiosity, Dr. Falvey. I've had a busy day and it's far from over. I would like to cut this interview as short as possible."

"Very well." He shifted the photograph another fraction of an inch. "Mrs. Hildebrand had a virus. She was running a slight fever and I sent her home to bed."

Nelson leaned forward, as though to loosen his Burberry. The face in the silver frame was middle-aged and gently pretty.

"A gallant woman," Dr. Falvey said.

"Your wife?" Nelson was surprised that his act had been noticed.

There was no reply. Nelson realized that the doctor had not heard the question. He did not repeat it. He said, "Are the Greenways your patients too?"

"No—that is, not regular patients. I did treat Miss Greenway recently when she was at the house—not for anything serious."

"Who sent Mrs. Hildebrand to you?"

The doctor looked as though he would protest again. The paper cutter made a faint scratch on the hard unblemished wood. He said, "I believe it was a Dr. Morganroth."

"What is his first name?"

The doctor met Nelson's eyes for a moment and looked away. "Jonas."

"I see. Dr. Falvey—will you please show me the medical histories of both the Hildebrands?"

The doctor stopped fiddling. He said with dignity, "You don't realize what you're asking. It's quite impossible."

"I may have to make it possible."

He stayed to ask a few more questions. The only gains he made were by default. He did not press the matter of the private files. Miss St. Clair showed him out and thanked him earnestly, as though he had cut the interview short as a special favor to her. He doubted that her dedication to Dr. Falvey would ever bring the reward she sought.

He drove to Garde Medical and stopped at the desk in the lobby. He made himself known to the woman in charge, who called someone to take over and gave him her undivided attention. She said that yes, for the length of a patient's stay they did file duplicates of visitors' passes and try to keep an eye on those who came and went. The attendants at the desk on each floor were asked to challenge anyone who seemed doubtful. This procedure was not customary in the average hospital, but Garde Medical received quite a few famous patients, and undesirables often attempted to crash their rooms. She showed him the duplicate slips of the people who had visited

Hildebrand on the previous day. With one exception the names they bore were the names mentioned by Alix Hildebrand. The exception was himself.

Nelson thanked her, as much for her well-bred suppression of curiosity as for the service. He walked toward the elevators and passed a bank of telephone booths. He decided that this was as good an opportunity as any to call Dr. Jonas Morganroth. Sometime later he emerged from a hot booth, Burberry over his arm, made further inquiries, and finally tracked Miss Leeds down in the staff cafeteria.

She was sitting at a table with three nurses. She recognized him and said brightly, "You're Nora's Mr. Grid-dely." He asked if he could speak to her privately and she excused herself to the other nurses and accompanied him to an empty table.

"I'm sorry to interrupt your meal," he said.

"That's all right—I'd finished. It isn't often I'm sought out by a handsome man." Her kind cheerful face sobered. "I called you Mr. Grid-dely in front of them to put them off. I know you're not just a friend of the Hildebrands. You're a detective, aren't you? You were there last night when—"

He nodded. "I'm hoping you can help me."

"But I've been removed from the case—temporarily. Mr. Hildebrand has a special nurse—"

"Yes, I know. It's the time you were on the case that interests me."

Regretfully she shook her head. "Dr. Courtland has already talked to me. I assisted him, you know, when we took Mr. Hildebrand to the operating room. He called me in today and asked me to quell any gossip that might be going the rounds. He told me that the orange juice had contained a lethal dose of morphine—and he wanted to know if I had any idea of how it got there. But I hadn't. Mr. Hildebrand is as nice a gentleman as I've ever met. It's frightening to think anyone would want to put him out of the way. As for that poor Miss Hogan—"

Nelson said, "Who brought the orange juice to the room?"

"Miss Hogan did—a little while before she went off duty. She mentioned that it was fresh."

"How does a nurse go about getting it?"

"Well—we take the thermos jug to the little pantry at the end of the hall, and we wait for it or leave it to be filled if there are jugs lined up ahead. Then we come back for it. That's so we won't be away from the patient too long."

"Is it common practice to leave the jugs there?"

"It is since they put the room numbers on them. Before that it was taking a chance. You see, if a nurse had broken her jug she might make off with any that had the juice she wanted—and it would be a nuisance to explain it to Supplies and get a replacement. But that doesn't happen now because whoever tries it can be caught red-handed."

"Is someone always in attendance in the pantry?"

"Usually. She might step out for a few minutes— Oh—do you think it was done in the pantry?"

Nelson said, "The alternative is that it was done in the room."

"But Mr. Hildebrand's wife was with him the whole day. The first thing he told me was that he wished I could get her to go out for some fresh air. He was teasing her—he said she wouldn't listen to him but she might to me."

"Were there any visitors present when you came on duty?"

"Just Miss Greenway and Mrs. Hildebrand." She thought for a moment. "No—Miss Greenway wasn't in the room—she was in the hall talking to someone. I didn't know who she was, of course, but Mrs. Hildebrand introduced us as soon as she came back in—and then I remembered passing her. She's different-looking, isn't she? I mean you wouldn't be likely to forget her."

"Who was she talking to in the hall?"

"I don't know. He didn't come back to the room. In fact, I'm not sure he'd been there at all. Later some people came from Mr. Hildebrand's office, and when they left Mrs. Hildebrand and his wife discussed them—saying how nice and thoughtful they were—bringing flowers and all—but I didn't hear anyone mention the man with Miss Greenway, so that's why I sort of had the notion he wasn't there to visit Mr. Hildebrand—just maybe a friend of Miss Greenway's who knew she'd be there and stopped in to have a chat."

Nelson's smile encouraged her. "Smart reasoning. Did you get a good look at him?"

"No—I only saw his back. Oh—!" The wholesome color of her skin grayed. She mumbled, "I—I didn't think to look."

"Of course you didn't," Nelson said reassuringly. "Were you left with any impression at all of his appearance?"

"I—he was tall—no—I'm not sure. Miss Greenway is so little she'd make anyone seem tall. He was dark—" She moved helplessly.

"If you saw only his back how could you tell his coloring?"

"I suppose I couldn't really. I guess his hat was dark. He hadn't taken it off, and by contrast with the camel's-hair coat—well—I just had a feeling he was dark—like—the way he was standing reminded me of—I can't think of his name but he plays gangster parts in the movies."

Nelson wondered if this was no more than the power of suggestion working upon her.

The pink was returning to her cheeks. She said with relief, "But it doesn't matter, does it? Miss Greenway will know who he is."

"Yes—that's true." Nelson shook hands with the good simple woman before she could examine the implications of her own words, escorted her back to her friends, and left the cafeteria.

On the third floor some hospital official—and Nelson credited Dr. Courtland—had ordered comfortable chairs to be placed at intervals along the corridor that led to Hildebrand's room. A few people, banished from the presence of their sick or taking voluntary respite, were using the chairs. The man seated near 301 aroused no particular attention. He did not rise as Nelson greeted him. He said, "Hello," and added that Dick was doing fine. He and Nelson might have been friends meeting in common cause. They conversed, muting their voices with what could have been deference to their surroundings. Nelson learned that Alix Hildebrand had come and gone in the last half hour.

Hildebrand lay with his eyes closed. His lids flickered as Nelson entered the room. The special nurse sat near a window reading a magazine. Nelson knew her well. Aside from hospital training, she possessed the qualifications necessary to police cases. He conferred with her quietly and in a kind of oral shorthand. Then she left the room.

As soon as the door had closed Hildebrand opened his eyes. He said, "You can tell your Lieutenant Danzig that someone tried to poison me."

Nelson drew a chair to the bed and sat down. He said, "Do you feel strong enough to talk?"

"What is there to say?—except that I'm supposed to consider myself lucky to be here at all." His voice grew a little louder. "But do you know—I can't seem to care. If I could change places with Miss Hogan I would."

"You're speaking out of physical weakness—and no wonder. You've had a rotten time. But you'll soon be back with Nora and—"

"Yes—Nora," Hildebrand said. He turned his face away.

"Look here," Nelson said, "we talked once before and I wasn't much good to you. Can you believe me if I promise that after a normal period of convalescence you'll go on pretty much as before?"

"As before—in a fool's paradise."

"Why do you say that?"

Hildebrand did not answer, and Nelson was afraid to guess at what he might have answered. He said, "By 'fool's paradise' do you mean obliviousness to the fact that you had an enemy?" He went on against Hildebrand's silence. "If that's what you meant you have plenty of company. Men who are free from malice themselves are always slow to sense it in others. If I'm right in believing that I know who made the attempt upon your life, it wasn't even motivated by personal malice. It was— Are you listening to me?"

Hildebrand said apathetically, "I'm listening."

"I said I think I know who tried to poison you."

"I heard you. But if I thanked you for your efforts in that direction I'd be lying in my teeth. She—my—she was just here. She told me that you'd taken Nora in. I can thank you for that sincerely—with all my heart—with all the heart I have. Don't ask me to work up any interest in whatever else you've done on my behalf. I can't find room for anything but regret that the attempt to kill me wasn't successful. It would have been such an easy escape from what's in store. Now I'll have to go on because of Nora—my one justification for an otherwise futile—"

Nelson said sharply, "Stop it. You're running away with yourself. Do you know a man named Henry Francis Hacket—a dark—?"

"No—and I'm not running away—nor can I run after or run from— I've got to stay and face it."

"The last thing I expected of you was self-pity," Nelson said.

Hildebrand's ears were closed to anything but the sound of his own laboring voice. "Do you know where I met her? In a rooming house—a property that had come into our hands. There was a buyer wanting it at once and we had to make a quick decision on whether the greater gain lay in keeping and remodeling or in selling. But I found a still greater gain—or so I thought. None of the men experienced in that phase of the business were available. I went myself. Just chance. She lived there. The woman who ran the place had asked her to listen for the phone and the bell while she was out shopping. She opened the door to me. She opened the door that had closed and locked when Nora's mother died. Fate in a rooming house."

Nelson did not try to stop him. Nelson thought, If he does not get this out of his system its poison will be more effective than any given drug.

"I forgot why I had come," Hildebrand said. "It was more than beauty. The beauty was there—not as it is now—but starved. She looked as though she had never had enough of anything in her whole life. I wanted to make up for it. I wanted to give her new light for her eyes—flesh for the bones that showed on her too thin face—closets full of clothes to replace the dress she wore—although even that was beautiful because she wore it. I kept coming back to the rooming house. I took her out. We got to know each other—but never better than in the moment of meeting. That was all I needed to know. At first she refused to marry me. She was a foundling, she said. A daughter of nobody. Something spawned and left to be raised by the state. In her earliest childhood, she said, before she was removed from the orphanage, she had listened to the other children's fantasies about their birth—about rich royal parents who would come to claim them. But she had indulged in no fantasies. Even then she had been filled with the cold certainty that no people with any heritage worth passing on would abandon their young. She had been neither hopeless nor bitter, she said. Merely determined to be a good parent to herself. And to that end she had prepared herself—listening—observing—learning what she could—trying to fashion the offspring that was herself into a human being worthy of respect and admiration. I said ridiculous things to make her smile. Her true parents must have been a god and a goddess, I said. One only had to see her to arrive at that conclusion. And if she had been denied the advantages of an earthly father and mother she had also been spared the disadvantages—the sometimes stifling possessiveness. Things like that, I said. I told her that she had achieved rare success as guardian of herself—that what she was and the way I felt about her proved it. But she answered seriously that she had not yet succeeded. Perhaps, she said, she had been too intense—tried too hard. Certain factors had interfered and she was not yet ready to marry. She had a job now, she said, and was going to school at night. The job wasn't much, but it could lead to a better one—and it was important that she stay until it did. She begged me to let her work out her own destiny. But I loved her. The job was in a shop and I didn't think much of it. It wasn't as though she had the stamp of a careerist. And finally I persuaded her. It wants more than persuasion, doesn't it? I should have stopped to take stock. I should have asked myself how it was possible that such a woman loved me. I'm a pretty dull fellow, all things considered. A businessman—not the imaginative type who seeks for anything beyond the fireside and the daily work. I should be thanking my stars that it lasted this long. I shouldn't blame her—I mustn't blame her—but that she could choose this time —a time when my resistance is so low—to tell me—" He stopped talking. He looked as though the graven bewilderment and despair upon his face were there forever.

Nelson said, "She told you? What did she tell you?"

"Nothing—no explanation. Just good-by."

Nelson said, "Good-by!"

"Why do you sound shocked? I thought I had prepared you for it—at least given you more preparation than I had. I don't want you to condemn her. In a way it was admirable of her because she might have gone without saying it—stolen away and left me to discover it by myself. But she had learned her manners well. She kissed me—she kissed me as though she meant it—and then she said, 'Good-by.'" He closed his eyes and translated aloud the image printed upon their lids. "It might have been that first day in the rooming house—so wan she looked. She wore green then too—but today it was an old wool coat I liked that I thought she had discarded long ago. So nice of her to wear it—"

Nelson said urgently, "How long ago did she leave here?"

"Fifteen minutes—fifteen years—and I'll never be able to let her go—never—"

"Hold onto yourself," Nelson said, "hold on hard." He glanced at the telephone, hesitated, and went out into the hall.

Chapter Fourteen

To the sentinel in the chair he said in passing, "Sit tight," and lengthened his stride. He prayed that he was not wasting precious moments, but with Hildebrand and perhaps the operator listening, it had been impossible to use the telephone in the room.

Before he entered a booth he flipped through a directory and recorded the numbers he needed. He called the Hildebrand house first. A maid told him that Mrs. Hildebrand was not at home. Next he dialed the number listed for Herbert Greenway. There was no answer. He called headquarters and gave a full graphic description of a redheaded woman in a green coat. He listed the places where he thought she might be found and outlined the course to be followed if he had guessed true. His hand was so tightly clenched around the receiver that pain shot up to his shoulder and aroused the forgotten bruise inflicted by Herbert Greenway's tackle.

He left the booth and breathed the comparative purity of the hospital atmosphere. He went back to get his Burberry in 301. For the moment he could think of nothing better to do. All he could think of was the river and what she had said about wishing she were dead.

In his absence the nurse had returned. She was standing before the closed door. She blocked the entrance of a small determined figure in trench coat and beret. The sentinel had arisen and seemed prepared to give her aid.

Nelson came up behind Lilith Greenway and said quietly, "You can't go in."

She wheeled around. She said in a gritty voice. "Try to prevent it. I intend to see Richard Hildebrand."

He took her arm. "Not today."

She said contemptuously, "Are you making it a family affair?"

"What do you mean by that?"

"You've arrested my brother. Now I suppose it's my turn."

He showed no surprise. "It will be—on a disorderly conduct charge if you try to make a scene here." He spoke to the nurse. "Go inside and stay there until further notice. I'll take care of this."

Lilith wrenched her arm free with unnecessary violence. She turned just as the door closed behind the nurse. It reopened anticlimactically and Nelson's Burberry was handed to him, but she did not see that. She was racing down the hall.

Nelson went after her. He stuck close, following her into an elevator. On the main floor she made no attempt to elude him and he made no attempt to detain her. He sensed her measuring eye upon him while he walked beside her to the exit.

She said, "You won that round," and was unexpectedly docile as he took her arm again.

"I haven't even started to play." He steered her to his car, helped her in without ceremony, and walked around to the other side. He saw the river, brown and dirty and pierced by needles of rain. He turned from it and slid behind the wheel.

"Do we just park here?" Lilith said. "I didn't know you cared."

He did not telegraph his intention. With one movement he swept beret and fringe back from her brow.

The beret fell to the seat. "Really!" she said. "Reall—!" Her hand went up to cover the gauze pad held down by flesh-colored adhesive.

He said with mock sympathy, "Poor girl—how did that happen?"

"I cut myself shaving."

He recognized the brand of humor. It was authentic Henry Francis Hacket. "Did you steal the razor?" he said. "Is that why you felt guilty enough to hide the traces with a new hair-do?"

"I'm vain. I can't stand showing my public anything but the perfect me. What else would you like to know?"

"Before we go into that it's only fair that I should give you my version in return for yours. You were in the stolen cab. You smashed the glass—or the impact smashed it—and you were cut by a flying chip. You were lucky it didn't land in your eye—but I'm afraid your luck is about to end. Now then—don't take it from there. Go back a bit further and tell me what led up to it. You needn't embellish—just a synopsis. I can fill it in."

She put the beret on, adjusting it with steady hands. "I'm in a hurry," she said. "I have no time for ridiculous conversation. I thought you were offering me a lift and I accepted because I came out without enough carfare." She depressed the button on the door.

"Sit still." He had started the car before she finished speaking. As it moved out of the driveway he secured the door. "You evidently had time to thrust your unwanted presence on a sick man. Did you think that since he had been disobliging enough to stay alive you might as well continue to blackmail him?"

"I wish we had a tape recorder," she said, "because I'm sure that in the presence of witnesses you'll deny all these libelous statements."

He ignored it. He said, "Or were you forced to see him because Alix had balked suddenly at helping you out with more cash or expensive gifts?"

She said calmly, "According to the law of averages, you're bound to be right sometimes. I do need ready cash—and if I can find Alix she'll give it to me—willingly—without benefit of blackmail—because she knows I'd do and have done the same and more for her. She might even be waiting for me this minute to ask some favor of her own. It's been a give-and-take relationship between us."

The car lurched. He swore. He righted his driving and himself. He said, "Where would she be waiting for you?"

"Heavens—how fierce you sound. What am I supposed to be guilty of now?"

"Where is Alix Hildebrand waiting for you?"

"I didn't say she was—I said she might be. I stopped at my apartment before I came to the hospital, and the doorman told me I had just missed her. So I said if she tried again to let her in and tell her that I'd be back as soon as I could. You see, I allowed for not being permitted to see Richard—especially if Alix wasn't there to support my cause—" She happened to glance at the speedometer. She said, "Join the police force and break the laws. Lucky for you I'm not a nervous female—or is it? May I ask where we're going in such a mad rush?"

He did not reply.

"Highhanded, aren't you? Is this the sort of thing that was pulled on my brother?"

He made a turn, his eyes intent on the traffic. "Who told you that your brother had been arrested?"

"My spies. I'm the brains of an international crime syndicate. I've spies posted all over."

His patience left him. "If that were so I'd have a certain amount of respect for you. But you're not the brains of anything. You're a petty little hanger-on of a petty little conniver who's dragged you in over both your heads—and you haven't even the frayed excuse of a miserable childhood to move a jury to clemency. Your aunt in Shenanga—Mrs. Dixon—will testify to that when the time comes—and the time is almost here. When I arrest you the charge won't be disorderly conduct or car theft or blackmail. It will be murder. If you have any conscience at all you can join me in the hope that it won't have to cope with yet another death."

Her eyes were like splashes of flat dark paint in the stark white of her face. She said, "I don't frighten." She pressed the back of her hand against her mouth, dropped it, and with the other rubbed at the indentations of her sharp little teeth. "You can stop trying to frighten me. I don't know where you got hold of my aunt's name—I couldn't care less—" Her voice quavered. "As for the other things you said—you have no proof—none—"

"I've proof—"

"I don't want to listen to any more. I won't listen—"

"Your brother had a duplicate key of the stolen cab—"

She struggled for composure, regained a degree of it. "Who says?"

"I've not only found the key. I've tried it."

"Well—why not? He had a right to it. He works for the owner—"

"He did work for him—which hardly gives him a lifetime lien on the cab." He regarded her briefly, thoughtfully. "So you didn't know he had lost his job? Yes—that could be. He was afraid to worry you—realizing that you needed his small income as well as handouts from Alix until you attained your rotten ambition. He was probably even unaware of the scope of your plans—just the dupe of a trusted sister who must have found his lack of intelligence extremely convenient. Perhaps the hit-and-run escapade started in this way. Perhaps you said, 'Bert—I'm short of change and I have to go to the Hildebrands'. Why should I take a bus or a subway when you have a cab at your disposal?' And to give you the benefit of the doubt in this one instance let's say that what followed was spontaneous. You happened to reach your destination at the same time that Hildebrand was nearing it on foot. Still allowing you that very narrow margin of credit, let's say that impulse got the upper hand. You saw and took your chance of gaining full control of his money rather than continuing on a dole of dribs and drabs. You didn't expect any difficulty in managing his wife when he had been removed, she being well under your thumb. So you leaned over the partition and grabbed the wheel from your brother. Then you stayed in the cab until it was out of the danger zone—left your brother to deal with it—and walked back, thinking to console the widow."

He was sure that at least a portion of what he had uttered was true. But she was a die-hard. Her voice started on a thin broken note and firmed as she went on talking. "No—no—and I'm as crazy as you are to bother to deny it. You don't believe it yourself or you wouldn't have arrested my brother—"

"I think your spies have been misinforming you."

"Think again. I know all about your visit to the apartment today—not that it got you anywhere—"

"It wasn't a total loss. I had enlightening talks with your brother—and with your intimate friend, Henry Francis Hacket. I'll admit they reacted rather impolitely—they ducked out—but I'd anticipated that and arranged to have them followed. I did not, however, order your brother's arrest."

"That's a lie. Frank told me when he called—" She clamped her lips.

"So Frank told you? What a ubiquitous fellow he is. The first time he cropped up was as a mistake Alix had made some years ago. It's broad-minded of you to have overlooked that and taken both sinners back to your bosom." He braked the car.

Lilith turned to him. "Alix told you that!" The measure of her fury was such that she did not realize they had come to a stop.

"To be continued in our next," Nelson said. He got out and went around to open the door for her. The attention was anything but polite. He caught her arm as she reached the asphalt and headed her toward the house.

"I'm not going up. I've changed my mind."

"You're going up and I'm going with you. The doorman might begin to have qualms about your status as a dignified tenant if I carry you under my arm—but if that's the way you want it—"

"No—"

"Then walk."

The doorman said as they passed him, "Your lady friend went up a few minutes ago. I let her in like you said."

Lilith did not thank him. Nelson did. When they reached the fourth floor he took her key and turned it in the lock. He gave her a little push that sent her over the threshold, and closed the door behind him. He did not like the living room, fully revealed from where he stood, and empty.

The privacy of her own four walls seemed to reassure Lilith. She said venomously, "That doorman's cracked. She's not here—he just wanted a tip."

"Try the bedroom," he said, and started for it.

She was at his heels. "This is my house. I don't give you leave—"

"You haven't a thing left to hide. Surely you don't believe I frittered away the shining hours when your brother and your 'house guest' deserted."

"You'll have to answer for that too—I'll bring suit against you I'll—" Then she said in mock weariness, "First my brother—then me—and now poor Alix. Why are you so interested in her all of a sudden?"

"Your poor Alix was driven out of her home because criminals decided to use it as a hide-out. Her next move after she had seen to the safety of Nora was to kiss her husband good-by and come to you. Do you understand? She may have gone down as we were coming up. She may have left you the usual note telling you you'd driven her to—"

Lilith darted past him. He strode after her and was temporarily halted by the door of the master bedroom slamming in his face. He thought at first that she had locked it, but it had only stuck. His shove drove it against the wall, and the sound of the impact synchronized with her choked cry, so that he was not sure he had really heard it.

He looked blankly about him and saw the green coat tossed over a chair. He took a few steps forward and stared into the adjoining bathroom. Lilith was kneeling near the tub, one white-knuckled hand clutching its rim for support. He had to pry the hand loose so that he could squeeze by her into the rectangular area of plumbing and tile.

The red head was pillowed by the base of the sink. The lovely lips met in a peaceful curve. Blood trickled from an outflung wrist.

He crouched and felt for Alix Hildebrand's heartbeat, held the back of his hand to her nostrils, willing the stir of air that would mean life. He snatched a hand towel from the rack, ripped it with his teeth, and tore off a strip. He made a tourniquet, twisting it tight with the handle of a toothbrush.

He was dimly conscious that Lilith no longer crowded behind him and thought grimly and fleetingly that she would not get far. He saw that the composed mouth was faintly blue beneath the lipstick but took heart because the stain on the tile was still fairly bright. She can't have been here long, he thought, and looked somberly at the razor on the sink. Only one wrist slashed. He lifted it and, feeling both thankful and foolish, removed the tourniquet. She missed the artery, he thought. She couldn't go on with it—fainted at the first sight of blood. Her head? He slipped his hand between the thick silken hair and its hard pillow and probed gently. He sighed. He dashed cold water in her face.

It brought her back to consciousness. She moaned.

He said, "It's all right now. You're all right." He lifted her in his arms and carried her to the bedroom. "Kick off your shoes—that's it." He stripped a blanket from the bed and deposited her beneath it.

She looked up at him. "I couldn't go through with it," she said. "Now I'll never be able to. I'll just have to go on living. I'm a coward."

"You're not enough of a coward."

"I tried the river first," she said. "But there was a policeman—he stared at me—and when I tried to find a deserted place he followed. So I came here—to see Lilith. I didn't mean to do it here. I was going to write her a note begging her never to let Richard know about me—but I went to the bathroom first—and the razor was there on the sink—and I—and I—but I couldn't. I got dizzy when I saw the blood—"

"Does your head hurt where you struck it?"

"No—"

He sat down. He was talking to her like a Dutch uncle when Lilith entered the room. Lilith turned her opaque eyes to the bed. Her words came hard and thin. "I got Dr. Falvey. He's coming on the double."

It struck Nelson that the steel of her voice was overtempered. He thought that it might break soon. He had no pity for her. He said, "A police doctor would be more to the point. Suicides—whether they come off or not—must be reported."

She said in that perilously hard voice, "Sure—why didn't you finish her off and be done with it?" She went to stand by the bed. There was something oddly protective in her attitude.

"Who else did you get in touch with besides Dr. Falvey?"

"You go to hell."

He went to the telephone in the foyer. He dialed, identified himself, and asked if Clevis had returned.

In another part of the building Clevis picked up the telephone and said, "I been waiting for your call. I wanted to tell you it was none of my doing. One of the mother's little helpers you sent could've been riding a white horse and blowing a trumpet. He stakes out in the delivery entrance of the apartment house two doors up—but first he walks by here to drop us a note. So far so good. Hank Tilman, my relief, who showed up about a half hour after you left, is holding the fort with me. I'm thinking of leaving but I decide to stick around a while longer in case. Pretty soon Greenway makes an exit from the house. It would have been roses all the way except that this enthusiastic J. G. hops out of his nest, crosses over, and joins the dance. A baby could've spotted him, and Greenway does. It's dinnertime—see—and hardly anyone on the street. Maybe Greenway's been warned to be careful. He starts walking toward your end—and he don't go more than a few steps before he takes a gander over his shoulder. He stops short—and what does his wet-behind-the-ears shadow do but stop short too—and there they are—practically staring into each other's kissers. Then Greenway makes a lunge for Junior G., who loses his head entirely. All I can give him is marks for agility. When the dust clears Greenway is wearing handcuffs and being marched off. I learn later that Junior gets some assistance from a prowl car on the avenue and books Greenway for assaulting an officer of the law. But the worst of it is the play has been observed—or else a curtain behind a closed window suddenly decides to move by itself—"

Nelson finally damned the spate. "Is the other one still in the house?"

"Must be. Far as I know, Tilman's still in the areaway—and you said you'd arrange to have the backyards covered."

Nelson was issuing orders when the bell rang and Lilith rushed to the door to admit Dr. Falvey. He lapsed into a kind of departmental jargon, but he need not have bothered. Lilith did not stop to listen. She towed Dr. Falvey to the bedroom.

Clevis said, "I get you."

"Good—do your best to raise Lindstrom."

As he hung up he heard what sounded like and was the whirring of an egg beater. He went to the kitchen door. Lilith threw the egg beater at the sink and transferred a brandy-flavored mixture of milk and eggs from bowl to glass. Nelson dipped a finger into the bowl and tasted it.

"A reasonable precaution," he said.

Lilith flung him a look of hatred. "Let me pass. Dr. Falvey says she needs—"

"All right—but don't stay to supervise. I want you out here." Sooner than he expected she joined him in the living room. She said, "Did you—have you called Bellevue?"

"Not yet."

"Don't report it. She's had all she can take."

"Why should you have a monopoly on dealing it out to her?"

"You don't understand."

"Make me understand."

"I—no."

"Then don't expect favors. By the way—you were right. Your brother *has* been arrested."

She said bitterly, "You were wrong again."

"How else have I been wrong?"

"He has nothing to do with it."

"To do with what?"

"The cab—anything."

"Careful—don't spoil your record by suddenly producing a trait like family loyalty. I thought that a phone call from your 'house guest' might have spurred you on to extort getaway money from Richard Hildebrand, but now you make me wonder if you weren't trying to raise bail for your brother. Didn't you know no bail is posted for a murderer?"

"Bert—a murderer! Don't make me laugh." She was far from laughter.

"There's nothing new about simple-minded men becoming the tools of unscrupulous—"

"No—stop—I won't let Bert be the—" Her hands punished each other.

"Won't you?" Nelson shrugged. "I'm not venturing an opinion about your brother's guilt or innocence—but think of the advantage his conviction would be to you and your cohorts. Surely, just because he happens to be of your own flesh and blood you won't allow sentimentality to stand in the way of self-interest—not at this late date. It isn't as though you have to worry about the danger that he might give you away. I'm sure he'll be glad to sacrifice himself for his beloved older sister. I'll bet he has a doglike devotion for—"

"You're mad! Suppose he did drive the cab? Richard wasn't killed. Why do you keep accusing him of murder?"

"I suppose it's too much to expect that you'd spare a thought for the nurse who was poisoned."

"What has that to do with my brother? He didn't—"

"You were at the hospital when Edris Hogan—who later died so horribly—went to get the orange juice for her patient. There were other jugs there, so she left hers—clearly stamped with the room number—and came back for it in a short while. By then she had been taken care of—in every way. This time it was planned murder. Your brother had the lethal dose ready and was hanging about until you found the right opportunity. You'd better sit down—your knees are shaking. Don't bother to fob this off with your customary humor or with denials. The nurse—as you know—was suffering from a hangover. When she brought the orange juice back to the room she drank some of it—perhaps at the sympathetic suggestion of Richard Hildebrand. It killed her. Don't interrupt. You'll have your chance. Your brother's mistake was in lingering there in the corridor after the deed was done. Miss Leeds saw him talking to you when she came on duty. She gave me a full description—"

Lilith cried, "She's mad too—they don't look anything alike— Oh God!"

"Now you begin to interest me," Nelson said. "You'll either have to continue or face the fact that Miss Leeds' testimony will lead to a conviction."

Chapter Fifteen

She sat down. It might have been no ordinary chair that received her. She might have been waiting pale and numb for the switch to be thrown. The words her stiff lips uttered were in the nature of a farewell speech.

She said, "I was coming to the end of it anyway—the end of Frank.

If I'd been built that way you might have found me instead of Alix on the bathroom floor. You've distorted everything just enough to make it off center. Frank was driving the cab. Bert wasn't even along. Bert never could keep track of his belongings. He had the duplicate ignition key made because he was afraid of losing the one Ross had given him. He left it lying around and Frank found it and asked what it was and Bert told him. You had this much straight—Bert didn't tell me he'd lost his job. I guess he was afraid of what I'd say. I'd bossed him since we were kids—for his own good, whether you believe it or not. So he wasn't going to tell me until he got other work. He was worried—poor guy. He never knew that Alix gave me money from time to time—as much as she could manage without asking Richard. Not that Richard's stingy—but he can't stand me—and she didn't think it according to Hoyle for him to contribute or for me to accept his contribution. So whatever I got came out of her allowance. She was stubborn about that. And it wasn't blackmail. She wanted to help me—my mother and father had been kind to her—she —never mind—"

"Get back to the cab."

"It was true that I was going down to the Hildebrands' that night and that I didn't have cab fare. I asked Frank for some, but he didn't have any either—as usual. He's always waiting for some big deal to come through—although Bert believes he pays the greater part of our expenses. Bert had just unlocked the door and gone to his room. Frank went to see if he had anything. I guess he didn't. I guess Frank knew he had lost his job. Frank had a way of getting things out of him. Anyway, he came back and said Bert hadn't been paid yet but that we could use the cab—we'd find it parked outside the owner's house. He said he'd drive me down while Bert was eating a bite of supper and be back in time for him to go after the evening trade. I didn't think anything of it. I realized that if Frank was being extra thoughtful it was because he was extra eager to have me collect the weekly dole from Alix. So he borrowed a cap of Bert's and we went to find the cab. He told me to sit in the passenger seat—it would look better—but nobody gave us a glance. You were right about the impulse too. Frank couldn't have guessed that Richard would choose the moment we reached the street to jay-walk. It happened in a flash. The cab headed for him and I tried to scream. I couldn't even squeak. I leaned over the partition and grabbed the wheel and swerved to avoid hitting him—but it was too late. Next thing I knew we were a lot of blocks away. Frank swore it was an accident. He told me to wipe my face—it was bleeding—and I did the best I could. I think I bashed the identification thing with my head when I hurled myself at the wheel. I went back to the Hildebrand house and Frank went on with the cab. He left it on a side street near us—and later he got Bert to put it in the used-car lot. He told Bert I had been driving it and would be in serious trouble if it were found too soon. Bert did it for me—that's his only part in it. I went straight to Alix's bathroom and tidied myself up. There was blood on my nylon blouse, but it washed right out. When Dr. Falvey came I told him that what with all the excitement and Alix fainting I'd smashed a drinking glass and a piece of it had flown up and cut me. He dug a tiny chip out of the cut and disinfected it and stuck on a bandage. I cut the bangs to hide it."

She tried to read Nelson's face. It expressed neither belief nor disbelief. "As for the poison," she said, "that's what closes my account with Frank. The cab business may have been an accident. I chose to think so. Now I have no choice—not if it's Frank or Bert. I'm through with him for keeps this time. I should have been through as of our first set-to in Shananga—but I'm a fool for punishment. Yes—he could have tried to poison Richard. I don't know where he got the morphine—but you can ask him that. When the Hogan girl came out with the jug she greeted me, and Frank wanted to know how come I was so clubby with the help and I told him she was Richard's nurse. I saw him edge over to the pantry—but she had pretty legs and I thought it was the wolf in him. When she went back to the room I noticed that he was leaning against the pantry hutch, staring after her. I stared too—to see if her legs were that good. When I turned around he was grinning, and I thought the grin meant that he was amused at my being jealous."

"Are you prepared to sign a statement containing all this?"

"Don't worry. I won't renege. You've hinted that I'm not much good—but I can be pretty bad and still not want my brother to pinch-hit for a murderer—even a murderer who's shared my bed."

"What was his excuse for coming to see you at the hospital?"

"Money. He hadn't dared to come for it the night before. In the morning, after Richard had been moved from Bellevue by Dr. Falvey, Alix asked me to pack a suitcase with things he'd need and bring it to Garde Medical. I was on the way there with it—but I thought Frank might be wondering about things, and since Alix had given me five dollars for taxi-fare—I decided to stop here first and talk to him. That was when I told him to meet me at the hospital in the afternoon. There hadn't been a propitious moment to ask Alix for money, but I intended to pawn her cigarette case before he came. I didn't realize I'd left it at your house."

"Your delicacy astounds me. With what you held over Alix I should think any moment would have been propitious."

"How many times do I have to tell you it wasn't blackmail? My parents were old-fashioned. They always said it was a poor house that couldn't support one lady. I was brought up with no business training—no special skills—and when they died without leaving a penny I went on being a lady at the expense of others—or I went on being a useless slob if you prefer that designation—and I'm sure you do. But I didn't blackmail Alix. She knew I'd never give her away."

"Then there was something to give away—for example, that she had what is euphemistically termed a nervous breakdown and that right after her foster parents moved to New York she was committed to Bellevue."

"She was cured. She wasn't insane in the first place—just sick and vague. In shock, I think they call it—because the way she'd been treated all her life finally caught up with her when that sweaty louse Voelker got it through his head that she was beautiful and tried to reap the benefits—which is a euphemism for you know what. You can ask Dr. Falvey if you don't believe me—or the psychiatrist—Dr.—Dr.—"

"Dr. Jonas Morganroth," Nelson said.

"Yes. I guess a man of his standing knows what he's talking about—and he pronounced her cured and said there was nothing to indicate she'd ever get into a state like that again."

"Barring accidents like you and Frank. When she turned the blackmail notes over to the police Alix led us to believe that her lover's name was Leon Myles—but a maid who was in the house at the time identified him to Richard Hildebrand as Frank."

"Alix never had any lover but Richard."

"What was the general object of her performance in my office? Did you and Frank put her up to it with the idea of casting doubt on Richard's sanity? That, of course, would be one way to get rid of him so that you could control the money."

Lilith said wearily, "I didn't know she'd gone to you until she broke down and told me afterwards. She knew Frank was sending the blackmail letters and she wanted to scare him into quitting. She didn't really mean to go into your building, but he followed her all the way and she had to. Then she didn't have the heart to go through with it because of her loyalty to me. She understood how I felt about him—and since letters referred to an art student she substituted a name for Frank's—the only name that for some reason or other she'd remembered from her class."

"Are you asking me to believe that Frank wrote the blackmail letters without aid or comfort from you?"

"I'm not asking you to believe anything but the truth. Frank had a yen for Alix when he was a boy, but he never got to first base. If it came to a showdown she'd have preferred Bert, who worships her—which should give you a general idea of how little she goes for my fancy man—"

She saw Nelson glance at his watch. She said, "I'm answering your question. The first time Frank turned up in New York he asked about Alix, and in the first flush of seeing him I made the mistake of telling him the whole story—including Bellevue—how she'd landed on her feet by marrying a rich man—and was taking art courses and so on to live up to him. I had no idea Frank would follow through by paying her a visit. That must have been the time the maid saw him and jumped to the wrong conclusion. I don't say he didn't make a pass. He would—naturally. Right after that—consistent with his habit of appearing and disappearing in my life—he dropped out for several years."

"And— ?"

"I went to California with another man—intention marriage. It didn't work, so I drifted back by stages and moved in with Bert, who was holding down a job. Then Alix got some unexpected dividends from stock that Richard bought for her and she insisted that we move to a better apartment. No sooner were we settled than Frank showed up again. He boasted of some deal that would net him thousands and said the minute it was settled he'd marry me. I didn't take the promise seriously—but I took him seriously. I never could help it. So he became a steady boarder. It seems he lost no time in starting to hound Alix—waylaying her on the street—popping in to see her at odd moments. So you see—he had ample opportunity to frame Richard without aid or comfort from anyone. Callers are usually shown to a room next to Richard's study. It's a big house. When they're home Alix and Nora spend most of their time upstairs—Nora in her playroom—Alix with her or in a sitting-room affair that Richard designed for her. Who would prevent Frank from slipping into the study downstairs and setting the stage with the crayon and the circulars?"

"You—as her dear close friend—since you had such a clear idea of what was happening."

"I didn't. Alix was so afraid the Bellevue episode would leak to Richard that she kept the blackmail all to herself. Then, when she couldn't stand it any more, she threatened Frank by going to the police—and then she told me—in that order—and I put a stop to it. I rounded on Frank. I said he'd have to get along on what I could give him until his ship came in—and he laughed and pretended it was a big joke and that he hadn't meant any harm."

"Did he make other jokes—about wouldn't it be wonderful if Richard got murdered?"

"No—I hadn't the slightest—" It ended in a groan.

"The hardest thing for me to accept is the stupidity you've shown. How was Richard engineered into calling for the blackmail pay-off at the record store?"

"I don't know—unless Frank called his office or had someone else call pretending to leave a message from Alix that he was to pick up the records. Nora had asked for some and he always used that store—it's near his building. He wouldn't think it strange of Alix to phone and ask him to pick up a package. By then Frank knew Alix had gone to the police and he had no intention of walking into a possible trap."

"Is Hacket his real name?"

"Yes—why shouldn't it be?"

"Has he never been arrested?"

"No."

Nelson said, "His luck's out. He should be here soon."

"Here? What a hope. He saw your men take my brother. He won't stick his nose outside without making sure the coast is clear." Hostility returned and lifted her from her chair. "You mean they've broken in and arrested him—you mean you knew it was Frank and not my brother and tricked me into confirming it—!"

"What difference does it make? You're through with him. You said so."

"I'll say this too. He won't be here unless he's knocked out and carried—"

"Yes he will—under his own power. Your brother will have telephoned him—under urging—to say that he got away—that the coast is clear—that he's home and that you've got hold of a large sum of money."

"He'd want to hear it from me."

"You came in soaked to the skin. You're in a hot bath."

"You think he'll fall for that!"

"I think so. He's not very smart either."

"Bert won't do it—he admires Frank he—"

"Not any more—because my men have convinced him that Frank has done something very bad to you—and I doubt if you have a corner on family loyalty. Why are you gritting your teeth? Are you afraid Frank will present a different version of the matter—one that involves both you and Alix?"

"Oh God!"

Dr. Falvey came into the room. He said without meeting Nelson's eyes, "Mrs. Hildebrand will be all right. Her husband's illness—lack of sleep—skipping meals—had combined to put her under great strain. Miss Greenway told me that you intended to report the matter. I don't think—"

"Very well, Doctor. You've just made your own report to me. I'll take full responsibility." He held out his hand.

The doctor met his eyes, took the hand, and shook it. He said, "Thank you, Captain."

Nelson accompanied him to the door. When he came back Lilith had disappeared into the bedroom. About to follow, he changed his mind and awarded himself a quiet five minutes of thought.

Presently he heard a stealthy sound in the hall outside the apartment. He was even more stealthy as he went to investigate. With no warning he flung the door wide and hauled Henry Francis Hacket into the foyer.

Frank was strong but he had no science. He landed only one blow before his arms were pinioned. Nelson propelled him to the living room and bounced him into a chair that faced the window. He was standing over him when the open door closed behind Clevis.

Clevis came around to the chair. He said, "He swallowed it," and chuckled. "Funniest procession you ever saw. We followed him nice and easy—me and Tilman—and the rest of the crew followed us—but he was so busy spending the dough that he thought was waiting he wouldn't have seen us if he'd seen us. Tilman's downstairs in case needed. I got hold of whosis, and he's on the way. Want me to warm this drowned rat up? I wouldn't mind pasting him one for myself—making me ruin two outfits." He shrugged out of the wet roomy coat donated by Sammy.

Nelson looked down at Hacket, who had not opened his mouth since his initial stream of profanity. Nelson said, "Lilith Greenway has come up with some interesting data. I brought you here to confirm it."

Hacket reached in his pocket and produced a cigarette. Clevis snatched it from him. "Smoking is bad for the nerve you're going to need."

Hacket said, "Where's Bert and—?"

"Bert's where my men took him. They prompted him to call you."

"The stinking, stupid—!" He dropped it. He said, "So what?"

"So what have you to say about Miss Greenway's statement that you're a blackmailer and a murderer?"

"Don't hand me that." His chest swelled. The smile that came to his face made Nelson's muscles twitch. "Maybe Bert was nudged into a phone call—but Lil would sooner cut off her right arm than cause me a minute's inconvenience. Wait till she gets back and finds you playing cops and robbers in her house."

Lilith said from the doorway, "I am back. I've been back for quite a while—longer than I realized." She walked around to face him. Her voice was completely expressionless. "And I intend to keep both my arms and whatever else you've left of me."

He looked incredulous. He started to leave the chair. Then Clevis and Nelson watched him undergo another change of front.

The smile he summoned was less arrogant, the voice ingratiating. "What did I do now, Lil? Why are you sore at me?"

"It won't work," she said. "I've told everything I know about you."

He stared at her. He shrugged and turned to Nelson. "What could she know? I don't confide in floosies. I use them—maybe to wipe my feet on—maybe to—"

Lilith closed in. She hit him across the mouth and he yelped. She looked at her hand as though it were something divorced from her that had aroused her curiosity.

"That was overdue," Nelson said.

"She'll regret it. She—"

"I don't want you to think we're entirely dependent upon her testimony. A nurse at Garde Medical has supplied a damning description of you—complete with the camel's-hair coat now hanging in your closet. She says you wore it on the day you doctored the orange juice."

"Excuse me while I bust out crying." He overreached. "Maybe you brought her back from the dead to say it."

"Will you repeat that?"

"If you didn't get it the first time skip it. I just thought you were referring to the dead nurse I read about in the papers."

"At least we're making progress. This morning you told me that you didn't read the papers. The nurse I referred to is the one who will appear in court. She's a sensible middle-aged woman—which is probably why you didn't recognize her. Yes?"

"Yes what?"

"You had your mouth open. I was waiting for words to come out."

"You wouldn't want to hear the words I've got for you."

"You don't want to hear mine either—but I'll go on with them anyway. I'll touch on the hit-and-run first and then flash back to the poisoning. You overlooked a print on the wheel of the stolen cab. It matches one I saw you leave in this room. I lifted it and took it along for comparison after you insisted upon giving me the run of the apartment today."

He ground out a rude directive.

"Yes—I know—you were sure you'd polished the wheel clean—but oversights happen. Now to get back to the morphine. It ties in with that big deal you've been bragging about. You were yanked out of the small-time circuit to assist in the robbery of the Fromm Drug Company. That makes you an accessory to the shooting down of a night watchman and to the theft of two hundred and fifty thousand dollars' worth of assorted drugs—although with cuts and dilutions much more could be grossed. The man who masterminded the robbery went West to his connections to arrange the details of disposal. You were left with the promise of a sizable percentage and a collection of odd medicines which you had been unable to resist palming. Your foresight in thinking they might come in handy paid off. Miss Greenway took some things of Hildebrand's to the hospital—stopping here first—and you quietly placed a bottle in one of the pockets. You reasoned the police were bound to think that Hildebrand—mad as a hatter—had poisoned his nurse and killed himself. It didn't occur to you that you should have transferred the residue of morphine to a less distinctive container—one that didn't have the firm's wholesale code mark on the bottom—"

The telephone rang in the foyer. Hacket jumped at the sound. Lilith looked uncertainly at Nelson and he nodded. She seemed glad to escape from the room.

Hacket had profited by the interruption. He said, "You've been talking Greek—understand? As far as I'm concerned it's all Greek."

Nelson heard Lilith's voice at the telephone. Then he heard her steps going toward the bedroom. Then the doorbell rang and Clevis went to answer it.

Hacket produced another cigarette and lit it, watching Nelson. Nelson made no move. He was listening.

Hacket said with a fine show of hardihood, "What's the matter—run out of Greek—or did you have to send for more of your comic stooges?"

Nelson stared at him. He said, "Do you know—I doubt if you'll ever hear from Melvin Johnson—Mike Jarmon—Mort Jasper, et al."

A pulse beat visibly in Hacket's temple. He said, "Who are they—triplets?"

"No—one man—and though I hate to hurt your feelings, I think he didn't employ you for your brains. I think he knew he wouldn't risk much in the way of reprisal when he double-crossed you."

"That's what he—!"

"Yes—that's what he thought."

"Thanks for the help. That wasn't what I was going to say. My mind always wanders when I'm bored. Sometimes it even makes me give out with the kind of double talk you've been spouting." He drew hard on the cigarette. He said, "You wouldn't've by any chance—uh—been speaking to this triplet character lately?"

"Wouldn't I?"

"Listen—I—what's going on?" He twisted around and looked over the back of the chair. He looked up at the monkey face of John Lindstrom. Lindstrom, flanked by Clevis and Tilman, nodded vigorously.

Hacket yelled. "It's a lie—I never saw him before in my life—he's a liar—"

Lindstrom said in an aggrieved voice, "That's a false accusation. How could I lie when I haven't said a word?"

"I'll get a lawyer—I'll—"

"You'll get a lawyer," Nelson said. "Even though you can't afford to pay for one the courts will attend to it for you. Take him away, Clevis. If he asks to see the warrant, show it. He's a stickler for formalities."

"No you don't—" Hacket was struggling in the grip of the two detectives. "What about her? She's not going to get off—she knew all about it—she—"

"You can put that in your statement. It will receive careful study."

"Let me loose—I've got a right to pick up a few of my—"

"You can send for what you need while you're awaiting trial. To stop and pack a bag now would disturb the present occupants of your room."

"Occupants? She's got someone else in!" He was beside himself.

Nelson said, "Don't try to understand. I'm still talking Greek. Have someone call the D.A.'s office, Clevis. Say we've an airtight case." He leaned down and whispered into Clevis's outstanding ear, "We will have. The suitcase he carried to the Hildebrand house might fill in the chinks. If not, he will. Be sure to notify the men assigned that tomorrow's party is off."

He thanked Lindstrom, joined the march to the elevator, returned, and went to knock upon the bedroom door. The voice of Alix gave him permission to enter.

She was sitting on the bed. She had brushed her hair, washed her face, and applied make-up. Her hands, with the one bandaged wrist, lay peaceful in her lap.

She said, "Captain—I'm ashamed and sorry." She did not look ashamed. She looked so radiant that for a split second he was again bedeviled. She said, "Dr. Falvey just called. Lilith spoke to him. He went from here to the hospital and he's told Richard—not about this"—she looked at the bandage—"about what you said I should have told him long ago. You were right." She all but made a song of it. "He wants me—he still wants me. So please, if I've committed a crime could I—could I pay for it after Richard comes home? Now I want to go to him—"

"Crime?" Nelson said. "Anybody's razor can slip. Put your coat on. I'll drop you at the hospital."

Lilith said, "Have they gone?" She did not look ashamed or sorry or radiant. She looked frozen.

He led her back to the living room. He said, "You're to go straight to headquarters and give your statement. I'll drive you there. It will take some days to prove whether what you've said is true or false. Meanwhile it might be a good idea for you to start getting some of the practical training that was omitted from your education. In the event that you don't get it in prison I recommend a business school. You'll be surprised at how much you might enjoy standing on your own feet."

Lilith did not register joy at the proposal; nor did she, as he expected, tell him what to do with his advice. She said, "What about my brother?"

"He'll be allowed to go home with you, provided he's given his statement. Neither of you is to leave New York until further notice."

He put the two women into the car's rear seat. They said little to each other. Perhaps they had said it all in the bedroom. Once he thought that money passed between them. He grinned wryly.

At the hospital Alix got out. She took his hand and pressed it. She said, "Thank you. Please tell Nora that we'll all be together very soon." It was obvious that she was overflowing with love. She leaned through the window and kissed Lilith. She said, "Try not to worry. You couldn't help it. I'll see you tomorrow."

"Sure," Lilith said.

He drove her to headquarters. She dictated the statement in a cold clear voice. He stayed on until she had signed it, and left her there to wait for her brother. Her parting words to him were charged with irony. "I might go to business school at that—if I can blackmail someone into financing me."

He was glad to observe that she looked less frozen but hoped she would never quite become her old self. He did not stop to see how Henry Francis Hacket was faring. He trusted Clevis to attend to him. He supposed that the men assigned to Lindstrom's office buildings would accept their reprieve with mixed feelings. They would be pleased to have a free Sunday after all and disappointed not to have a hand in breaking the celebrated Fromm case. Hacket, however, without being conscious of it, might harbor some clue as to the whereabouts of Mike Jarmon, et al. If so, it would be squeezed out of him.

Driving home, he noted that the hands of the panel clock pointed to a quarter after ten. He thought that was not bad. He remembered his promise to take Junie to the zoo and hoped for fair weather tomorrow. He thought that the zoo would be a pleasant change. He would take Nora too. He would let Junie suggest it. He thought of the detective he had sent to Shenanga. He thought that if all the waste motion spent in solving a case were laid end to end it would span the world.

In spite of abridged sleep he was wide awake. He made irrelevant resolution to go to bed early, and not in the guest room. He visualized the scene between Alix and Richard Hildebrand. He saw Richard's face stripped of the pains and fears of the last few days. It looked fine. He saw the face of Alix. It looked fine too, but it was strictly for Richard. He wondered what Sammy had cooked for dinner and if there was a sizable portion of it left.

He garaged his car and vowed silently that short of a city-wide massacre it would not be used again that night. He walked the short distance to his home. It seemed to him that the rain was abating.

Kyrie lay on the sofa reading to music. She looked up from her book. Then she arose. "Grid—you do look tired."

He was surprised. "Do I? Well—everything's wrapped up."

"Good—I'm glad. Who—?"

"I'll tell you about it later. I'm all kinds of hungry."

"Sammy hasn't gone upstairs yet. I'll go and have a consultation with her."

He blocked her way. "I said all kinds of hungry."

"I don't wonder. You probably haven't eaten since tea. What am I going to do with you?"

"I'll tell you," he said.

"Oh?" She shook her head. She said firmly, "No you won't—not on an empty stomach."

THE END

DEATH OF THE PARTY

RUTH FENISONG

Chapter One

As Matt climbed the stairs to Rennie's apartment he promised himself that it would be the last time. This was routine procedure. So was his rehearsal of the parting speech which he intended to deliver in a gentle but firm voice. "I'm thinking only of you, Rennie. I have nothing to offer and I won't have for years. Our one sensible course is to make a clean break. This sort of thing might be all right for some girls—but not for you. It—it's—" His mind always balked at the word "sordid." It was impossible to apply it to anything connected with Rennie even though she lived in a run-down house in a run-down neighborhood and was carrying on a run-of-the-mill affair with a pinchpenny factory worker.

He halted on the second landing to let someone pass. Snow had melted on the collar of his shabby overcoat and was trickling down the back of his neck. Squirming, he thought angrily, But it isn't a run-of-the-mill affair. That's a big lie.

The rest of it was a big lie too. He was not thinking only of Rennie. He was thinking only of himself.

His status of factory worker was temporary, merely a part of the stretch toward goal. In order to reach that goal he had to follow a straight road, and no vistas to the right or the left must be permitted to halt him. Yet if, as he had been led to believe, women held love above all else, how could he tell Rennie that ambition came first?

Three nights a week he went to school. The other nights should have been devoted to study, but two of them he spent with her. And the days that followed those nights doubled in length, and as likely as not the foreman caught him dozing over his machine. If he lost his job he could find another, but until he did, time and money would be squandered. A family crisis had cut short his formal training as a physicist. With the crisis finally resolved, he had decided not to return to the university until he had paid the debts incurred and saved money enough to insure his energies against being dissipated in outside chores. He supposed that a wife and children might come later as by-products of success. Now they could be nothing but obstacles.

He heard a door on the second landing open. Rennie called, "Matt?" and he said, "Yes." He began to climb again, picturing her before he saw her, steeling himself so that the actuality would not puncture his resolution. It was tonight or never, he thought. If he put it off any longer it would be never. So it had to be tonight. He would throw out all of that prepared stuff and say whatever came spontaneously. The important thing was to say "Good-by" and make it stick.

The narrow doorway framed her. She had a small beautiful body and a small alert face. She had eyes that lighted the dim hall.

He did not mean to kiss her. A kiss was no fitting prelude to a farewell scene. It should come at the closing, if at all. And then it should be no more than a token demonstration to show that there was no hard feeling on either side. He kissed her because he could not help it. He sniffed her dark sweet-smelling hair and set his lips to her sweet wide mouth. She clung to him for a moment. When she freed herself he braced his jellied knees and followed her into the apartment, his mind and body pulling in opposite directions.

She took his hat. She hung his wet coat on the shower rod in the bathroom. The whole of the apartment could be seen at a glance. Mainly it was a rectangle broken by doors: the hall door, the closet door, the bathroom door, and the door to the kitchenette. It had a gate-legged table, a bookshelf, a lamp, two straight chairs, a chest of drawers, a studio couch, and a radio on an end table. Sometimes it even had a vase of flowers. It looked all right when Rennie was in it. When she was not, it looked like what it was, a furnished room for a tenant in the low-income bracket.

He sat down weakly on the couch. He picked up the newspaper she had bought, read a few headlines, and put it back on the end table. His interest in news was generally limited to items concerning science. A moment too late he realized that a straight chair would suit the occasion better. Rennie came from the bathroom before he could shift without making a point of it.

"Are you hungry?" she said.

He was always a little hungry because meals were so carefully budgeted. "No," he said, "I ate in the cafeteria." He had told her that he was putting in overtime at the factory so that she would not have to share her food with him. Lately he had been troubled by the thought that she was depriving herself and that she looked peaked. That was one of the excuses he had used to postpone the evil hour.

"I bought you a shirt and two sets of underwear and two pairs of socks," she said. "It's a present. They had a sale."

"Thanks—it's present enough that you bought them. Does this cover it?" He took a ten-dollar bill from his wallet. That left it quite flat.

"And then some," she said. She went to her purse and gave him bills and coins in exchange. "I told you it was a sale. I'll make some coffee. In a blizzard like this there can't be too many hot drinks."

"Don't bother about the coffee, Rennie. Sit down."

"I want it myself." She left the door of the kitchenette open. He watched her as she measured coffee into the drip pot, set the kettle of water upon the stove, and cut slabs from a Dundee cake.

She said over her shoulder, "Why don't you take your shoes off? They must be wet."

"I didn't do much walking—just from the subway." A better opening might not occur. He said soundlessly, I'll keep my shoes on because I'm not staying—not tonight or any night. He said aloud, "Rennie—" and was stopped by the clink of breaking china. "What was that?"

"I dropped a cup."

"I'll pick up the pieces." He started to rise.

"Stay where you are."

"But you might cut yourself."

"I deserve to cut myself. I'm a clumsy idiot."

"You? That's the first awkward move I've seen you make."

"How little we know about each other," she said. She kicked at one of the fragments.

The words and the petulant act were unlike her. He wondered fleetingly if his state of mind could possibly have been communicated.

"Temper," she said. "Sorry. I'll sweep them into a dustpan later."

He answered absently, "I'll do it before I leave."

"Oh sure. I can just see you stumbling out of a sound sleep to tidy the kitchen."

That was his second opportunity. He let it pass. She was facing him with the laden tray in her hands. He got up and took it from her. He set it down on the gate-legged table and said, "The coffee smells too good to take chances with."

"That's right—rub it in."

They sat opposite each other. Surely it was a reflection of his own guilt that made her smile seem forced, her face too pale. He cursed his conscience for making high opera of a situation that countless other men took in stride. He said, "Isn't that lamp casting a sicker light than usual?"

"I put in a new bulb yesterday. It must be your imagination." Coffee slopped into the saucer as she poured it, and she passed the cup to him without appearing to notice.

By no stretch of the imagination was that par for her. He said explosively, "What's wrong, Rennie?"

"Wrong?"

"You heard me. Is the job getting you down?"

"Of course not. The job's fun—sometimes."

"But not today?"

"Today wasn't much fun."

"I thought so. Look, Rennie—"

As though she took the command literally, she fixed her eyes upon him.

"What I never could understand," he said, "is why you chose to work in that cheap department store. You're fairly well educated. You could—"

"I don't say 'like a cigarette should' is what you mean. Drink your coffee." She transferred her stare to his cup. "Did I do that? I'll get you a clean saucer."

"Never mind. Let's keep to the subject." He blotted the saucer with a paper napkin. He drank and said, "There must be plenty of jobs you could do that wouldn't take so much out of you physically. You're intelligent enough to—"

"What makes you think so?" Her voice was so brittle that he hardly recognized it. "Our relationship hasn't exactly been an exchange of ideas."

It was true. In the six months since their first meeting little time had been spent in serious conversation. She knew that he wanted to be a physicist, and he knew that she had come to New York to escape a domineering father. That was about all. Sometimes, motivated by an impulse to prove his worth, he had tried to translate his background and his hopes, but usually she stopped him. "Let's not dig back into our pasts or worry about our futures. If we do we might break the spell of now." Her lack of interest had deflated him and he had renewed his ego in the one sure way. Almost all that they knew of each other had been learned by touch.

"But now that we've arrived at the old-unmarried-couple stage," she said, "why should I withhold anything from you? The sad fact is that I've had no practical training. I can't type or take shorthand—I'm too untalented to be an actress—and too small to be a model."

"For Pete's sake! Were your parents raising you to be a lady or what? People shouldn't have kids unless they're prepared to give them the tools needed to face this world."

She said stiffly, "No doubt you're right."

"Rennie—quit it."

"Quit what?"

"Acting this way."

"What way?"

"Like a—like an actress." He tried to make a joke of it. "Maybe you could be one. Maybe you have a hidden talent—"

"It won't stay hidden long."

He said uncertainly, "I shouldn't have criticized your parents. It's just that I don't like to think of you wearing yourself out behind a counter." What he meant was that he might have felt more comfortable about leaving her if she did not have to stand on her slim feet all day with nothing to anticipate but coming home to a lonely flat. And it would be lonely. Aside from her father and the people in the department store, she had never mentioned the existence of friends or relatives, male or female. Nor had she offered any explanation for the singular lack of attachments in her life. Perhaps, he thought with belated understanding, she had refused his confidences because she might be expected to return them.

"Haven't you any ambition?" he said. "I'm not against selling if that's what you want to do—but why pick a Fourteenth Street dump when one of the better stores would jump at you? Where do you expect to get—taking all kinds of guff from all kinds of people who don't know their own minds?"

"Who does?" At his puzzled look she added, "Know his own mind?"

"I do." Or do I? he thought.

"As for ambition," she said, "I don't suppose I have any—not in terms that you could understand."

"Try me." It was ironical that on the verge of bowing out he should be so eager to know more about her.

"My aims are not so grand as yours. I'm not a budding scientist. I'm just—just—" She began to laugh.

"What's funny?"

The laughter choked her. It brought tears to her eyes. They overflowed and nothing was funny.

That settled it. He was all she had. He could not do what he had come to do, not while she was down. Confused, he thought, If this is weakness make the most of it, and got up and went to give her comfort.

She edged away from his reaching arms. "B-budding," she said, "just budding—that's me. I've thought of a hundred ways to tell you. I've even thought of not telling you. The weather's right for melodrama—isn't it? A blinding snowstorm and a fallen woman trudging through it in search of some secret place to hide her shame."

His throat felt rough. He scraped it with a sharp cough. He said, "It's impossible."

She choked again. "It couldn't be done and she did it." Her chair almost toppled as she thrust it back. She sped around him to the chest of drawers and rummaged for a handkerchief. She mopped and blew before she turned to face him. "You made me admit that today wasn't fun—and how right you were. I spent my noon hour in a doctor's office—with a Woolworth ring on my finger just in case. And it was 'in case.'"

He said nothing aloud. Deep inside he carried on a zany conversation with himself.

She threw brittle words at him. "You ought to take your expression to a lab. I'll bet it has emotions unknown to science."

His voice sounded rusty. "Isn't—couldn't the doctor have been mistaken?"

"He says not. He says it's gone far enough to be certain."

"Did you have to wait until—?" He bit his lip.

She stared at him. She said, "I wasn't particularly worried at first. I thought the cold I'd had might have delayed me. That can happen. Then I began to take stuff that one of the girls at the store recommended. She swore it had worked for her but it—"

"You little fool—don't you know things like that are never any good?"

She said aloofly, "Be tolerant of me. I haven't had much experience."

"You could have made yourself deathly sick—"

"Oh."

He wondered what the sudden smile was doing on her lips. He attempted to analyze his emotions without benefit of a lab and met with signal failure. Since he was no longer free to walk out, surely it could not be relief that kept isolating itself and floating to the surface. How could relief figure in anything that meant indefinite delay or even a full stop to his career? But there was still a way. The obliging girl in the store might know of a—

In a blinding flash he saw an ugly illicit scene as Hogarth might have engraved it. He closed his eyes to shut it out. He opened them and there was Rennie with that smile wavering on her lips, and over his dead body would one of those dirty-handed murderers touch her.

He said flatly, "We'll have to get married."

Her smile vanished. "Have to?"

"Of course. I've saved money—enough to take care of—"

"Keep saving it," she said. "There's no 'have to' and there's no 'of course.'"

He thought that she was too upset to understand. "You poor kid—did you think I'd run out on you?"

"I don't know what I thought."

He wanted to bring the smile back. He would have taken her in his arms, but her small set face held him off. "Rennie—listen to me—naturally you're mixed up—it must have been a hell of a shock—but you can stop worrying. It's my responsibility and I'm ready to—"

"Be quiet." There were ways of saying it. Her way was unmistakably hostile.

"Now see here—"

"I appreciate your readiness to offer the big sacrifice," she said. "So sorry I can't accept."

"I hope you know what you're talking about." He was trying to make all due allowances, but he could not keep the injury out of his voice. "I can't do anything more than—"

"No—you can't do anything more," she said, "and it may surprise you to learn that nothing you did in the first place gives you the right to gallop to the rescue."

"I don't get it. You can't be hinting that—"

"You don't get anything. I was referring to you and your responsibility. Can you really believe I'm some wretched little weakling who was unable to resist your manly charms? I really hate to disillusion you—and wouldn't if your ego wasn't strong enough to make immediate recovery—but if there was seduction done I did it—not you. On the day we met I would have settled for anybody—that's the sort of mood I was in. After all, you couldn't call it a romantic meeting—could you? A Social Security office where we swapped brilliant observations about the weather while we waited for cards that would permit us to labor for our board and keep. I'll go so far as to say that I didn't exactly find you repulsive, but it wouldn't have mattered if I had—so now you know."

He translated his urge to do her violence into shouted words. "Too bad the pickings that day were so slim for both of us." By the look of her she would have preferred violence. She said tiredly, "Act three—curtain."

"Who am I to argue with the director of this piece?" But as he said it reason returned to unclench his hands and clear his darkened face. He saw where the trouble lay and tried to remedy it. "Rennie—I know you didn't mean what you said—and you know I didn't. Let's start again. I *want* to marry you. If I sounded any other way it's because I was knocked off base."

She arose and started to clear the table. She said with no more than casual interest, "Why do you want to marry me?"

He took a step toward her, his arms outstretched. The cups and saucers in her hands blocked him.

She shook her head. "That's the answer I expected—but unfortunately it comes with no guarantee against normal wear and tear."

He dropped his arms. "Are we discussing merchandise—or what? Put those dishes down."

She carried them to the kitchenette. She set them in the sink and turned on the water.

"Rennie—do you have to do that now?"

She might not have heard. She turned off the water and said, "Is it still snowing?"

He walked to the window and raised the blind. He stared unseeingly at the white flakes swirling into the court. He said, "It's not too bad."

She came out of the kitchenette. "Then you won't mind going home."

He turned. He studied her briefly, shrugged, and strode the few paces to the bathroom. He pulled on the light above the washbasin and was confronted by his reflection. At some stage of the proceedings he had upended his fair hair. Otherwise he looked the same. His face was like rough stone sculpture from brow to strong jaw. It needed a shave. He scowled at it because it had not had the decency to age in the past hour. He retrieved his shabby coat and put it on. When he came out, shapeless old hat in hand, Rennie was sitting on the couch, busily reading the newspaper.

He said in a melodramatic voice, "So I'm the one who's being cast out into the snow."

She dropped the newspaper. She said politely, "Forgive me for not seeing you to the door. Please leave your key as you go out."

"That would be inconsiderate of me. You might be asleep when I get back."

"You're not coming back."

"Yes, I am. I'm only going for a long walk to give you time to unravel yourself." Her manner was such an odd combination of militancy and defenselessness that although he had nothing to laugh about he almost laughed. "Anything you'd like me to bring? Cigarettes—ice cream—pickles?"

"Luckily," she said, "I can't be more revolted than I am. The sooner you go, the sooner I can bolt the door."

He thought that it was giving her a bit of trouble to keep her mouth straight. He said, "Bolt it—but slide the bolt back gently when I knock. We wouldn't want to disturb the neighbors." He made what he considered to be a jaunty exit.

Chapter Two

As soon as he reached the sidewalk his air of nonchalance fled. From every standpoint it was a rotten night. He had given Rennie his weather report without sufficient evidence. The snow was thick underfoot. It fell steadily, supplying endless ammunition for a sharp-shooting wind that aimed straight at him. He turned up his frayed coat collar and tugged his hat as low as it would go.

In the snug flat it had seemed man-of-the-world wisdom to give Rennie a little while to regain her good sense. Now it seemed folly. He had said he would take a long walk. But who in his right mind would take a long walk on such a night? He should have said, "Sleep on it. I'll see you tomorrow." Then he could have gone back to Brooklyn instead of practically asking for pneumonia.

He headed east, trying to use his external misery as a cover for the war that waged inside. He cursed the thrift that had made him stave off having his shoes resoled and kept him from buying gloves. The reason for that thrift had vanished, to be replaced by something far removed from reason. He had played one hell of a joke upon himself.

And a hell of a wife and mother Rennie was going to be. It meant nothing to her that he wore no overshoes or that his hands were chapped. He thrust them into his pockets. Her thoughtlessness did not bode well for the kid. He would be the one who saw to it that the kid was wrapped up warm. His kid. Slowly the real battle came into the open.

She wanted me to get down on my knees and say "I love you." She got pretty sarcastic with that "big sacrifice" stuff. But it is a big sacrifice. Besides—how could she expect me to say "I love you" in cold blood?

It occurred to him then that if it could not be said in cold blood it meant nothing. By way of experiment he said loudly, "I love you, Rennie. I love you."

The wind flung it back to his stinging ears and it rang true. A pedestrian plodding a few yards behind him came to a dead stop.

Matt was unaware that anyone shared the street with him. He had received a stunning revelation.

He thought foolishly, And me so sure it was only good old sex. No wonder it couldn't be handled with the "So long—nice knowing you" routine.

He very nearly turned to run back to her. But he did not want to make any more mistakes. She's not going to believe I was hit by a bolt of lightning. What she'll probably think is that it's too cold out for me. I must go easy—find exactly the right equation to cancel that pompous nit-witted performance.

He remembered a bar on the west side of Seventh Avenue that he had often passed but never entered. He would enter it tonight. The thought of warmth inside and out quickened his stride. A drink was definitely in order to celebrate his coming marriage. Why not? Other young couples had managed the simultaneous building of a family and a career. But even as he reached for assurance, worry creased his forehead.

Glumly he went over in his mind an article he had read in the Sunday *Times*. It had stated that mathematics and physics were a young man's field, and that as a general rule if a man had not made his mark in that field before the age of thirty the betting was strongly against his ever making it. The article, written by Norbert Wiener, had gone on to say that at twenty-five the apprenticeship should be completed and the journeymanship begun, with the master years to follow in short order. The writer pointed out that under the best of circumstances there was little time to develop since the work involved the athleticism of an intellect in its peak years, and therefore an early start was more valuable than massed experience.

Matt's outthrust jaw seemed to hold the strength and temper of a cold chisel. He was twenty-three. All right—he was twenty-three. He would be the exception to the rule. Nothing so drastic was involved, just sticking to his factory job until he had fattened his savings sufficiently to provide for Rennie's support as well as his own. Even in the factory he was picking up useful pointers on automation. He did not intend to make that his field, but it was bound to come in handy. And adding practical experience to the credits he was earning at night school, the future did not look too grim.

He told himself that he had much to be thankful for. Not if he searched the world over could he find a less demanding girl than Rennie. The house in which she lived with apparent happiness proved her indifference to her surroundings. Lucky for him that she was not the spoiled daughter of wealthy parents. When the time came to return to the university he could rent the cheapest possible lodgings near it, and she would not mind in the least. Perhaps he might get a second chance at the scholarship that had been offered to him when his father met with the accident. Of course, after the hospital bill was met, he would have to set aside a sum for the kid's upkeep; food and clothing and here and there a doctor bill since even healthy kids needed professional care. Rennie's own needs seemed negligible. So far as he knew, she had not bought a new dress during the entire period of their relationship. Sometimes when he went for a walk with her she would stop to gaze at the shopwindow of a fancy store, and although he was ignorant of such matters, in his opinion her clothes compared favorably with those on display. Whether he was right or wrong about that, not once had he heard her complain because she could do no more than gaze. She seemed devoid of discontent and frustration, and she did not spin the fantasies of someday having money to burn what were common to many girls who worked for a living. All to the good, he thought, as was her confessed lack of ambition, which left her entirely free to share his.

He had reached Seventh Avenue. He started to cross to the bar on the opposite corner. Midway he changed his mind. What was the matter with him? What kind of celebration would that be? The thing was to buy a bottle of wine to share with Rennie. The wine would speak for him, show her how he felt. Maybe champagne. It did not have to be imported, and he could while away almost as much time in making his selection as he would have spent nursing a drink in the bar. No need to cross for a liquor store. There were several on this side of the avenue.

He made an about-face. Someone gave a warning shout in the moment before he dropped to his hands and knees and then lay sprawling on the snow-packed asphalt.

Above him he heard voices. A man said comfortingly, "The lights were with you, lady. It wasn't your fault."

"I tried to avoid him—"

"Sure you did. He had no business being there in the first place."

He said to himself, This isn't your night. Get up, you dope. And he gathered his limbs to obey the injunction.

A stocky shape bending over him said, "Maybe you ought to stay put, bud—till we raise a cop."

"I'm all right." I must be, he thought absurdly, because the fall didn't even knock my hat off. He muttered, "I wasn't hit by the car. I just slipped trying to dodge it."

"Well—if you say so. Here—I'll give you a hand."

The helpful bystander led him to the sidewalk. He was able to stand there quite firmly in spite of the fact that his legs felt a bit slack.

His repeated assertion that he had suffered no injury dispersed a thwarted group of excitement hunters. Traffic, momentarily arrested, resumed its course, the Samaritan faded out of the picture, and so far as the victim was concerned the incident was ended. This was not the case with the woman driver.

Still a little shaken, he wished that she would call it a night. She had pulled the car over to the curb and was insisting that he get in beside her.

"You'd better not walk," she said. "You might be hurt without realizing it. I'll drive you home."

"I'm not going home."

She said persistently, "I'll take you wherever you're going."

All he wanted was to find a sheltered place where he could explore the extent of the damage, not to his person, but to his pants. In dusting off and readjusting his flapping overcoat he had been disturbed by currents of air that should have been excluded by material.

He said with ill grace, "If you're afraid I'll change my mind later and sue, forget ft. I haven't even bothered to get your license number."

That only made her more persistent. "It's for my own peace of mind," she said, and leaned over to hold the car door open.

A passing drunk paused to advise him. "Patch up the tiff, brother. Don't play hard to get when she's sticking her mouth out at you." He came close to peer at Matt with bleary eyes. "Down on your luck, eh? Well—take my word for it, pride don't pay. Sell it while you got a customer."

Sensitive to the possibilities of drawing a second crowd, Matt glanced apprehensively at a few people on the corner waiting for the lights to change, nodded to the woman, and started to walk away. Both the car and the drunk followed. The drunk, trying to grab a handful of his overcoat, was the greater evil. With a groan of exasperation Matt fended him off and made such a fast dive for the car that the bridge of his nose struck the low hood.

The latest blow brought tears to his eyes. He growled, "Anything for a quick getaway," and slammed the door hard.

She made a quick getaway, and for the first few minutes he leaned back against the upholstery, just glad to be out of the wind. His knees felt sore, and so did the palms of his hands. Friction burns, he thought. Probably cinders scattered to prevent slipping. A fat lot of good they did me. Exploring furtively, he discovered the source of the air currents. No wonder his knees hurt. There were rents in the worn cloth over both of them.

Without turning her head the woman said, "Lean back again. Your nose is starting to bleed."

That was the crowning indignity. He was conscious of the warm gush in his nostrils as she spoke. He pulled out a handkerchief and applied it. He thought savagely, I couldn't have cooked up more of a mess for Rennie if I'd worked at it. I'll scare her out of her wits.

His room in Brooklyn had been picked for its convenience to the factory. If he went there to make himself presentable it would be hours before he could get back. Rennie had no telephone. She would think he had taken her at her word and deserted.

He craned for a glimpse of his face in the rear-view mirror. He could not see much under the jammed-down hat. The wadded bloody handkerchief was no help either. But what he did see was nothing to show to Rennie. Were those scratches on his cheek—or smears? Only a good wash would tell, and the chances were that he would get short shrift in a drugstore if he asked to use the lav after investing a few cents in iodine. Looking as he did, he'd be classified as a tramp wanting in from the cold. But there were public washrooms in Grand Central or Penn Station where a coin would buy a private cubicle supplied with towels and soap. He might even wangle a needle and thread from an attendant. The whole operation, including the subway back, could be done in well under an hour.

He said through the handkerchief, "If it isn't out of your way would you drop me at Penn Station?"

"Do you plan to spend the night there?"

He had no immediate reaction to the question, but there was something in her tone that he did not like. He had taken no notice of her appearance while he stood on the street trying to get rid of her, and he could not make much of it now. She was burrowing into a fur coat, and she wore a kind of nun's wimple arrangement that hid her hair completely and presented him with hardly anything more than a view of a short straight nose. Not that he wanted anything more if the perfume she used was an indication. He disliked perfume unless it was mixed with Rennie. In the closed car this brand smelled like a tropical jungle.

"I'm sorry," she said. "I didn't mean to pry—but that drunken man was right, you know. Pride doesn't pay."

Delayed reaction caught up with him. Lady Bountiful in person. She thought he *was* a tramp—that he had not asked her to drive him home because he had no home. He was amused, but sourly. He said, "They have cops in the station who keep an eye out for sleeping bums."

She made the clicking sounds of sympathy.

"Also," he said, keeping his voice level, "I could be going to the station to catch a train."

"Are you?"

"No." He took the handkerchief from his nose and stared at it. Only a spurt, he thought, caused by that collision with the hood—and it wouldn't have happened if she wasn't such an officious number. He spoke with deliberate crudeness to pay her back for her presumptuousness. "Dames should be careful about picking up characters like me. They could get into bad trouble."

The sound of her caught breath gave him a mean satisfaction, but she said calmly enough, "That might be true on a lonely country road. It's no risk with so many people around."

Automatically he looked out of the window. He wondered stupidly when and where she had cut across to join the crawling traffic on Fifth Avenue. "Penn Station is west," he said, "so I guess you're not going my way after all. Just drop me off at the next corner." He tried to read the street number. It was veiled in snow. Ninth or Tenth Street, he guessed.

"Is that clock on the dashboard right?" he said.

"Yes—it's right."

It was five after ten. It seemed impossible that he had left Rennie less than three quarters of an hour ago.

She stopped before they reached the next corner. A car, parked near the entrance of a modern apartment building, pulled out. She wheeled neatly into the space it had vacated.

He was trying to decide whether it would be quicker to take a bus or to walk to the subway on Sixth Avenue. With his hand on the door release he said, "You didn't have to park. If I tried hard I could have made the sidewalk without getting knocked down." Then he was ashamed of his ill humor. She had only meant to be a do-gooder. "Well—good night—and thanks."

She too was out of the car. She caught his arm and said, "Wait—"

He said some of the words that had been intended for Rennie. "Let's face it—we've got to part—cruel as it may seem."

"You're coming in with me," she said. "Undoubtedly you can use a drink—and certainly you can use a pair of trousers to replace your torn ones. After that we'll see." She sounded desperate.

We will—will we? he thought. So she hadn't missed a move he'd made in the car. In the nick of time he stopped himself from giving a good tug to dislodge the fingers that clung to his arm. If she lived here she had a bathroom and there would be no need to go to Penn Station. He might even accept the trousers and mail them back to her. He said with the vague idea of not sailing under false pretenses, "Can I get washed up?"

"Yes—you'll find what you need, including disinfectant."

He did not know if she meant disinfectant for the unsavory person of a tramp or for his wounds. He did not care. Obviously she was in worse straits than he to have extended the invitation at all. Trousers fine. Disinfectant fine. As for the rest of what she had to offer, No ma'am, and thank you kindly.

She steered him away from the main entrance of the building to a separate door raised from the sidewalk by three short steps. Over it was set the small bronze equivalent of a shingle.

He hung back. "Isn't this a doctor's office?"

"Yes."

Rapidly he revised his estimate of her. "I don't need a doctor—anyway he won't be in—they don't sleep in these places—they have daytime office hours—"

"Ordinarily he wouldn't be here. He is tonight." She was twisting the doorknob. A soft chime sounded as the door yielded. Voices and hi-fi music came from behind another door to the right of the entry.

"Come along," she said.

He crossed the threshold and heard the committing click as the outer door closed behind him. He thought that either the doctor was throwing a party or that music was part of his therapy. He took off his hat and muttered, "Look—it sounds busy in there. I don't want to tear him away from anything. Just point out the bathroom to me and—"

She hesitated. She whispered, "I didn't realize how young you are."

He could not return the compliment, so he said nothing. Her eyesight was evidently a lot better than his. In the dim light of the entry she was little more than a fur coat and a wimple.

She was gesturing toward a third door. She whispered, "Through there—you'll come out on a hall. It's the first door on the left."

"Are you sure it's all right for me to—?"

"Yes—I'll explain to the doctor. Good night."

She seemed to have forgotten the matter of the trousers. In fact she seemed as anxious now to be rid of him as she had been to detain him. Well, he could hide the rents from Rennie until everything else was mended between them. "Thanks," he said, "and thank him too. I'll sneak out quietly."

He went through an office containing a desk, a metal typewriting table on wheels, filing cabinets, and several chairs. All had a look of newness. Sniffing fresh paint, he wondered if the doctor was new as well.

The hall beyond the office was dark. He stepped into the first room on the left, fumbling for and finding a wall switch.

The overhead light was strong. It blinded him for a moment. When his eyes had adjusted he saw cabinets stocked with drugs, instruments, and clinical receptacles; a diathermy machine, a small sink, and a series of shelves bearing towels and white hospital gowns.

The examining room, he thought. She got the layout wrong. The examining table looked more used than the rest of the equipment because a patient was sleeping on it.

Matt said, "Excuse me," and went into reverse. At once he was prompted to move forward again. Screwy that anyone should be sleeping on that hard thing unless he'd had too much to drink—or unless—unless—unless—!

He was at the table, leaning over it. He was staring into the sightless eyes of a dead man.

Chapter Three

The eyes and the crusting blood at the mouth's corners told the story. The short straight knife skewering tie to shirt was redundant. Matt's hand shot forward to pluck it out. A whisper of caution stopped him. Don't touch. Don't touch anything!

In the space of seconds he passed through a series of stages: shock, curiosity, and a primitive fear that urged him to flee the room, the building, the neighborhood. That portion of universal guilt that most men taste in the presence of crime was active within him.

His reason tried to gain the upper hand. The woman knew him to be on the premises. Therefore his flight would be suspect.

A hum of talk and music drifted back to him. Was one of the occupants of the front room a murderer? The doctor himself? Or was this the doctor wearing a scalpel for a tie pin?

It did not seem plausible, but he would take no chances. Before he faced anyone he would call the police. That was the law.

The man looked small in death, and old. Violence had barely ruffled his sparse gray hair. His popping stare was hypnotic. Matt had to tear his own eyes away. He was sweating. He noted this in passing and longed to be out in the bitter cold again.

He went back to the office where the new telephone waited on the new desk. He did not stop. His feet, obeying no conscious impulse, carried him on to the dim entry hall.

If there had been free choice before, that was where it ended. The door to the right of the entry opened and he was confronted by a short burly figure swaddled for the street. Looking past him, Matt saw a seated group; all men.

The burly figure started at the sight of Matt, recovered, and said loudly, "What have we here?"

His voice brought the group to attention. One of its number arose, set down his highball glass, and turned off the record player. The lamps in the room rayed out to brighten the entry. Matt blinked in the sudden spotlight and drew the bloodstained handkerchief from his pocket to dry his face. He said, "We have plenty."

The group of men swarmed toward him. There were five or six of them, each a well-groomed citizen who could afford to be contemptuous of outsiders.

"Which of you is the doctor?" Matt said. He had not intended belligerence, but they were crowding him.

The burly man said unpleasantly, "So you're here to consult the doctor—are you?—recommended, I'm sure, by a grateful patient—" He left no chink between his sentences for affirmation or denial. "Dream up another tall tale fast. The doctor has never practiced—and won't start until tomorrow."

Matt took quick estimate of the round red face and said without hope of reaching whatever intelligence might live behind it, "Didn't she tell you?"

A rangy man with a haughty cynical face raised an eyebrow. "She?"

One who seemed younger than the rest of the swarm detached himself and said in bedside tones, "I'm Dr. Stewart. Can I help you?"

"You'd better get ready to help yourself—unless there's a simple explanation for the corpse on your table." The moment he said it, a simple explanation occurred to him. He was not familiar with New York police procedure, but back home the old general practitioner was also the coroner and had been known to perform an autopsy in his basement. He said, "You don't happen to be a police surgeon? I mean, did they send you a—?"

The doctor's blank face told him that he had not scored.

The reaction of the others was quicker. Someone had sneaked behind him to pinion his arms. He gave a low protesting growl and began to struggle. A free-for-all resulted. The well-groomed citizens had been transformed into an angry mob. His nose began to bleed again. There was a doctor in the house, but the doctor was busy, trying ineffectually to restore the mob to guest status. If that was a sample of the way he worked, Matt had no faith in him.

He had managed to wrench his arms free. He flayed about with them, but he was outnumbered. The rangy sportsman type sent him spinning across the threshold of the room, where he made contact with the upholstery of a chair. Someone said, "Attaboy, Rolfie," and the sportsman took a bow.

Two of the company guarded Matt while the rest trooped back to the examining room. Presently the guard changed and he took advantage of the general excitement to reach for a highball glass near his chair. The strong drink had been merely splashed with soda. He gulped it down and grimaced and thought that they could have afforded better whiskey, but it helped him to sit out the pointless talk around him.

"Who the hell left the front door open?"

"Hackett was supposed to be the last one to— I mean we thought he went out."

"He's out all right. Permanently."

"Poor old Gene—I can't believe it—leaving early because he had to catch a train—" The speaker looked like a king-sized mouse.

"He caught something, Stanley. I don't understand—"

A bronzed playboy type said, "Nothing to understand. Just as he opened the door it hit him that he wanted the john—so he went back—"

"And that left the way clear for this bird."

Reminded of their prisoner, one of them shook a fist at Matt and actually said, "Come clean if you know what's good for you."

The bromide received uncritical support. With the exception of the doctor, who was calling the police, all made menacing sounds.

"You thought the place would be empty—"

"You were after drugs—weren't you?"

"What surprises me is that it doesn't happen oftener. These separate entrances are a cinch. No doorman to—"

"You couldn't let it go at breaking and entering you—"

Someone said judicially, "Now wait a minute. We've got to be fair." He nodded at the playboy type. "If Palmer's theory is correct and poor Gene left the door open while he went to the john, it isn't a case of breaking and entering."

"Technicalities be damned—it's a case of murder."

Matt was yanked from the chair. "Talk—you son of a bitch."

He pushed at the too-close red face with spread fingers and the burly man backed away. He was tired of being manhandled. He noted with whiskey-flavored pleasure a discoloration on the rangy character's cheek. It meant that at least one of his random blows in the entry had struck home. He flexed muscles he did not know he had in preparation for another free-for-all. The doctor forestalled it by returning to the room.

The doctor made an unnecessary announcement. "I'm afraid no one can leave until the police arrive."

Matt was beginning to sort out his enemies. The one with the judicial accents had a melon-shaped head and a melon-shaped paunch. They called him Frederick—or Fredericks. He was consulting his watch. He said, "The call is put through to the Communications Bureau at Spring 7-3100, where an announcer notifies the nearest radio car. It should arrive any minute."

For confirmation, two stalwarts tramped into the room, warded off a deluge of gratuitous theory and information, and backed out to pay a visit to the corpse. The one who came back to stand in the front room's doorway had weary eyes that conferred upon each unit of the group exactly the same amount of suspicion. To Matt, the group's sore thumb, he seemed an unbiased soul.

The burly man stepped into the uneasy silence. "You got here soon enough, officer. I'll grant you that—but why rest on your laurels?" He pointed at Matt. "With the exception of this hoodlum who entered unlawfully and when intercepted tried to fob us off with a ridiculous cock-and-bull story which I'll come back to presently—we're all ready to give an account of ourselves. My name is Callender—Henry C. Callender." Again he left no space between his words for insertion. "The other gentlemen and I want to keep Dr. Stewart out of this. Aside from our grief at the untimely death of Eugene Hackett, that is our main concern. Dave is the son of one of our late and valued friends and we regard him as a protégé. Nothing must interfere with his career—but fortunately we are not without influence—"

Here the radio policeman took advantage of the slight meaningful pause. "Look, mister—"

Henry C. Callender overrode him. "The truth is, we can't help feeling a measure of responsibility for the way an innocent gesture of fellowship turned out. Dr. Stewart has just been qualified. He moved into these offices today with the intention of starting his practice tomorrow. In addition to providing his equipment, we decided to launch him with a surprise celebration. He was here making sure that everything was shipshape for the reception of his first patient when we barged in. Naturally we didn't count upon any such tragic outcome and you can well understand that if it isn't handled discreetly—"

It was the re-entrance of the second policeman that halted Henry C. Callender. "I guess they're having a job to raise the precinct 'lieut,'" he said. His eyes toured the room and came to a definite pause when they reached Matt. He began a low-voiced exchange with his partner.

Callender said loudly, "I hesitate to tell either of you officers your business, but wouldn't it expedite matters if one of you took down our statements? I've already given a good part of mine and I don't want to have to go through it unnecessarily—"

The second policeman waded in fast. "My advice is, don't waste your breath on us. We're not detectives. Our radio car was a couple of streets away when the word went out from the 'trouble turret.' All we're here for is to check if your call was or wasn't a hoax and report back—which I just did. The real parade hasn't started yet."

"Why didn't you say so instead of—"

Matt did not follow the rest of Callender's monologue. The euphoric effect of the drink was wearing thin. He got out of his chair and no one pushed him back into it. He edged over to the least inimical-looking man in the room, the one who suggested an eyeglassed Rotarian mouse. He said desperately, "That woman must have mentioned how I came to be here—"

The man averted his head as though the sight of Matt were more than he could bear.

"Look," Matt said, "if she didn't explain she didn't—but at least tell me her name and where she lives—"

The man put distance between them, moving gingerly, as though he were skirting a midden.

Matt was still in the dark as to the identity of his furred and wimpled nemesis when the parade started.

It marched in without fanfare or special order. There were representatives from the medical examiner's office, from the local precinct, from the Homicide Squad, from the Bureau of Criminal Identification, and from the office of the district attorney, all too intent upon upholding the standards of their departments to bother about the spectators. Henry C. Callender, roped off with the rest, had to bide his time until the fingerprint powders, the camel's-hair brushes, the feather dusters, the magnifying glasses, and the photographic equipment had been restored to their portable cases.

The departure of the technicians and the removal of the corpse to the morgue left a lieutenant and two detectives from the precinct, a contingent from Homicide West, complete with a squad stenographer, and an assistant from the D.A.'s office. Matt thought somberly that it had been a pretty good showing, considering the hour. Even more somberly he wondered what Rennie would be thinking.

His respect for the city's processes decreased when the assistant D.A. and the melon-shaped party recognized each other with mutual expressions of delight. It developed that they were members of the same club and they indulged in light chitchat, which was interrupted by a man who seemed to be the brass of the homicide contingent. He had crisp curly white hair over a sane personable face. He was addressed as Captain Nelson, and at a few words from him the precinct lieutenant opened the meeting.

"To expedite matters," he said, "you can give your names and addresses and occupations to the stenographer. Then we'll take your individual statements inside where there's a desk."

After this information had been recorded, the doctor was the first to be called to the inner room. He came out wearing a bewildered expression.

The tanned playboy said anxiously, "They weren't rough on you—were they, Dave?"

Henry C. Callender bristled with fatherly indignation. "They'd better not be. I'll know how to deal with any high-handed—"

"They're sealing up the offices until further notice. It seems I can't start tomorrow after all."

Callender said, "Don't worry—we'll see about that."

The detective who remained in the room with the suspects broke it up by speeding the doctor on his way. "That's right. If you have nothing to worry about don't worry. Go home and get your beauty sleep."

Matt, whether by chance or design, was the last to be questioned. He grew increasingly nervous as one by one the others were beckoned into the sanctum through which a comparatively lighthearted version of himself had passed several hours back. None who emerged gave him so much as a glance. The avoidance was blatant, and in a few instances it seemed to be flavored with guilt, as though the accuser dared not meet the eye of the accused. As an added discomfort he was seized with a fit of yawning. He could not control it. Time after time his mouth gaped wide. He would have given much for leave to sleep. I must be phlegmatic as anything, he told himself. A fine situation to sleep through.

Finally, with five disposed of and the mouse type still in closed session, he was alone in the room with the detective. He tried to take his measure and decided that he did not look like much of a detective—or, for that matter, much of a man. He had a clownish face with black buttons for eyes, and his loose bag of a suit emphasized the meagerness of its contents. He could be overpowered easily, Matt thought. He dismissed the thought as impractical before it led to anything, but not before the little man grinned at him and said, "Take it easy while you can."

His tone, if not exactly friendly, was without animus. Because it had become a novelty to be so addressed, Matt responded in kind. "You must be a mind reader."

"Hope. You just had that look—and that certain ripple went over you. We get so's we recognize the symptoms."

"You *are* a detective."

"What else?"

Matt saw no profit in antagonizing him. He went on talking in the hope that the sound of his own voice might restore his lost entity. "Well—you haven't spent your time out here trying to dig for helpful information."

"What helpful information could *they* give me?"

Matt was heartened by the scornful utterance. He missed its implication.

"And if something went by me the chief will fill me in later. I'm practically his right-hand man."

"Which one is your chief?"

"Captain Gridley Nelson."

"The tall white-haired—?"

"Yep—the white-haired boy of Homicide West—and all points East if you ask me—not to mention the Bronx, Brooklyn, and Queens, on account of their squads don't boast a near match to him."

"Then why did he let someone else take over?"

The little man continued to be forthcoming. "That's regular procedure. The precinct man catches the squeals and carries the case—by the book, that is. But sooner or later it's up to Homicide—barring it's cut and dried and packaged like this one."

"Packaged? You mean you know who killed him? But you're letting them all go home."

"All except."

Hope straightened Matt in his chair. "The man who's in there now—the one with the glasses? I thought they were keeping him longer than the rest but—"

"Be yourself—will you?" The detective leaned over him. "Now that we're real private and cozy I'll do you a favor and let you get it off your chest."

"Get it off my—?" He realized then that the affability, the readiness to instruct him had been designed as a softening-up process. He cursed his stupidity for accepting it at face value and said with cold restraint, "No favors, thanks. I'll go through channels like the rest."

"I had a hunch you'd be stiff-necked. You've got the jaw for it. But you'd be surprised at how loose you can get when the pressure's on. I've seen it happen time and again to the bravest of you characters." The clown implicit in his appearance had vanished. "Why not look at it this way. You're a young fellow. Could be if you don't have a record you'll sidestep the chair. Say murder was far from your mind and the guy jumped you and you lost your head—"

"Nice of you to cue me—but those aren't the right lines."

The little man shrugged to his ears. "Don't say I didn't warn you. Those precinct boys are minus in the finesse department. Here's where you could grab a chance to cross them up so's they won't have an excuse to work you over."

"Try for your promotion elsewhere," Matt said.

"You got me wrong. Worming a confession on a bungle like this wouldn't rate me an extra coffee break." He fixed his button eyes on Matt's lowering face. "Tell me one thing. How long have you had the habit?"

"The habit?" He yawned, but not for effect. "Oh—I see." He shook his head. "You've been listening to Henry C. Callender. However—since you're trying so hard I will tell you one thing. I—" He meant to give a definitive assertion of innocence covering both drug addiction and murder. He was cut off by the entrance of the eyeglassed mouse, who stepped on his foot in a rush toward the chair where he had left his hat and coat.

The detective watched him, clown's mouth stretched wide. He said reprovingly, "Walk—don't run—to the nearest exit."

The mouse said as though he expected an argument, "I was told I could go."

"Sure you can—and good night to you."

The sound of the outer door closing was not loud but it gave Matt a headache. He was not soothed by a voice calling from the inner room, "Okay, Clevis."

"That's me," the detective said. "And that means you. You left it till too late, Jack. Now I've got to throw you to the lions."

Chapter Four

Heaped ash trays and stale air had robbed the new little office of its gloss. The homicide captain and one of his men stood near the filing cabinets. He acknowledged Matt's entrance with a nod. His deep-set eyes were friendly. The rest of the company went on with what they were doing.

They were as busy as actors on a set stage at the rise of the curtain. The precinct men were in a huddle at the desk. The stenographer sat before the metal table, hammering away at the typewriter keys. From a perch on the desk's edge the assistant D.A. leaned over to study a sheaf of papers. He said something to the precinct lieutenant, addressing him as "Gates."

The bell on the typewriter pinged. The lieutenant reached out to take the finished page from the stenographer. He added it to the bottom of the sheaf. Then, as though to refresh his own memory, he began to read aloud from the top page.

"Dr. David E. Stewart, M.D., resides at East Fifty-second Street. Maurice Fredericks, City Councilman, Park Avenue. Henry C. Callender, president, Callender chain of supermarkets, Inc., Central Park South. Donald Palmer, stock broker, Plaza. George Rolfe, Rolfe Racing Stables, Inc., West Meadows, Connecticut. Stanley Ackerman, vice-president, Ackerman Motels, Boston."

He had been reading tonelessly. When he came to the last name on the list he grimaced as at an anticlimax and flavored his nasal voice with a tinge of unbelief. "Matthew Berthold, factory worker, Brooklyn."

The assistant D.A. passed a hand across his lips to cover a smile.

The homicide captain appeared to be studying his custom-made shoes.

Matt stepped forward and said clearly, "I'm Matthew Berthold."

The clown called Clevis prodded him. "Wait till you're asked," and Lieutenant Gates raised his eyes from the sheaf of papers and pretended to see Matt for the first time.

He beckoned peremptorily and Matt walked up to the desk. Several chairs had been brought in to supplement those that belonged in the office. He was not offered one. He stood tall, trying not to be conscious of his torn trousers, regretting that at some point he had sloughed off his overcoat and left it in the other room.

Gates had twisted his chair around to get a better view. "So you're a factory worker," he said.

"Yes—temporarily." Ego prompted the qualification.

Gates said knowingly, "That goes without saying. I wouldn't be surprised you've had quite a few temporary jobs. No use wasting time on that phase of it." He was evidently tired of craning his neck. He gestured, and Clevis pushed a chair against Matt's legs. He buckled, suppressing the exclamation that arose to his lips on a wave of resentment. Deliberately he lengthened the process of settling himself.

"Comfortable?" The lieutenant had a rabbit's face. He twisted it into a pseudo-hearty expression. "What's the rest of your story? Take all the time you need."

Matt realized that he did need time as soon as he tried to form an opening sentence. Instead of devoting the long wait to worrying about Rennie, he should have spent it on an editing job. Because, of course, Rennie had to be kept out of it. If he was so unwary as to mention her name, routine might dictate that they question her. And routine or not, a police visit out of the blue was enough to alarm anyone.

Aware of the suspect pause, he said, "I'm trying to find a good starting-off place—"

"Start anywhere at all. We're born listeners."

"Well—after I got through work tonight I felt like going to a movie, so I came to New York. I'd heard that the Greenwich Theater was showing a re-run I'd been wanting to see, so I got off the subway at Eighth Street. I started to walk to the theater, slipped in the snow in front of a car, and was almost run over. It was my fault—not the fault of the woman driving the car—but she seemed to feel responsible. I wasn't hurt except for scrapes and scratches—but she thought I might be and she wanted to drive me home. I couldn't let her take me all the way to Brooklyn, so I refused. She kept insisting and I got in and said she could take me to Penn Station. The fall had messed me up and I didn't want to—I thought I could go to a washroom in the station and get cleaned up before I—" He stopped and, out of habit that months of abstinence should have broken, fumbled for a cigarette. He withdrew his hand empty, but the moment's passage had refilled his mind. "—before I went home. From the attitudes of the people I've been running into I was right in guessing I look like a tramp—and my landlady is a stickler about keeping up the good name of her rooming house. If she happened to be around she might have shut the door in my face." He could not see how his effort at lightness had been received by the homicide captain, but the rest of the faces told him it had failed. He threw more words into the heavy listening silence. "Instead of taking me to Penn Station the woman stopped the car in front of this place. At first I thought she lived in the main apartment building and that I could get presentable there as well as in the station—and that she might let me have a needle and thread to mend my pants, which I'd torn when I fell—or, better yet, I could borrow a pair of her husband's. She'd suggested something like that during the drive. But she steered me to this entrance. The door was on the latch and we walked in. She said she knew the doctor and he'd be here even though it was past office hours. She was right. The place was far from empty. She pointed out the bathroom and said I could use it and she'd explain matters to the doctor. All I wanted was a wash and some disinfectant for my knees. I walked into this office from the hall as directed, and through it to the hall beyond. Then I went into what she said would be the bathroom and switched on the light." As soon as the editing job was out of the way he proceeded with ease. It did not occur to him that his objective handling of the statement's meat could be interpreted as callousness. "At first I thought someone was asleep on the examining table. I started to back out but didn't make it. I suppose my subconscious must have registered the absence of breathing before my ears did. I went to the table and saw the dried blood and the scalpel sticking out of him. I'd learned enough about the law to keep my hands to myself. I stood there taking it in for a minute or so. I could still hear voices and a record player going in the front room." Unable to resist, he stropped his voice to a fine edge. "I caught myself wondering if your influential tycoons realized they were holding a wake. That posed the problem of whether I should announce my find to them first or call you first. I guess you can take it from there."

Lieutenant Gates said, "Guess again."

Matt had leaned back in his chair as for an earned respite. The tone jarred him forward. "I concluded that it would be wiser to call you first and take no chances on the doctor and whoever he had with him. I can give no logical explanation of why I didn't follow through. I must have been in a kind of shock. Anyway, I walked past the telephone. I'm sure you've been told the rest."

"We've been told six times that you couldn't walk past the telephone or past the front room fast enough, and we could give you a logical explanation for it without trying. The only trouble is, we have to get it on record in your own words."

"You've got it in my own words. The stenographer's been taking it down."

"Sure he's been taking it down—but he knows as well as you and I do that it's not getting us anywhere. So how about starting again?"

Matt's strong features assumed a stupid cast. "You want me to repeat what I've just said?"

Gates shook his head. "That wouldn't make sense—would it?"

"No," Matt said. "It wouldn't. Because it would come out exactly the same except that some unimportant minor detail might have been left out."

"It's what you might call unimportant minor details that we're after." His show of patience was like thickly applied paint. "Say, for example, an unimportant minor detail like the name and address of the woman who was supposed to have brought you here."

"I don't know her name and address."

"Just between the two of us, that doesn't surprise me. What does is that you don't dream one up for her. It strikes me you've got the imagination for it—but in case you've been overtaxing it we'll go on to another unimportant minor detail like how it's tough Brooklyn's got no movie houses—especially on such a stormy night." He kept swiveling his rabbit face toward the homicide captain and the assistant D.A. He was like a man who finds himself before television cameras for the first time and is determined to make the most of his opportunity.

"I told you I wanted to see a special picture."

"Would it be too much to ask you *its* name?"

It was not easy without closing his eyes to visualize the marquee of the Greenwich. "A foreign film," he said. "French." Unexpectedly and for what it was worth it came to him. "Translated, it means 'Forbidden Toys.'" He corrected himself. "'Games.'"

"French too," Gates said. "Nothing like having an education. I've been remarking to myself you're no slouch with English either. Well—you won't be the first or the last who didn't take advantage of his advantages. 'Forbidden Toys,' you said. Funny thing—but that knife or scalpel or whatever you call it fits that heading to a T. Which brings us up to still another unimportant minor detail—mainly the little something you had to do with sticking it into the corpse." He waved an admonishing finger. "I'm not finished. Didn't you have your innings without interruption? Now let's say that somewhere between switching on the light and backing out you—"

Matt said furiously, "Is this a courtroom—because if it is I haven't seen the jury go out and I haven't seen them come in—"

"All in good time. Matter of fact, you haven't seen a thing yet." Then he barked, "Stand up."

The change of tactics was sudden. It brought Matt to his feet.

Gates stood up too, his head incongruously small on a long high-shouldered body. "Blow your nose."

"What?" He almost laughed. Then, because no one else seemed amused by the absurd command, he tried to read sense into it, concluded doubtfully that his nose had started to bleed again, and reached into a pocket.

"We're waiting."

"I left my handkerchief in my overcoat. I—"

"Too bad you didn't get a chance to flush it down the drain." Gates motioned to one of the detectives. "Bring the coat in."

Matt's nose did not feel as though it were bleeding. He touched it gingerly, decided that the lieutenant had been speaking some departmental code, and shrugged. He had been holding his head high and stiff. He lowered it.

"Not feeling quite so proud of yourself—eh? You're all alike when it comes to a showdown," Gates said. "Raise your arms."

Still on the subject of his nose, Matt said, "All right—but I don't think it's bleeding any more. You're probably misled by the leftover traces of the last bout. I haven't looked in a mirror since I bumped—"

He realized that the lieutenant's hands were sliding over his person; that the yield of his pockets was being transferred to the desk. He cried in outrage, "Hey—!"

"Now we're getting somewhere," the lieutenant said. He waved back the man who had returned with the coat. He nodded at the stenographer, who added another squiggle to his notes.

Matt gazed through fog at the heap on the desk: pen, pencil, a depleted roll of caffeine candies, the key to Rennie's apartment, the key to his room, his savings account book, a library card, a comb, a publisher's advertisement torn from a newspaper, his wallet, and some coins. He reached out to reclaim his possessions.

Gates struck at his hand without rancor. "Not when you're going so good. You might interrupt your train of thought. Go on."

"Go on with what?"

Gates addressed the stenographer. "Read it back for him."

The stenographer read flatly, "'I haven't looked in a mirror since I bumped—'"

"Okay. Take it from there."

Matt's throat constricted.

"I thought a smart boy like you would see the light in time," Gates said encouragingly. "You can sit down again if you want to." He sent a self-congratulatory message around the room and sat down himself. "You bumped—"

Matt swallowed hard. His throat opened unexpectedly wide. He shouted, "I don't want to sit down. I've had enough. I bumped into the top of that woman's car. I was in a hurry but I forgot to stoop. That's the beginning and the end of it. Did you search your tycoons or were you afraid to disturb the set of their custom tailoring? If you can give any reason except my clothes and my failure to supply a Park Avenue address as to why I should be singled out for special attention I want to hear it."

"I'll give you several. For a start, you've been putting more feet in your mouth than you've got. Right off you said you hung back when the woman offered you a lift. Then all of a sudden you were in such a hurry to get in you bumped your nose. Right?"

"There was a drunk bothering me. The only way to get rid of him—"

"There was no drunk—there was no street accident—there was no woman."

"What you mean is that the Park Avenue crew found it convenient to forget about her."

"That will do. Fun's over." The lieutenant turned to yank Matt's coat from the man who held it. A search of it netted him three objects. The first was no more than a flash to Matt as it caught the light. The second was a flat box that meant nothing to him. He tried to recall what he had been carrying. He was fighting sleep again. This fact seemed incredible to him, but it was true.

The flashy object and the box were added to the possessions on the desk and concealed by Gates's frame. The third object was the stiffened handkerchief. Gates clamped a corner of it between thumb and forefinger and swung it back and forth like a pendulum. "Yours?"

"Yes—mine. Blood and all—thanks to the bump."

"Lucky that's something we don't have to take your word for."

"Lucky for me."

"You think so? Ever heard of blood typing?"

"Yes—when I was a freshman—and blood grouping—and benzidine tests and precipitin tests." He was dopey but calm. He had nothing to worry about except Rennie, who waited not quite alone, with her ear to the hall door. "And I still say that's my blood."

"I've got eyes. I can see the stain around your nostrils."

"Then why—?"

"So you had a nosebleed and here's what it buys you. We don't generally reveal evidence, but being you're such a fine upstanding so-and-so, I'll make an exception and tell you the late Eugene Hackett has blood on his knuckles. How about it?"

"The late—? Oh!" His mind produced an echo of a voice saying, "Poor old Gene."

"You make the connection? So did Hackett—right smack on your nose before you knifed him. Trying to dent a big bruiser like you must have swung him around, because the first stab he got was in his back. Then you decorated his chest to make sure he wouldn't tell on you."

Matt spoke slowly to keep his voice steady. "I'd like to see the laboratory report that proves my blood was on his knuckles."

"Maybe I'll show it to you as a favor, provided you rate a favor. Meanwhile the benzidine test done on scene shows it's human blood and that's enough to go on with."

"Thanks for admitting I'm human."

"Don't let it go to your head. You keep this up you won't be able to tell what species you are."

The assistant D.A. had left his desk perch. He said, "Stasis has set in. I vote for a change of locale."

A conference followed. The homicide captain moved forward to take part in it. Matt's physical presence was ignored, or he thought it was until his restlessness brought a flanking tactic that sandwiched him between two detectives.

The conference did not last long, but to him it seemed interminable. It was keyed low except for occasional words and phrases that flew above the muted register to brush against his ears. In catching them he realized that there was general agreement as to the change of locale and dissension as to how he would be charged.

Standing there, he became resigned to his arrest. He could say no more than he had said. It remained for them to verify his story, a job that would probably be deferred until his landlady was up and about and his foreman had come on duty. So it would be an overnight affair and there were only a few hours left to the night. What were a few hours in jail? It had happened to the best of men. It would be quite an experience, and one day when the years had worn away its cutting edge it might even make a suitable tale for his children. His child—Rennie—

Anxiety nudged his jaws apart. He yawned to end all yawns. He looked with longing at the roll of caffeine candies on the desk. But caffeine was not needed to alert him. The flashing object near it did the trick. He yelled, "That hypodermic syringe isn't mine—neither is that box of—"

It broke up the conference. Gates left the inner circle. "Now you're talking," he said. "Stolen property—and not much of a haul, considering what it will cost you."

Matt said dully, "I've heard about it but I never believed it. Corrupt—all of you—planting that stuff in my overcoat pocket to—"

"Same old song." Gates looked pained. "Know something? I'd kind of expected you to be more original."

They took him to the station house and booked him on the charge of burglary. They rolled up his sleeves and his trouser legs, and when they found no telltale marks their contempt for him swelled rather than diminished. He was not even stealing to support his habit, they said. He had not even that excuse. They took a sample of his blood, which he thought was stupid of them, since there was more than a sample on the handkerchief. They examined his bank book and clucked over it and said he was doing pretty well for himself, wasn't he? Or could it be that he was not Matthew Berthold after all and that the book too had been come by dishonestly?

By that time it had become a valiant effort to give them a "yes" or a "no." Moreover, he was no longer sure of his name or of anything else. Nor could he distinguish between the units of "they" popping out at him with such jack-in-the-box rapidity.

Now and then "they" were impelled to provide physical aid in the business of keeping his head from sinking upon his chest because his neck had given up the job of supporting it. Once they were even impelled to give him some sort of stimulant so that his eyes would stay open. In the beginning there had been voices in the place. But after a while there were only loud noises and sometimes barking, as though a pack of dogs had been let loose. He was not afraid of the men-shaped dogs but he wished they would go away. They were like stage dogs, except that instead of answering questions with barks they barked questions and denied the answers.

"Describe the car."

"What make was it?"

"What was the license number?"

"Describe the woman."

"Where were you born ... date ... what did you do before you had this alleged factory job ... how long have you been in New York? How ... When ... Why ...?"

It was a long night, or at least he supposed that it was still night. Else why should they be so extravagant with the electricity? But at last they did turn out the great bulb that was roasting his eyeballs, and for a too-short while he slept.

They did not bark him awake. The man with the white hair aroused him, speaking in a voice with the dominant characteristic of profound sanity. Now the questions were asked quietly and, aided by breakfast and a cigarette, Matt was able to make the proper responses.

A little later several of the pack returned to escort him from the building. Fortunately they could not stop his breathing, and the cold wintry air that he gulped before he reached the waiting car helped him more than the breakfast or the cigarette. The nature of his ordeal had so distorted time that it would not have surprised him to emerge into a change of season. But the snow still fell.

He was transported to the Central Criminal Courts Building on Centre Street and somewhere around midmorning was arraigned before a magistrate. The magistrate set bail for a hearing at a date he did not catch, and the bail was so high that even by recourse to his confiscated savings book he could not have raised it. So he was forced to await developments in a cell in the Tombs. The cell's upper bunk was empty, for which he was grateful, since he had no desire for conversation. He assured himself that the wait would be a short one. He had gathered enough information along the way to be convinced that the burglary charge was merely a holding device. It meant that for all their vaunted certainty, their attempts at brainwashing, they could not charge him with murder. He made the most of that, and he tried to make the most of the lower bunk in the cell. It was important to refresh his mind and body, because when they came to tell him that it had been a mistake he meant to cut them down with a few well-chosen words. And in his present state he might destroy what dignity was left him by bawling like a child.

But too many figures collected in the space behind his closed eyes: Rennie, heart-sick at his defection, the woman in the car, the corpse, the magistrate provided by his fitful dozing with a black cap, Henry C. Callender blasting into the ear of the white-haired captain, assorted clowns, dogs—

His stifled groans scattered them. He sat up, and for a moment it appeared that the nightmare would not carry over. But no one had come to deliver him.

As the door slid to behind the guard, Matt gazed at his first prison meal. For the first time in memory he had no appetite.

Chapter Five

He had thinning hair and a thick middle. His fleshy nose was marked by broken veins. When the man who had answered the door did not step aside, he pushed past him into the impressive white house. "Tell Mr. Marshall that William Strachan wants to see him."

"Does he expect you?"

"I've got a standing invitation."

"Wait here."

James Marshall's man went in search of his employer and found him writing checks on the second floor of the house.

"There's a William Strachan to see you."

Strachan, assessing the furnishings in the hall below, thought with disdain of the fee he had received. But the windfall of such a lordly client had taken him off guard and he had named the first sum that came into his head. A type like Marshall was as anachronistic to his office as he himself was here, and could, with a little handling, be made to up the ante. He blessed the ad in the Red Book for changing his luck.

He rearranged his watering mouth as Marshall came into view. He said cordially, "Good afternoon, Mr. Marshall. I tried your office first but— "

The cordiality was all on his side. Marshall said, "What do you want? My business with you was concluded some time ago."

"Yes, but I just happened to be in that department store again and all of a sudden I got the idea that there might be something else I could do for you."

Marshall said, "This way," and led him to a comfortable square of a room with an open fireplace.

Strachan sat down in response to a nod of permission. Marshall stood near a glass wall that gave on to a wintered landscape. Strachan admired the scenery because it was expensive. He dismissed it in favor of more important matters and yearned openly at a fully equipped bar.

Marshall said, "I didn't hire you to spy. I merely wanted to know where she was and what she was doing. After you found that out I gave you no further instructions."

"When you hear what I have to say you'll thank me for keeping you in mind."

"Well?"

Strachan breathed asthmatically. "I rushed out here as fast as I could—walked from the station because there was only one cab and—"

"Scotch?"

"Rye if it's all the same to you." He shook his head as his host reached for a siphon. He drank the whiskey neat and made an "aahh" sound. He said, "Not to boast, I've earned more than a couple of drinks—"

Marshall did not appreciate the dramatic pause. "If you have anything to say—say it."

"Right you are. I found the guy responsible for keeping her away." He took out a few sheets of paper. Before he had time to unfold them his hands were empty.

James Marshall read rapidly. Watching him, Strachan thought with envy that all this citizen had to show for his years was a fortune and a few gray streaks in a healthy head of hair. Middle age had done no damage to his handsome face or compact body. Even without money a man like him would have no trouble getting what he wanted. Women, for example, would tumble like ninepins—

Marshall had finished reading. "You're sure about this?" If the report had played upon his emotions there was no evidence of it in his voice.

"Now look, Mr. Marshall, I know my business."

Marshall looked. His dark blue eyes were almost black. Strachan shifted uneasily and straightened the set of his old Billy Taub suit.

It was only by fluke that he had stumbled upon the girl yesterday.

He had gone to the Fourteenth Street store to take advantage of a sale in shirts, which showed how far down he was in his luck. With time to kill he had wandered about, amusing himself by dressing an imaginary woman from the skin out. He had not killed time. Instead it had worked for him. Suddenly there was the girl, behind a counter featuring lingerie.

It had been easy to follow her home to the remodeled tenement in the village. It had been easy to lurk in the entrance and keep tabs on who pushed what button. It was sheer speculation, of course, but who knew what it might lead to? And he had nothing better to do.

He stood pat until the first and only caller showed. The caller had a key, but he had pressed the bell a couple of times to announce his arrival. There had been nothing furtive about him. He had not even noticed the footsteps behind him on the creaking stairs. He had behaved as though it were quite in the cards for him to be playing house with such a juicy plum for a partner. In fact he had shown no eagerness to get on with it. The ascent to the landing where the girl received him was stop and go all the way, and Strachan had been hard put to lag a discreet distance behind him. He seemed like a rough customer, strong as a bull if you went by looks. He should have been able to take the stairs at a fast run, so evidently it was mental and not physical trouble that slowed him down. Judging by later events, he must have had plenty to mull over.

Marshall said, hardly moving his lips, "Did you look through the keyhole after he entered the apartment?"

"No." To dispel any idea that he had been remiss in his duty he would have explained that the bed was out of keyhole range. But he could have sworn that in some way the simple negative had pleased Marshall, so he let it stand.

"You listened, of course," Marshall said dispassionately.

He had tried. He had heard a dish break, and subsequently he had heard enough to tell that they were quarreling. But he had missed the nature of the quarrel. Somebody on the floor had managed to scrape up the payments on a television set and was setting his money's worth in volume alone. And right next door water kept gushing out of noisy pipes. He had not mentioned the quarrel in his report. He had based his omission on the premise that if they were splitting up anyway it might detract from the credit due him. He said knowingly, "I heard plenty."

Marshall did not ask him to particularize. "Your report says he left the apartment at ten after nine. Doesn't that indicate he could have been a casual caller?"

Toward the end of the climb Strachan had passed the preoccupied lover on the stairs and reached the cover of the flight above just as the girl opened her door. He grinned, remembering the revelatory embrace. "I'm afraid not," he said. He wanted to add that she would have to be pretty desperate to get that close to a casual caller. He refrained because under the circumstances Marshall might see no humor in the observation. "Him having a key and all," he said.

"Is there anything more I should know?"

Strachan's tongue varnished his lips. "You asked me to find Dorene Marshall and paid me for it. I guess that was all you really wanted."

"Is this a complete report or not?"

"Well—there are some things I don't like to put in writing, Mr. Marshall—not if I want to protect my clients. A man in my profession has to be prepared for everything—like I could have been held up or dropped dead on the way here—and how would you feel if it came to light that she's been monkeying around with a murderer?"

He saw with relish that he had taken Marshall down a few pegs. Heady with success, he got up and restocked his glass over and above the first generous measure. Now that there was no hurry he took it back to his chair and sipped like a gentleman. "You understand of course that the steps I took went beyond the call of duty."

Lines striped Marshall's forehead and parentheses had been drawn around his mouth. "I understand what you want me to understand." Without warning he snatched the glass from Strachan. "Get on with it and do your wallowing later."

Strachan tried to summon a long-neglected dignity. He flinched as the glass met the bar's surface and wondered that it did not splinter. "I don't have to take any insults from—"

"You don't have to lay yourself open to them. People who work for me do so on the understanding that I pay for value received. I don't bargain."

Strachan said appeasingly, "It's not that I don't trust you—but I'm a fellow likes to have things cut and dried." He took out a small notebook, opened it, and said to forestall confiscation, "Just a few jottings in my own private code so's I won't leave out anything important. After I—"

"Skip the footnotes," Marshall said.

"Well—I hung around till he left. Then I tailed him. Of course it was a dirty night—but with his collar up and his hat pulled down he looked more like a thug than ever—and not a thug who'd done much good for himself. I could see why, too, because he acted as if he didn't have all his buttons. For instance, once he stops and yells something into the wind. I'm a couple of feet behind, so I don't get what he yells because—"

The glance Marshall flung at his watch seemed violent enough to shatter its crystal. Strachan accelerated. "It's easy to see by the way he's walking that he's got no particular destination, but after he gives that yell it looks like he might go into reverse. Only he doesn't. He walks on until he gets to Seventh Avenue and starts to cross the street. That's where he does go into reverse—right in the middle of traffic—and smacko—he's down for the count. At first I think the car hit him and that he'll be out of circulation for a while—or for keeps. But I'm wrong. He recovers on the spot and is helped to the sidewalk, where he insists it's all his fault and he's okay and it's not necessary to report the accident. I'm mingling with the rest of the rubbernecks by this time. As soon as they're satisfied the excitement's a dud they move along. Lucky for me it happens near the corner. I make for it and merge with a cluster that's waiting for the light to change. There I can watch what's going on even if I can't hear but snatches of it. The light changes about four times, but there are always enough new crossers ganging up to cover me. The car that did the trick is parked and the lady driver is yakking away and motioning to the victim to get in. She's got a kind of distinctive voice—I think I'd recognize it anywhere. He keeps shaking his head but she won't take no for an answer, and it keeps on until a drunk comes along and puts in his two cents. Whatever he says results in a win for the lady. Our boy dives into the car, which takes off. Due to my training I've got the car made from A to Z, including the license number. If not for that I could have been left at the post. Also, the weather and the heavy traffic are with me. I manage not to lose it. All the same it's tough going." He gave a few illustrative wheezes. "If I just didn't happen to catch a cab while it's dumping its passengers this wouldn't have meant a thing to me."

He riffled the pages of the notebook and produced a clipping. He said expansively, "Maybe it will save time if you read it yourself."

The clipping was no more than a few paragraphs. Marshall made short work of it. When he looked up the lines in his face had been ironed out. "This Matthew Berthold is the man you tailed?"

Strachan said, "You hit it in one. And I can see you feel as relieved as I do. Factory worker, thief, murderer, or what have you—we got to give him credit for keeping her name out of it—at least so far."

Marshall said evenly, "How would it work to his advantage to involve her? She couldn't serve as an alibi if this account is accurate."

"It's accurate, but like everything in the newspapers there's a lot more to it." He did not meet Marshall's eyes.

"It satisfies me as it stands," Marshall said. "It's obvious that this Berthold committed a crime and tried to lie himself out of it. Since he'll be granted a just trial I'm quite willing to yield what interest I had in him to the electric chair."

"Well, I don't know." Strachan's voice swelled with righteousness. "I wouldn't want to condemn anybody out of hand myself. In all fairness I guess we should give the police more time to check his story. Meanwhile it would be smart to face the fact that they'll try to drag all kinds of information out of him—the people he's been seeing—his recent activities—his friends—stuff like that." He avoided Marshall's appraising stare as though he were dodging a missile.

Marshall walked over to him. The way he handled his body hinted at a caged violence. His voice did not change. "I congratulate you on your sense of fair play. What might arise if he should reveal the name of Dorene Marshall is irrelevant. Inside of a few hours she'll be untraceable." He had taken out his wallet. "This concludes our business. It's payment in full for the extra work you assumed."

Strachan accepted the carelessly tendered bills. He made no attempt to rise. "Aren't you forgetting something? I'm a licensed private detective—bound over to co-operate with the police where co-operation is indicated. I tailed Matthew Berthold and the woman to the doctor's office. I saw them go in. A couple of minutes later she came out alone and drove away."

"Satisfied that she'd done her duty, I suppose."

"Sure—but that's not the point."

Marshall's right eyebrow did a solo climb. It gave his face a satanic cast. He said with an insulting lack of interest, "What is the point?"

"The item you read isn't my only source of information. When I take on a job I stick with it, and I've been pretty busy between last night and now. I've got it on sound authority that Berthold's story rates a big horse laugh from the precinct lieutenant—mostly because his description of the woman and the car are too hazy to be taken seriously. The check as of noon today proves he lives where he says he lives and works where he says he works. But plenty of workingmen have committed crimes—so that doesn't cut much ice. The one thing that could shake the police about his being guilty is if they found the woman and the car."

"Undoubtedly an appeal will be made for her to come forward." Marshall had the air of a civilized man forcibly buttonholed by the town bore.

"And maybe she will and maybe she won't. You can't always tell. She had the earmarks of a spoiled rich dame. It might not suit her book to get mixed up in it. Which kind of leaves me with a problem."

"In other words," Marshall said, "you're struggling with your conscience."

Strachan's smile was smug. "That's right—and I'd appreciate some advice from a man of the world like you. Of course my evidence may not help the poor jerk in the long run, but decency says I should present it."

"And what says that you shouldn't?"

"Well—I—" His eyes roved and settled on the bar's surface. He seemed to be making a sweating effort at telekinesis, but the whiskey glass stayed where it was. He swallowed air and said, "I wouldn't want to do anything that wasn't to your advantage." He caught and twisted the tail of his fleeing confidence. "I go all out for my clients. You don't have to worry that I'd—"

"To put it bluntly," Marshall said, "my worries have nothing to do with you—but who can resist an appeal for advice? If you haven't run afoul of the law and have nothing to fear from an encounter with the police, then by all means get in touch with them at once."

Strachan's mouth hung open. He closed it and forced it apart again with blustering words. "You want to think this over. If I do go to the police I'll have to begin at the beginning and explain how I happened to be tailing Berthold. You wanted your name kept out of it or you wouldn't have picked me out of the Classified in the first place. If you weren't shunning publicity you'd have put Missing Persons on the job or got some—"

"More reputable investigator," Marshall said. "Sorry—I'm afraid I can't spare you any more of my time. When I told you that I don't bargain I should have added that neither do I respond to blackmail." He strode to the door.

"Wait a—"

Marshall quit the room without a backward glance. Strachan started to follow, got as far as the bar, and retrieved his glass. The whiskey was excellent, but he grimaced as though it tasted of dust and ashes. He was accustomed to defeat, yet never before had he been so sure of his cards. The bastard! he thought. The big heel of a bastard!

On the third drink he heard the sound of a starting motor. The bastard could have given me a lift to the station. Just because he's well-heeled he thinks he can lean all over a guy. I'll fix him.

He poured one more, still sober enough to keep a cautious eye out for the appearance of some underling who might question his right to the bottle.

Chapter Six

Rennie summed up her night by exonerating Matt for his failure to return. She, who at an early age had based her judgment of men upon the behavior of a particular man, should have known better than to demand the impossible. She had caught one of the species in a trap and, not content with his acceptance of a suddenly narrowed world, had expected him to thank her for it. And the cliché that "love breeds love" was a blatant lie.

At seven o'clock in the morning she stopped trying to sleep. Neither a bath nor the smell of coffee awakened a physical hunger. Nevertheless, after making the tossed bed and discarding her robe for a dress, she forced a breakfast of sorts down her rebellious throat, hoping that it would satisfy the "passenger" she carried. For from now on the going would be hard enough without courting extra hazards.

Yet she could not quite believe in the finality of Matt's exit. She went over it again as she had done throughout the night: the things she had said, the things he had said, the way he had looked as he walked out the door. He had meant to return. She could have sworn to that.

In the night she had been so tightly bound by her own misery that she did not even want to ascribe his desertion to anything but the fact that she had offered him an out and he had taken it. She had refused admittance to the fear that he might have met with an accident, dismissing it again and again, treating it as a symptom of the neurotic state into which she had sunk. Now as it reassailed her she fended it off with bitter self-scorn. How naïve, how romantic to imagine that nothing short of an interfering fate could keep him from her side. Much more likely that he might still return, that he was delaying purposely, punishing her for the manner in which she had received his hard-wrung assurances. She chewed on that theory for a moment, not liking the taste of it, but extracting what nourishment it offered. It offered very little. Matt was not that way. If his nature held the smallest vein of sadism, then it was well concealed.

She got up from the table. The fear got up with her, dogging her steps. She tried to ignore it. Soon it would be time to leave for the department store. Business as usual. Business for as long as she could meet without dismay the shrewd appraising glances of her co-workers. At least the job would take her mind off—

The fear made a sudden lunge. It gripped her so relentlessly that she could fight no longer.

Her pocketbook was on the desk. Feverishly she seized it. Two ten-dollar bills, two dimes, a nickel, and a few pennies. She would have to call the hospitals—all the hospitals—but the factory first to ask if Matt had signed in. Only, of course, he hadn't.

In the beginning there had been no need for a telephone. It was merely an added expense, and it had pleased her to live as nearly as possible within the limits of her weekly wage. It fostered identification with the other sales girls, making her feel less of a masquerader. Above all, it drew her closer to Matt, who had always struggled for his needs. These reasons seemed spurious now. She would have given much to see the familiar instrument and its companion books in the room.

She was at the closet, tugging her coat free. They would change a ten-dollar bill in the drugstore on the corner if she bought something. Something to insure the return of adequate silver. And when that was used up she would buy again.

The drugstore was crowded with people waiting for seats at the counter or lining up to pay their breakfast checks. She purchased a lipstick that cost a dollar and three cents with tax. She asked for dimes and spilled a few and scrabbled for them. She had almost spilled herself in her rush down the stairs. That would not do. She must keep a cool head. Planted before the chained directories, she threw the Red Book open and willed the print to settle down.

There were about three columns of hospitals. So sure was she now of what had befallen her lover that she mislaid her intention to call the factory. He had meant to come back. And if he had meant to come back he would not have strayed far from the neighborhood. St. Vincent's was nearest. Or did they take all emergencies to Bellevue no matter where the accident had happened?

There was a ball-point pen and a circular in her bag. She used them to record the precious numbers, shut herself in, and deposited the first dime.

A series of voices, curt, kind, harried, or indifferent, sang the same refrain. "No patient of that name has been admitted ... No patient ... No Matthew Berthold ... No ma'am ... No ... No ..."

She emerged from her final session in the booth, a small casualty with darkened eyes and bitten mouth.

Snow was piled high at the street crossings, and she wore no overshoes. Grimly sensible, she rode the one station to work. Her descent into the subway seemed a fitting prelude to the years ahead.

In the department store she punched the time clock, her card recording tardiness of half an hour. The floor manager waylaid her to deliver a minatory speech but cut it short to ask if she were ill. She shook her head and marched to her counter, where she backed the denial by beating her sales record. There was an urgency about her that fired the shoppers. She did not quite know what she was proving but she went on proving it until midafternoon.

She was in the rest room, stonily sitting out the allotted "relief" period, when a girl handed her a tabloid newspaper. "Want this? I've finished with it."

She accepted it to be polite but let it drop to her lap as soon as the girl had gone. At the entrance of several newcomers she picked it up and pretended to read to avoid conversation.

She turned the pages aimlessly. At first the type that caught and held her eyes had only the significance of association. FACTORY WORKER HELD IN VILLAGE SLAYING.

It reminded her that she had meant to call the factory. And in fancy she heard a male voice saying, "Sure he's here, lady. Where else would he be?" And afterward, if factories were anything like department stores, the joke would be relayed. "Your girl's chasing you. If you want out how's about passing her along?"

She released her hold on the paper. She pressed her palms to her temples. She thought, I spent a lot of dimes but I saved a lot of pride.

Turning from a mirror, one of the girls caught sight of her vulnerable exposed face. "Got a headache?"

"I've earned it."

"Big night—huh? That'll teach you."

"Yes—that'll teach me." She used the paper as a shield again, her eyes guided by chance or instinct to the story beneath the arresting line.

She could barely digest it. It lay like a lump in the pit of her stomach, sending up waves of dizziness. She lowered her head to her knees and kept it there. She had never fainted. This was no time to begin.

"Hey—what's the matter with her?"

"Get her a drink of water."

She rallied. She raised her head and drank from the brimming paper cup. She said, "I'm all right."

"You don't look it. You ought to go up to the infirmary and lie down."

"They say the new virus sometimes starts with—"

She thought, The virus I've got is as old as the hills.

"Nuts to the infirmary. Somebody should take her home and put her to bed. She shouldn't go by herself."

"Thanks," she said. "If I could just sit quietly for a while—"

"You sure you don't want—?"

"Let her alone. She knows what she wants. Anyway, her color's better."

"Okay—but stay here as long as you have to. There's no bonus paid for dying on your feet."

She waited until they had straggled out. Then she made her way to the public telephones on the floor below. The minutes she spent in the booth were as futile as those of the morning. The difference lay in her reaction to them.

She said to the lawyer's secretary, "Please let me speak to Mr. Decker. It's urgent."

"Mr. Decker left a little while ago."

"One of the partners then—"

"I'm sorry. They've left too. If you give me your—"

"You're sure my—you're sure there's no one I can—?"

Excitement lifted the secretary's voice. "This isn't—you aren't—?"

"Do you know if Mr. Decker was going straight home?"

"I believe so. He didn't mention an appointment in town."

"Thanks."

"Wait—where are you—?"

Rennie hung up. It did not occur to her to seek out the head of her department for a "by your leave." She went to the locker room for her coat and left the store.

She took a taxi to her apartment. As soon as she was safe inside she packed a suitcase, carefully including a warm sweater and vitamins that the doctor had prescribed. Her mission might be prolonged for more reasons than one, and under the circumstances she had to be prepared. Responsible for herself alone, she would have run barefoot to Matt's rescue.

Despair and its attendant moods had been erased. Initial shock had made way for the acceptance of Matt's plight as temporary, a challenge that she could meet. But she could not meet it unarmed, and to be armed meant to employ the best lawyer she knew.

The trains ran hourly to Edwin Decker's house and she would board the next one. She would waste no more time in telephone booths. No communication over the impersonal wires could accomplish half as much as face-to-face entreaty.

She was ready to close the suitcase when the downstairs bell rang. She forgot to remove her finger from the buzzer, pressing until it must have sounded as though the mechanism had stalled. Matt! The maniacs who arrested him have come to their senses. I won't need Uncle Ted. Then she was at the door, listening for the footsteps.

The knock was imperative. She cried, "Who's there?" and could not wait for an answer. She flung the door wide.

James Marshall said, "Hello, Rennie."

She had no room in her crowded heart for surprise. She said, "You were in Uncle Ted's office when I phoned." Before he could reply she muttered the contradiction: "No—I didn't leave my address."

He was staring at her. She despised him, yet could have thrown herself into his arms and leaned and leaned against his arrogant strength.

He said, "Are you going to keep me standing in the hall?"

She found and used a seasonably cold voice. "I'm not going to keep you at all—not even long enough to ask how you traced me." But she stepped aside to let him enter.

He crossed the threshold, reaching behind him to close the door. His eyes stayed fixed upon her, renouncing all else in the room. He said, "May I sit down? I feel as though I've climbed the Matterhorn."

"I didn't choose a walk-up with you in mind. However—you contributed a few things to my education—small superficial courtesies included—so do rest until I put my galoshes on."

She thought she knew by rote every nuance of her father's face. But the expression her words produced was difficult to classify. On anybody else she would have called it pain.

He sat down. He gave the suitcase a casual nod. "It seems I got here in the nick of time."

She leaned forward from the edge of the bed, intent on the zippers of her galoshes.

"So you've been in touch with Edwin," he said, "and he hasn't let on. I can't help thinking that's stretching professional ethics too far."

"I've only called him once. He wasn't there."

"You always did run to him with your troubles."

"There was no one else to run to."

"Then you *are* in trouble?" He watched her struggle with the zippers. He said, "I'll do that," and went to kneel at her feet. "There." He arose and looked down at her. "It isn't the only time I've helped you to dress—is it?"

"I'm supposed to be softened by that. I'm supposed to hark back to my childhood and weep on your comforting shoulder."

"It's yours if you've cause to weep."

"I haven't—and if I had I wouldn't usurp the privileges of your girl friends."

He shook his head. "Whatever else being on your own has done for you, Rennie, you're still a prig."

She flushed. "I doubt if I was ever a prig. Jealous would be more like it. Psychiatrists say that everyone has more or less of an Oedipus complex. I won't deny my normal share but I've managed to cope with it." She got up. "What I couldn't cope with was your rotten bad taste."

He barred her way. "That was an unfortunate incident—"

"A planned incident."

"All right—planned. You had said you would be away for the weekend."

"Don't apologize. I should—for returning without notice."

"I'm neither offering nor asking for an apology."

"This is where we both came in," she said, "and I for one would be bored to sit through it again." She picked up the suitcase.

He took it from her and set it out of her reach. "I'd hoped you might grow a little during the past long months "

"I've grown," she said. It was wrenched from her. "How I've grown."

He appeared to ignore it. "That was one of the reasons why I postponed this visit."

"I could guess at other reasons but I don't like to be repetitious."

"You'd be wrong as well as repetitious. I didn't run to the police because I didn't want you plastered all over the front pages—but I wouldn't have been deterred by that if I hadn't trusted you so fully. I counted upon your integrity, Rennie, to keep you safe no matter what—"

She cried, "You should have allowed for inherited traits—" Unnerved by his searching eyes, she looked away. She said, "I'm not condemning you for having whatever it is you have that mows them down. What I can't understand is why you didn't marry one of them—just for expediency. Surely it would have made your private life less complicated." She whipped herself on, wanting to anger him, to force him into some word or deed that would restore the crumbling wall of hostility she had built against him. She wanted this for his own protection. "Even a Don Juan must arrive at some point," she said, "when he tires of playing the field."

He would not lose his temper. He said gravely, "Soon after your mother died I did consider remarrying—purely for your sake—"

"Thanks very much."

He said, "But my heart wasn't in it—and, that being so, the atmosphere created would have done the impressionable child you were more harm than good. I loved your mother. I couldn't replace her. I could only replace the less important aspects of the relationship."

"What a beautiful rationalization. I'm sure I'll be the better for having heard it." She was edging toward the suitcase.

He stopped her. "That's too heavy for you. I'll carry it down as soon as I've finished."

"Let me pass. You've made me miss a train as it is. Why did you have to find me? How *did* you find me?"

"That will keep—"

"It will as far as I'm concerned—but you might not get another opportunity to—"

"Then I must make the most of this one." His touch on her shoulder was gentle. "I'm your father, Rennie. Surely you can spare me a little while—"

"You don't want a little while. You've come to take me home, haven't you?"

"Yes."

"Well—I'm not going."

He said, "I think you wanted me to find you, Rennie. You didn't even use the simple precaution of changing your name."

Tears stung her eyelids. She would not shed them. "Don't feel flattered. I was just afraid to give the Social Security people a false one. I needed a Social Security card so that I could sell underwear."

"I know about your job," he said, "and today I was briefed on other of your activities."

She thrust his hand from her shoulder and moved until her back was to the wall. "So much for your trust in me," she said. "You gave me a break by not going to the police. Why should you run the risk of publicity when you could avoid it by paying your own spies? But the one you hired couldn't have been up to movie standards or he'd have forced his way in here for some manly fun and games."

"Rennie—try to put yourself in my place. I've never been a very patient man—but I thought if I gave you enough leeway you'd realize how unfair you'd been and return of your own accord. When you didn't—"

"Your fatherly grief urged you to call out the dogs."

"Don't scoff. I missed you—and today I told myself that perhaps you wanted to come back and couldn't because of your stubbornness. So I decided it was up to me to make the first move. When you have children of your own you'll understand how—"

She struck the hard irrevocable blow. "The time is not far off. In fact it's set as definitely as medical opinion can make it. And let that put an end to your hearts-and-flowers motif."

From a level above the shattering words she saw her handsome father age. But she could not stop herself. "For once you're thrown, aren't you? It's something your hired detective couldn't have prepared you for. Well—look at the bright side. Perhaps it will be a boy to perpetuate your name, since he may not have one of his own—"

"That's enough!" The tone was lethal, but the arm he had raised fell heavily to his side.

She said in a small shaky voice, "That would have been the final touch of melodrama. Now will you leave?"

"Is it Matthew Berthold?" He winced at her muted answer. "You know that he's been arrested?"

She nodded. "And I know that it's a mistake."

He walked over to the table. He said with his back to her, "You're sure it's Berthold?"

She felt no relief at being spared his gaze. The desire to hurt him was spent, leaving a terrible emptiness. "There's been no one else," she said, "though I grant you the right to think there could have been. I love Matt. I always will."

"You want to marry him?"

"It's a question of what he wants."

James Marshall said dryly, "A factory worker is hardly likely to run from an heiress."

"You don't understand."

"I'm trying to understand. Believe me—I'm trying."

"The factory's only a steppingstone toward completing his education as a physicist."

"That's what he's told *you*."

"That's what he's told me—not boasting to give himself stature—but simply—and with no ax to grind. Because he believes that I'm an ordinary and rather ambitionless salesgirl."

"And if he's guilty?"

"He isn't. Please—it's no use going on with this. I must help him."

"How?"

"I was leaving for Uncle Ted's when you came. He'll—"

He turned to her. "My car's downstairs. I'll drive you there. The roads aren't too good and we won't be able to make much speed, but it's better than waiting an hour for the next train."

She said, "That's—that's good of you."

"Rennie—Rennie—!"

She flung her arms around him.

"All right," he said to her hair. "It will be all right—"

Chapter Seven

At six o'clock that evening Captain Gridley Nelson threw open the window of his office and tried to make the chill sooty air of the courtyard substitute for a night's lost sleep, a bath, and a change of clothing. The snow had stopped in the morning, but it continued to fall upon his desk in the form of reports ranging from the first U.F. 61 to follow-ups turned in by the men assigned to gather information pertinent to the murder of Eugene Hackett.

Nelson did a little jig step to flex his long legs before he reinstalled himself behind the desk. Absently, and unnecessarily, because he could have recited it by rote, he reread the "Pedigree" of Matthew Berthold.

Under "Check Relevant Matter," the prisoner was summed up feature by feature, including blond hair, hazel eyes, and small ears, the tally ending with the observations that he was right-handed, fast-talking, and bore no distinctive marks. Nelson, remembering Berthold's general demeanor and the character and intelligence of his roughly cast face, found the descriptive terms wanting.

Clevis shambled into the office and shut the door upon the activity outside. Clevis looked at his chief but did not express the concern that thinned his clownish mouth. He said airily, "Here's my contribution," and added another paper to the heap. "I'm going off duty now—but I'd as soon swap shifts with one of the boys if—"

"That won't be necessary."

Clevis lingered. He shook his head as Nelson started to read his report. "Don't bother. I didn't find her—the radio didn't find her—television didn't find her—and she didn't find herself. And even if we'd more to go on we could have come up with the same zero."

Nelson was rather fond of the little man. He eyed him now without affection.

"Barring," Clevis said defensively, "she's a dame can't read, see, or hear—why wouldn't she come forward?"

"There's an obvious answer or two. She might be involved or she might be shy of the limelight for other reasons."

"First I'd have to believe she ain't one of those figments of his imagination."

"Bias is hard to shake, isn't it?"

"You got some kind of bias too. You didn't like the way they ganged up on him. You always take a shine to the underdog." He cleared his throat. "Well—maybe I'm out of line. Good night, Captain."

"Good night."

But Clevis did not go. Nelson's unshaven face seemed to fascinate him. "Captain—this is none of my business but—"

"But you're going to say it anyway. All right—say it."

"Haven't you been home since last night?"

Nelson smiled. "You make a better detective than a nurse."

"All the same—it beats me—"

"What beats you? And since you're evidently not in a hurry to go off—stop shuffling your feet and sit down. I haven't the energy to follow a moving target."

Clevis took the straight chair beside the desk. Encouraged by Nelson's smile, he said, "I'd be in a hurry if I had a home like yours to go to." He boasted constantly of his chief's background, of his inherited wealth. More than once he had exchanged blows with newcomers to the squad who suggested that the custom-made clothes, the scale of living were products of some secret source of graft. Aside from basking in reflected glory, he had genuine admiration and respect for the prematurely "white-haired boy" of Homicide West. Yet sometimes, as in this instance, he found his dedication incomprehensible.

"Cigarette?" Nelson pushed the package toward him.

Clevis lit up and relaxed, a man off duty, chatting with a friend of long standing. "Good thing your missus is away. She wouldn't be too happy with the way you're knocking yourself out."

"Especially when it's in the bag," Nelson said.

"Well—it fits the bag better than anything else we got. It don't make sense to me that those friends of the doc would pick his office to stage a crime—not even if they're crime-minded. Also, they check out as being what they say they are—"

"So does Berthold. His landlady and his foreman confirm his address and occupation."

"Sure—but they don't exactly go to bat for him—besides which he lives in a crumbier joint than he has to on the take-home pay he gets—and from the looks of him, what money he spends goes for books on high explosives and stuff. The landlady says it wasn't natural the way he studied them—till all hours—like electricity was as cheap as water. And in the next breath she complained that a couple of nights a week he didn't come home at all. Also his foreman, while admitting he was a good worker, had a beef about him asking so many questions he wouldn't be surprised he was one of those iron-curtain characters."

Nelson said, "Books and an intelligent curiosity are enough to give anyone grounds for suspicion. But let's try to be broadminded. They don't prove conclusively that Berthold's a murderer. Early this morning what was left of him muttered something to me about working in a factory so that he could afford to further his education as a physicist."

Clevis settled down to acting as a clarifying agent for Nelson's thoughts. It was not the first time he had been so used. "No getting around it," he said, "Berthold's a fast talker."

"So it states in his 'pedigree.' I suppose it's meant to be a synonym for 'articulate' or 'inventive,' since his speech isn't particularly fast. At any rate his ambitions have been substantiated by his college. He was a physics major—a scholarship student—and the grant he received might have been sufficient to see him through except that his father died after a lingering illness and he had to leave so that he could support his mother."

"Who's supporting her now?"

"She died about seven or eight months ago."

"Schmalz," Clevis said. "All their stories are smeared with it." At Nelson's sigh he said, "So I'm jumping the gun a little, but none of it proves he's clean any more than there's final proof he stabbed Hackett."

"I'm glad to hear you say that. It shows that your mind is not entirely closed."

"My mind's as open as the next."

"The next being Mr. Henry C. Callender, seconded by the precinct."

"Much as I hate to be in their corner, facts are facts. It don't stand to reason Henry C. Callender or ex-City Councilman Fredericks or the Ackerman creep or the rest of them are guilty, so it's got to be the old saw about someone wandering in off the street—namely Berthold."

"He wasn't the only one who wandered in off the street."

"Not that dame again! Listen—I went to the alleged scene of the alleged accident and I canvassed the shopkeepers—a couple of which were open at the alleged time. The most I got was if anything happened they didn't notice—it being a neighborhood where things happen steadily." He grinned. "Having an alleged open mind, I admit this don't signify for or against Berthold. Neither do the sneers I get when I ask can they put me onto any outstanding drunk who might have been around—because drunks are likewise a neighborhood glut and not outstanding. But what does signify is Berthold's say-so that a small crowd collected. That means there had to be passers-by or it couldn't've. And among the crowd there had to be at least a few who heard or read all about it when the news broke this morning." He drew breath. "What I'm getting at is, we don't even get a crank call on it. So I say it never happened."

Nelson said, "He didn't tear his clothes or bloody his nose in a struggle with the late Eugene Hackett. There was no sign of a struggle or of his blood in the room or on the corpse."

"He could have mopped up. From the state of that handkerchief he could have been mopping up the stockyards."

"You know better than that."

"Yeah—the lab boys would have spotted something. But didn't Lieutenant Gates say there was blood on Hackett's knuckles?"

"Proving that fantasy isn't limited to those on the wrong side of the law. The knuckles on Hackett's right hand were slightly swollen. That's all."

"What else do you want? Berthold had bruises to explain why."

"I noticed a bruise or two on the doctor's friends."

"Sure—Berthold tangled with them later when they stopped him from taking a powder."

Nelson said tepidly, "That sounds plausible."

"You don't like it? All right—how about this? He didn't get his lumps from the corpse. He's in a brawl before they meet, or falls down someplace, and that gives him the idea to ring in the dame and the car. How's that for plausible?"

"Very. All we lack is a plausible motive for the crime."

"Simple." The black button eyes gleamed. "He was prowling the streets trying to pick up a dishonest penny to speed his return back to college—and the doc's office looked like good pickings—and being the door's ajar and no one's watching, he sneaks in—"

"He knew the place wasn't empty. Light showed through the blinds."

"He makes it for a night light on account of doctors don't keep such late office hours. And he figures the unlocked door for carelessness."

"What does he figure when he's inside and hears the sounds of merrymaking?"

"That everyone's safely occupied. So he tiptoes to the back. Maybe he's a little drunk. I got a whiff of alcohol when we had a chat in the front room."

"Not much of a whiff—not according to the sample taken of his blood."

"That so? Well—at least it goes to show he ain't such a model he don't treat himself to a drink once in a while."

"He didn't treat himself. After the guests had urged him to stay he had a part of a drink on the house. It had been set down next to the chair he took—and it had been drugged."

Clevis whistled. "I thought his eyes looked that way."

"Gates was sure of it—and exceedingly disappointed when examination disclosed no further signs of a habit."

"That lieut's a clunk," Clevis said slowly. "Pros don't mix it with whiskey."

"Yet it was mixed with whiskey. Bourbon. Only one bottle of it had been tapped. I sent for it and for the glass containing bourbon dregs. Both contained Demerol, according to the lab."

Clevis said lamely, "Demerol was in that box of ampules he lifted."

"Did he doctor his own drink with it?"

"That ain't so farfetched. All killers are some percent psycho."

"Have you seen a duplicate of the medical examiner's findings?"

"No—I didn't think the autopsy'd be far enough along yet to find much of anything."

"It's far enough along to have found Demerol in the bloodstream of the corpse."

Clevis's eyes lost their gleam. He said reproachfully, "You could have told me that in the first place. You know good and well it cancels my theory. I was working on what friend Callender said about the door being ajar because Hackett interrupted himself on the way out to go back for a leak. I figured he picked the wrong room and started a rhubarb when Berthold tiptoed in—and Berthold panicked and got him by grabbing the scalpel from the handy instrument cabinet. But that Demerol—"

"Never mind the Demerol. Did Berthold strike you as a panicky type?"

"Hell—by the time we got around to him he'd had a chance to collect himself."

"By the same reasoning he'd also had a chance to collect more for his pains than a small quantity of a synthetic drug and an inexpensive hypodermic syringe."

"I don't know. I guess G.P.'s don't keep heroin around, so he stole the next best thing." Then he said, "Planted on him, you think?"

"It wouldn't surprise me."

"Not by the precinct boys?"

"I hope not."

Clevis had begun to take more than token interest. "Were there fingerprints on the glass?"

"Berthold's large thumb over smears."

"How about the time of death?"

"The usual leeway on either side of the clock—which means anywhere from around nine until the M.E. arrived."

"That don't help him. It includes the time he gave for entry."

Nelson shrugged his wide shoulders. "At any rate," he said, "by now the precinct and the D.A.'s office must realize that they can't make the burglary charge stick. Unless they get more evidence they'll have to free him when the thirty-six hours have passed."

"Why can't they make 'burglary' stick? Admitting he was framed, how can he prove it?"

"The framer probably banked on his putting his hand into his pocket to finger the plants absently or to haul them out for inspection. But he did neither. He shed the coat—with the result that there were no prints—and the lieutenant's handling left it that way."

"Couldn't Berthold have wiped them clean himself? Nope—my brains slipped. They wipe prints off of what they leave behind—not what they take with them." Suddenly, and after his fashion, he became a champion of Berthold. "The poor dope—he doesn't even have the sense to scream for a mouthpiece."

"I'd call that another point in his favor. It didn't seem to occur to him that he'd need one. If he were even slightly connected with the underworld it's fair to assume he'd know some of the tricks."

"Let's hope if and when he gets to court he don't draw a shyster to defend him. The way I see it, they won't let him go. They'll either hold him as a material witness or take a chance on a murder charge." Clevis scratched his head. "What's eating me? We got a murder and we got a 'collar'—and everybody's happy—the D.A., the precinct, the newspapers—"

"I'm not. Are you?"

"I could force myself. Maybe we're looking at this from the wrong angle."

"I'll look where you point."

"Say it turns out to be a premeditated job—?"

Nelson nodded.

"Well—take college and those books he buys. They don't spell 'dumb.' So why couldn't he have arranged it all to make us think what you had me thinking? Ain't it possible we could dig up all the motive we need if it's established that he and Hackett weren't strangers?"

"Provided it *can* be established."

"There's a Mrs. Hackett. She maybe saw Berthold around or heard mention of him."

"She's been notified—and she'll be questioned—but it will have to keep until she returns to New York. Probably tomorrow if she's not too hard hit to travel."

"Where is she?"

"Miami."

"Say—that's where your missus and the boy are. How's about sending me down to oil up the investigation? I could do with some red-hot sun." He gave a hollow cough.

"I'm afraid we'll have to brave the winter winds together."

His car was parked near the building. He dropped Clevis off at a bus stop and drove home. At a few moments before eight he let himself into his house.

A very tall straight shadow swept across his path to the stairs. It spoke in the deep rich voice of Sammy, his housekeeper-cook. "I glad Miss Kyrie away. You ain't fit for her to see."

"How can you tell?" He switched on another lamp.

"I don't need more light, Mr. Grid-dely. You worked all last night and you didn't even come home this morning to freshen yourself."

"Isn't this your day off?"

"I on again. You staying long enough to put something on your stomach, it ready by the time you come down."

"It's a deal—on condition you serve it in the kitchen and keep it simple."

He went upstairs. His young son's room looked unnaturally tidy. The bedroom he shared with Kyrie complained of her absence. He glimpsed himself in her mirror, frowned, and glanced apologetically at the extension telephone. Before he put in the customary call to Miami he bathed and shaved.

Back in the bedroom, he gave the operator the number. He was buttoning on a clean shirt when Kyrie's voice came, intimate and sweet.

"Grid?"

"Were you sitting at the phone? Sorry I'm late."

"No squawks. You've been so punctual it spoiled me. When you didn't call on the dot I thought my luck had changed. Are you still at the office?"

"No—I'm home."

"I wish I were."

He shut his eyes for a moment. He could see her plainly: slim, ash blond, and violet-eyed. He said, "You've earned a vacation from me—how's Junie?"

"Fine—just this one week in the sun has clobbered the virus. In fact I think we could—"

"No—you're to stay until the weather improves here."

"Is it still snowing?"

"It's stopped—but it's chill—and he's had a pretty bad bout."

"He's waiting to talk to you. Shall I put him on?"

He spoke to his son, and then Kyrie came back. "Hear that door slam? The hotel's giving a special show for children. I had to extend his bedtime."

"I hope I didn't make him miss any of the show."

"Be flattered. He wouldn't budge until you called. Sammy's off today, isn't she?"

"No—she's getting dinner for me."

"Good. You sound as though you need it. When did you have your last meal?"

"Let's not waste these few precious moments on nonessentials."

The deliberately maudlin tone of his voice made her laugh.

"The trouble with you is, you have no sentiment," he said.

"And the trouble with you is, you're a good actor—but not good enough. If you had lunch at all today it was watery coffee and a droopy sandwich at your desk. I'll bet you're working on something more than average distasteful."

"Let's just say that the precinct involved is acting more than average distasteful—and stop being so perceptive."

"I couldn't not be—living with you all these years. I knew you were tired and phony cheerful the moment you spoke."

He said on impulse, "Kyrie—have you ever been to the Aintree Hotel at Miami Beach?"

"I know it by sight."

"What sort of place is it?"

"At least twice as big as this one—and five times as gaudy. I think it draws the very sudden rich—gamblers and overnight successes at something or other. Is it connected with your case?"

"Probably not in any way that counts."

"Too bad. I was hoping that since I couldn't lure you south, business might—with time out for the vacation you didn't take."

"Next summer we'll—"

"No rash promises, Grid. Only—please take care of yourself."

"I will. You too. Any message for Sammy?"

"I think I'd like to give it direct."

"All right. I'll call down and tell her to pick up the phone. Hug Junie for me."

"Who's going to hug me for you?"

"Nobody had better try. More tomorrow, Kyrie."

He finished dressing and went down to the kitchen. Sammy was setting a cocktail shaker and a glass on a tray. She said, "I just going to bring this to you. Miss Kyrie's orders."

"Thanks, Sammy. It will taste better here." He poured the whiskey sour and sat at the kitchen table to drink it. He said innocently, "What did you and Miss Kyrie talk about?"

The tall woman looked down at him. "You mean do I tell her you working all night?"

He smiled. "That's exactly what I mean."

"What sense it be to worry her?"

"I deserve to have arsenic in my food for thinking you would."

"Folks wearing theirselves to death don't need no other poison," she said.

He watched her put the final touches to his meal. He had made Junie stop coaxing her to go to Florida at her firm announcement that she preferred the climate up North. Now he was selfishly glad she had stayed, whatever her reasons.

"Has Junie been writing to you?" he said.

"I got me a little old inky postcard this morning. I think he using the sand as a writing desk." Then she said, "I sure going to feel happy to see that child again."

"Another two weeks and he'll be back."

She set the thick broiled steak and the salad before him and cut chunks from a loaf of French bread. "That going to do you? Seem like you too hungry to start messing with cooked vegetables."

"They'd just be a distraction. This is perfect."

"You eat before it stop sizzling," Sammy said.

She got QXR on her radio to keep him company and busied herself in the pantry while he ate. When she returned she looked at the empty plates and nodded serenely. "I expect you feeling better now, Mr. Grid-dely."

"There are too many detectives in this house."

The phone rang while he was drinking coffee. "Sit still," Sammy said. "It left to me I going to tell anybody you can't be disturbed."

But she came back to say that a Mr. Thurlow was on the line. When Nelson took the call he was greeted by the pompous and reproving voice of the assistant D.A.

"Captain Nelson? I've been trying to reach you at your office—"

Nelson glanced at his watch. It was five after ten. He said, "Occasionally I come home."

"Yes—of course—I didn't mean to intimate—everyone knows your reputation for hard work." He took time to get to the point. Nelson, who did not like him, did not help him. "In regard to the Hackett case—I'm afraid it's a bit more complicated than at first glance."

"I didn't assume it was simple to begin with," Nelson said. "What complications are you referring to?"

"Well—it seems that Berthold appears to have made some rather surprising connections in high places."

Nelson waited.

"You've heard of Edwin Decker?"

"Yes—I know Mr. Decker." Nelson's triangular body straightened. He moved his broad shoulders as though he were shedding the last remnants of fatigue.

"I've been notified that Decker went to the Tombs to see Berthold. It seems he's prepared to go bail for him and to undertake his defense. What do you make of that?"

"Too bad," Nelson said, meaning, "Wonderful."

"A man of his caliber—a famous criminal lawyer—" Thurlow spoke as though he were coping with a mortal wound. "Of course we could have Berthold shadowed until the case comes up—"

Nelson refrained from saying, "What case?"

"Or in view of the possibility that the burglary charge might not stand up in court the D.A. could appear before a General Sessions judge and ask that Berthold be held as a material witness until sufficient evidence is gathered to book him for murder." He paused for a comment that did not come. "I was wondering if you had any suggestions. I don't mind admitting that I'm baffled."

"By the implication that Berthold is not the friendless derelict he seemed at first glance?" Nelson was enjoying himself. "I don't see why that should baffle you. It merely places him on an equal footing with the other suspects."

"Suspects? City Council Fredericks—or Donald Palmer or—?"

"It isn't necessary to go through the list of them," Nelson said kindly. "I have it pretty well committed to memory. By the way—was Decker outgoing enough to mention who had stimulated his interest in Berthold?"

"No—and my informant seems to think that Berthold doesn't know either. But that's nonsense."

"I wouldn't be too sure," Nelson said. "Someone might be paying hush money to a screaming conscience. That would leave Berthold as much in the dark as you are."

Chapter Eight

When the guard said, "Your lawyer's here," and ushered a stranger into the cell, it seemed to Matt that he was entering yet another phase of the Kafka-like plain to which he had descended. Obviously in that frustrating half-world it would be useless to protest that he had no lawyer, so he shrugged and sat on the edge of his bunk to await developments.

The lawyer was a thin, loose-jointed man with graying hair. He had a clean odor that freshened the harshly disinfected air. He brought another intangible with him, a kind of power that Matt felt through his numbness.

"I'm Edwin Decker," he said in a resonant voice.

Matt nodded and took the proffered hand, surprised at its warm bony grasp, since dreams should be composed of no such vital substance.

The guard went out and locked the grille. Matt wondered if he had misunderstood, if Decker were just another prisoner sent to occupy the cell's second bunk. His clothes were no clue. Of good wool and cut, they could have come to him at second hand and been molded to his spare form by wear.

"Should I know you?" Matt said.

"My ego says you should. What modesty I have admits the possibility that you don't." His glance around the cell achieved the transition from pleasantry to grim purpose. "Why didn't you send for a lawyer?"

"I had no lawyer to send for. I supposed a reasonable facsimile of one would be provided when the time came." He had an odd sensation that Decker was memorizing him. "I don't know any of the ropes. This is my first non-offense."

Decker said abruptly, "Move over," and sat down next to him. "I'll cut this as short as possible—the object being to get you out of here."

Matt, who toward evening had stopped listening for the sounds of deliverance, said, "You make it sound easy—but the cost of bail these days has skyrocketed like everything else." He held fast to bravado. "You'd be surprised at the price tag on common theft."

"Are you guilty of theft?"

"No."

"Of murder?"

"No. Are you the lawyer they picked for me?"

"A reasonable facsimile."

"You have my sympathy. You're stuck with a beaut."

"We'll see about that." His voice deserved a bigger house than the narrow chest from which it issued. He recited almost word for word the statement Matt had given.

Matt listened, an inhabitant of the Kafka world again. When the recital was over he nodded objectively. "Maybe they're not entirely to blame. It doesn't sound like much." In deference to the impressive voice he added, "But if anyone could convince me that I was telling the truth—you could."

"Thank you." The severe planes of Decker's face were altered by a smile. He said, "For a man in a spot—even an innocent man—you're a bit detached."

"Frozen is the word. Since last night I haven't been able to produce a single thought to warm myself by—and it isn't for want of trying."

"Then I take it there's nothing you can add to the statement?"

"No. The truth is, I'm beginning to share their doubt that the woman who picked me up exists."

"If she does we'll find her."

"The police didn't." The hope conjured up by Decker's assurance was as sharp as a sword. Matt backed away, distrusting its bright edge. "And that homicide captain would have tried. At least—at least I think he would."

"These things take a little time," Decker said.

"Time!" For Matt a year had passed. The blade of hope dulled and blunted. So far as he knew, this man selected at random from "their" roster was no more than a third-rater. Or he might even be an agent sent to elicit what "they" insisted had been deliberately withheld. Matt looked him in the eye. "Do you think the woman exists?"

"Yes."

"Would you mind telling me why you should believe me when nobody else does—except maybe Captain Nelson?"

"If I'm to defend you, belief is a reasonable starting point. My belief, however, has certain reservations."

"I knew there'd be a catch to it. What are they?"

Instead of answering, Decker asked a series of questions. Some of them back-tracked to the ground covered by the statement. None of them served to widen it. He went on digging. "Wasn't there anyone on scene whose manner stood out beyond what was called for by the circumstances?"

"I didn't notice," Matt said. "My own circumstances stopped me from making more than general observations."

"Such as?"

"Things like how insulated and sleek they seemed—the spouting Callender—and the fellow with a tropical tan in the middle of winter—and the one with the overstuffed paunch who called the D.A.'s man by his first name—and a four-eyed mousy little twerp who treated me as if I had the plague. The size of it is, I was extra-touchy. I saw them as they affected me—and nothing I saw would make them murderers."

He slumped as the questions continued. Many of them seemed irrelevant, dealing not with the case but with his parents, his background, his future as a scientist, and what he had been doing to insure that future. He answered because he felt that Decker was trying to do his job. Once or twice he was seduced into expressing enthusiasm, which petered out as he remembered how problematical his future had become.

To change the nature of the questions he said, "What about the murdered man? He's haunted me all day—among other haunts." He realized the implication of his words and reddened guiltily. "I mean—wondering what sort he'd been—and why he was killed."

"You'd never met or heard of Eugene Hackett?"

"Where would I have met him? In night school—or at a quick-lunch counter? As for hearing about him—I haven't time to read the social columns."

Decker appeared to disregard the irony. "Hackett was a rich man with a sizable piece of many profitable enterprises. So far as his publicity goes, there were no black marks against him. I expect that he had the average number of friends and enemies attracted by men of wealth. He was sixty-five years old— "

Matt said, "He looked older," and added carefully, "That is, his corpse did." He half expected Decker to pounce.

Decker merely said, "He left no children, and no one but his wife benefited materially by his death." Without emphasis he elaborated, "His wife, by the way, is vacationing in Florida."

"How do you know all this?"

"I've been in touch with his lawyer, who was courteous enough to tell me his will in substance."

Matt nodded, impressed in spite of himself by such thoroughness. He was unprepared when Decker said, "To go back to my reservations concerning your story—you did not ride in from Brooklyn to see a movie."

"Didn't I? Look—I appreciate the way you're trying to take hold, but you've also been ringing in a lot of things that have nothing to do with—"

"Character witnesses have often swayed a jury. My advice is to spare no one who could act in that capacity. Obviously you took a long subway ride last night because of something or someone more important than a movie. Even second-run movies are expensive to a man on a budget."

"And even skinflints have their moments of extravagance," Matt said. "I don't think we're getting anywhere, Mr. Decker, so maybe I should give you and your reservations some advice in return for yours. Why not drop the case and let them hire another boy?" He was acting the fool and he knew it, for although logic implied that if Decker were good at his profession he would not at his age be on tap to defend indigent prisoners, there was that about him which inspired trust.

His heart plunged as Decker stood up. Yet he went on playing the fool. "Congratulations for having the sense to back out. There'd be no glory in sticking—or money either. I've got a little but—" Rennie came, as she had come all day, between himself and thoughts of self-survival. "But I've other demands on most of what I've saved."

"I'll get busy," Decker said, and moved toward the door.

Matt's "Thanks anyway" was ambiguous, because of course the man was saving face. Then he said, "Wait—"

"Yes?"

An account of the murder had surely appeared in the newspapers, and Rennie was a reader of newspapers. What he wanted was to ask the deserting lawyer for writing material so that he could have him mail some sort of reassuring message to her. But Decker would be certain to read her name and address, and there was the risk that he would deliver it to those who supplied his bread and butter. It was better to leave Rennie without reassurance than to take that risk. Talk about character witnesses. An unmarried girl carrying the child of the defendant. He could imagine in what direction that would sway a jury. Rather than have her so exposed he would go jet-propelled to the chair.

Decker had turned, was watching his face. He jumped from the treadmill of his thoughts. "Never mind."

Decker called for the guard, who came immediately to release him. The single overhead bulb in the cell went out and there was only the lighting in the corridor to think by.

At intervals during the day Matt had dropped into a feverish doze. Now he was wide-awake and he wondered how many hours of the night remained. He toyed with the notion of summoning the guard to ask the time, but decided it would not be worthwhile to invite anger or ridicule, not even to break a monotony harder to bear since Decker had come and gone. Decker had torn from him the saving veil of depersonalization. Coming to grips with reality again was a painful process. He would have to get a real lawyer, one of his own choosing, but who? And how? And where? Would Captain Nelson come if he sent for him? Would he give him advice as a friend?

Except for meals which he could not eat, Matt had received no attention throughout the dragging hours of imprisonment. Either the inmates of the Tombs went without exercise, or he had not been "in" long enough for exercise to be considered essential. He stood up and stretched experimentally, as though he expected rebuff from atrophied muscles. There had been activity in the other cells, doors sliding open and shut, footsteps along the corridor, but to what purpose he could not determine. With each emergence from unrestful sleep he had heard voices, some pitched to ordinary level, some raised in anger, and some, incredibly to him, in jest and laughter.

The comparative after-hours quiet stifled him. He had an impulse to rip it apart. How to become stir-crazy in one lesson, he said to himself. Like those movies where prisoners beat against their bars and scream for freedom. Somehow remembrance of the clichéd sequence steadied him. But I've got to get out, he thought more calmly. There's a built-in solution to every problem. I've got to figure this one. If no one else can find that woman, I must. She's the hidden key—she—

He saw her as she had appeared in the car and in the entry's shaded light. He saw her fur-swaddled height, her straight dark-fleshed nose, the rest of her a blur except for a glimpse of mouth and upper teeth. A short upper lip, and teeth white by contrast to—? Dark-skinned. A brunette. With that complexion she was a brunette.

It seemed little to go on, but there had been less before. Would it help the homicide captain—or Decker?

It was as though he had been drugged. His mind would not hold to any given line. Decker. There was no use pretending that he did not regret the loss of Decker. Third-rate or no, the man had been interested to the extent of boning up on the case. "*I'll cut this short*," he said, "*the object being to get you out of here*." And he said, "We'll find her." As easy as that. Well—he had cut it short all right. He could have spared himself the trouble of asking those unprofessional questions that all but demanded a biography of Matt's parents.

Not that Matt had minded answering. The memory of his parents, of his love for them, held nothing painful except that it was memory.

His father had been the principal of the small town's elementary school. His death was caused by injuries received in the burning building after the children and the staff were safe outside. He had lingered too long in an attempt to rescue some of the records, and when the firemen reached him he was pinned beneath a fallen beam. He lived for a suffering while, crippled in limb and lung. When he died, Matt's grief was pocked with resentment for his mother's anguish, for the change in both their lives, and for what he considered the mock-heroics of overconscientiousness that had destroyed a decent, blameless man. He was unaware that much of his father lived on in him, that his own determination to spare Rennie the publicity that her association with him might bring could be categorized as mock-heroics.

His father had left a small mortgaged house, a modest insurance, and nothing else of material value. It was impossible for Matt to return to college and keep up the payments on the house. Nor were there jobs available at home. His mother had chosen to be uprooted rather than to be lonely. So she had accompanied him to New York. They rented a small apartment, and on the basis of recommendations from former instructors, Matt was admitted to Columbia. He worked after classes to supplement the dwindling legacy and managed well until his mother became ill. The symptoms of a common cold turned out to be the onset of a fatal influenza. She had made a valiant effort to live, but the loss of her husband and concern for her son tipped the scales.

Medical attention, hospital bills, and funeral expenses devoured the remainder of the nest egg. Matt took the full-time job in Brooklyn and installed himself in a room convenient to it. He was motivated solely by dogged purpose. Then came Rennie. And then came—?

He was pacing the cell like any movie prisoner. He stopped and turned toward the sliding grille. Here was the guard to tell him to stop moving about, disturbing the innocent sleep of his fellow cutthroats. He made a grim sound that was nearly laughter.

The high overhead light went on. The guard said in a not unfriendly voice, "You've sure got something to laugh about, boy. You've been sprung."

Chapter Nine

What happened then, although a marked improvement, was as indigestible to Matt as the events of the preceding night and day. He dressed, followed the guard, obediently signed for the return of his trifling possessions, listened to without hearing a speech that sounded like an incantation, had his hand shaken by a brisk man with a brief case who forthwith disappeared, and was given to understand that he could do likewise.

The gates of the gloomy structure had become invested with a certain beauty by virtue of their transformation from entrance to exit. He walked through them conditionally free, yet too overawed by the turn of his luck to dwell upon the fact that bail still leashed him.

Outside, while he tried to take bearings, his name was called. Unable to account for this phenomenon, he glanced over his shoulder, convinced for a fearful moment that "they" had changed their minds.

The resonant voice said, "This way," and, half poised to bolt, he saw the car. Before he reached it he recognized the figure at the wheel.

Decker said casually, "Can you drive?"

Matt said, "Yes," remembering, how many lives ago, his father's old sedan and all the old familiar roads it had traveled; remembering a souped-up job that he and a friend had shared, and rushing on to remember a stint at college as chauffeur for a crippled professor.

"Good," Decker said. "Later perhaps you'll take over. I don't enjoy night driving. Too old for it. Get in."

Matt hesitated on the sidewalk. "I might take you out of your way. You see—I've got to—I've got to see a friend." Rennie, he thought gladly, I can go to her now—tell her what's happened—make light of it so she won't—

"If it's anybody you prefer not to involve," Decker said, "postpone it. Shadowing is common procedure in cases like yours."

"But—" He moved his neck as though the leash had materialized to chafe him. He scrutinized the seemingly deserted street.

"If there *is* a shadow you don't expect him to be in plain sight, do you? Get in."

He obeyed, renouncing with a long-drawn sigh the sight and sound and touch of Rennie. He would watch out for a phone booth and send her a telegram. That would have to do.

As soon as the car started he said, "I haven't thanked you. The fact is, this business has left me in a kind of fog. I didn't even connect you with my release. There was a man with a briefcase and I thought he—"

"That was my assistant. He didn't wait because he was in a hurry to get home."

"Oh." He did not attempt to reconcile his previous summary of Decker with an assistant or with a large smoothly gliding car. He twisted around in his seat and could not see the prison, and for the moment that was all that mattered.

"How did you manage it?" he said.

"Relax. I'll tell you in good time."

"Look—I live all the way out in Brooklyn—this is an imposition—"

"You don't live in Brooklyn anymore."

"I don't—?"

"Your rent was due at noon today, and your former landlady's a stickler for the cash-on-the-dot system. I'm told your room's been rented."

Matt groaned. "My books and papers—"

"She'll undoubtedly keep them safe until you send for them."

"Can she—? I haven't been convicted—is it legal for her to put me out like that?"

"Legal or not, it won't be worth your while to fight her."

"What about my job?" He did not need to ask.

"As soon as you get out of your present difficulties they'll have to rehire you, but undoubtedly you can do better."

Matt said in a low harsh voice, "Sure. I won't worry about a thing. It's fun to live dangerously—never knowing where the next swipe's coming from just that it's coming—" He could have gone on and on, but he used his teeth and his lips to hold back the useless anger. It was not Decker's fault. Decker had performed a miracle—or anyway a temporary miracle. And the car's swift forward motion, the windows lowered a little and scaled by a clean cold wind, were no small mercies. He breathed deeply. He said, "Sorry to take it out on you—but if we aren't going to Brooklyn, where are we going? Hadn't I better hunt for a lodging instead of—?"

"It's late. Any place prepared to admit you without luggage would be very expensive or very questionable. I'll put you up."

"I'm under enough obligation as it is."

"I'm no altruist. It's in my interest to keep an eye on you."

"I won't jump bail if that's what you mean."

"I don't think you will—but I've had a pretty full day—and to put it bluntly I don't propose to make it fuller by doing the rounds of hotels to get you bedded down."

"You won't have to. I'm capable of—" He stopped because it seemed unnecessarily stiff-necked to argue about where he spent a night that but for the grace of his benefactor would have been spent in a cell. "All right. It suits me if it suits you."

He sat back and watched Decker's authoritative manipulation of the car. Night driving did not appear to trouble him in spite of what he had said, but perhaps he had only been making conversation to ease an awkward moment. He was a nice guy. To make him small return Matt said, "If you do want me take over say the word. Just tell me where you live and the best way to get there."

"Barns Village—Westchester. You can do the last half."

"Barns Village!"

"Don't use that tone. It isn't in darkest Africa."

Matt did some mental arithmetic, adding Barns Village to the assistant and the expensive car. The homely name was misleading. It was one of the wealthiest suburbs in the East. Even he had heard of it.

"In fact I've seen literature that refers to it as within easy commuting distance," Decker said.

Matt was shaking his head. "Stung again," he said. Then he said, "Stop the car—I want out."

Decker's voice was rough with concern. "I can't stop here. What's the matter—are you sick?"

"Good and sick for letting myself be fooled. They wouldn't send a lawyer to go bail for me. They'd wait until the case came up. My wits were addled or I'd have—"

"Is that all? Don't be too hard on yourself—"

"Hard on *myself!*"

"Your wits were addled because you swallowed a glass of drugged whiskey."

"What?" He had ascribed his condition to the stupefacient ingredients of shock. He said angrily, "So I was wrong all the way. One of my bright notions was that the woman had something to do with framing me. But she couldn't have drugged a glass of whiskey on the chance I'd drink it. How would she know I'd help myself—?"

"I think we can safely assume that the drug wasn't meant for you. It might well have been intended to dull the perceptions of some guest whose acuteness was feared by the murderer."

"Sure—and that points to the murderer being another of the guests."

Decker said, "Fortunately we aren't required to fix guilt. All we have to do is prove your innocence."

Matt's "We?" was sired by disillusionment. "This guest whose guilt we don't have to fix knows I didn't kill because he has one sure way of knowing. And you have one sure way of knowing who he is."

"I don't follow your reasoning."

"Oh yes, you do. He's hired you to defend me. A belated attack of conscience wouldn't let him go all the way—not when he could afford a high-priced lawyer to ease it." He expected Decker to deny or equivocate. He did not expect him to sound amused.

Decker said, "An ingenious theory. Supposing it were true?"

"You led me to believe—"

"I led you to believe nothing. You led yourself. Furthermore it shouldn't matter to you who retained me. What should matter is that I'm undoubtedly superior to any lawyer you'd have the opportunity to select."

"I'd rather take my chances with—with an ambulance chaser."

"That's hardly a realistic attitude. It might be that in your effort to reach goal you've been neglecting to feed yourself properly. The amount of Demerol you took should have worn off by now."

"Demerol be damned! You're shielding someone—that means you're guilty too. How do I know you won't double-cross me if your real client has another change of mind?"

"I thought that scientists had begun to emerge from their ivory towers. If yours hadn't been windowless and soundproofed you'd know that I'm considered to be one of the top lawyers in the country. I'm prepared to document that claim when we reach my house—not out of vanity but to convince you that I'd have to be certifiable to risk my good reputation by indulging in any practice that would destroy it. Meanwhile—if I swear that my interest in you has nothing to do with the doctor, his guests, or the woman who picked you up—will you be satisfied?"

"For all I know your word isn't worth a —"

"For all I know your protestation of innocence has the same value. We'll have to take each other on trust"—he braked for a red light—"or part company."

"I vote for that," Matt said. His fingers grasped the handle of the door.

Decker said, "I was instructed to break it to you gently—to wait until a bath and a meal had weaned you back to a reasonable perspective—but I'm beginning to doubt you ever had one." His voice sizzled. "Let that door be. You're a stubborn, hotheaded young fool. I never believed in the cliché that love is blind, but it's obvious that Dorene's vision is impaired, to say the least."

"Dorene?" For a split second the name meant nothing to Matt. "Rennie—"

"Yes—Rennie." A trick of mind had made him say "Dorene." She had been named after his dead sister, but barring moments of sternness with her, he always used the diminutive.

Matt was saying, "Oh no. How in God's name did you—?"

"Calm down. It's very simple. She read of your arrest in the afternoon paper." He reduced the heat of his voice to a dry simmer. "Since you've known her so well you should have known that she's a fighter. Naturally she—"

"Naturally she came to you," Matt yelled. "What do you take me for? By your own boast you're at the top of your profession—a rich man. So a poor kid who slaves in a department store naturally decides to retain you—and naturally you stand on your hind legs to beg for the peanuts she throws your way. Try again. Tell me anything—count on the Demerol to work for you."

"Wait a minute—"

He could not wait a minute. The traffic light had changed and someone in the car behind was pressing a horn. To him the outlawed sound was a final contemptuous raspberry. He got the door open and hurled himself to the road. Decker shouted after him, but he did not look back. He counted upon the traffic to render the trickster helpless. A nice guy—a very nice guy! He squeezed through a minimal space between fenders and spun when he reached the sidewalk, directing his racing steps away from the oiled and treacherous society of Barns Village. Once or twice he looked back. No one followed him. That story of a police "shadow" was probably as phony as everything else.

What does he take me for—what do they take me for? He marched to the rhythm of it. I'll show them—I'll show them all. That was a better marching tune. It spurred him on through the first lap. Then he slowed down, timing his stride to a less stimulating beat. Lucky for me we hadn't reached the highway. I'd be a fine sight stumbling along a grassy shoulder. Just what I'd need would be for a third helpful Joe to catch me in his lights and offer assistance. I mustn't trust anybody but Rennie—bless her. She waded in to help—only I wish she hadn't.

He thought that the type of lawyer within her reach had presented no problem to Decker and his nameless client. He thought that Decker in his exhaustive inquiry had learned of the minor colleague's fumbling efforts; had made contact with him, even employing attractive concrete means of persuading him to bow out. Preoccupied with this, he came to a subway station and walked on until subliminal prompting sent him sprinting back. It was not the subway he wanted, but after two changes a train brought him to familiar territory.

There was a couple welded together in the musty vestibule of Rennie's house. The female tore herself loose with a tremulous squeal. The male groaned tortured obscenities. But Matt had constituted no interruption or threat to their pleasure. He neither saw nor heard them. He rang a bell, dimly realized that it was the wrong one, and muttered undirected apology as the latch was released. He lumbered up the stairs, projecting all of his senses to the third floor before his body reached it, experiencing more sharply than reality that which he willed to happen there.

On Rennie's landing he stood ready to assault the blank scarred face of her door, but the prevailing quiet stayed his hand. A knock unheralded by his special ring might sound ominous coming at this hour. He drew the key from his pocket. He discovered with relief that she had not used the bolt, and let himself in quietly. If she should wake and cry out, he had the words of reassurance near his lips.

He heard no outcry. He could not even hear her sleeping breath. But because the words were ready he uttered them with infinite gentleness. "Rennie—it's Matt—don't be afraid. Rennie—sweetheart—"

The room was airless. On the coldest nights she flung the window wide. The room was airless and empty, a fact he had known and denied in the very moment of entering. He groped for the standard lamp and switched it on, and was mocked by the smooth bland surface of the bed and by the untenanted neatness around him.

He looked into the kitchenette and the bathroom. He looked in the clothes closet. There were several gaps on the usually tight-packed rod. He slid the clothes along it in search of her missing winter coat. Then he sat down and stared at the floor.

Where had she gone so late? What errand undischarged had sent her into the cold streets? She would come back of course and find him there and everything would be— At any moment she would walk in the door and everything would—

After a while he got up. He removed the bedspread and folded it as he had seen her do. He shed coat and shoes and loosened his collar. Then he lay supine, eyes open, and waited as she had waited on the night before.

Chapter Ten

Edwin Decker did not savor the prospect of facing his niece. He toyed halfheartedly with the alternative of driving back to town, spending the rest of the night at his club, and mending his fences before he saw her. But a disappointed Rennie was better than a Rennie left to imagine the worst, and moreover, he was unable to reconcile even this most absurd form of moral cowardice with his temperament. He drove on, acutely conscious of the empty seat beside him.

Up to a point, he thought, he had handled matters well, stretching the truth for the young man's good where stretching was required. For example, he knew that there would be no police shadow since he had hinted that he did not intend to let the young man out of his sight. He also knew that Matt could demand his Brooklyn room and get it at little more cost than the imprecations of the landlady. These inventions had been necessary in order to lead Matt to Rennie. It would have been wiser, of course, to state at the outset that he was Rennie's uncle. But she would not have it that way.

Even in normal circumstances, she said, Matt showed the kind of pride that had gone out of fashion. Probably, she said, he would take an old-fashioned attitude about her money, and certainly he would feel deceived. Yet she knew that his offer to "do right by her" had sprung from love and not, as he believed, from a sense of obligation. Therefore, only she could ease him into acceptance of the true state of her fortunes. So please let her be the one to tell him—please, Uncle Ted.

When he hesitated she had begged to go with him to the Tombs, to reveal the truth then and there. He had denied her firmly on the grounds that she had taken all she could stand, that there might be reporters present, and that she would gain nothing but notoriety. He thought it politic to leave his main reason for denial unstated, fearing that she would quarrel with it. He wanted to get a line on the young man without her there to cloud his judgment. He was determined, should Matt Berthold prove less than half she said he was, to let him rot in jail. Rennie had no temporary alliance in mind. She would marry for keeps or not at all, and in her uncle's opinion an illegitimate child was preferable to an undesirable husband.

He had compromised by granting her first request. In the light of hindsight he thought that perhaps this had been her sole object and that the follow-up was merely a bargaining tool. There was nothing wrong with her wits, he thought. *She* should have been a lawyer.

He scowled at the windshield. And what had she become? There was a designation in the books for— To hell with that. She was a fine decent girl to whom no opprobrious term applied, and it was up to him to see that none was ever used. With the best of intentions her father would bungle. After her mother's death he had bungled everything but financial affairs. And if the sum total of a man could be called a fault, then the plight of his daughter was his fault. He had overindulged her materially and underindulged her spiritually, and it was from him and not from Edwin Decker's sister that she had inherited the wayward—

He knew he was being unjust to the two of them. It had taken considerable pluck for Rennie to strike out on her own, to get a job, to adjust to a life so far removed from accustomed luxury. And if she had sinned—! The syllable snarled in his head and he annihilated it. What she had done, outcome aside, was intended as a deliberate slap at her father. Deliberate emulation to depose a clay-footed idol who had never asked for a pedestal in the first place. Decker did not know what had brought her disillusionment to a head, but he did know that a Rennie at bay would refuse to accept the convention-drawn dichotomy that separated masculine and feminine behavior.

He could not remember paying a coin at the toll box, yet here he was on the highway. Somewhat cheered that the worst of the drive was over, he picked up speed. But the cold and the snow had laid death traps and he had to slow down again. Maybe James will have persuaded her to take a sleep, he thought. He can be very persuasive when he tries. And if he got her to lie down and close her eyes for a while she might be good for the night. Which would suit me fine. But he knew it was wishful thinking. Awake or asleep, she would hear the car and come running to embrace the missing lover.

He had put her through a grueling interrogation, getting as much useful information as he could before he went into action. His reactions as her story unfolded had been a complexity of dismay, anger, pity, and over all a constructive urge to protect. He had no child of his own. She occupied the high place in his heart. He hated to recall her purple-shadowed eyes, her small tired face strained further by the lawyer-client relationship which he had instituted so that he might reach conclusions disencumbered of sentiment.

And he had reached them. All would be well. She and the young man would have their chance at the happy ending. And who knew but that a marriage so inauspiciously embarked upon might turn out as well or better than the average mating. He had married after a year's engagement, and two years after that his wife had left him. She had regarded his work as a spiteful rival, resenting each moment he gave to it. Decker sighed and thought that in the final analysis Matt Berthold was a lucky man. It would not be Rennie's fault if he failed to achieve his ambition.

On the whole he had been favorably impressed by Matt Berthold. He had observed closely a good cross section of people under stress and, making due allowances, he thought that the young man would do. There seemed to be nothing shabby about him in spite of his disreputable clothing. He had a forthright eye, and that cock-and-bull tale about coming from Brooklyn to see a movie was in his favor too. He was practicing chivalry in an age that had little use for it; a prodigal brand of chivalry, since he must have realized that the slightest suspicion of a lie could serve to negate his statement in its entirety.

When I was about to leave, Decker thought, and he asked me to wait, I was sure he was ready to tell me about Rennie. But he clung to the lie as though all knighthood hung upon it. No one was going to sully the reputation of his lady if he could help it.

Decker swore. He shouted, "Dim those lights, you oaf," to an offending car. The chain of his thoughts showed no perceptible break. A knight, huh? There was irony for you. Some knight to take advantage of— Don't be an old fossil. No one took advantage of Rennie. Berthold was a man—not exactly a man of the world, but not a monk either. He had merely bowed to the natural law of his species.

He would be easy to find again. No doubt he had headed for Rennie's apartment. And her "Uncle Ted" could have done the same, except that for all his questions it did not occur to him to ask her for the address. But Matt would wait there for her. At least it would keep him from searching for a lodging. He would wait the night and as much of the next day as might go by before he gave up hope of her return. So the thing to do was to have him intercepted by a member of the firm who lived in Manhattan, and that as early as could be arranged. If he was still in the "Doubting Thomas" stage, Strachan, the private detective who had seen him with the woman, could be dangled as tempting bait until Rennie made him see reason.

A telephone call made by James Marshall had revealed that his man had driven Strachan to the railroad station. He had not stayed to see him board the train. The fellow had been drunk, drunkenly insistent that he should "blow."

James should have hung onto him, Decker thought. Instead of a contemptuous suggestion that the little crook take his evidence to the police, he should have hauled him to the nearest precinct. But James had no interest in justice unless it bore upon his own affairs.

Again Decker recognized that he himself was being unjust. James, at the time, had no way of measuring the importance of Strachan's evidence. He wanted what Decker wanted and what Berthold wanted, to keep Rennie out of it. Berthold had been nothing to him but an anonymous jailbird.

Whereupon Decker was quick to acknowledge that but for Rennie he too could have accepted Berthold's misfortune with only passing interest. For regardless of the public's fond assumption that falsely accused prisoners were a rarity, it simply was not so. And however philanthropically inclined, a man could not go to bat for all of them.

Meeting his brother-in-law on that small patch of common ground, he could admire his attitude toward the would-be blackmailer. Anyone so threatened would do well to follow suit, he thought. But too few dared. James, he conceded, had a certain aptitude for appraising his fellow men, and a certain integrity as well. It assumed odd shapes, but it was there. It was even manifest in dealing with his ever-changing women. He never failed to warn them in advance of the limited extent of his interests. Decker had extracted this from a woman who had tried to compensate for lost virtue by airing her troubles in court. No wonder that Rennie—

He pulled up at the Barns Village railroad crossing to sit out the passing of a train. It was a long train, but he was not impatient. There were only two more miles to go and at the end of them was Rennie.

She did not rush to meet him. She and her father were in the main living room. She was sitting on a couch, hands folded in her lap, decorous as a child who had been promised a treat for good behavior. When Decker entered alone a question formed in the room and hung like an icicle beyond the reach of the snapping logs in the fireplace. She looked past her uncle and seemed to be listening for the answer.

Decker went to her. "Don't look like that. It's not as bad as you think. It's not bad at all. I bailed him out but he got away." Rapidly he made full explanation.

Rennie was neither appeased nor comforted. "Why did you let him go?"

"What else could I have done—stuck in the middle of traffic? Did you want me to abandon the car and count upon my aging legs to outsprint him?"

"I should have gone with you."

"And made matters worse?"

"No—I'd have told him everything—forced him to understand why I—"

"Suppose *you* try to understand? Believe me—after spending a day in that cell he was in no receptive frame of mind. You might have lost him for keeps."

She jumped up. "Of course! He's in the apartment. There won't be much traffic now. If I hurry I can make it in—"

"Sit down. You're going nowhere."

"I am. You muffed it—"

He was glad to see the return of her color and vitality. He said, "Yes—I muffed it—and not without considerable assistance. It's my business to lead a horse to water and make him drink—but I can't do it when amateurs like you insist upon tying my hands."

"We're wasting time. Did you put your car away?"

"I did. And your father's car is in the garage too—and the garage is locked—and the key is in my pocket." He allowed himself the luxury of temper because the situation required it. "After this you'll think twice before you decide to sail under false pretenses."

Her father stopped being a bystander. "Don't be hard on her, Ted."

"She's being hard on me."

Rennie, a study in arrested motion, was staring at him. To keep her arrested, he said, "But I can take it. What I can't take is her willful intention to place in jeopardy the health of my grand-nephew-to-be by subjecting him to a hazardous drive on an iced highway merely to gratify one of her selfish whims." He gave it his all. His resonant voice quavered. "It's plain she thinks I've grown so old and addled that I'm not to be trusted."

For a moment she looked uncertain. "I'm sorry, Uncle Ted—I—" But he could not fool her for long. They understood each other too well. "You're a fraud," she said. "Not an old fraud either—and you know I trust you, but I can't let him stay there worrying about me. I went through the same thing last night—waiting and waiting—imagining that every sound outside must be the right sound. It was sheer hell—so please don't try to stop me—"

"Be sensible, Rennie—"

"Give me the keys or I'll hitch a ride. I mean it."

"What proof have you that he'd stay after he found the place empty?"

"For heaven's sake!" Her cheeks were bright with a furious impatience. "Where else would he go? To search for me in the streets among the professionals?"

"That does it." Decker took a key ring from his pocket. "Good-by and safe journey—and a bit of parting advice. Be sure to get a lawyer you can respect to pick up where I've left off."

She took the keys as though they were red hot. She said, "Uncle Ted—that's not like you."

"And you're not like the niece I used to have. Excuse me—I'm going to what I choose to consider my well-earned bed. I hope you know your way around Brooklyn in the event the fellow's decided to beard his landlady."

James Marshall moved in again. He said firmly, "None of this is necessary. I'll go to the apartment. It's high time I met my future son-in-law."

Decker thought that he noted a slight alteration in Rennie's mutinous face. Her father said, "Your uncle and I want to do what's best for you and it's definitely not best for you to take a long drive. You're in a highly excitable state—"

"I am not."

"Very well. You are not—but neither are you as tactful and clearheaded as you'll be after a night's sleep. Even if you make the trip safely you'll be in no condition to handle the situation as it should be handled."

"And what about you? You couldn't even hold onto that detective you hired."

He refused to be drawn. "I didn't know then that I'd want to hold onto him. That makes all the difference, Rennie. You should be the first to agree that I usually get what I want." He added in the same low key, "And so do you—except that in this instance I wouldn't gamble on your chances. I'm not saying that Berthold is superficial enough to fade out because you look like something left on a scrap heap, but he wouldn't be human if he didn't regret his bargain."

Rennie's mouth opened. She uttered something, but there was no fire under it, and her cheeks had lost their bright flags. Her father took the keys from her unresisting hand.

Decker gave him silent applause although he doubted that the postscript had done the trick. More likely the accumulation of fatigue and frustration had caught up with Rennie. The poor child was so tired that she hardly knew what she was doing. Like the tag end of an army in retreat, she moved slowly toward the stairs and slowly climbed, clutching the curving banister for support.

Behind her the two men exchanged rueful glances. When she was no longer to be seen, James Marshall jingled the keys in his hand.

"Is the garage really locked, Ted?"

"Yes, but my car hasn't been put away. You can use it."

"No, I'll be more at home with my own."

"Well—good luck." Decker managed to make it sound optimistic. He would have given a heavy slice of his income to witness the meeting between his brother-in-law and Matt Berthold.

"Any instructions?" Marshall said. Coming from him, the question was humble.

"Ad lib it. You're a past master." He wished that Marshall would accept instruction to let matters stand but had no hope that he would break his promise to Rennie. He was too deep in his parental role, and it was too bad that he had not assumed the role sooner.

Marshall left. When the car started Decker exhaled the breath of relief. Until then he had been fearful that Rennie would pull herself together and rush from the house, hell-bent on running her own errand.

He looked at his watch. It was five after three. He poured a stiff drink and sat down with it. He took a few swallows and put it from him, deciding that a few aspirins would do more toward providing a few hours of sleep. He intended to rise at six and planned a similar awakening for the man he had slated to shanghai Matt. By that time Marshall would have had his innings. And if either or both attempts were unsuccessful, nothing worse could happen than another temporary setback for Rennie. Apart from that, the status quo would hold. For whatever Matt Berthold did, he would not jump bail. He would appear in the right place at the right time. Decker had to believe that or kiss his flair for judging character good-by.

His housekeeper entered the room. She and her husband had been with Decker for a long time. He smiled at her and said, "What are you doing up so late?"

"I thought I might be wanted." She was a responsive woman. She did not need a reading of the household barometer to know that it had dropped abnormally. "Can I get you anything, Mr. Decker?"

"No, thanks. I'm sitting here because I'm too lazy to drag myself to bed."

She hesitated and said on a note of cheer, "It's nice to have Miss Rennie staying with us again."

"You might look in on her and see that she's comfortable."

A little later he went upstairs and met her tiptoeing out of Rennie's room. She whispered, "She fell asleep in her clothes. I got her shoes off without disturbing her, but I'm afraid to undress her for fear she might—well—I'll just get some light blankets so's she won't catch cold."

He looked into the room. From her position, Rennie had been sitting on the edge of the bed when she succumbed. Her arm was curved around a pair of galoshes. Her coat lay on a chair.

He understood why his housekeeper had hesitated to undress her, not for fear of breaking her sleep but of ending it. Even slightly refreshed, she was capable of putting on coat and galoshes and going to the city, though it might mean a hike to the railroad station.

He helped to tuck some blankets around her, extinguished the light, and crossed his fingers.

Chapter Eleven

Gridley Nelson flung out an arm to gather to him a Kyrie who was not there, opened his eyes, and sat up. He could have gone back to sleep for an hour and still made an early start, but it did not seem worthwhile without the drowsy murmur that had so often protested his desertion.

Lacking the noisy ritual of a small boy greeting the day, the house was unnaturally quiet as he dressed. Sammy was downstairs. She had never quite accepted his occupation as being suitable to a gentleman, but she gave him a good breakfast and a grudging "Godspeed." He was in his office at a quarter of an hour before nine o'clock.

Men had been sent to the newspaper morgues, and to Hackett's New York office to gather what information was available from his employees. Nelson digested their findings. Hackett had invested in the Callender Supermarkets, was a client of Donald Lawrence Palmer, Stockbroker, owned a piece of the Ackerman Motels, and even had a finger in such an unpredictable venture as the Rolfe Racing Stables. But since he had also invested in various other enterprises, this meant nothing but that he had respected and backed the business acumen of his friends, all of whose affairs seemed to be thriving. George Rolfe, in the idiom of the detective, was "queer for horses." Of course he had good years and bad years, but they seemed to average up and at present he was one of three bidders for an exceedingly famous and valuable British two-year-old which had been the biggest money maker of the past season. The only time that Stanley Ackerman made the news was when he attended Rotary Club meetings. He was doing more than well, although the motels that were situated in the East showed a loss in winter. Callender had no financial worries either. People had to eat. The credit rating of ex-City Councilman Fredericks was not high, but he would not benefit by Hackett's death. And Donald Palmer stuck to business and fishing with very good results.

Nelson sent for Clevis and Judd, both competent men. He told them to pay visits to Dr. Stewart and the sponsors of his debut to the medical world. The line to be taken was a difference of opinion in the statements and a request that each go over his again. They were to report back if and as soon as they unearthed anything that warranted further attention.

By noon he had heard from neither of them, but that did not necessarily mean failure. No appointments had been arranged. The policy was to take the men listed off guard, and if they were not at their respective addresses time would be consumed in tracking them down.

The morning had not passed without interest. At half-past ten a Sanitation Department employee came to see Nelson. He was a giant dressed in redolent working clothes. Under his arm he had something wrapped in newspapers. The clerk who brought him in kept his distance and backed out fast.

The giant looked at Nelson and said in a small reedy voice, "I guess you're the head man. I didn't ask to see you, but the cop on the desk thought I better. I had it in my head to leave this and blow." He placed the newspaper package on the top of a filing cabinet and unwrapped it. "Of course it could've belonged to a butcher, but the aprons they wear ain't that shape—and it ain't torn or anything, so why would a butcher throw it in the garbage?" He waved the unsavory cloth so close to Nelson's nose that he sympathized with the fastidious clerk.

"Where did you find it?" he said.

"That's just it." He refolded the garment with housewifely neatness and planted it on the spread newspaper. He rubbed a hand over his sprouting cheeks. "In my line of business I come across all kinds of stuff. I wouldn't have given it a thought except my partner on the truck happens to mention a big shot was murdered last night in our territory. So we're dumping cans near the building where it happened and this falls out. Like I'm telling you, maybe it's beef or liver blood, but my partner says maybe it ain't and what's the matter I don't recognize it's the thing you wear for a checkup at the clinic. The upshot is we toss and I lose. I want to leave it at the nearest station house, but I get an argument it should go to the Homicide Squad because my partner once flunked an exam for cops and knows the ropes."

"You found it this morning?" Nelson said.

"No—yesterday—around seven-thirty." The giant was both defensive and apologetic. "I put it aside, seeing as how I had to come to this neighborhood today on an errand for my wife. I'd already got permission for that—it being against the rules to knock off work without. Anyways, I could be dumb to bother in the first place, so I didn't see no harm in sleeping on it."

There was nothing to be gained by a lecture. Nelson thanked him, took his name and address and the location of the prize-yielding garbage can.

The giant supplied the information but was obviously not quite ready to leave.

"Yes?" Nelson said encouragingly.

"Excuse me—I wouldn't want to stick my nose where it don't belong—except my partner will be at me to tell him is it nothing or something."

"If it's something you'll read about it in tomorrow's paper—probably with a mention of the part you played."

"Say!" Before he left he insisted upon giving his partner's name so that they could share equal billing.

Nelson sent the garment to the lab. The blood would be analyzed, and serology tests would be applied to those portions that should have absorbed sweat. He was almost ready to bank upon the outcome. The nature of the find, plus the location in which it had been discovered, was too significant to be dismissed as coincidental. The blood would be Hackett's blood, and if the material had blotted up sweat it would be the sweat of a thoughtful murderer who had covered himself against revelatory stains before stabbing his victim a few more times to make sure of a thorough job. And then it would follow that the wardrobes of Dr. Stewart, Callender, et al., be overhauled without co-operation from the owners, in order to find a soiled shirt apiece for the purpose of comparing exudations.

And so much for the state versus Matthew Berthold.

He was going too fast. He slowed to skirt a looming pitfall. There would be no sweat. The clothes beneath would have absorbed it before it reached the gown, unless the wearer had stripped. Yet not even the cocksure precinct lieutenant could dig up a reason for Berthold to run out after he had done the deed, dispose of the incriminating evidence, and return to invite arrest.

But the still anonymous murderer, a villain of excessive confidence, *had* run out and returned before the police arrived. He must have done. No—wait. It could have been thrown from a window to be retrieved and disposed of later. Could it? Nelson, remembering the windowless examination room, shied. The blood on the gown had scarcely dried. Would anyone, however confident, have chanced an encounter while he carried it to another of the offices? Doubtful.

As for concealing it on his person, none of the group had worn an overcoat while being questioned, and any suspicious bulge would have attracted notice. Fredericks had sported a rather prominent potbelly, but since his clique seemed to accept it as a permanent fixture, probably his signal crime was gluttony. Nelson grinned before he got on with it. The gown could have been hidden in any of the heavy overcoats, but Clevis had been in the front room to expedite departures, and little escaped Clevis.

So it's got to be the old saw about someone wandering in off the street. Namely Berthold. The words of Clevis came back to him verbatim. He examined them, and as before discarded the conclusion, this time with tangible justification. *Not that dame again!* Clevis had said. But it could well be "that dame again." Nelson discounted as implausible that she had quit the scene of the crime and purposely knocked Berthold down to provide a scapegoat. But she could have taken advantage of the accident, and not necessarily with a lasting frame in mind. Rather she might have converted it to a red herring of sufficient odor to distract attention from—well—from the man she sought to protect.

Which leaves us where it finds us, he thought, and could have wished to share the initial belief of Clevis that she was a myth, since a promising young man's future no longer depended upon her. He took time out to regret the young man's needless ordeal and, as so often happened in the course of an investigation, he had to caution himself against becoming sidetracked because some unfortunate by-product of murder engaged his sympathies to an extent that threatened clear thinking. If Berthold was out of the woods, he and his squad were not. They had just about glimpsed the light through the trees and were faced with a laborious trek before they could reach it.

He called the lab to ask if the job on the gown had been started and was told that it had. He asked for speed and was told he would get it, and knew that he would not. Science set its own pace, and he had been trapped by inactivity into making a futile request. Not for the first time he resented the demands of his desk. He wanted to be out doing leg work with his men.

At twelve thirty-five Clevis checked back to account for his morning. Clevis had drawn as his share of the list Callender, who lived on Central Park South; Palmer, who was staying at the Plaza while his apartment was being repainted; and Ackerman, who stayed at the Guelph Arms when he visited New York.

Clevis had taken them alphabetically. He had missed Ackerman by five minutes and refrained from pumping any of the hotel staff as to a probable destination for fear of defeating his purpose. He had proceeded to Central Park South, catching Callender on the wing, and extracting from him nothing but arrogantly expressed annoyance. He had been forced either to accept a brush or to resort to physical means to detain his quarry. He had accepted the brush and pretended to fade. He was adept at becoming a part of his background, and Callender, reassured if he needed reassurance, had bellowed an East Fifty-second Street address to a cabdriver. Dr. Stewart lived on East Fifty-second Street. Clevis thought it would be a good idea to see if anything was cooking there even though the doctor was on Judd's list. He thought that he just might manage to get within hearing distance of a conversation, say from a crouch outside the apartment door, provided the building was not soundproofed. All he got for his pains was a meeting with Judd as he entered the lobby. Judd was on the way out. Callender had not shown. He might legitimately have changed his mind en route, or he might be a real foxy guy with illegitimate reasons to outfox Clevis. As for Dr. Stewart, according to Judd it was a miracle he had ever got a license to practice. Judd sized him up as a guy with nothing to hide and no place to hide it. Clevis and Judd had lingered awhile on the chance that Callender might still turn up. They had separated after consuming all but the crumbs of an hour, Judd bound for the city councilman's address and Clevis to the stockbroker's. He had telephoned Palmer's office first in the role of a client with loose cash to invest. He was cordially informed by Palmer's secretary that she would be glad to make an appointment for him and regretfully informed that he could not speak to Mr. Palmer, who was out. He went at once to the Plaza, but "out" did not mean at home. Then he had taken a subway to the Wall Street office to see if it might mean "in conference." The office setup was easy to case. While the receptionist had her hands full picking up and laying down telephones, he had managed to slip past her to a door that said, "Donald Lawrence Palmer." The "sanctum" behind it was neat but empty. He would try again later. He was telephoning from a store nearby and could stick around unless Nelson had an interim mission for him. He said tentatively that the widow Hackett had got back from Miami a few hours ago.

Nelson did not fall in with the suggestion that Clevis add Mrs. Hackett to his list. He instructed him to continue as before and stimulated his interest with an account of the garbage man's visit.

Clevis wanted to know if he could use the gown as bait to catch reactions. Nelson advised him to refrain until further notice.

By one o'clock Nelson felt that he had earned a respite from sedentary occupations. According to word from police and press representatives covering the airport, Vida Hackett had arrived at eleven o'clock and gone directly to her apartment. The gist of her one brief statement to the reception committee was that she had nothing to say.

It was, however, possible that a tête-à-tête in familiar surroundings might extract from her something stored and forgotten that could be donated to the investigation. He decided to try for the donation in person. He would have lunch first to avoid intruding upon hers.

Outside the temperature had risen a little but, the sun had lingered only long enough to convert yesterday's snow to today's slush. Walking to the least repellent restaurant in the neighborhood, Nelson thought with satisfaction of Kyrie and Junie on the Florida sands.

In the restaurant he pushed mediocre food around his plate, swallowed some of it absently, paid the check, and walked back to headquarters to get his car. He drove across town and up Fifth Avenue to the high Seventies.

The Hackett residence was a narrow brown slice of a building between two large apartment houses. Its door was opened by a woman in a black quilted robe.

He introduced himself and presented the credentials of his office. She read them with more than average care. She said, "What is it you want? I'm Mrs. Hackett."

He thought her admission superfluous since a maid or a visitor would wear more formal attire so late in the day.

Prompted by cold or modesty, she drew the robe closer, hiding its green lining and her sunburned chest. She said evenly, "My servants are away. I haven't had time to call them back." In the same uninflected tone she said, "I haven't even had time to make myself believe that my husband is dead."

"I know." His deep pleasant voice was sympathetic. "Sudden tragedy often supplies its own anesthetic—a sort of protective numbness to make it bearable." He made mental notes as he spoke. Her hair was a subtly encouraged blond, cut and curled quite close to her head. She had drawn her mouth to her own specifications. Under the red coat its natural shape was secret. He wondered if the lines marking her brow and raying from her eyes had been deepened by grief or merely by the strain of clinging to youth. She was junior to her late husband by many years, yet not so many as she took pains to advertise.

She had been making her own notes. She lowered her eyes as he spoke again. He said, "I'm sorry if this appears to be an intrusion—but if you'll allow me to come inside for a few moments—"

She turned abruptly and he followed her into the hall. She closed the door and walked toward the rear of the house, murmuring about the breakfast room being the only one not shrouded in dust sheets. Dogging her steps, he studied the long back braced by tension above the uncontrolled hips. She entered a small room that might have been cheerful on a brighter day. Now the shades were drawn and a lone lamp shone upon a table bearing a cup and saucer and a thermos jug.

He held the chair she had obviously vacated when the bell rang. She sat down and he took a chair on the opposite side of the table.

Again she offered superfluous information. "I was just about to have some coffee." She added tepidly, "Would you like me to get another cup?"

He said, "No, thank you." He had taken it for granted that they were alone in the house, yet he heard a scuttling sound overhead, followed by a thud that he identified as some light object dropped or fallen. She must have heard too, but she offered no explanation, and he no comment.

She coughed and apologized. "I had rather a bad sore throat in Miami. I'm just getting over it, but talking makes me a bit hoarse."

He had not noticed any hoarseness. He took the apology as a hint to cut his visit short.

She was staring at his hand on the table. "My husband stayed at his club while I was away," she said. "Someone was supposed to come each day to dust and air the house, but servants are apt to be careless without supervision. I'm afraid the furniture's been rather neglected."

He seemed puzzled. Then he said, "Oh—sorry." The table was clothless and he had been fingering its fruitwood surface. "I wasn't testing for dust—just a form of doodling without a pencil."

She looked as though she wished he would doodle elsewhere. Her eyes were narrow and gray, very light in contrast to her tanned skin. They showed no trace of tears, but even the flattery of the shaded lamp could not gloss over the discolored patches beneath them. Perhaps, he thought, an inability to get relief by crying was what made her sound so near the breaking point.

"Please don't let me keep you from having your coffee," he said.

She lifted the thermos jug and tilted it over her cup. Her slim-wristed hand was steady as she poured. She took the coffee black, setting the cup down after a few sips.

She said, "You asked for a few minutes. I'm giving them to you. I assume it's customary for police officials to make calls on occasions like this—but I've neither slept nor relaxed for a moment since my husband's death—and while I appreciate the interest shown, I'd appreciate privacy more."

"I can understand that," Nelson said. He could feel the force of her will urging him to get on with it, ready to rush him from the house as soon as his errand was stated. But he had found that delaying tactics often brought better answers than those produced by questions. "I assure you I would have postponed the call if time wasn't important to the investigation."

"What investigation? I thought an arrest had been made."

"That's true—but not on a murder charge. The fact that Matthew Berthold is out on bail points to the weakness of the case against him."

"He's out!"

Nelson did not like the shrill protesting sound of her exclamation. He said, "It was in the morning papers."

"I haven't seen the papers. Nothing in them could change the only thing that—that I care about." She closed her eyes and covered them with her hands.

He waited with some apprehension for the gesture to develop. "Mrs. Hackett—?" Then he said firmly, "I don't like this any more than you do. A moment ago I was admiring your courage and control. I've spoken to many women in comparable circumstances—some who gave way to hysteria and some completely lacking the intelligence to realize that I wasn't deliberately adding to their burdens. I've been congratulating myself that you belonged in neither category—that you would readily give what help you could."

Whatever she was, she was no fool. She showed her eyes again, now slightly reddened by the pressure of her hands. She said with tight composure, "And to how many women in comparable circumstances have you delivered that 'pep talk'?"

He said solemnly, "In general it's effective."

"Perhaps—but if I were the hysterical type I would have given way before this. I'm afraid, however, that I do lack the intelligence to grasp how I can be of help to you. So far as I know, my husband had no enemies."

"He did have friends."

"His closest friends were with him that night. The police have as much information about them as I have—possibly more."

"Aren't they your friends too?"

"Gene knew them before he met me. For his sake, naturally I accepted them. I hate to confess this, since several of them took the trouble to call me in Miami to express sympathy, but sometimes I've found them a little heavy in the hand."

"Do you think one of them could be a murderer?"

"Of course not. They were all fond of Gene—and he of them."

"Yet you seem to have certain reservations about them."

"Purely personal ones. They're businessmen who enjoy talking shop." Her shrug was self-deprecating. "No doubt the fact that I was so often bored is more of a reflection on me than on them. They're all quite a bit older than I am and could hardly be expected to have the same outlook." She spoke like a woman trying to be frank and fair, but much was hidden behind her shuttered face.

Nelson tried to raise the shutter. "Your husband was older, too—perhaps a bit older than Fredericks or Callender or Ackerman—and certainly no contemporary of Dr. Stewart or Donald Palmer or George Rolfe." He pronounced the names deliberately, underlining them with deliberate pauses.

So far as her response to the tactic went, one member of the group was as another to her. She said indifferently, "It couldn't have been age then, could it? I suppose I'm not introverted enough to analyze my likes or dislikes—but on the other hand I'm not quite as extroverted as they are. I do think there's more to life than business—with poker—drinking and an occasional round of golf for relaxation. I prefer books and music and the theater and good conversation."

"Did your husband share these tastes with you?"

"To some extent—but after all, in spite of a few experiments on television, the stage hasn't been reached where we drop a card into an IBM machine and wait for it to come up with the perfect mate. Love as I interpret it isn't all that exacting—and I happened to love my husband. His male companions I could take or leave." She went on a little huskily, "I only hope I didn't make it too obvious that I chose to leave them."

"That seems to take care of the social end of it," Nelson said. "What about the people your husband met in a business way—his associates—those he had dealings with?"

She sighed. "Are you married?"

"Yes."

"Well, I expect that each day you have a great many encounters your wife knows nothing about. And that was true of Gene to an even greater degree because his business interests were so varied. It seems to me his New York office would be the logical place to start such an inquiry."

"Men have been known to unburden themselves to their wives—to drop a name or two in connection with the disagreements or quarrels that crop up in any sort of work."

"Gene wasn't the sort to bring his worries home." Again the air of frankness enveloped her. "You see, I was quite young when we were married—and he'd got into the habit of treating me more like a child than a helpmeet. Perhaps that was partly my fault. I should have encouraged him to discuss his problems with me—but the truth is, I reveled in being taken care of—in being shielded from unpleasantness. And now I—" She paused as though to tighten the leash upon herself. "I really don't know why I'm talking to you in this way. It could be that you don't in the least resemble my mental image of a police officer."

"The movies and television seldom do us justice," Nelson said. "Did you know beforehand of the party that was given to launch Dr. Stewart?"

She nodded. "Gene always insisted that I go south for the worst of the winter months—but of course we spoke to each other frequently—and the last time he called he mentioned the party. Only he said he wouldn't be able to attend."

"Oh?"

"When the arrangements were made," she said, "he didn't realize that he had an important engagement that night. His secretary had mixed things up and he was due at a convention in Philadelphia."

"But he did go to the party."

She repeated slowly, "He did go to the party."

Nelson wondered if the bias he was developing lent her delivery a theatrical flavor. "I suppose the others persuaded him."

"No, they wouldn't have had to do that. Gene probably thought it over and decided to take a later train to the convention. He was a man of strong loyalties, and Dave Stewart's father had been a member of the inner circle. He'd had reverses, and he died without leaving enough to provide for his son's future—so Dave was taken on as a protégé and put through medical school. Then everyone chipped in to rent and equip an office for him. They were like kids—as proud and pleased as though they'd passed the medical exams themselves. Especially Gene. I can understand why he felt he had to be there to wish Dave luck—but if only—if only—" She raised her hand to her mouth to crush back the rest of it.

Her face, unshuttered for a moment, looked tortured. In spite of his bias Nelson found the performance convincing. He took his leave, which helped more than anything else he could have said, and she recovered sufficient poise to show him out.

At the door she said, "There are funeral arrangements to be made. When—?"

"You'll be notified of the release. Today perhaps." She would be asked to make official identification of the body, and he had meant to accompany her to the morgue. During the last stage of the visit he dropped that project because of a conviction that he had witnessed as many of her rationed emotions as she was likely to display.

Chapter Twelve

Walking to the side street where he had parked his car, Nelson reviewed several aspects of the visit, among them the sound he had heard overhead. He thought that a dog or a cat would have signified its presence with additional sounds, unless in settling down for a nap it had displaced some small object. But nothing had been said about Mrs. Hackett stepping off the plane with a pet in her arms, although the plain-clothes man at the airport had supplied a description worthy of a fashion expert.

Enlarging upon the theme, he halted, hesitated, and crossed to the park side of the avenue. Granted that a pet had been left in a kennel to be sent back as soon as Mrs. Hackett arrived, she was scarcely the type of woman to invite it to sit at table with her. Yet he could almost have sworn that the chair he had sat in had been warm, and that his doodling hand had discovered the circle left by a cold wet glass. The warm chair could have been imagination. The drink and the sounds were not.

The park looked chilled to the snow-pocked bones of its trees. A few of the benches in front of its stone boundary were occupied even on this mean day. Spaced along the line, a woman behind a baby carriage or an old man behind his thoughts sat facing the traffic. Nelson joined their company. Turning his coat collar up, he did not rate a second glance from passers-by.

By sitting sideways he could trace a long diagonal line to the Hackett steps. He had to crane to see over buses, but the low styling of the modern cars was with him.

Very soon he began to respect the stamina of the old men and the young mothers. Fifteen minutes passed in which no one left the Hackett house and no one entered to plague or comfort its bereaved mistress. He gave himself five minutes more. Then he stood up, stamped his cold feet, and walked to the curb. He would have liked to wait longer, but he could ill afford the time since there was no guarantee that an hour or two or three would produce results. Nor was there guarantee that a visitor kept under wraps would be relevant to the case.

He lingered like a good citizen until the light had changed. Reaching the opposite sidewalk at a point about five doors down from the Hackett house, he turned for one last look.

A man was descending the steps. At the foot of them he stopped to button his overcoat. That done, he adjusted his hat and made a survey of the traffic before he headed in Nelson's direction.

Nelson got a general impression of his build and walk but none of his face. To bar the possibility of his own being recognized he stepped under the canopy of an apartment building. His quarry approached slowly, still interested in the traffic. Nelson, sheltering in the doorway of the building, could barely glimpse his profile, but it was impossible to associate the type of clothing he wore with any of the suspects.

Nelson gave him a small lead and took off after him. As he moved with carefully measured stride his eyes photographed all that the man's back presented.

He had a short thick figure squared by the padding of a belted blue coat. The coat exposed about eight inches of blue trousers. A multicolored scarf lumped untidily above his collar. His hat was a brown snap-brim. The heels of his brown shoes wanted new lifts. He was not too steady on his feet. Punch drunk—alcohol drunk—or just bad co-ordination?

Nelson, who had tailed no one for a long time, could not under oath have said that the present essay was based upon anything more than common garden curiosity. It might even be based on less, he thought. Merely an excuse to dodge the waiting desk.

It turned out to be the shortest tailing job on record. He had decided to terminate it himself by catching up with the man and saying, "Mrs. Hackett forgot to tell you something. She wants you to come back." If it produced nothing revealing, at least the face could be filed with the other data for future reference. Why future reference should be needed was another unanswerable question. Mrs. Hackett's acquaintances, whether they resembled bookmakers, touts, or ex-fighters, were no concern of the Homicide Squad. The murder had been done while Mrs. Hackett was in Florida. There were no grounds for supposing that she had hired a killer. But if she had, the killer would hardly have left it to luck to provide a weapon. Nor would he have risked the dangers of a well-peopled place.

She had stated with a ring of truth that her husband meant to forgo the party and that his presence was due to a change of mind. That could be checked with the secretary who had allegedly mixed his appointments. If verified, it scrapped a theory of premeditation as applied to the widow and her doubtful visitor and advanced the investigation not a bit. The whiskey had been drugged and the scalpel wielded by someone on the inside. Mr. Belted Coat could not have been inside unless every last one of the known insiders was in cahoots with him. As candidate for the man most likely to be visible in that gathering he would have piled up more votes than Matt Berthold.

The play was taken from Nelson. Belted Coat stopped short, gave a piercing whistle, darted into the street and into a taxi. Nelson, slow to profanity, did not use one of the words that occurred to him. But he was quick to reach the curb and note the cab's license number before traffic surged forward again.

Although Belted Coat's intention had been telegraphed, Nelson had counted upon taxis being scarce because of a law that denied them the privilege of cruising for fares on Fifth Avenue. They were scarce all right. There was not another empty one in sight. Luckily, he thought, little if anything was at stake. But the advice he gave to members of his squad boomeranged to hit him square in the ego. *Proceed on the premise that nothing is unimportant. Take nothing for granted.*

Discomfited, he walked back to the side street to reclaim his car. A fine example he had set. And come to think of it, what did the fellow mean by being so extravagant? He should have taken a bus and got his shoes heeled with the money saved. The absurdity did not soothe his ego but it did make him smile.

Driving downtown, he thought that the license number of a cab was not much to show for his self-imposed assignment. But at least it was something he need not file away for future reference. He could use it to locate the driver and ask where he had dropped a fare picked up at such-and-such a time at such-and-such a spot. If only to satisfy the boy in me, he thought. The dull boy made by all desk work. Doctor, lawyer, Indian chief—bookie, boxer, gambler, thief. What was it Kyrie had said about the Aintree Hotel in Miami? Something to do with the sudden rich—with gamblers. Kyrie, come home. I need you—I'm slipping.

A big gaudy place, the Aintree. Presumably for big-time operators dressed up in cashmere or camel's-hair, with or without belts. Miami was crowded at this season of the year. Kyrie was content to stay at a family-type hotel. Mrs. Hackett might not be. She might have chosen the Aintree for lack of more suitable accommodation. And it would develop that there was no connection; that the lad who got away was a plumber come to estimate repairs in the upstairs bathroom. Still, the Aintree seemed an odd sort of makeshift, considering that Hackett had counted among his properties a fine new house in the Virgin Islands.

Back at headquarters, Nelson asked a clerk to trace the license number. His desk had sprouted a fresh crop of papers. He went through them rapidly, putting aside items of first importance. These included an account of Judd's activities written at three-fifteen. Before he could read it word came in that a tenement dweller a few blocks from the building in which he sat had shot and killed his wife and two children.

Nelson, accompanied by several members of the squad, rushed to the address, expecting to find a berserk killer. They found a defeated soul calm in the midst of carnage. He was scarcely out of his teens. His thin blank face showed neither remorse nor fear. Sure he had done it, he said. His wife had been no good. And when he lost his job she had stopped trying to hide it. His kids were luckier dead than living as they had lived. He would have thanked his own father to shoot him at birth because then he would not have grown up to pick the same kind of wife that his mother had been. He had meant to shoot himself, but the gun had jammed. It was as rotten as everything else he had ever touched.

At twenty minutes to five Nelson returned to his office. He was sick at heart. The importance of the work on hand seemed microscopic compared to what he had just seen. He asked himself drearily why it was constitutionally impossible for him to reach the state of immunity that protected good surgeons and good nurses and, yes, good policemen, so that whatever they did was all in the day's work. It would never be all in the day's work for him. One of the little boys had been Junie's age—

The clerk he had entrusted with the license number came in to tell him that it had been issued to the Chilton Cab Company. The driver of the cab in question worked an early shift and was expected to check in at five. Word had been left for him to call Nelson.

Nelson went to the water cooler, wishing that it contained scotch or brandy. He filled a Lily cup several times and drank until his dry throat felt easier. He seated himself and picked up Judd's report, glossing over part one because its substance had been relayed by Clevis.

Judd had gone from the doctor's house to the Bellaire Hotel on Lexington Avenue. The desk clerk had told him that Mr. George Rolfe was in the lobby and indicated two figures standing near the elevators. Judd did not have to ask which of the pair was Rolfe. One of them had "cheap chiseler" written all over him and could scarcely have been the owner of the famous stables in Connecticut. Nor did he seem to be receiving much encouragement from the owner, although he was talking to him at a great rate as Judd approached.

Reading between the lines, Nelson was able to round out Judd's wordage with what he knew and what he imagined he knew. He recalled the rangy, tweedy Rolfe as seen on the night of the murder, and it was not difficult to visualize the look of disdain on his thin features as he tried to get rid of the button-holer. Judd had been more successful, or less, depending upon the point of view. "The minute he got a gander at me he beat it out of the hotel," Judd said.

Here Nelson supplied a footnote. Judd was a good man, but no matter how he tried he could not dispel the impression that he had teethed on a night stick.

George Rolfe, however, showed no fear of the law. Judd asked if the chiseler had been annoying him, and he nodded and answered to the effect that Judd's arrival had been opportune. He guessed that the fellow was drunk. At any rate he stank of stale liquor. Judd asked if he knew him, and Rolfe's "No" made it sound like a silly question. Judd suggested that he had probably wanted to make a touch, but Rolfe seemed to have no further interest in the subject. He said that if Judd had any business with him it had better be transacted upstairs. And he said if it was in regard to the Hackett murder he was as much in the dark as the police.

He had a suite decorated with a lot of individual touches, like pictures of horses and trophies. When he caught Judd noticing he said it was a home from home. He had leased it when the hotel was built so that he could have a place to stay on his trips to New York. He offered Judd a drink. Judd declined and watched him down a stiff one.

He did not object to Judd's visit or to being taken over his statement. He rubbed a bruise on his cheek and said that Berthold had packed a mean wallop. He rang in a few changes on his statement, but that was natural. Anything too pat was open to suspicion. Judd, who had plowed through the lot, thought that Hackett had said good-by to everybody and reached the outside door before he turned back to visit the bathroom. But the way Rolfe told it today, in the first stages of the party Hackett complained of a bad headache, and the doctor advised him to swallow a couple of aspirin and lie down in the examination room where he couldn't hear the celebration. Doc said that with a little rest and quiet he would feel fine. Hackett had taken the advice. He said that he did not want to be a wet blanket so he would rest until it was time to catch his train. Then he'd sneak out, because if he looked in to say "Good-by" it might break up the party. A while later, not much after ten, Rolfe thought, and could not be more specific, he said he heard something in the hall and took it for granted that it was Hackett leaving. He supposed the others had heard too, but no one mentioned it. They were all talking, and the hi-fi they had bought for Doc was grinding away. Besides, someone had complained of a draft earlier and closed the door to the hall. No, he could not remember who had closed it. Judd asked if anyone had been out of the room at the time he thought he heard Hackett, to go to the can or something. Rolfe could not be sure, but he said he did not believe so, or he might have put the sounds down to the missing member and not to Hackett. That could have been loyalty. They were a close-knit group. Judd told him his ears must be pretty good to hear anything with the door shut and the hi-fi playing and all, and Rolfe said people who lived in the country got accustomed to tuning in on the faintest whisper of a leaf. Be that as it may, Judd wrote, according to Rolfe, nobody had actually seen Hackett start to leave, and that business about his going back to the can was pure conjecture or just plain lying. It might be important or it might not.

Nelson tugged at his hair. Matt Berthold had entered the offices after ten, and *if* there was no reason to doubt Rolfe, it was Matt he had heard. Or else, since he admitted that he could not swear to the time, his ears had been attuned to the going or coming of the unknown murderer. But his story did not mean necessarily that the other guests had been guilty of deliberate concealment. They too could have heard what Rolfe heard, and by the time the police arrived they might have become so sold on the theory they had formed of

Hackett's about-face at the door as to be convinced that they had actually witnessed it.

Judd had checked in at three o'clock to type the report and was probably in the ready room awaiting further assignment. Nelson rang to ask for him, but he had "stepped out for a minute."

Nelson turned to the next page of the report. Pumped on the subject of his friends, Rolfe had suggested civilly that it would be more profitable for Judd to get information straight from the horse's mouth. He, himself, had nothing to hide, he said, and was sure that this held for all concerned. He had been on excellent terms with both Hackett and his wife, although he had to grant that she was not his line of country. When asked what he meant by that he said he meant nothing, really. Perhaps, being a confirmed bachelor, he found all women frightening.

From the Bellaire, Judd had proceeded to the apartment house of Councilman Maurice Fredericks, near Sixtieth Street and Park Avenue. Fredericks was at home and had corroborated his original statement in every detail. Nelson gathered that the melon-shaped politician was somewhat impatient with the revisions made by Rolfe. He said of course he had heard Hackett leave, hi-fi and closed door notwithstanding. He said that Judd was mistaken if he thought his perfectly good hearing would be impaired by the few drinks he had taken. He had always been able to handle his liquor like a gentleman and always would. He appeared hurt by the suggestion that the late Eugene Hackett had antagonized anyone to the point of ruthless enmity, or that anyone who knew him would want him out of the way. He consumed time by delivering a fulsome eulogy which boiled down to, "Gene was a prince. Everybody liked old Gene. Maybe he had made himself slightly ridiculous by not choosing a second wife nearer his age and station, but a man would not be human if he didn't have a few blind spots."

Judd could get nothing else from him on the "marriage bit." Fredericks insisted that there was nothing else to get. He detested gossip, he said, and had not intended to imply anything against the little woman. She had suffered a dreadful loss and he had been the first to offer his condolences. The rest of the session was larded with irrelevance. Judd called the role on his friends and was assured that every last one of them was a prince, witness their positions, their financial standing, their golf scores, the lengths to which they had gone in order to give Dave Stewart a proper start. Fredericks considered himself blessed to be counted among them. And if Judd wanted his opinion it had been a grave mistake to set bail for that evil intruder. Mark his word, Berthold was guilty, but fortunately his friend, the assistant district attorney, had the case well in hand and justice would be done. He had terminated the interview with a politician's handshake.

Nelson went through the papers on his desk to see if a report had come in from the laboratory during his absence. It had, but it was incomplete. Translated into lay English, it informed him that so far as could be determined the blood on the examination gown matched Hackett's blood. There was an inference made that the wearer had dried clammy hands by rubbing them along the sides of the gown. But the garbage man's find was impregnated with fish and meat and vegetable leavings and it might be impossible to isolate the traces of sweat. Further tests would be attempted.

Nelson looked up to see Judd standing in the doorway. He told him to come in.

Judd said worriedly, "I'd skipped lunch, so I just ran down for a bite."

"You earned it." He nodded Judd into the desk-side chair and picked up the receiver of a ringing phone.

"Captain Nelson? I'm Lou Gargulio. My boss at the Chilton Cab Company said I should get in touch with you." The voice was businesslike, the voice of a man with a clear conscience.

"I'm interested in a fare you picked up this afternoon." Nelson gave the time and the street.

"Oh, him—sure," Gargulio said. "I dropped him at Ninth—off Fourth Avenue—wait a second—I'll get my book."

While Nelson jotted down the building number, Gargulio said, "You mean the jerk's in trouble—I hope."

"He seems to have made a strong impression," Nelson said.

"Strong's the word. He stinks up the cab so's I could tie one on from breathing—and then he don't have nothing smaller than a twenty. He peels it off a roll which is too big to be honest—him looking the type who bets at the two-dollar window—and I dive into a store and get down on my knees they should break it without I invest in something I got no use for—and he's so much obliged he gives me a dime tip."

To make certain that Gargulio had not confused his fares, Nelson said, "Can you remember what he was wearing?"

"He wasn't no Brooks Brothers customer." For proof, Gargulio mentioned a few sartorial details.

"Did he say anything to indicate that his own office was in that building?"

"Yeah. When I griped about the twenty he said to wait—he'd run up and pay me from the petty cash. But for all I know, he could have lost himself, so I wasn't having any."

Nelson thanked him and hung up. He stared thoughtfully at Judd, whose blunt features began to show apprehension.

Judd said, "Did I do something wrong, Captain?"

"No—sorry—I was thinking. Will you describe the man who was talking to Rolfe in the Bellaire lobby?"

Judd squinted as though he were reading the description from an optometrist's chart. "Short—thick-set—flabby red face—small fat nose—light blue eyes—at first I made it he worked for Rolfe—or wanted work—like a trainer or groom—but when I came closer I saw his complexion was more out of a bottle than out of doors—blue overcoat with heavy shoulder padding—brown hat—he didn't take it off—the hair that showed over his ears was sandy."

"That's good enough," Nelson said.

Judd sat very straight. "You mean he's in it?"

"He could be." Nelson got up and went to the rickety clothes tree. "You didn't see Rolfe give him money?"

"Like blackmail maybe?"

"Maybe."

"No—and if any was slipped to him before I came in he wouldn't have been hanging around. You think Rolfe was lying about not knowing him?"

"Not necessarily." Nelson was putting on his coat. "Let's hope that whatever the man works at he works at late. Get your coat and meet me downstairs."

Chapter Thirteen

In Rennie's apartment the hour came when Matt's heavy eyelids betrayed him, and for a little while he breathed peacefully. Aroused by a knocking at the door, he did not have to struggle over the bridge between sleeping and waking. He took it at a leap, realizing at once where he was and what had led to his being there alone. He had not turned the standard lamp off. It competed strongly with the dull light of morning that showed through a strip of window uncovered by the drawn shade.

Rennie would not knock, he thought as he went shoeless to the door. He opened it without hope.

"Yes?" he said, and turned from the man to look at Rennie's electric clock. It was a quarter to seven.

The man said oddly, "I was afraid I'd miss you."

He had a cultivated voice. For some reason Matt's hackles rose to it.

"I was held up—I—"

Matt said, "Don't apologize—it's early enough. If you're looking for—for the lady of the house, she's not here."

"I know that." The man was no door-to-door salesman. He carried only the wares of assurance backed by a handsome well-bred face and good clothing.

Matt stared at him. "What did you say?"

"I said that I know Rennie isn't here. May I come in?"

Matt reached out to help him over the threshold. His foot kicked the door shut. To his tired angry mind the man was all of a piece with the tormentors who had used blows and accusations to undermine the structure of his life. But now the tormentor was the intruder. His grip upon him tightened. "Who are you—what's Rennie to do with you—?"

"I'm James Marshall." He looked at the clamp fastened to his arm, and as he looked it loosened and dropped. "You *are* Matthew Berthold," he said, almost as though he hoped for a denial.

Matt nodded, and seemed to see in the handsome face an aping of his own despair. If that were so, Marshall made quick recovery. He said, "We've a great deal to discuss. We might as well sit down to it."

"No." Matt was denying the nightmare's crowning blow. The man was older than he had appeared to be in the hall's dim light. Old and sophisticated—the type that young girls were so often flattered into. "No—we have nothing to discuss. Rennie didn't find it necessary to tell me you existed—and why should she? I meant nothing to her—she said so herself. I was fool enough not to believe it—but that's another story. Get out of here—" He shook his head. "But that's unreasonable—I don't want to be unreasonable. You have more right to the place than I—and you're welcome. I'll leave." Pain blinded him to the fact that he was half dressed. He took a step toward the door.

"Leaving seems to be your specialty," Marshall said, "with or without shoes."

Matt looked down at his feet. He walked over to the bed, stooped, and groped for his shoes. He sat down to put them on.

Marshall said, "If you meant nothing to Rennie I wouldn't have come."

"It's none of my business," Matt said, not knowing what he said, "but why *have* you come?" He was bent over, fumbling with his shoelaces. He could not bear to look at the man. "It can't be to demand the usual means of satisfaction unless you're hiding the horsewhip or the gun. Of course you're the injured party and if you want to take me on with your bare hands, I'll have to accept the challenge even though you're twice my age—but I don't mind telling you I've always been bored by violence."

Marshall said, "You seem to be confused about a number of things. I don't wonder at it but—"

"Where's my jacket—my overcoat—?" His jacket was on the floor. He grabbed it and put it on. His overcoat hung among her things in the closet. But it did not seem decent to open the door and reveal it there. Confused is an understatement, he thought, because why should sharing her closet strike him as more intimate than sharing her bed? He bent again to finish tying his laces.

"I'm here to find out just how much Rennie means to you."

"Funny thing about that. I'd oblige with an answer if I were flesh and blood—but I'm not. I've turned to stone. It happened all of a sudden." He straightened. "Look—must you wallow in it? Hit me with a glove or something—or do what you have to do and get it over with. She's gone back to you—or you wouldn't have known about me. That settles it as far as I'm concerned—and should settle it for you, provided you've taken her back. You have—haven't you?" He stood up, towering over Marshall. He drew breath and held it for fear of missing the answer.

"It isn't a question of taking her back," Marshall said. "I've never let her go—and won't until I'm sure it means her happiness."

"Very touching. So you've come to look me over before you decide. Take your time—don't be deceived by my rough exterior—a heart of gold beats beneath these slept-in rags—sometimes I even shave. Maybe I fall short of your high standards, but that superior air of idle richness must have taken generations to—"

"Shut up. Rennie told me you'd be difficult. She called it pride—I don't. Not if this is an example of it—"

"For God's sake, what kind of a man are you!"

"A man who loves his daughter and wants what's best for her."

"Daughter—!"

"Don't you understand anything? I'm James Marshall."

Matt wanted to weep. Instead he shouted, "So you're James Marshall! No doubt it's a name to conjure with from the way you make it sound—only it doesn't mean a thing to me. But all right—you're Rennie's father—and I do have something to say to you. Why didn't you take care of her? How could you let an innocent young girl run the risk of staying alone in a place like this? Look at you—a tailor's dummy—living off the fat of the land while she stood on her feet eight hours a day because you were too selfish to train her for a better job. And you stand there bleating about her happiness. Don't you realize what could have happened to her?"

Marshall's face had reddened, but it was not the red of rage. He sat down at the table, turning away from Matt to say in a choked voice, "Your reaction is very interesting and very unexpected." He cleared his throat and after a moment met the younger man's eyes. "That was a virtuous high-sounding speech—but evidently it doesn't occur to you that you had a little something to do with what did happen to Rennie."

"I—hell—!"

"Quite."

Matt drew in air again. "Don't misunderstand—don't think you have to play the heavy father. I love Rennie. I had it all figured out—I—"

"Yes?" Marshall said.

"I'd saved some money—it would have taken care of—we could have been married—and when the baby came we— Look—I don't owe you any explanation."

"What do you mean by 'could have been married'?"

"Don't worry—we will be married—and you couldn't stop it if you tried. Your interest is too much, too late." Matt strode over to the table. "There might be a small delay because of—because I'm in a—" He broke off. "What's it to you? I should be with Rennie now. Is she all right? She must have been terribly—"

"She's all right. She sent me for you."

"Then why didn't you say so? I'll get my coat —"

"And go as you are? It strikes me as not improbable that you have a razor here. If so, now would be the time to prove that you do shave occasionally. Rennie's not apt to be reassured by the way you look."

Matt, glowering down at him, saw for the first time a troubling resemblance to Rennie. He stalked into the bathroom and slammed the door. He stripped himself of the stale-smelling clothes, turned the shower on, and got under it. His morale began to climb as he soaped and scrubbed. After he had shaved and brushed his teeth and combed his wet hair he remembered almost with joy the new clean shirt and shorts and socks in the bottom drawer of the bureau. Using a towel for a loincloth, he went to claim them without a glance in Marshall's direction. When he had put them on, the disreputable outer garments could not destroy a sense of well-being. He felt as though something hopelessly lost had been recovered in some unlikely place.

He came out of the bathroom again fully clothed and very nearly in his right mind. The nod that Marshall gave him was a friendly comment. It seemed to call a truce which he decided to honor on a temporary basis.

"I'm ready," he said, and took his hat and coat from the closet.

"Have you had breakfast?"

"No." At the mention of it his dormant hunger set up a shamefully eager response.

"Does Rennie keep anything on hand? I could do with coffee if you can make it."

"I can make it, but wouldn't it be quicker to have it on the way?"

"It's barely eight o'clock. There won't be many places open."

"All right."

He filled the kettle at the kitchenette tap, measured coffee precisely, and took the remains of a packaged loaf from the breadbox. As he worked he thought that he could afford to humor Rennie's father in the small matter of getting breakfast for him. He did not look like a man accustomed to early rising and was undoubtedly in need of a pickup. But if he had an idea that belated concern for his daughter entitled him to a vote on larger issues, he could think again. Matt wondered with no great interest what he did for a living. It did not occur to him that Marshall's evident prosperity had bearing upon his own future, but he resented the selfishness that had kept him from easing Rennie's path. He told himself that from now on Rennie would be well looked after. And then his face darkened and he stood transfixed with a piece of hot toast in his hand. I've got to do something. As soon as I've seen Rennie I've got to find that woman. Where do I start? I should have asked that lawyer how long I had. Maybe I should have hung onto him. He might have furnished a clue—led me to whoever it was who hired him—

Preoccupied, he set the food on a tray and carried it to the table. James Marshall was preoccupied too. Matt did not notice that he hardly touched his coffee until he himself had drunk two cups of it and eaten all of the heavily buttered toast. Then he looked across the table at the nearly full cup and said, "Finished?"

"Yes, thank you."

"I thought you wanted it. No good?"

"Excellent."

"Well—I'll wash these and then—"

"Leave them."

"I guess you haven't had much experience with old houses. Roaches come when—"

"Never mind. Rennie won't be back. If she's left anything that she wants I'll send for it and have the place cleaned at the same time."

"Who says she won't be back?"

"She does."

"Oh." He could not argue with Marshall about what Rennie chose to do.

"Cigarette?" Marshall said.

"I've sort of broken the habit. I don't want to start again. Hadn't we better get going?"

Marshall lit a cigarette and inhaled deeply. He returned the gold case to his pocket. He made no move to rise.

Matt tried not to sound impatient. "Do you live far from here?"

"Connecticut."

Matt grunted as though he had been hit in the stomach. Connecticut meant at the very least an hour spent in traveling each way. Added to the time spent with Rennie, it would eat far into the day. I can't afford it, he thought with sickening disappointment. Too much to do. I'll telephone her. A talk will have to hold us both until—well, for a starter I could go to see that doctor. The woman wouldn't have taken me there if she hadn't known him, so it follows that he must know her. I'll get him alone and force him to listen to me. He didn't seem like such a bad—

He said to Marshall, "I suppose you have a telephone at home." Marshall looked surprised. "Yes—why do you ask?"

"Because I've just realized I can't go back with you. I'll call Rennie and—"

"Rennie isn't at home—she—"

"I thought you said—"

"I haven't said anything yet. You go off the handle so fast you haven't given me a chance."

Matt grasped the table's edge. "If anything's happened to Rennie and you haven't told me—"

"There. That's an illustration of what I mean. Nothing's happened to her. She's with my brother-in-law in Barns Village. You didn't give him a chance to explain either—with the result that you've caused everyone, including yourself, a lot of unnecessary trouble."

"The lawyer—Decker—?"

"Yes. Rennie begged him to take your case, but he would make no promises until he saw you. He did see you and he came to the conclusion that you were worth saving—which makes you a fortunate young man —"

"Sure—and a worthwhile charity case. What I could scrape up wouldn't do more than buy his commutation ticket to Barns Village."

"Will you let me finish? Rennie and her Uncle Ted are very close. Yet in spite of his affection for her he wouldn't have touched the case if you hadn't impressed him favorably. As for charity—you're marrying a wealthy girl—"

"The hell I am. If you think because you've got a sudden rush of generosity that Rennie and I will accept handouts from you—"

"I haven't offered you a handout. My—Rennie's mother left her quite well off."

Matt tried to digest it. It would not go down. He said, "Wait—I'm getting a glimmer. Rennie was left some money and you managed it for her—and let it slip through your fingers—" He stopped to stare at the fingers. They were smooth and fine and they were pulling another cigarette from the gold case.

"May I have a word now?" Marshall said. His face was the face of a man praying for patience. His voice was level. "You might grow on me in time—but at the moment I'm extremely doubtful of my brother-in-law's judgment. I did not play ducks and drakes with Rennie's inheritance. I invested it for her."

Matt said uncertainly, "I wasn't accusing you of dishonesty. Why should I—I don't know anything about you—or about investments, except that they're chancy."

"Chancy or not—Rennie's money is a good deal better than intact."

"I—I'm floored. It doesn't make sense. If it's true, why would she take a job in a store like that—grub along in a dump like this?"

"I don't know. She might have picked the store because it was unlikely she'd run into people she knew there—or perhaps because it was as far removed from her own environment as she could get—perhaps to prove something to herself—or to me. She wanted to punish me—but that's another story and has nothing to do with you."

"Neither has her money anything to do with me." He could not keep the defiance out of his voice. "Of course I'm glad she won't have to grub any more, but that's all it amounts to as far as I'm concerned." He got up. He walked over to the window and yanked at the shade. He looked through the dirty glass.

Marshall said, "Good. I was afraid that this pride I've heard so much about might obscure the intelligence I've heard so much about. Not that you'd get very far by treating Rennie to the poor boy's noble renunciation of the heiress. Once she's made up her mind, I doubt that even a force like you could alter it. Then there's the child to consider. Financial security for a child is not the be-all and end-all of—"

"Keep quiet—let me think—I've got to think."

"I'll give you something profitable to think about. You've assumed that my concern for Rennie is something new. It isn't. You may not approve of the means I used to show it, but that's neither here nor there. The point is that the means worked out to your advantage. When Rennie left my house I hired a private detective to find her—and for reasons of his own he exceeded his instructions. He saw you enter this building on the night that Hackett was killed—and when you left he followed you. He witnessed the street accident and its outcome—and he got the license number of the woman's car."

Matt had come away from the window. He forgot Rennie's money. He forgot everything but the sudden shining light at the end of the long black tunnel.

Watching his face, Marshall said, "I'm sorry, Matt."

"Sorry!"

"That you were put through it—but you were no more than a name to me, and I couldn't allow myself to be blackmailed."

Matt did not know what he was talking about. And he did not care. "Have you found out who owns the car—her name—?"

"Not yet. You see—"

"Give me the license number. I'll go straight to the police—to Homicide—Captain Nelson—"

"Strachan didn't tell me the number. We tried to get in touch with him yesterday but—"

"What's his address?"

"It might be wiser to let Ted handle—"

"Look—I don't need an expensive lawyer to do what I can do myself. Will you please—?"

"Very well." Marshall stopped sitting like a permanent fixture in Rennie's chair at Rennie's table. "I'll drive you to Strachan's office."

"I don't need— Okay, let's go."

Chapter Fourteen

They were waylaid on the sidewalk in front of Rennie's house. A neat young man with a neat mustache gave Matt a doubtful glance and greeted Marshall by name. The two talked briefly while Matt shifted from one foot to the other. He was on the verge of breaking it up when the man took himself off.

Marshall's car had a dented fender. Otherwise it was the type of car that seemed to run in the family. Matt got in beside Marshall, thinking of the woman's car that he had been too muddled to observe.

Marshall made reference to the sidewalk encounter as he pulled away from the curb. "I suppose you gathered that Jerome was on the way to see you."

"Me?"

"He's a junior member of Ted's firm. He'll tell him that everything's under control."

Matt said a heartfelt "Yes—it is." Then he thought that Marshall deserved some sort of acknowledgment even though what he had brought about was the result of spying upon Rennie. So he added, "Thanks to you," and carried the friendly motif further by expressing token interest in the dented fender. "Were you in an accident?"

"Last night—early this morning rather. I skidded off the road into a tree. I'm thankful Rennie wasn't in the car. When my brother-in-law returned alone she wanted to set right out. Fortunately we managed to dissuade her."

"Oh lord." A little of what he felt for Rennie spread to include her father. It tempered his first harsh judgment. "You weren't hurt?"

"No—just angry. It was my first accident since I learned to drive."

"I'm that way too," Matt said. "I can take something rotten happening when I've practically asked for it. It's different when it's not my fault."

"I think it always is one's fault," Marshall said, "directly or indirectly." It smacked of the heavy-father role, but Matt let it pass.

They found a parking space near Fourth Avenue. Matt was rather surprised to be led through the entrance of a dilapidated old building. In view of the casual talk of wealth, he had expected a more imposing front for someone hired by Marshall.

Marshall explained as they started up the narrow dirty flight of stairs. "I picked Strachan out of the telephone book. I wanted to avoid publicity, and after sizing him up I doubted that he'd court it. Of course if he failed to find Rennie I'd have taken other steps."

There were three or four doors on the first landing. The one nearest the stairs was Strachan's. It did not give when Marshall turned the knob. Matt stooped to read the penciled sheet of paper tacked below eye level. "It says he won't be back till four-thirty."

"For all we know, it might have been written yesterday or the day before—or last week."

"What time is it now?"

"Twenty-five to ten." Marshall rattled the doorknob. "I've a good mind to—"

Matt said, "What I don't need is to be rearrested for breaking and entering—and where would we begin to search for a small item like a license number?"

"You're right. Anyway, it's probably in that book he carries. Well—we'll have to return at four-thirty. We'd better postpone the trip to Barns Village. With the roads as they are, there's no telling how long it will take."

Matt followed him down the dark stairs and out into the street. The day now hung about him in heavy dragging folds. He said tentatively, "Before you brought Strachan into the picture I was planning to pay Dr. Stewart a visit." At Marshall's questioning look, he elaborated. "The fellow they gave the party for—"

"Yes—I know."

"I suppose his office will be closed, but I could look up his home address in the book. I think I will anyway. Maybe we're taking too much stock in that four-thirty business. If Strachan doesn't come back today—"

"Don't worry. If he doesn't Ted will send experts in search of him."

"All right—but meanwhile why sit back and wait? That woman didn't pick a doctor out of a hat. It stands to reason she and Stewart are acquainted—and with time to mull it over and a little prodding from me he might remember—"

Marshall was shaking his head. He chose his words carefully. "I'd let it alone if I were you. Regardless of how unjustly it came about, you're out on bail—you reminded me yourself that it's a ticklish position to be in when I wanted to force Strachan's door. And you might make it worse by going to Dr. Stewart's home. He might be reluctant to see or talk to you, and if you insisted—or lost patience with him and did anything that could be interpreted as a threat—those responsible for your arrest could very well jump to the conclusion that their case had been strengthened."

He looked relieved when Matt said, "I see what you mean."

"We'll go to Ted's office and—"

"No." He had thought of something that he *could* do, and in spite of frustration upon frustration he brightened. "I'll call Rennie. We passed a drugstore—"

"Of course. That comes first."

In the drugstore they pooled their coins. Matt was the one who gave the operator the Barns Village number. Marshall had the delicacy to stand away from the booth.

The connection was made, and because he wanted so much to hear it, Matt thought for a quick heartbeat that the answering voice was Rennie's. He said her name.

"Who's calling, please?"

He might have known, he thought, that members of the family would not answer their own phones in Barns Village. But before he could humor the secretary or maid or whoever was on the job to screen callers, Rennie herself said, "Darling—where are you?"

He said stupidly, "It's Matt."

"Do you think I'd call anyone else darling? I was listening on an extension. I've listened every time the phone rang—waiting for you to say 'Rennie' the way you say it. Did my father—?"

"Yes, he did. I—"

"Don't say anything yet. Don't say anything you could be sorry for. I've been sorry enough for the two of us. Oh, Matt, are you very angry?"

He was smiling at the black instrument as though it were a beautiful living thing. He said gruffly, "Anger isn't exactly the—"

"I'll never forgive myself for behaving like that—talking the way I did and sending you out into that mess."

"Stop right there. I didn't take any notice of your nonsense—and you didn't send me into the mess. Anyway, I'm free of it—or nearly."

"Of course you are. I knew you'd be as soon as I got Uncle Ted to—"

"Could you please kindly leave Uncle Ted out of it for a couple of minutes? I—"

"Matt, you *are* angry. I wasn't really sailing under false pretenses. I didn't tell you about the money because it didn't and doesn't matter."

"Oh, that," he said. "I haven't decided what's to be done about that yet."

"Matt—Matt—you're wonderful. I'll do whatever you say. If you want we can go right on living in the apartment and—"

"No, we can't—it's full of cockroaches by this time. I didn't wash the breakfast dishes."

"Wait till I get my hands on you."

He thought of how long he had been waiting. Her next words seemed telepathic.

She said, "I know just how awful it must have been—going there and not finding me—and worrying on top of everything else you'd been through. I wanted to come in but—"

"Yes, your father told me."

"What time did he get there?"

"At the crack of dawn. I thought he was a salesman."

"He is in a way—or you wouldn't—" Then she said, "When can we be married?"

"What do you mean, 'Salesman in a way'?"

"Never mind—"

"I'm as immune to salesmanship as a guy can be. I like to believe that I make up my own mind—and before we rush into marriage there's something I've got to tell you."

He heard her catch her breath. He said quickly, "Something I neglected to say last time—so here goes. Rennie—I love you."

She broke the little pause. "It doesn't count over the phone. It's got to be implemented by the usual informalities. I'm coming in—"

He managed a firm "No, you're not. The roads are bad—and anyway I'll be busy."

"Doing what?"

He said inspirationally, "For one thing, I've got to go to Brooklyn and see that my books and papers are safe."

"Yes, you've got to do that. You wouldn't want to lose those notes you've been making on the thermonuclear thing."

"Where did you get—how come you know about that?"

"You told me."

"But you didn't listen—"

"I always listened. I'll be the listeningest wife in the world. Matt, going to Brooklyn won't take all day. What else do you have to do?"

"You'll be the nosiest wife in the world. I've plenty to do—and later I have to see a man about a dog license."

"You mean that private detective? Isn't it lucky my father was so sneaky?"

"Rennie!"

"You sound shocked. Anybody could tell you were brought up to respect your parents. That's part of why I—"

The operator cut in to say that the three minutes were up. Rennie told her to reverse the charges, but Matt inserted more coins, making a mental note that he owed Marshall sixty cents.

Rennie said, "Where are you phoning from?"

"A drugstore. We tried to see the detective, but he won't be back until four-thirty."

"We?"

"Your father and I. He's standing outside. Do you want to talk to him?"

"No, I'll see him later. I won't drive in. I'll rest this morning and take an afternoon train. You can meet me at Uncle Ted's office when you're through with the detective and we'll have dinner together."

He said, "Okay," and thought that one of the things he would have to do was draw his money from the Brooklyn bank.

"I'll get Uncle Ted to take us."

"You'll do no such thing—"

"Why shouldn't he? You're a client of his, aren't you?"

"Now listen to me —"

"Matt, I'm only teasing. We'll go to the automat."

"Wrong again. I owe you a celebration. I meant to have one right after you got so coy about the little stranger."

"Did you—did you really? You don't mind?"

"Mind! But get this straight—he's going to respect his parents."

"How could he help it? Darling, I don't want you to spend any more money. I'll hang up. Don't forget—I'll be at Uncle Ted's. There's usually somebody working late there, so it won't matter if you're delayed—but get there as soon as you can. I could have come in with him this morning, but he stole away without waking me."

"He showed good sense. I'll meet you there, but that doesn't mean I'm his client. What's his address?"

"Ask my father. And—Matt—be nice to him."

"Who?"

"My father. Uncle Ted can take care of himself. He's like me—strong. I used to think my father was too—before I got mature."

"If he could weather a blow like me I guess he'll do."

"I'm so glad you like each other."

"Like each other? You're lightheaded."

"Yes, I am. You're responsible for that—as well as for my maturity.

See you—darling."

Marshall was talking in another booth. He terminated his conversation as Matt passed, and joined him.

He looked at Matt and said, "I needn't inquire about Rennie's health."

"She coming in by train this afternoon. She'll go to Mr. Decker's office."

"Fine. We can join her after we've seen Strachan."

Matt did not want the pronoun "we" to become too much of a habit. He said pointedly, "Meanwhile I'm sure you have business to attend to—and so do I." He remembered Rennie's injunction to "be nice," and went on with more grace, "I've got to go to my room in Brooklyn. I've books and papers that are important to me and the landlady might get careless with them."

"All right. For the time being we can lock them in the luggage compartment—unless you have a better storage place."

Matt had planned no further than a round-trip subway ride. He tried to compare at long distance the capacity of a station locker with that of the car's trunk. "I could store them in Rennie's apartment," he said.

"I don't think it would be wise. Ted mentioned the possibility of the police keeping track of you. Your comings and goings might lead to inquiries about who had leased the apartment, and some enterprising sob sister might use Rennie as the subject of a story."

Matt said, "There's been no sign that I'm under surveillance, and if I were, being seen with you could accomplish the same result."

"I could offer an acceptable explanation. For instance—my brother-in-law is acting for you. He negotiated the bail bond and I'm guarding his investment."

"Are you?"

Marshall smiled. "No, but I've made a bargain with Rennie to hand you over to her safely—and I intend to stick close to you until I've done it."

So Matt found himself in the car again, this time behind the wheel because he had suggested that Marshall must have had a bellyful of driving after his recent collision. Besides, he knew the way.

He had never driven in New York. For a while it took most of his attention. It was good to be in command, even if what he commanded was only a machine that responded without quibble to the slightest pressure. Soon his reflexes took over, freeing his thoughts and his vocal cords for simple exercise.

He discovered that it was not difficult to be nice to Marshall. In the course of the drive he gave more easily of himself than he would have thought possible a short while ago. He had expected Rennie's father to be curious and he had expected to resent his curiosity. He had not expected the warm, intelligent interest projected by Marshall in putting him through his paces. He found himself talking enthusiastically about his work.

As they neared the rooming house, Marshall said, "From the sound of that theory you've been working on, it seems to me that all you need is a laboratory and a go-ahead signal."

"Sure—all I need is the earth. Without a degree, who's going to think I'm entitled to a job that would give me the lab and the go-ahead nod?"

"I realize that you have to complete your studies—but you shouldn't have to work for your degree the hard way. You should be subsidized."

Matt said, "No, thanks."

"I didn't mean by me. The government's shouting for nuclear physicists."

"Shouting is about all," Matt said. Then he said nastily, "You could pull the necessary strings, no doubt."

"As a citizen of this country I might consider it my duty to try." Marshall refused to be baited. "Even if your future and Rennie's weren't linked."

He practiced a form of string-pulling in the rooming house. It was no more than a look and a few authoritative words to Matt's landlady, but it stopped midway an abusive monologue on murderous beasts who had the nerve to infest decent establishments. Marshall, just by his appearance, worked the further miracle of civility. She offered to help with the packing and at his bidding fetched some twine and a carton large enough to contain the overflow of books accumulated during Matt's tenure.

Matt's reaction to this hovered between admiration for Marshall's handling of the situation and disgust for his own callowness which would have met it with unproductive rage. Rage, he thought disconsolately, was the ineffectual weapon of the poor.

Refusing Marshall's assistance, he jammed clothes into his suitcase, and on second thought unpacked again to change into his cleaned and slightly better suit. When he had closed the suitcase he gathered up his more important possessions and fitted them into the carton. The room, denuded of everything but narrow bed, bureau, table, and chair, had never looked meaner. Nor had his prospects. He was homeless and jobless and he would not have blamed Marshall for turning upon him and commanding him to get out of Rennie's orbit. He could almost have issued the command to himself.

Marshall had drawn the chair to the window. His head was bent over a notebook picked up at random. "I envy you," he said.

Matt gave the statement its due. "Ha!"

"My education along these lines is elementary—but the little I can understand makes me want to start life over."

Matt held out his hand for the notebook. Surrendering it, Marshall said, "You're one of the lucky few who obviously knew at an early age where you were going. I didn't."

Matt's silence was expressive. It said, You're one of the lucky few who didn't have to know because you were there.

"My father was wiped out in the crash of '29," Marshall said. "I was in my senior year at college and my tuition had been paid, so I managed to finish. Then I went job hunting. I had connections, of course—"

Matt said, "Of course."

"But most of the people I tackled were in the same boat as my father—and the others took a jaundiced view of my qualifications. Those were Depression days and the openings that existed went to experienced men. Finally, out of sheer kindness I was given a menial job with a firm that had weathered the crisis."

"And rose to the top of the ladder by leaps and bounds," Matt said.

"Not exactly. But I wasn't held back by the fact that on the way up I happened to fall in love with and marry a rich girl." His eyes seemed to take fresh stock of his surroundings. He nodded as though satisfied. "I recognized this room the minute I saw it. It has a strong family resemblance to my first home from home. I was pretty sorry for myself—"

"I don't feel sorry for myself," Matt said. He secured the carton neatly with the landlady's twine. "I appreciate your reminiscences and the motive behind them—but if you think you've drawn a parallel, you haven't. Being a financial genius—or whatever you are—hasn't got much to do with being a so-called egghead. The terms alone point up the values of our society."

"It rests with men of your generation to balance those values," Marshall said. He watched Matt tie the last intricate knot. They left the room, he carrying the suitcase and Matt the heavier load.

They drove to a gas station, refueled the car, and went to the bank where Matt's savings were deposited. He withdrew every cent since he had banked there only because it had been a convenient place to cash his pay check. Marshall asked him what he intended to do about the factory, and he answered that according to Decker there was not much he could do except collect his back wages. Marshall said they might as well attend to it while they were in the neighborhood, so they drove on to the factory.

The paymaster, a dehydrated individual who seldom had words for anyone, seemed morbidly pleased to see Matt and thirsted openly for the details of his predicament. Matt was not disposed to gratify him. He escaped without encountering any of his co-workers. Later, he thought, he might get in touch with the few whose company he had enjoyed. There was a pink slip attached to his check. It did not have a depressing effect because he had received an unexpected bonus by way of severance pay. He supposed that the union would fight to reinstate him if he presented his case, but knew that he would not present it. He rejoined Marshall, who had waited in the car, and before they drove away he turned with mixed feelings to take a last look at the squat gray buildings.

Marshall asked with surprise how it had got to be three o'clock. No wonder he was hungry, he said. Matt told him that the only restaurant in the vicinity was a counter place, and Marshall said it wouldn't be the first time he had eaten at a counter. He did not even cast a dubious glance at the dubious coffee and hamburgers, nor did he quibble when Matt paid the check. Matt's savings, stowed in an inner pocket, gave him a sensation of affluence. He would have liked to order more food, but he was anxious to start back to Manhattan. He thought that between now and going to the detective's office there might be time for him to find a temporary lodging where he could leave his belongings and lay his head that night.

The traffic had increased, but they were making fairly good time until they found themselves behind a long funeral procession. They could not pass it. They had to crawl along until the endless line of cars turned down a side street. Matt guessed that he would have to postpone hunting for a room and that he would be lucky to make the detective's office on time. Marshall consoled him by saying that Strachan would not have bothered to leave a note if he meant to rush in and rush out. Obviously he intended to be open for business after four-thirty, and reaching him a few minutes late could make no difference.

They were ten minutes late and could not find a parking place. Marshall, infected by Matt's impatience, offered to relieve him of the wheel. "I'll park. You run on ahead and hold him—provided he's turned up at all."

Matt said, "Right." He jumped out of the car and was off at a sprint.

He rammed against someone in the entrance of the run-down building, muttered an apology, and kept going. He raced up the narrow stairs to the first landing and wheeled to take the few remaining steps. Before he reached the office he thought he heard sounds of occupancy. The note was gone from the door and the door gave.

He was met by a gust of wind as he stepped inside. His first thought was that Strachan must be a fresh-air fiend. Then he tripped over a body on the floor, and before he could right himself or have a second thought he was sent to join it by a blow on the side of his skull.

He struggled for several minutes to regain full consciousness. He heard a groan that was not his own, and crawled over to the body that had tripped him. It muttered thickly, "I give up—you win—you bastard—in my hat." Then it closed its eyes and was quiet.

Matt squatted on his haunches and fingered the aching spot behind his ear. He heard another voice that belonged to Marshall. With difficulty he caught some of the words.

"... never should have let you out of my ... are you hurt ... what ...?"

Matt looked around him at the fair-sized cheaply partitioned space, closed and opened his eyes, and looked again. Nothing had changed. A chair was overturned. The metal file with all its drawers extracted had bled a lot of paper. So had the ravished desk. The window giving on to a fire escape was open.

He pointed a languid finger at the stuffed bundle of clothes on the floor and muttered, "Strachan?"

"Yes—I'd better—"

He could have laughed at Marshall's fastidious expression, except that he could not laugh. Marshall picked his way toward the telephone on the desk and was halted by the policeman in the doorway.

The policeman strode in, hand at holster. There was a small crowd behind him. He waved them back. A man in the foreground said with shrill triumph, "Officer, I told you it sounded like murder—see—there on the floor—and the big thug crouching over him—"

"On your feet," the policeman said to Matt. "Too late to roll him now."

Matt opened his mouth but stared wordlessly at the pointing gun.

Marshall spoke. "Put that gun away. We had business with—"

"You sure did. Come around here where I can keep an eye on the two of you."

"Listen," Matt said groggily. "Just listen—give yourself a chance to learn something." He had pulled himself upright. He was trying to bring the blur of the policeman's face into focus, but what he saw did not look promising. "You got here too late," he said. "The fire escape—" He turned and stumbled toward it, because it seemed simpler to communicate by illustration than by talk. He was standing with his hands braced on the sill when the policeman fired.

He did not connect the shot with himself. He felt no pain. But as he came away from the sill it seemed to him that sanity had entered the room symbolized by a familiar face and voice. Captain Nelson of Homicide to the rescue, he thought. He said in what he believed to be a loud strong voice, "In his hat."

Chapter Fifteen

Nelson and Judd had entered the loft building with no particular plan for ferreting out the man they sought. Climbing the stairs, they had been directed to Strachan's office by the sound of the shot. Nelson would have preferred to find it by trial and error. He had cut a straight path through the confusion while Judd telephoned for an ambulance and dispersed the crowd. Judd, armed with further instructions, had picked up Strachan's coat and hat and exited with the stretcher-bearers. Matt, who had answered one brief question concerning Strachan's hat, limped out under his own power.

Nelson, the patrolman, and Marshall remained in the office. Marshall had tried to accompany Matt to the hospital, but the patrolman insisted doggedly that he was under arrest.

All three men were angry after their fashion. Nelson was the only one who concealed his anger. He lowered the window, closed the door, and asked the patrolman to give an account of himself.

"I was walking my beat, Captain, when a man ran up to me and said there was a commotion in the office next to his that sounded like somebody getting the works. I went back with him and sure enough there's a man stretched out and a thug rolling him—"

"You idiot!" Marshall had righted the overturned chair and was sitting on the edge of it. "That thug was loosening Strachan's clothing—trying to do what he could for him."

The patrolman's face reddened. Otherwise he ignored the interruption. "I told him to stand up." He did not look at Marshall.

"Handsome here began to talk his way out of it, but I ordered him to step forward where I could keep an eye on him. Meanwhile the big fellow is mumbling like crazy about the fire escape. Well—there was the stiff—I mean the man laying in front of me—and a couple of other things like the chair ready to trip me up. By the time I'd get to the window or bring help by blowing my whistle it would be too late—so I did my duty as I saw it. I didn't shoot to kill—all I meant was to stop him from—"

Marshall said through pale lips, "He wasn't attempting to escape. He was attempting to show you how the escape was made. I hope you're discharged and never get another job as long as you live. You blundered in here cold. You didn't ask a single question and wouldn't listen when I tried to explain. Strachan needed a doctor urgently, but you had no time for such trivia. He looked dead to you and that settled it. If he does die it will be on your head. As for that fine boy who's worth a dozen of you—if you've injured him seriously I'll—"

"All right," Nelson said. He had let him get that far because a portion of his words relieved the pressure of his own anger. He said to the patrolman, "What's your name?"

"Leader, Captain. Conrad Leader." He added his precinct number. "I've been on the force six months." He offered the information like a schoolboy, uncertain of whether he was about to receive praise or censure.

"I thought so," Nelson said. "Well, Leader, you did your duty as you saw it. Next time see it more clearly."

"Yes, Captain." His voice was respectful, his face mulish. "Could I say something?" At Nelson's nod he said it. "What about him? He's complaining I didn't give him a chance to talk—but he still hasn't said a thing. If he's not an accomplice why was he standing by as cool as—?"

"I'll talk to you in private, Captain," Marshall said.

Nelson gave him a measuring look. "You're in no position to make conditions. I'm taking you into custody."

The patrolman said eagerly, "Wouldn't I save you trouble by making the arrest myself?"

"I'm leaving you here to hold the fort. Be sure that the snow on the fire escape isn't disturbed. There's a footprint there that's asking to be cast. As soon as it's attended to you can go."

"What about my report? This—this man won't give me his name or the name of the man I—"

"Postpone the report until further notice. I'll take the responsibility."

The patrolman did not look pleased to be relieved of his "collar." He managed a halfhearted salute.

Nelson said nothing until he and Marshall had quit the building. Then he said, "Wrong direction," as Marshall faced toward Broadway.

"But I left my car in a—"

"It can be picked up later." He headed for Fourth Avenue, setting a fast pace.

Marshall, striding beside him, said, "I hope you'll fix the parking ticket. Well—you've done me a service so I'll grant you the right to call the turn, but could I make a phone call first?"

"If it's a short one."

When they came out of the drugstore Marshall said, "Thank you—and thanks for sparing me the publicity that could attend the inclusion of my name in a police report."

"Berthold is out on bail. I imagine he wanted that publicity less than you do."

"I realize that. Where are we going? I vote for the nearest bar."

"If Leader had his way you'd be drinking a bitter brew at the precinct." They had reached Nelson's car. He gestured Marshall into it and took the driver's seat.

Before they were well under way Marshall produced a wallet. "If you're willing to assume that I didn't steal this you'll find identification to prove that I'm James Marshall, a member of the New York Stock Exchange, and a board member of several well-regarded corporations. I believe it also contains a receipt for my last income tax, as well as an invitation from Princeton to be present at a class reunion. I remember reading somewhere that you're a Princeton man too. I bring that up at the risk of seeming to curry favor."

Nelson said dryly, "I'll try not to be influenced one way or the other." He did not say that Marshall's name and reputation were familiar to him. He stopped for a red light and examined the wallet. Returning it, he said, "What's your connection with Matthew Berthold?"

Marshall offered him a cigarette. He refused it. Marshall lit one and said, "I became interested in him when he was brought to my attention as a young man of promise. May I ask how you happened to appear in Strachan's office?"

"After I've asked you the same question."

"Recently I had cause to employ a private detective. Strachan handled the job successfully, so I thought he might be useful in helping Matt to locate the woman who had driven him to the doctor's office. She could be an important link in establishing his innocence."

"Very plausible—except for a glaring inconsistency. In the process of earning those impressive credentials it must have been necessary for you to be a fairly good judge of your fellow men—which makes it hard to believe you would trust a type like Strachan to succeed where the police had failed."

"Your crowd granted him a license to be a detective—which means that we both had poor judgment."

"He may have rated it at the start—but a license isn't insurance against deterioration. Was the initial job you gave him of the same nature—locating someone?"

"It was a personal matter."

"My curiosity isn't personal. I'm attempting to discover why anyone able to afford the fees of experts should hire Strachan."

"You sound like a lawyer."

"Speaking of lawyers—is yours Edwin Decker?"

"Yes. Is this where I should start to scream for him? As a matter of fact, Edwin Decker happens to be my brother-in-law."

"Did you instruct him to act for Berthold?"

"What if I did? You can't quarrel with *that* choice."

"No—I can't. It must be convenient to have a lawyer in the family. I suppose Mr. Decker obliged you by taking the case in spite of what he might consider more important commitments—unless he has his own interest in Berthold. The young man doesn't happen to be a member of the family too, does he?"

Marshall said sarcastically, "Of course—he's my illegitimate son—" Then he winced and his voice rose. "Damn it—most men of means indulge in some sort of philanthropy along the way. Why should you question my interest in the young man?" He tried to recapture his casual manner. "I would have fared better by going along to the precinct with that flower of New York's Finest."

"I doubt it." Nelson thought that, except for a check on Berthold's parentage, the illegitimate angle would not have seemed too farfetched. In addition to rumors concerning the older man there was that about his appearance that suggested more than a fair share of success with women. He wondered why Marshall, having introduced the angle himself, had choked on it. He said experimentally, "If he *were* your illegitimate son I'd keep your secret for the sake of your daughter."

"What a gentleman you are." Again his disturbance was plainly communicated. It lowered his guard. "I take it you were listening in the next phone booth."

"You carry her picture in your wallet. She's very like you."

"Oh— Yes—I suppose she is."

"Was it your daughter who asked you to help Berthold?"

"You're a clever man."

Nelson said, "Mr. Marshall, I had to know why you're sponsoring him. When I talked to him after he'd been questioned all night he was a friendless waif. How could your sudden championship be anything but suspect? Influential men have been known to grind dirty axes."

"Matt and my daughter are going to be married. Does that satisfy you?"

Nelson said quietly, "Does it satisfy you?"

"No, I'm a monster straight out of Greek tragedy. I wanted to dispose of her impecunious suitor. Therefore I provided a corpse and commanded a faceless siren to lure him to it. Is that what you have in mind?" He waited a moment for Nelson to react. Then he said with passionate sincerity, "All right—I wasn't satisfied at first, but I am now. I suppose since I've gone this far you might as well have the rest of it."

He told the story, eliding the nature of the quarrel that had caused Rennie to strike out on her own. He said that he had not thought it would need a mastermind to discover her whereabouts. A reputable agency might insist that he go to Missing Persons. Then it would be bound to leak to the press, making Rennie even more at odds with him. So he had picked Strachan at random. When Strachan told him that she had an apartment and a job to keep her busy, he decided to let matters rest. The experience would do her no harm. She would tire of it and come home in her own good time. He had reckoned, he said ruefully, without Matt. The youngsters had met and fallen in love, and there it was. Here he made another elision. Only a mind keyed to nuances could have inferred that the relationship had been anything but decorous.

When he had finished he said, "You needn't tell me that I should have brought Strachan and his evidence to the police. I realize now that in a way I'm just as responsible as that patrolman for Matt being shot—but at the time my concern for Rennie made everything else seem unimportant."

Nelson did not labor it. He said, "You're luckier than you deserve to be."

"Am I? Rennie doesn't know about the shooting. I just told her

Matt and I would be delayed. Poor child—she's—the whole business has—"

"Where is she?"

"In Ted's office."

"Did you speak to him too?"

"No—not since morning—and then he advised me to leave Strachan to him. He wanted to meet me there, but I resented the inference that I couldn't handle it myself."

"He should have advised you to leave him to us."

"He couldn't be sure that Strachan wasn't throwing a bluff to extort money from me. He wanted to know exactly how much the evidence was worth before he presented it." Marshall seemed unaware that the car had come to a dead stop. "Besides, he wasn't too pleased with the smug bird-in-hand attitude of the police and the D.A.'s crew."

"So he decided to confound them in court with the rabbit trick," Nelson said. "We might as well get out."

"I didn't realize—where are we?"

"Headquarters. But you're a free man. You can get a taxi on the corner and go back to pick up your car. Sorry we inconvenienced each other."

Marshall said in dismay, "I thought—I hoped we were going to the hospital—"

"Your future son-in-law is in good hands. And I don't think there's much to worry about since he showed such strong and lucid resistance to being carried out on a stretcher."

Marshall joined him on the sidewalk. "But I don't even know where you had him taken—and shouldn't you be there when Strachan comes to—if he does?"

"He will. I share the intern's opinion that his unconscious state is as much due to alcohol as to the beating he took. He's so far from feeling pain that he could undergo surgery without anesthesia—and when he does awake sufficiently to identify his assailant, someone will be standing by."

"To hell with his assailant!" Lack of sleep and the day's demands were catching up with Marshall. Under the building lights his handsome face was a tired gray. "What I'm concerned with is the license number—and Matt. You agreed with me that it was important to keep Matt out of it—and the hospital is sure to report a bullet wound." He followed Nelson into the building. "I won't be brushed off. If you think I intend to face Rennie without knowing where—"

Nelson took pity on him. "Matt's at my house," he said. "By this time he will have been treated by an excellent doctor and made comfortable by my housekeeper. She's been instructed to keep him there at least overnight."

Marshall took a deep breath. "That—that was very decent of you."

"I acted in the interests of my job. I want the Strachan business kept under wraps until all the facts are in on the Hackett case—and my house seemed the safest bet to prevent a leak." He saw more questions coming and forestalled them. "I've work to do. The sooner I start, the sooner we'll get our answers." He gave Marshall his home address. "Pick up your daughter en route—and when you get there ask my housekeeper to give you the drink you voted for a while back."

Marshall said, "You've been—"

Nelson shook his outstretched hand and left him.

The wall clock struck seven as he entered his office. He frowned at it. He shucked off his coat, sat down at his desk, and called Sammy. She told him what he wanted to know about Matt. The doctor had removed the bullet from his leg and diagnosed the injury as a flesh wound. There were no symptoms of serious concussion from the blow, but it was too early for a definite opinion on that score. Nelson said that she could expect more visitors, and she sounded pleased to learn that the young man's girl was one of them. She said he seemed to be fussed more about something else than his health and maybe his girl was it. Sammy took in stride the invasion of Nelson's work into her territory but was disturbed when he asked her not to hold dinner for him. She advised him to get along home as quick as he could. He told her that she had no cause for uneasiness and assured her that the young man was not a criminal. She answered scornfully that she could see that with her own eyes and scolded him for sending two policemen to stand around giving the house a bad name. But she repeated firmly that he had better get along home.

He hung up with the feeling that Sammy too was "fussed" about something and that whatever it was it would have to wait until he had time to draw her out.

Obviously, to Marshall, intent upon protecting his own interests, the Strachan affair had meant only a delay in getting the license number. He had not stopped to make any connection between the Hackett murder and the man who had administered the beating to the alcoholic detective. As Nelson saw it, Strachan's life had been spared because he had told his assailant that the number was committed to paper and filed where it would be found by the police should anything happen to him. In substantiation there was the disordered office which indicated that Matt had interrupted both the search and the beating. And if Nelson's theory was correct and Matt had been recognized by the assailant, the similarity of his errand would also have been recognized, as would the possibility of his success.

Therefore, Nelson's own roof had seemed the safest and least obvious stronghold for Matt against a violent, desperate man. Provided, he thought, that my reasoning holds water. He looked for holes in it. In view of the facts, what else could Strachan's several appearances mean but that he had enlarged his market for blackmail? Perhaps, in his drunken fog, he had not even bothered to trace the license number. He might have been making the rounds of Hackett's friends, hinting that he could be persuaded to quash a scandal involving all of them, or called upon the victim's widow to promise justice for a stipulated fee. And through it all he had been wearing the license number in the sweat band of his hat and had revealed the hiding place to prevent another beating when he confused Matt with the manhandler.

Nelson could have called the Motor Vehicle Bureau from Strachan's office, but it had not seemed advisable to do so in the presence of Marshall and the patrolman. He had merely fingered the hat casually before he passed it to Judd.

Judd seemed to be taking his time about reporting the findings. Still, knowing the woman driver's identity would not break the case by a long shot. Her connection with the murderer would have to be established. And there was a connection. Otherwise, why the beating and the search?

He called the ready room to find out who was there. Clevis answered, recited the list, and a few minutes later made a personal appearance.

"If you've turned in your report," Nelson said, "why don't you go home before you're stuck with something? This makes two nights in a row for you."

"Either way I get stuck. My wife's got a visiting mother to keep her warm—so I'm not in a hurry to call it a day. But believe me, there's worse I could call it. I saw Donald Lawrence Palmer finally."

"Well?"

"I'd stake my all and almost did his only crime is fast talking—and I do mean fast. He nearly had me sinking my life's savings into a deal by the name of Mutual Funds. Him throwing the big pitch for my couple of bucks might have made me suspect he was hard up enough to kill for gain—except that Dun and Bradstreet says different. I guess big business gets that way on small suckers. I asked him the usual questions and added a few subtle teasers like how come a feller his age hangs out with such an old crowd and he frankly admits they're his clients and it pays him to socialize with them. A real open guy. So I'm encouraged to be a chum and ask him where he gets the sun tan—thinking could it be he was in Florida holding hands with Mrs. Hackett—but at the same time I ask myself why a handsome rich job like him would want to bump off the husband of a dame with such thick ankles—and anyway he starts bragging about a new sun lamp that—"

Nelson said, "Hold it," and answered the ringing telephone. "Yes ... Go ahead, Judd...." He listened. He said slowly, "No—how could you—you're not expected to be a mind reader.... Where are you now? ... I see ... Yes—that should be good for a while, but get right back there to be on the safe side. You'll have company soon.... That's right."

Clevis's big ears had scooped up every word. He said as Nelson hung up, "Sounds like Judd's onto something."

Nelson scribbled an address. "Give this to Bonino. Judd will fill him in when he gets there."

"Why Bonino? I'm—" He looked at Nelson's face and went. Nelson stood up. He stopped in the act of putting on his coat to pick up the phone again. "Send Clevis back."

Clevis came on the run. He said hopefully, "Yes, sir."

"Did Bonino leave?"

"On the double."

"Good. What was that you said about thick ankles?"

Clevis grinned. He took a folded newspaper from his pocket. "Get a load of her stepping off the plane this morning."

The story had made the front page. The picture was captioned, "Tragic Homecoming for Mrs. Eugene Hackett." Nelson stared at it for so long that Clevis said, "Hey—she must have something I missed." He watched slack-mouthed as Nelson rummaged in the top drawer of the desk and produced a magnifying glass. He muttered, "No disrespect—but are you kidding?"

"Somebody is." Nelson exchanged the magnifying glass for the telephone. He asked for Long Distance.

Chapter Sixteen

Driving uptown with Clevis, Nelson gave him a summary of the day's developments. He concluded with, "Your contribution was bigger than you thought."

Clevis was modest. "I don't know my own strength." Then he said, "It begins to look as if we've got so much evidence we can hold some of it over for the next case."

Nelson laughed, but both he and Clevis were grimly serious as they left the car and joined Judd, who stood near the hotel's entrance.

Judd said, "The clerk told me he came back at about six-thirty and went into the restaurant about three quarters of an hour later. He's still there. Bonino's covering it from the lobby—it's got no entrance from the street. You going right in to—?"

"I'll let him finish his dinner," Nelson said. "Stand by."

He went into the lobby with Clevis. A few people sat about wearing the uncertain expressions of those who wait. The dapper Bonino got up from a leather chair. Bonino smiled cordially as though he were giving them "Good evening," and said, "I guess he's having second portions of everything."

"Cover the service exit around the corner—just in case."

Bonino nodded.

Nelson and Clevis sat down on a settee that afforded the view they wanted. Clevis took out his newspaper. He said from behind it, "I wasn't exactly on the ball at first. When you asked for that Miami number I would have made it a sudden urge to call your missus—except I couldn't tie it in with the magnifying glass."

Nelson said, "Oh lord!" and tried not to think of Kyrie waiting for his evening call. A few minutes later he thought of no one but George Rolfe, who was sauntering out of the restaurant. He got up to intercept him. Clevis stayed where he was.

"Mr. Rolfe—"

Rolfe turned, seeming only puzzled in the moment before he smiled. And before he smiled he jammed his hands into his pockets as though he were wearing something more casual than his well-cut charcoal suit. "I'm sure I know you but—?"

"Nelson—Homicide. We met at the party for Dr. Stewart."

The bruised area on Rolfe's cheek had spread. It showed dark through a layer of ointment. He said pleasantly, "How could I have managed to forget?" and answered himself, "I suppose because you look more like a social acquaintance. Is this a chance meeting?"

"No—shall we go to your room?"

Rolfe said, "Either you fellows need reorganization to avoid an unnecessary duplication of effort or you're uncommonly thorough. A man came today to ask me to go over the statement I made. Are you on the same errand?"

"Not exactly," Nelson said.

"Well—I have to go upstairs anyway to get my hat and coat. Walking off a meal is my sole means of exercise in the city—but I can spare you a few minutes."

He headed for the elevator. Clevis was in it when it started. Rolfe did not give him a glance until he unlocked his door and Clevis edged past him into the lighted foyer of the suite. Then he said, "Oh—of course. I should have recognized him even quicker than I did you. No conflict about his being a social acquaintance. This must be more important than I thought if it takes two of you."

He went into the living room. He placed the visit on a short-term basis by neither sitting nor offering chairs. He said with humorous resignation, "Shoot the questions, gentlemen."

"We haven't come to ask questions," Nelson said. "At least not primarily. We've come to give a progress report."

Rolfe said, "From the size of my taxes I often think I'm supporting all of the public bureaus single-handed—yet I'm overwhelmed by such service. Is it rated by everyone who happens to be present at the scene of a crime?"

"No. You've been singled out because you figure more prominently than the others."

"My dear man—"

"I'll become less dear as time passes." Nelson might have been bringing a refractory child to order. "Take your hands out of your pockets."

Rolfe's thin brown face looked amused. "With or without the gun?"

"I haven't accused you of carrying a gun. The weapons you're concealing are your bare hands."

"So much for my vanity," Rolfe said. "I have a score of my own to settle with the hoodlum who broke up Dave Stewart's party." He removed a hand from his pocket and raised it to touch his cheek. "He gave me this as well as the swollen knuckles when I waded in to restrain him."

"Allowing for the various stages of bruises, Mr. Rolfe, it's unmistakable that something has been added to yours since the night of the murder. At the time everyone was subjected to close scrutiny—but for no better reason than that you were reputed to be an expert horseman I took particular note of the shape and strength of your hands. They were unblemished except for occupational calluses between the fingers."

While Nelson talked, Clevis had slipped unnoticed into the bedroom. He came out carrying a soiled shirt. He said to Nelson, "For the serology boys—in regard to you know what."

Rolfe's calm broke. "This has gone far enough!" He strode toward Clevis.

Nelson interposed himself between them. Clevis wrapped the shirt in his newspaper. He whispered to Nelson, "None of his shoes are damp and I couldn't find rubbers."

Rolfe went into a moment of silence, shrugged, and addressed himself to Nelson. His tone was mild. "I'd prefer an explanation of this clown's extraordinary behavior to that progress report you mentioned." He sat on the arm of a chair.

"It amounts to the same thing," Nelson said. "Today one of my men interrupted a conversation you were having with a blackmailer who hurried off to visit the next prospect on his list—Mrs. Eugene Hackett. My unexpected appearance at her door impelled him to run upstairs and hide. Mrs. Hackett did not see fit to ask my help. After I left she got rid of him—presumably at the cost of a few drinks and a down payment, since the driver of the cab he hailed noticed that he was loaded on both counts. Possibly Mrs. Hackett then did what most lone women under stress would do. She got in touch with an intimate friend to ask for advice—you. But whether or not that's true, you were sufficiently provoked to go to the blackmailer's office and demand that he surrender his valuable little property—the license number of your car. I'll make an informed guess that alcoholic courage accounted for his resistance to your demand and to the blows he managed to deliver in self-defense."

Rolfe said indolently, "I don't think much of any of your guesses."

"Call it a logical conclusion then—borne out by the wear and tear on your hands."

"I hate to admit it because it sounds so sordid," Rolfe said, "but I went for a stroll in Central Park this afternoon and was accosted by a degenerate. He was so persistent that I had to resort to my fists."

"Was the encounter witnessed?"

"No—not a soul in sight."

Nelson said, "Do you want me to go on with this—or would you prefer to have your lawyer present?"

Rolfe stretched and dropped to the chair's seat. "My heavy dinner's made me sluggish. I can't seem to understand what you're talking about—or why the license number of my car should be a valuable property—and least of all why I'd want a lawyer."

Clevis muttered, "Maybe he'll understand a cell—and the walk they let him take after a dinner to end dinners."

Nelson put it more delicately. "Unless you can give me an acceptable explanation for the fact that Matthew Berthold rode to Dr. Stewart's office in your car you will be charged with the murder of Eugene Hackett."

Rolfe said, "I don't know how my car figures in your investigation, but I'll take your word that it does. Well—I'd left it outside Dave's place with the key in the ignition. Living in the country's made me careless of things like that. Has it occurred to you that Berthold could have stolen it—driven away—decided that it was too risky a haul—and driven back to find pickings more easily disposed of?"

"That," said Nelson, "is one of the few things that did not occur to me. Continue."

"I should think the rest is obvious. Strachan spotted him—realized that he wouldn't be a rewarding target for blackmail—and switched to me. That is, he—"

"Then you admit that Strachan tried to blackmail you—and that you were interested enough to get his name and address."

"Who knows what he wanted? He thrust a card at me—"

"Incautious of him, but of course he'd been drinking—and you had probably insisted that you'd negotiate only at his office, where you were again interrupted—this time by Matthew Berthold."

Rolfe crossed and recrossed his legs. "You can't seriously think I had anything to do with the murder of poor old Gene. What motive would I have—or do I strike you as a homicidal maniac?"

Nelson looked down at him. "Eugene Hackett was far from poor."

"I was speaking in terms of his death—not his finances."

"And I was speaking in terms of motive. I'm afraid you'll have to settle for a ride instead of a walk, Mr. Rolfe."

Rolfe did not stir. "I gave you the explanation you asked for."

"I found it unacceptable. I'm willing, however, to admit that you neither talk nor behave like a man who has anything to fear. So I'm going to give you a chance to co-operate with the law. Of course if you have any reason for refusing—"

"Why should I refuse? It seems to me I've been extremely co-operative so far." There was a handkerchief in his breast pocket. It stayed there although he must have been aware of the sweat gathering on his forehead and upper lip.

Nelson ignored it too. "What I have in mind calls for your hat and coat. Clevis will get them."

"I'll get them myself." He got up and pushed Clevis aside with a rough gesture. It was his one overt show of hostility since Clevis had appeared with the shirt.

When he was in the bedroom, Clevis whispered, "It's okay, Captain. Ninth floor—no fire escape, poisons, or firearms—and his razor's electric—but he's playing it so cool he might try to shake us when we hit the street. He either had a thought about footprints and ditched the shoes or he's wearing them. Maybe I spoke too soon on having too much evidence."

Rolfe came out dressed for the street. He looked correct and slightly supercilious. He said, "Captain, I'd hate to think that a man of your caliber would resort to tricks to get a suspect to come along peaceably. That's the phrase used in making an arrest—isn't it?"

"I promise that when I take you to headquarters it will be without tricks," Nelson said.

"You haven't disclosed the form my co-operation's supposed to take."

"Would it surprise you if we went to Bellevue to give Strachan an opportunity to identify you as the man who beat him up?"

"No—nor would it worry me. Who could consider his testimony reliable even if he should take it into his unreliable head to identify me?"

In front of the hotel he nodded to Judd as to an old acquaintance and stood at ease while Judd went around the corner for Bonino.

Seated between Judd and Bonino in the moving car, he spoke to the back of Nelson's head. "Did I understand you to say that Strachan is at Bellevue, captain?"

"Yes."

"Then why are we going uptown?"

"You yourself pointed out that Strachan could be classified as an unreliable witness. Happily we're not entirely dependent upon him."

Rolfe leaned forward. Bonino and Judd leaned with him. He sat back, and so did they. He laughed without mirth. "I seem to have been set down in a line of Tiller Girls. If I'm to be of service the least you can do is brief me."

Clevis said, "You won't need briefing. All you got to do is what comes natural."

Rolfe shrugged and was silent. He made a few attempts to look out of the side windows, but Bonino and Judd blocked his view. For the rest of the drive he kept his eyes on the broad windshield. When Nelson stopped the car at the corner of Mrs. Hackett's street he was not surprised. Nor did he protest until he had been assisted to the pavement.

"March," Clevis said.

He did not move. He said to the watchful men, "I refuse to be a party to this."

"A party to what?" Nelson said.

"How do I know? But whatever your object is in calling upon a bereaved woman, surely it doesn't justify a wholesale invasion of her privacy."

"Have you reason to believe that Mrs. Hackett cared so little for her husband that she doesn't want to know who killed him?"

"If you have such knowledge—which I doubt—you could find a more tactful means of breaking it. The newspapers say the servants are on vacation and that she's alone in the house. If that's so, how do you think she'll react to a group of strangers on her doorstep?"

"The sight of your friendly face should reassure her."

"Sorry," Rolfe said. "I'd be better at quieting a horse than soothing a nervous grief-stricken woman."

"You did offer to co-operate."

"I've changed my mind. I don't like your methods."

Clevis and Judd closed in. "What say we book him, Captain, while you call on the widow? That way he can't complain of wholesale invasion. Course she'll be pretty shocked when you tell her who's in stir—but comes to grief-stricken women, you're as good as a head-shrinker. You just let them talk themselves out."

Rolfe said, "Don't think I'm affected by your efforts to intimidate me." It was too dark to see his face clearly, but his capitulation sounded like the result of an inner debate. "However, since she hasn't anyone else to look after her, as long as I've come this far I'll see it through."

They walked to the Hackett house. Clevis and Nelson escorted Rolfe up the steps while the other two men waited below, but not too far away to block retreat should Rolfe change his mind again.

The first floor of the house was lighted. Rolfe said in a loud voice, "I wouldn't blame Mrs. Hackett if she didn't let us in."

Nelson murmured blandly, "I'm sure she will if she hears a familiar voice. Ring the bell."

Rolfe made no further attempt to give warning. He rang, and at the sound of footsteps within, Nelson and Clevis flattened themselves on either side of the door.

She opened it cautiously on its chain and saw only Rolfe. The chain was off in a moment and the door wide. "George—I hoped it would be you even though you said—"

"No cause for alarm—these gentlemen asked me to—" Clevis shoved him over the threshold and held the door for Nelson. Judd and Bonino came up the steps.

Inside the entrance hall, Nelson said without preliminary, "Strachan recognized you today, didn't he, Mrs. Hackett? Recognizing people is his business and he had less on his mind than Berthold did."

She turned and led the way to the nearest room. She was wearing a low-necked black jersey dress and had thrown a cardigan about her shoulders. She drew it closer and sat down in a slip-covered chair. She said, "Strachan?"

Rolfe had propped himself against a piano shrouded by a dust sheet. He said, "Strachan's a disreputable little character who's going around blackmailing people. The captain has an idea that he came here."

"The captain will do the talking," Clevis said.

Nelson had no taste for it. This was the stage of his job that he relished least. He said bleakly, "It won't help anyone's cause to draw this out. Mrs. Hackett—you were in New York on the night your husband was murdered."

Her deep tan seemed to fade as he watched. She looked at Rolfe. "I—"

Nelson said, "I'd advise you to say nothing until I've finished—nothing at all. The fewer retractions you have to make later, the less harm you'll do yourself. You may have had no purpose in coming to New York than to see George Rolfe. But you didn't want your husband to learn of the trip. You enlisted the help of your maid so that if your husband called the Miami hotel in your absence she could sub for you—pleading a sore throat or a poor connection or both to account for the difference in voice. But first—to prevent anyone in the hotel from giving you away inadvertently or even maliciously, you had pretended to discharge her. You were of an approximate size and height, and when you took the plane for New York you wore her clothing, and sun glasses and a scarf to conceal your hair. Meanwhile she had kept to your room and asked in the unrecognizable voice of a sore-throat victim that the waiter leave her trays outside the door. Then she received telephoned instructions from you as well as notification from the police, and was still posing as you when she stepped off the plane this morning. The reporters saw nothing strange in the fact that a woman so recently bereaved should want to cover her suffering face and be unwilling or unable to speak to them." He glanced involuntarily at her slim ankles. "But the camera was more astute."

She was staring down at her hands, and now it was Rolfe who tried to catch her eye. Nelson went on, "I'm trying to give you the benefit of the doubt as far as is humanly possible. I do not believe you were a willing accomplice in your husband's murder. I have evidence to bear this out. You, of course, were here when the maid arrived in a taxi this morning. It won't be necessary to tell me where she went after reassuming her own identity. At my request the manager of the Aintree in Miami made inquiries. She had been friendly with a girl on the hotel staff who asked for her address—and to keep up the fiction of being fired she gave her parents' home. She was there when I telephoned tonight—and horrified to hear that you were in trouble. She said Mr. Hackett was old and what he didn't know hadn't hurt him. She said you only went to New York to be with your boy friend—and she didn't blame you—especially since he'd stopped writing or calling and it had begun to look as though it were out of sight out of mind with him. She said you'd chosen the Aintree because it was one of his hangouts and you'd hoped you could get him to come down—"

Rolfe said, "Fantastic—isn't it, Vida? I'm supposed to be your boy friend. Under any other circumstances I'd be flattered, but—"

"But as it is you wouldn't mind having a horsewhip handy to protect her honor," Clevis said, "or maybe a scalpel would do. He's sweating again, Captain, and the joint's cold at that."

"You came to New York, Mrs. Hackett. The party for Stewart had been arranged some time ago, and Rolfe had said he would be there. He had probably not encouraged you to visit him in Connecticut—"

"You're right for once," Rolfe said. "With all due respect to the wives of my friends, women are strictly taboo around my stables."

"You're overdoing it," Nelson said, and turned back to her. She had changed neither her position nor her masklike expression. He had the feeling that he was trying to reach a deaf-mute. "You thought you could see Rolfe before the party and arrange to meet him afterward. You weren't afraid of running into your husband because of the Philadelphia convention. You called Rolfe at the Bellaire and he told you he had no free time—or at any rate he told you something that made you rather desperate. You said you would go to the party too."

"I'm disappointed in you, Captain," Rolfe said. "That's not even good fantasy. If a couple were engaging in a bit of furtive dalliance, would they appear together at a stag affair thrown by friends of the woman's husband? And while I have the floor let me ask you if that tall tale of a spiteful servant has any more weight than a yarn spun by Strachan? I happen to know that Mrs. Hackett did fire the girl for insolence—and naturally she was taking her revenge."

"When did Mrs. Hackett tell you she'd fired the maid?"

"When I called to offer condolence. I don't mind telling you that, having done that, I considered I'd discharged my duty toward the widow of a friend."

"Evidently the widow of your friend did not agree. I won't pretend to have all the details straight—you'll supply those in time. But when Eugene Hackett turned up at the party after telling everyone that he couldn't make it, you began to worry about what might happen if his wife made good her threat to turn up as well. You didn't want to antagonize Hackett. He owned shares in the businesses of all his friends and he had invested substantially in yours. You were on the verge of touching him for more funds. You had a run of hard luck this year—backing horses that let you down—and losing more than you could afford to lose. Hackett was not a sportsman. Perhaps he'd been hinting that he wanted to withdraw his money so that he could invest it in something more predictable. Stewart's party started with a tour of the offices to show how well they'd been equipped. You saw the Demerol and palmed it. Probably you had no chance to put some in Hackett's glass, so you drugged an opened bottle of bourbon. He preferred bourbon to scotch or rye, which was what the others were drinking. But he had a headache and left a half-finished glass which Berthold drank later. I think you knew that a small quantity of Demerol would be harmless. You merely wanted Hackett to be sleeping it off should his wife make an appearance. He did lie down to get rid of his headache—but the convention was on his mind and he awoke in time to catch his train. He—"

The woman raised her head. Her eyes and her voice were dull. She said, "Don't go on—please—" She brought her hands together, the fingers whitening as she twisted them.

Rolfe rounded on Nelson. "I hope you're proud of yourself. If she has a nervous breakdown because of the gibberish you've—"

She said, "It's no use, George. He knows. We were fools to think we were safe—"

Clevis and Judd had to muzzle him. She did not look his way. Her eyes seemed sightless. "After I called George I came here and changed my clothes. It seemed too much trouble to get my car out of the garage, so I thought I'd take a cab—but it was such a rotten night that I couldn't get one. I took a bus. I was angry and hurt because I'd come all that way to be with him and he'd brushed me off. I was going to tell the others at the party that I thought Gene would be there—that I'd got lonely for him and had come back to surprise him. I meant to act disappointed not to find him—and to get George to take me home. George must have been listening for me. He heard the outer door open and came out into the hall, closing the room door behind him. The others didn't notice—what with the music and talk. When I saw him I wasn't angry anymore. I threw myself at him. We were in each other's arms and he was whispering for me to go and he'd come to the house later—and Gene came from the rear of the offices and saw us that way. George whispered that none of us wanted an open scandal and we went back to the examination room and Gene struck him in the face and threatened to break him. Then George was holding the scalpel and staring at the floor—and I panicked. I wanted to throw up—it kept me from screaming. I ran—I didn't stop until I got to the door and the street. I saw George's car. I had to sit down and rest to keep myself from being sick. After a few minutes I saw the ignition key in the lock and I drove away. I drove for a long time. Then I had to go back—I had to know the worst. And on my way that man fell in front of the car." Something in her eyes flickered. Her voice sharpened a little. "He didn't look like much," she said. "I—" She stopped.

Nelson said quietly, "You thought he looked more capable of murder than George Rolfe—and that gave you the idea that his unexplained presence on the scene might divert the police."

Suddenly she was alive again and at bay. She pressed against the back of the chair. "He looked like a tramp. It would only have been a temporary inconvenience for him. They couldn't prove him guilty."

"So you led him into the trap."

"No—I didn't think it out—I didn't know what I'd do."

"Until you got there and found that all was as before and that somehow your lover had managed to stave off the inevitable police.

Did he tell you how he put on an examination gown and stabbed your husband again to make sure he was dead? Or was that done earlier—and did he give you the gown to dispose of before you ran out?" He saw the truth in her face. The pity he had felt for her drained away.

"Rolfe is a man who makes the most of his opportunities," he said. "He couldn't risk having your husband live to tell the tale—especially since his death meant wealth—even though he would have to marry a woman he'd tired of to get his hands on it."

She was twisting her hands again. "No—no—he loves me."

Nelson turned to Clevis. "Take them away."

Judd and Bonino were forcibly restraining Rolfe.

"He don't look so good anymore," Clevis said. "No trouble now in sizing him up as a murderer. I'll call for the paddy wagon. You coming too?"

"I think you can manage without me."

"Don't worry about a thing. We'll have both signed statements before you turn over in bed."

Nelson drove home, and only when he reached his door remembered that Matt Berthold would be there. He thought, Well, I'll be able to ease his mind, and sighed and wished it could wait until morning. He was tired and depressed. He wanted to put behind him all aspects of the Hackett case.

Then, when he opened the door, a minor miracle happened. A slim figure with ash-blond hair came running to him.

"Kyrie," he said, "how—?" But he had asked too many questions that winter night. He kissed her hungrily and smelled and tasted spring.

When he released her she said, "Don't you take time to read the weather reports? Last night we had a freeze in Miami—and more of the same is predicted—so Junie's better off in his own snug house."

"Let's go up and see him. Is he asleep?"

"Yes—soundly—although he went to bed under protest. Hadn't you better show yourself to your company? Grid—will it be all right about young Matt? He's sweet and so is his girl—and if you'd stayed out much longer I'd have fallen for her father."

"No wonder Sammy wanted me here in a hurry." He smiled and hugged her. His malaise was gone.

Matt lay on the living-room couch, and a dark-haired girl who seemed no more than eighteen leaned over him. The two were not embracing but they gave the impression of being entwined. James

Marshall and Edwin Decker sat near the fireplace, a tray of drinks between them. They arose as Kyrie came into the room with Nelson, and Edwin Decker shook hands with him. Matt started to rise, but the girl pushed him back.

"The doctor says you're to stay off that leg." She stood up and went to Nelson. She held out her hand. "Captain, I'm Rennie Marshall. I'm going to marry that accident-prone character on the couch and I thank you for all you've done for him. We're leaving right away because we don't want to spoil Mrs. Nelson's homecoming."

Nelson looked down at her, liking the small alert face and the clear eyes that gave it beauty. "I'm the police, see? And you don't leave until I say so."

"But we've had an indecent amount of your hospitality—including a wonderful dinner and—"

"I won't detain you by force," he said, "but I thought you might be interested in learning that Matt is no longer a suspect."

He told the story, condensing it as much as possible. If they were thirsty for the gory details they could read the newspapers.

They were not. When he had finished there was a lingering silence. Matt broke it to say deeply, "Thank you, sir." Rennie had gone back to sit beside him. He gave her a very young smile.

Decker spoke. "I've never been so happy to lose a client."

Rennie said somberly, "How could that woman—how could any woman—?"

"You're not to think about it," Matt said. Then he said, "Was she—is she a brunette, Captain Nelson?"

"No—a blond. Why?"

"Later I remembered that her skin was dark."

"Sunburn."

"Oh."

That seemed to exhaust everyone's curiosity. Presently Matt was helped to the guest room, and Rennie and her father and her uncle took their leave.

Sammy brought Nelson a tray. The food had an extra flavor with Kyrie for company. She talked about Junie and about the high spots of the Florida vacation. Then she said, "Matt will go to Mr. Decker's house tomorrow if the doctor says it's all right. He'll stay there until the wedding."

"When's that?"

"Next week. Rennie says she hopes their son will be as charming as ours."

"Oh?"

"Yes. Stop looking like a puritan."

"Am I?"

"You were for a split second. Poor kids—it isn't going to be all moonlight and roses for them. Both her father and her uncle have worked out a sensible plan for him—but I'm afraid he'll be stubborn about it. It's obvious he wants to be a self-made man."

"There's no such thing. Nobody ever made it without some sort of help along the way—and material help's the easiest kind to return."

"You tell him that, Grid. He has great respect for you. He looked at you as though you were the oracle of the world."

"I'll see what I can do—but at the moment I'd rather be the oracle of the bedchamber." He got up and pulled her to her feet.

She said in a muffled voice, "Did I call you a puritan?"

THE END

www.ingramcontent.com/pod-product-compliance
Lightning Source LLC
LaVergne TN
LVHW021801060526
838201LV00058B/3192